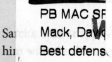

Sa... ...ed
hi... ...ay
by a second blow that... Arr... ...ght-
headed and his mouth filled with the coppery tang of
blood from his split lower lip.

"Done talking yet, Vulcan?"

"In fact . . . no. I am not."

"Then let's see if we can make you tell us something
useful." Over his shoulder, Prang shouted, "Bring her in!"

The suite's double doors were pulled open. Two Klingons dragged in Amanda by her arms. Prang grinned at
the sight of her. "Is she how you did away with Gorkon?
Did you send your own mate to seduce him on the dance
floor?" When his men presented Amanda to him, Prang
leered at her. "Maybe she was the one who did the deed.
Came to him in the night. Slipped poison into his drink.
Then vaporized him to destroy the evidence."

Amanda was horrified by the accusations. "You're
mad!"

Prang backhanded her across the face.

Sarek watched his wife fall to the floor. For the first
time in his diplomatic career, he contemplated whether
it might in fact be logical for him to answer the Klingons on their own terms—by crushing every bone in
Prang's body.

STAR TREK®

THE ORIGINAL SERIES

LEGACIES: BOOK 2

BEST DEFENSE

David Mack

Based on *Star Trek*®
created by Gene Roddenberry

POCKET BOOKS

New York   London   Toronto   Sydney   New Delhi   Centaurus

Pocket Books
An Imprint of Simon & Schuster, Inc.
1230 Avenue of the Americas
New York, NY 10020

This book is a work of fiction. Any references to historical events, real people, or real places are used fictitiously. Other names, characters, places, and events are products of the author's imagination, and any resemblance to actual events or places or persons, living or dead, is entirely coincidental.

First Pocket Books paperback edition August 2016

POCKET and colophon are registered trademarks of Simon & Schuster, Inc.

For information about special discounts for bulk purchases, please contact Simon & Schuster Special Sales at 1-866-506-1949 or business@simonandschuster.com.

The Simon & Schuster Speakers Bureau can bring authors to your live event. For more information or to book an event, contact the Simon & Schuster Speakers Bureau at 1-866-248-3049 or visit our website at www.simonspeakers.com.

Manufactured in the United States of America

10 9 8 7 6 5 4 3 2 1

ISBN 978-1-4767-5310-2
ISBN 978-1-4767-5315-7 (ebook)

For all those architects of imagination in whose footsteps I am privileged to walk . . .

and for Leonard

Historian's Note

The events of this story take place after the *Enterprise* crew's mission to the diplomatic conference on Babel ("Journey to Babel"), one week after their mission to Argus X ("Obsession"), and roughly six weeks after a foreign spy escaped from the *Enterprise* having stolen the mysterious alien artifact known as the Transfer Key (*Star Trek: Legacies*—Book 1: *Captain to Captain*).

Since wars begin in the minds of men, it is in the minds of men that the defences of peace must be constructed.

—UNESCO Constitution, 1946

One

Una limped alone in a land without shadow. Two merciless suns, high overhead, scorched the white salt flats. Had it been hours or days since she had crossed the dimensional barrier to this forsaken place? Time felt slow and elastic. The glaring orbs of day seemed never to move.

Perhaps this world is tidally locked to its parent stars.

It was a rational explanation for the endless noontime, yet it fell short of explaining what truly felt askew to Captain Una about this bizarre alien universe. Plodding toward a distant sprawl of hills backed by rugged mountains, she was plagued by the sensation of running while standing still, as if in a dream. Far ahead, haze-shrouded hilltops bobbed with her uneven steps and lurched in time with her wounded gait, as salt crystals crunched beneath the soles of her dusty, Starfleet standard-issue boots.

Both halves of her uniform—its black trousers and green command tunic—were ripped and frayed in several spots. It was all damage incurred on the planet Usilde in her home universe, during her harried escape through traps wrought from brambles, nettles, and thorns. To reach the citadel created by extradimensional invaders known as the Jatohr, Una had been forced to defy the taboos of the indigenous Usildar, who both feared and despised the alien fortress, which had appeared without warning years earlier in one of their rain forest's larger lakes. What Una knew and the Usildar did not was that the alien stronghold was also the key to traveling between this blighted dimension and the one she called home—which meant it was also her only hope of rescuing the other members of an ill-fated *Enterprise* landing party, who had been exiled here eighteen years earlier while she had been forced to bear helpless witness.

I am no longer helpless. And I will bring my shipmates home.

She swept a lock of her raven hair from her eyes, noted the delicate sheen of perspiration on the back of her pale hand. Peering ahead, she found no tracks to follow, no road to guide her journey. Her training nagged at her. It demanded she proceed based on careful observation and rational deduction, but there were no facts here to parse. Only level sands and blank emptiness, stretching away to a faded horizon. And yet, Una knew she was moving in the right direction. It wasn't that her Illyrian mental discipline gave her any special insight into this *universum incognita*; it was something more basic and less rational. It was instinct. A hunch. A feeling.

Doubts haunted her. She slowed her pace and looked back. As desolate as she found the landscape ahead of her, it was a feast for the senses compared to the vast yawn of nothing at her back. Nothing interrupted the marble-white void of the sky or the featureless expanse of the desert stretched out forever beneath it. Waves of heat radiation shimmered in an unbroken curtain, giving the boundary between earth and air the sheen of liquid metal. But nothing else moved here. Nothing living flew in the air; nothing walked, crawled, or slithered across the parched soil. There was no wind to stir so much as a mote of bleached dust from the ground.

The hills looked just as barren, and the mountains behind them were forbidding. But for all their threat of hardships, they also promised shelter and a break from the monotony. And so Una pressed on toward them, confident her shipmates would have made the same choices eighteen years earlier. *Martinez would not have let himself or the others perish in the open desert,* she assured herself. *He would have sought shelter, water, and resources—all of which are more likely to be found in the mountains than on this sun-blasted plain.*

Una wondered if she would recognize her old shipmates after so long apart—or they, her. The last time Martinez and the others had seen Una, she had been an eager young lieutenant, a helm officer aboard the *Enterprise* under Captain Robert April. Back then, they had perpetuated her Academy nickname "Number One" because of her history of taking top honors in nearly every academic and athletic endeavor with which Starfleet could challenge her. Rather than chafe at the sobriquet, she had appropriated it, after a fashion: because her native Illyrian moniker was all but unpronounceable by most humanoid species, she had chosen to serve under the name "Una" since her earliest days at Starfleet Academy. In later years, after she had climbed the *Enterprise*'s ladder of rank to serve as executive officer under the command of Captain Christopher Pike, it had been a welcome coincidence that Pike had proved partial to addressing his XO as "Number One," a holdover from ancient Terran naval traditions dating back to that world's age of sail.

Perhaps the only former crewmate of hers who could pronounce her true name was Commander Spock. She had long admired his penchant for favoring his cool, logical Vulcan heritage over his more emotional human ancestry. In his youth, of course, he had exhibited a disturbing tendency to betray his heightened emotions by raising his voice on the bridge—an unseemly habit Una had helped him overcome, in the interest of honing his sense of decorum as an officer. Where many of their peers might have bristled at Una's catechism, Spock had taken her counsel to heart with a near-total absence of self-consciousness.

Spock and I have always understood each other better than most people do. But his devotion to logic blinds him to the power of hope.

If not for the compassionate understanding of Spock's captain, James T. Kirk, the current commanding officer of the *Enterprise*, Una's mission might already have ended in failure. She had taken a grave risk in stealing the Transfer Key—a device of not only alien but extradimensional origin—from its longtime hiding place in the captain's quarters of the *Enterprise*. Having recently perused Kirk's report of a similar device he encountered in an alternate universe, and Spock's report of how a transporter malfunction had opened a pathway to that universe—first by accident, then a second time by design—she had gleaned new insights concerning the alien gadget she and Captain April had seized on Usilde in 2249. With that resource at her command, Una had planned to power up the now-abandoned Jatohr facility on Usilde and open the doorway between her universe and this one, to which her shipmates had so long ago been cruelly exiled by the Jatohr. To make that opportunity a reality, she had risked ending her career in a court-martial and jeopardized the imminent Federation-Klingon peace talks to return with the Transfer Key to Usilde—an action that had served only to attract the Klingons' attention to the primitive planet and the advanced alien technology it harbored.

Regardless, Una had hoped there would be time to save her friends and escape with the Transfer Key. To her dismay, the other five members of her Usilde landing party, as well as four officers "blinked" off the bridge of the *Enterprise*, were nowhere to be found when, at last, the gateway between universes was opened once more. And so she had made a fateful decision: She struck a bargain with Kirk and Spock. They would keep the Transfer Key safe from the Klingons and return to Usilde in sixty days to reopen the door between universes. Which meant Una had that long, and not a day more, to find her lost shipmates and return with them to her arrival point in the desert—which she had marked with an X, scorched into the salt with the phaser she had borrowed from Kirk—for their long overdue homecoming.

It was an outrageous proposition. A mission doomed to fail. Una didn't care. She had beaten impossible odds before.

She would either bring her shipmates home . . . or die here with them.

Two

Captain James T. Kirk strode the corridors of the *Enterprise* with a sense of purpose. On most days, under normal circumstances, he made a point of affecting a relaxed air in front of his crew. On occasion he was even known to share a genial smile with those junior officers and enlisted personnel he passed en route from one part of the starship to another.

This was not one of those days.

His mind was preoccupied to a peculiar degree, bent toward grim memories of recent events. Just a week prior, the *Enterprise*'s survey of Argus X had resurrected an old horror from Kirk's past, a gaseous creature that drained iron-based blood corpuscles from living beings—in effect, a vampire masquerading as a cloud of sickly sweet vapor. It was the same alien monster that eleven years earlier had killed over two hundred of Kirk's shipmates on the *Starship Farragut*, including his commanding officer, Captain Garrovick.

That score was now settled. The dikironium cloud creature had been exterminated. Despite his commitment to Starfleet's core mission of peaceful exploration, Kirk felt no remorse for having slain the gaseous fiend, which was capable of interstellar travel. It had posed an unqualified threat to the safety of humanoid life throughout the galaxy. If he were ever to encounter another of its ilk, he would terminate it with the same ruthless dispatch.

If only all my command decisions were so clear-cut.

Weeks had passed since he and Spock had ushered Captain Una—a former first officer of the *Enterprise* under Chris Pike and most recently the commanding officer of the *Starship Yorktown*—through a portal to an alternate universe. At the time Kirk had felt skeptical of her nearly fanatical devotion to her lost shipmates. As a captain he sympathized; she had been a lieutenant, commanding a landing party for the first time, when her crewmates were lost. But they had been missing in action for eighteen years. Wasn't it time she moved on?

Then, last week on Argus X, his nose had caught that cloying sweet odor, and all his rage and grief from a decade earlier had come rushing back, animating his every word and deed until his errand of justice was served. In the shadow of those terrible events, he understood Captain Una's actions more clearly than ever.

The past is never forgotten; it's always with us.

Junior personnel strove to avoid drawing Kirk's hard stare as he quick-stepped through the *Constitution*-class starship's curving gray corridors, but there was one officer who was desperate to snag a moment of his attention: his new yeoman, Ensign Kalliope Dalto. A dark-haired, doe-eyed woman from the human colony on Rigel IV—wispy of frame but whip smart and relentless in her pursuit of excellence—she dogged Kirk with tireless patience, a data slate full of ship's paperwork tucked under her arm.

In a more charitable mood, Kirk would have halted

the chase and let her push the fuel-consumption reports and quartermaster's requisitions into his hand somewhere back by the turbolift. Unfortunately for Dalto, Kirk was still stung by the betrayal of his most recent yeoman, Ensign Lisa Bates, who had absconded from the *Enterprise* with a powerful and dangerous alien artifact known as the Transfer Key. The gadget had been entrusted to Kirk's care by Captain Pike, who had inherited the responsibility from Captain April.

And I was the one who lost it.

Bates had been beamed off the *Enterprise* by a Romulan bird-of-prey, revealing her true allegiance even as she rubbed Kirk's nose in his failure to detect a spy who had toiled at his side for months. Coming so shortly after the promotion and transfer of Lieutenant Janice Rand, perhaps the best captain's yeoman with whom Kirk had ever served, Bates's betrayal had struck an exceptionally cruel blow. Of course, it was unfair to take out his resentments on his newest yeoman, but history taught him it was a tradition as old as the sea.

It seemed, however, no one had apprised Dalto of that fact.

She caught up to Kirk just before he reached the door to the conference room. Her timbre was polite but assertive, neither showing nor brooking disrespect. "Pardon me, Captain!" As he halted and turned to face her, she extended the data slate and stylus to him with a courteous smile. "Today's reports, sir."

He frowned but stifled a sigh as he signed one report after another, then handed the stylus and slate back to Dalto. "Thank you, Yeoman."

She tucked the stylus into its slot on the side of the slate. "Commander Spock and Lieutenant Uhura are waiting for you in briefing room one."

Kirk arched one eyebrow and shot a sidelong glance at the door behind him. The panel on the bulkhead beside it identified it clearly: BRIEFING ROOM 1.

He forced a mirthless smile. "Thank you, Yeoman. Dismissed."

Dalto returned the way they had come, heading back to the turbolift with unhurried grace. Kirk continued on his way, into the briefing room—where, as Dalto had duly informed him, his first officer and senior communications officer both stood awaiting his arrival, a portrait of opposites: half-Vulcan Spock with his pale, almost greenish complexion and bowl-cut sable hair, human Uhura with her flawless brown skin and elegant coif. They both faced the door as Kirk entered. He motioned for them to be at ease. "As you were." They moved to stand behind their customary seats at the asymmetrically pentagonal conference table.

Though Kirk often found the briefing room's windowless, clamshell-curved blue-gray bulkheads and dark blue carpeting claustrophobic, today he welcomed its privacy. He sat on the narrow side of the head of the table, which cued Spock and Uhura to take their seats.

"What have you found?"

Spock's delivery was as dry as the deserts of his homeworld. "Not as much as we had hoped, Captain. The Klingons have intercepted and destroyed all Starfleet reconnaissance probes launched into the Korinar Sector."

"What about long-range scans?"

"Inconclusive," Spock said. "We've detected increased Klingon starship traffic near the Usilde system, but how much of a presence they have established on the surface is unclear."

Kirk swiveled his chair toward Uhura. "Signal traffic?"

"More than usual," she said. "All of it encrypted, as expected."

"I presume we've applied the usual ciphers?"

A nod. "Yes, sir. No luck so far."

Their news left Kirk frustrated. "Until we know what kind of welcome to expect from the Klingons, we can't risk going back to Usilde."

His declaration discomfited Spock. "Captain Una is counting on us to facilitate her return from the alternate universe."

"I'm aware of that, Mister Spock. But at the moment, the Klingons don't seem inclined to let us visit. Not that it would matter if we could." He asked Uhura, "Any leads on the stolen Transfer Key? Or my former yeoman?"

"Reports from Starfleet Intelligence suggest the bird-of-prey that picked up Ensign Bates remains active in the Kaleb Sector. But they don't know if she or the Key are still on board."

"That's not much, but it's a start. Stay on top of that, Lieutenant. If any ship or starbase spots that vessel, I want its coordinates and heading relayed on the double."

"Understood, sir."

"As for Usilde, we're out of time for playing it safe." Kirk reached forward and thumbed open a vid channel to the bridge. The face of Commander Montgomery Scott, the *Enterprise*'s chief engineer, appeared on all three screens of the triangular tabletop viewer. "Mister Scott? Set course for the Korinar Sector, warp factor six."

"*Aye, Captain,*" Scott said in his Aberdeen brogue. "*Warp factor six.*"

Kirk switched off the monitor. Spock fixed him with a questioning look. "Are you sure that's wise, Captain? With the Organian peace talks about to commence on Centaurus, such action could be construed by the Klingons as a hostile provocation."

"I promised Captain Una we'd help bring her and her people home. So the Klingons can take it any way they want—but whether they like it or not, we're going back to Usilde."

———————

If there was a name for the disorientation that plagued Sadira's transition back to living among Romulans, she decided it most likely would be *tishaal-rovukam*—a Rihannsu word whose closest English transliteration was "situational whiplash."

She had spent the past several years living under the alias Lisa Bates, playing the part of an eager young Starfleet officer and, most recently, dutiful yeoman to none other than Starfleet's highest-profile young starship commander, Captain James T. Kirk. Had she aspired to a career on the stage, she might have considered it the role of a lifetime. As a sworn officer of the Tal Shiar, the clandestine intelligence service of the Romulan Star Empire, she had found it a degrading slog.

At least my servitude with Kirk was brief, she reminded herself. *And an unqualified success.*

Clanks of colliding metal and the hiss of plasma torches filled the cramped engine room of the *ChR Velibor*. Sadira stood with her back to a gray-green bulkhead, careful not to impede the mechanics and technicians who labored under the watchful eye of the *Vas Hatham*–class bird-of-prey's chief engineer, Lieutenant Ranimir. Hovering behind him were the ship's commanding officer and ranking centurion. Neither Commander Creelok nor Centurion Mirat made any effort to disguise their disapproval of the alien device that was being married to the bird-of-prey's main power core—a task imposed on them and their crew by Sadira, who had been given free rein by her superiors to test their new prize, the Transfer Key.

Creelok made a point of avoiding eye contact with Sadira as he asked with growing impatience, "How much longer, Ranimir?"

The engineer frowned at the alien device his team had grafted to the engine room's main console. "Hard to say, Commander. This device is unlike anything else I've ever seen. Before we hooked it up, I didn't think it would be compatible with our power supply—but it seems to have adapted itself to our network in less than a day."

His report visibly alarmed the centurion. "It adapted itself? How?"

"I wish I knew, Centurion." Ranimir pointed at a row of primary system readouts. "Its energy consumption has doubled since we brought it online, and it's still increasing."

Creelok's steep, angular eyebrows knit with concern. "At what point does it pose a threat to the safety of the ship and crew?"

"I won't know that until I see it." Ranimir tapped a red button on the console. "I set up a kill switch to cut its power. As a precaution."

"Sensible," the commander said.

Sadira moved closer to join the discussion. "Will it work while we're cloaked?"

"Since no one will tell me what it does," Ranimir said, "or how much power it needs when activated, there's no way I can answer that."

"I am not interested in your excuses. The device needs to work while our cloak is active."

Ranimir traded worried looks with Creelok and Mirat. "I can't promise that."

"I did not ask for your promise, only your compliance." It was clear to Sadira that none of the *Velibor's* crew liked taking orders from her. She wondered if it might simplify matters for her to affect the mannerisms she had cultivated for her Lisa Bates persona—an identity she had spent years honing in a model human settlement on Romulus.

Adopting a more dulcet tone of voice, Sadira added, "Ranimir, I know that I'm asking a lot of you, and of the ship, but my orders come from the highest levels of the Tal Shiar. So let's start over: If we assume the Transfer Key will increase its power consumption once activated, what can we do to prevent it from interfering with the ship's operations?"

Her sop to diplomacy eased Ranimir's anxiety, if only to a small degree. "I've isolated the Key's power supply to reactor one, and the cloak is running off reactor two. As long as we don't try to fire any other weapons or raise shields while operating the Key, I might be able to make this work."

She softened her aspect with a smile. "Excellent news, Ranimir."

The commander and the centurion remained dubious. Both men were gray and wise, veterans of a generation of space service. They would not be easily swayed by soft words and empty pleasantries. Creelok slid his narrowed gaze in Sadira's direction. "I don't care who gave the order. I don't like having this alien technology wedded to my ship's controls."

Mirat nodded in agreement. "I concur. This sort of test should be done under controlled conditions, in Romulan space. Not on a ship deployed in hostile territory."

"Your concerns are noted." To Ranimir, Sadira added, "Keep working. I want the Key operational by the time we reach the Ophiucus Sector."

Satisfied she had made herself clear, she walked away. Only after Sadira exited the engine room and started up the corridor to the lift that would return her to her quarters did she hear the echo of another set of footfalls at her back. She turned to face Creelok. He dropped his voice to a confidential register that did nothing to mask its obvious venom.

"You might want to consider passing your requests through the chain of command."

"Why should I?"

"Because I was commanding starships before you were born. I don't care who you work for—I won't have some arrogant girl-child snap orders at me in front of my crew."

She taunted him with a smirk. "I think you will."

"Respect has to be earned, Major Sadira. You'd do well to remember that."

"And the Tal Shiar can have you killed and your ship placed under my command any time I deem fit. You'd do well to remember *that*." She drew her dagger and in a flash pressed its blade to Creelok's throat. "And just so there's no misunderstanding, *Commander*—I don't make requests, I give orders. And I expect them to be followed." She sheathed her blade as the doors of the lift opened beside her. "Have the Key online before we reach the target—and when you get back to the command deck, increase speed to warp seven." She backed inside the lift and added as the doors slid closed, "I have a schedule to keep."

———

To most people, Sarek's stern Vulcan mien was unreadable, but he could always count on his intuitive human wife, Amanda Grayson, to see through his façade. She entered the diplomatic reception and proceeded directly to his side, like a memory unbidden but still pleasant to recall.

Her gaze was keen, her voice discreet. "You look disappointed."

"I would say dissatisfied." He gestured toward the various buffet tables, which were set in two corners at opposite ends of the hotel ballroom. "I asked that the buffet tables be spread about the room, with mixed cuisines on each." With subtle looks, he directed her attention to the cluster of Federation diplomats gathered on one side of the ornate gilded room, then toward the Klingon diplomatic contingent huddled on the opposite side of the huge space. "Instead, the catering staff put all the Klingon delicacies in one corner, and all the Terran and Vulcan dishes in another. It is not conducive to the casual intermingling of strangers."

"You're telling me. It's the political equivalent of a junior high school dance." She looped her arm under and around Sarek's. "I guess it's up to us to break the ice, then."

She was, as usual, correct. As the ranking member of the Federation diplomatic team, Ambassador Sarek was expected to set the tone and serve as an example to his subordinates. He doubted his colleagues would mimic his effort unless expressly ordered to do so, but for now he concurred with his wife: decorum required he greet his opposite number.

"Very well," he said.

He crossed the room with Amanda on his arm. Their every step made her silvery dress shimmer as its rippling fabric reflected the warm glow of the chandeliers. In contrast, his attire, though equally formal, was quite simple: a tailored black cassock and a gray mantle, both as fashionable in their cut as they were flattering to his trim physique. His only accessory of note was the ornament of jeweled gold he wore around his neck, an ancient family heirloom that had been passed from sire to scion for over ten generations. In spite of its objective worth—or lack thereof, in an age when science could manufacture gold and gems at will—to Sarek its value lay in its historical significance. To him it was a symbol of continuity. Of longevity. Of life.

All the same, he was not surprised that no one else in the room paid the least attention to the decoration on his chest; all eyes were on Amanda and that mesmerizing dress of hers. If not for his lifetime of cultivated mental discipline, Sarek might have enjoyed a moment of pride when he noticed that even the Klingons had taken note of his wife's elegance.

The cluster of foreign dignitaries parted as he and Amanda neared. From their midst emerged their leader, Councillor Gorkon, and his chief attaché, Councillor Prang. Gorkon was the taller of the pair, aristocratic in his bearing, deliberate and arch in his mannerisms. In every way, he was a son of privilege; he had been born to power and wielded it with almost criminal indifference. Prang was another story. His wild eyes, broad shoulders, barrel chest, and muscled limbs betrayed his service as a celebrated warrior of the Klingon Defense Forces—one who had blundered into politics by way of an advantageous marriage that had elevated him from the ranks of the common folk to a seat on the Empire's vaunted High Council.

Sarek honored Gorkon with a long nod. "Welcome, Councillor."

"Thank you, Mister Ambassador."

Amanda chimed in, "Did your new wife accompany you?"

Before Gorkon could answer, Prang replied with naked contempt, "We Klingons do not bring our mates on *official business*. It—"

Gorkon interrupted Prang with a dramatic clearing of his throat. Then he plastered a false but polite smile onto his face and said to Amanda, "As it happens, Illizar and I are not yet married. The wedding was briefly postponed."

"My apologies, Councillor," Amanda said. "I was not aware."

He dismissed the awkwardness with a small wave. "It's of no consequence. The wedding is set for next month, on Qo'noS." Returning his focus to Sarek, he asked, "And how is your health, Mister Ambassador? I understand you had surgery not long ago, on the *Enterprise*?"

"Yes, to correct a cardiac ailment. I am fully recovered."

Sarek noted the Klingons' intelligence-gathering capabilities had remained robust, even in the aftermath of the armistice forced on them and the Federation by the Organians—a fragile peace that both sides were here on Centaurus to fortify by negotiating a mutually binding treaty.

Thinking it best to shift the focus off of himself, Sarek turned toward the table of Klingon culinary delicacies. "I hope that our chef was able to prepare these dishes to your liking."

"Yes," Gorkon said. "The *pipius* claws are quite succulent. And I commend your kitchen for knowing not to chill the *gagh*—the worms are so much feistier at room temperature." He cast a look across the ballroom and furrowed his ridged brow. "If I might be permitted one gentle criticism? I might have suggested interspersing the food tables." A toothy grin. "To encourage more casual interaction between our respective contingents."

A sage but humble nod. "A sensible notion, Councillor. I shall take it under advisement for future events." Out of the corner of his eye, Sarek noticed Amanda doing her best not to betray her amusement at the irony of Gorkon's critique.

The small talk rankled Prang. "Who cares about food and trifles? We came to let the Federation sue for peace. Tell me, Ambassador: What are you prepared to give up in exchange for the Empire letting your people live?"

It was instructive to Sarek that Gorkon suppressed any trace of a reaction to Prang's rhetorical challenge. Like a true statesman, Gorkon appeared content to observe how Sarek chose to respond to the younger Klingon's blustering. Sarek stalled by folding his hands in front of his waist while considering his next words. "The questions you ask are most direct, Councillor Prang. If only the answers to them could be as simple. However, I think you know as well as anyone does how complex and delicate a negotiation it is that lies ahead of us."

Prang sneered. "You talk a lot, but say little."

A demure shrug. "I strive for precision."

"An admirable trait," Gorkon said, putting an end to Prang's verbal bullying. "And a necessary one, at a time when so much is at stake."

"Indeed." As was customary in matters diplomatic, both Sarek and Gorkon had indulged in the art of understatement. What both men understood—and were too wise to voice aloud—was that neither side would profit if these negotiations ended in failure. It had been less than nine months since Starfleet and the Klingon Defense Forces had made the mistake of squaring off against each other on the planet Organia, whose native inhabitants—a race of beings who had long since evolved into forms of pure energy, gaining in the process nigh-godlike abilities—had reacted by threatening to neutralize the military capabilities of both interstellar states unless they agreed to an immediate cessation of hostilities followed by a formal peace. At that point, both powers had been forced to set aside old grudges in the name of self-preservation.

Gorkon, speaking under his breath, issued curt orders to Prang and the rest of the Klingon contingent, who promptly dispersed and fanned out into the room to initiate the awkward process of pretending to enjoy mingling with their Federation hosts. As a swell of Terran classical music filtered down from unseen speakers somewhere overhead, he listened, then cracked a smile. "Debussy. Wonderful! Mister Ambassador, may I have permission to ask your wife to dance?"

"My permission is irrelevant. My wife makes her own decisions, and I respect them."

"A wise policy." Adopting a courtly air, Gorkon honored Amanda with a graceful bow. "Madam, may I ask the honor of sharing this dance with you?"

"You certainly may." Amanda took Gorkon's hand. She shot a look of coy amusement at Sarek as the lanky Klingon escorted her onto the dance floor and led her in a classic waltz.

The gathered dignitaries observed the moment with varying degrees of surprise as Gorkon and Amanda whirled around the ballroom with balletic flair. Some of the Federation VIPs regarded the scene as an oddity, but the scowls and raised eyebrows among the Klingons suggested they viewed it as more of a perversion.

Either way, Sarek hoped it was a good omen for the rest of the conference. Because as peculiar a notion as friendship between the Federation and the Klingon Empire might seem to some, he knew for a fact that it was both powers' only remaining hope for survival.

———

The night had been too long and too full of drink for Gorkon to endure one of Prang's signature rants, but the hot-tempered, callow young councillor had never been one to know the joy of an unexpressed thought. As they and their delegation plodded back into their ridiculously luxurious suite of rooms in a commandeered residence hall on the campus of New Athens University, Prang slurred, "Could you have made a bigger fool of yourself, Gorkon?"

Not nearly as inebriated as his detractor, Gorkon turned and confronted Prang. "Were your slander not perfumed with the reek of bloodwine, I would cut your throat."

A sullen glare, then a cocksure smile. "Did you enjoy dancing with Sarek's wife?" He snorted and stumbled sideways. "Did she smell like flowers?"

"She was a superb dance partner. As for your second, less delicate query . . . let's just say that's a fine example of what makes you unsuitable for this kind of work."

"If anyone doesn't belong here—" Prang jabbed his index finger against Gorkon's chest. "It's *you*. You talk like they do. You dance to their music. What next, Gorkon?

Eat their cooked food? Drink that swill they call *coffee*? Serve them the Empire on a platter?"

Their contretemps had become a spectacle. The rest of the delegation had surrounded them, and it was evident more than half were sympathetic to Prang and his sloppy rage. Gorkon knew if they turned against him, the entire mission could be compromised.

Gorkon sucker punched Prang in the gut. The younger man doubled over. Gorkon kneed him in the face, then cracked an armored elbow into Prang's back. As the junior councillor fell facedown on the floor, Gorkon punched him in one kidney, then kneeled on the fallen man's back.

"Listen to me, you stupid whelp. This isn't some back-alley knife fight. There are no points here for bravado." He grabbed a fistful of Prang's hair and hoisted the man's head at a sharp angle from the floor. "You scoff at the Organians' warning, but I saw it happen with my own eyes. An entire fleet paralyzed in deep space. They could *end us*, you fool."

Gorkon stood, pointed at a man near the suite's double doors to the corridor. "Close those." Once the entrance was shut and privacy restored, he continued, raising his voice to speak to the other ten members of the diplomatic team. "We did not come here to pick a fight. We are here to negotiate the terms of a peace that we and our people can accept."

Pivoting slowly, he sought out familiar faces, then aimed his accusatory finger at each of them in turn. "Durok. You work for Imperial Intelligence. They told you to bug the suites and offices of the Federation delegates. Orqom. You're no mere translator. You were sent by the High Command to insinuate surveillance software into the Federation comm relay here in New Athens. Marbas. The Order of the *Bat'leth* wants you to arrange a visit to a Starfleet vessel so you can steal its command codes. I order every one of you to abort your secondary missions *now*, upon pain of death at my hand."

He punctuated his spiel with a swift kick into Prang's ribs. "And *you*, Prang. You're the worst of all. You sent *yourself*, because you and your allies on the High Council mean to sabotage these talks before they get started. Please convey to Councillor Duras my heartfelt regrets for the failure of this pathetic gambit he concocted."

Prang spat a mouthful of magenta-tinted bloody sputum on the floor, then glowered up at Gorkon. "You're the fool, Gorkon. You think I don't know the chancellor's orders? He wants *concessions* from the Federation—more than we could ever have taken by war."

"We all want things we cannot have. Chancellor Sturka is no exception." He walked away from Prang and growled to the others, "This is over. Go to bed."

Withdrawing from the field of rhetorical battle was the only prudent choice, Gorkon knew. Prang had scored a more palpable hit than he'd realized. It was true the chancellor had ordered Gorkon to make outrageous demands in exchange for a peace treaty with the Federation. What was too dangerous for Gorkon to admit to his underlings was that the chancellor expected to get all that he wanted and more, and Gorkon was at a loss for how to placate him with the far less substantial gains these negotiations were certain to yield.

In a game of political poker with existential stakes, I

have been sent to the table with a losing hand, Gorkon lamented as he retired to his private chambers. *Worse, I've been ordered to bluff the infamous Ambassador Sarek of Vulcan.* The weathered Klingon frowned and shook his head. *If only I were still a starship commander. The answer was always simpler then: kill everyone and let the politicians cope with the fallout.* He chortled softly at the ironic nature of his dilemma. *Which makes this, as the songs of old liked to say, poetic justice.*

Three

Even in silent-running mode, the bridge of the *Enterprise* hummed with an undercurrent of intense energy and focus. Lieutenant Uhura's voice cut through the tense sonic backdrop to snare Kirk's attention. "Captain? Mister Spock reports the *Galileo* is ready to launch."

Kirk answered over his shoulder, "Tell him to stand by, Lieutenant."

He swiveled his command chair to face the science station, where Ensign Jana Haines hunched over the hooded sensor display. Trim and golden-haired, the science officer was in her early forties, an uncommon later-in-life applicant to Starfleet Academy. She looked up as Kirk asked, "Ensign, are we still picking up that Klingon cruiser on long-range scans?"

"Negative, sir," she said. "Its last known heading took it back into Klingon space."

"Let's hope our luck holds." He turned toward the main viewscreen, which showed a static field of stars. One of those points of light was the Libros system, home to the planet Usilde and an alien machine that could open doors between universes never meant to intersect.

Technically, the Libros star system was located in neither Federation nor Klingon territory—hence its official status as being of "disputed" sovereignty. To Kirk's discontent—and to the detriment of Captain Una and her

shipmates from the *Enterprise* of eighteen years earlier—
the Federation tended to interpret "disputed" as meaning
"hands off," while the Klingon Empire almost always took
such ambiguities as an invitation to plant its flag.

They certainly did in this case, he brooded.

Looking around the bridge, Kirk found the number of
unfamiliar faces troubling. Lieutenant Stiles manned the
navigator's post—normally Chekov's station on this duty
shift—next to helm officer Lieutenant Beggs Hansen, who
filled in for Lieutenant Hikaru Sulu. Both of them were
eminently qualified for their roles, but in times of crisis
Kirk had grown accustomed to surrounding himself on
the bridge with the *Enterprise*'s best officers. Though he
had been reluctant to deprive himself of the counsel of all
but one of his most accomplished officers, he knew it was
the best strategy for success—not least because Spock had
assured him it was so.

The soft pneumatic swish of turbolift doors parting turned Kirk's head just enough to note the arrival of
Doctor Leonard McCoy, the *Enterprise*'s chief surgeon
and his trusted friend and adviser. The lean, perpetually
exhausted-looking physician emerged from the lift and
descended the short steps into the command well of the
bridge to stand at Kirk's side. Though he had a reputation
for emotional outbursts, on this occasion he lowered his
voice to a confidential volume that did nothing to conceal
his ire. "Jim? Have you lost your mind?"

"This is neither the time nor the place, Doctor."

"I disagree. You're about to put four good men in the
Klingons' crosshairs. Now seems like the perfect time for
me to ask: *Why?*"

Kirk shot a glare of reproach at his friend. "Because it's what *needs* to be done. And you of all people should know that on *this* bridge, my orders are *not* up for debate."

His rebuke prompted McCoy to deliver his rebuttal as a whisper. "Dammit, Jim. How can you take a risk like this, the night before the treaty conference?"

"Because I made a promise, Bones. To Captain Una."

"But if Spock and the others are caught—" McCoy looked around to make sure his next words were safe from eavesdroppers. "It could start a war. Or they could be charged as spies—"

"And put to death," Kirk said, finishing the grim thought. "I know. And so do they."

"Seems an awfully high price to pay for a *promise*," the doctor grumbled.

"Your objections are noted, Doctor."

Rebuffed, McCoy apparently had nothing more to say as he withdrew from the command well to loom over Uhura's shoulder on the upper deck of the bridge. Kirk let his friend retreat from the conversation as he stewed over the unsettling truth he had been forbidden to share with anyone else on the ship except Spock: It had never been Kirk's decision to send the bulk of his senior staff on a covert operation to Usilde. After he told Starfleet Command of the Transfer Key's existence—and its theft by a Romulan sleeper agent—they had dictated this mission to him in spite of his objections.

Most galling of all had been the addendum that directed Kirk to take full personal responsibility for the mission—so that if it backfired, it could be dismissed as a rogue operation, the brainchild of a maverick starship captain acting without authority. The rationale for the order had been apparent to Kirk from the start. It was there to safeguard the treaty negotiations from any blowback that might occur if the mission went sour. And because Kirk would ultimately be responsible for the conduct of all personnel under his command anyway, it had been deemed preferable to portray him as a renegade rather than as a commander who had lost control of his ship and crew. In the abstract, Kirk agreed with his superiors' reasoning, though he harbored concerns that it might foster a false impression of his command style and encourage copycats.

Can't worry about my image, he decided. *If this is what Starfleet needs me to be, or seem to be, then that's what I'll deliver.* Kirk had always considered himself a loyal officer, a by-the-book man who put his mission, his ship, and his crew ahead of his self-interest. And so he would remain— no matter what mistaken impressions history might have of him in ages to come.

But that didn't mean he had to be reckless.

He turned once more toward Uhura at the communications console. "Lieutenant? Any signal traffic to or from Usilde on Klingon military channels?"

She pressed a deep brown hand gently to the receiver tucked into her ear, listened with keen attention for several seconds, then shook her head at Kirk. "None, sir."

"Very well, then. Inform Mister Spock the *Galileo* is clear to launch."

As Uhura relayed his order down to the ship's shuttle

hangar, Kirk said, "Mister Stiles, aft angle on-screen, please."

"Aye, sir." Stiles keyed the command into the forward console, and the image on the main viewscreen changed to show the aft section of the *Enterprise*'s cylindrical secondary hull. A few seconds later, a small silver flash shot from the starship's open clamshell hangar doors. Within moments the brilliant streak of motion retreated into a pinpoint of light that shrank and disappeared into the endless spray of stars.

From behind Kirk, Uhura confirmed, "The *Galileo* is away."

"Thank you, Lieutenant. Monitor their emergency channel at all times until their return."

Kirk stared at the stars, alone with all the doubts he knew he could never share. Had he done the right thing? Had he just jeopardized the treaty negotiations, and with them, the fates of billions of sentient beings? Most damning of all, had he sent his friends and shipmates to their deaths? Only time would tell, but for now all his misgivings had to remain his alone.

Because that was what it meant to be a starship captain.

———

Journeys of a thousand miles may all have begun with single steps, but Captain Una had long since forgotten the step that launched her upon her interminable path.

It was easy, in the monotony of the desert, for one's mind to wander. Even with a distant landmark upon which to fix one's gaze, the endless flats, the barren horizon, and the empty sky all conspired to lull one into a walking hypnosis, a perpetual dream state of denial.

Una blinked and found herself in the high-walled confines of a rocky mountain pass, with no recollection of how or when she had transitioned from the salt flats onto a narrow trail strewn with jagged stones and drifting veils of beige dust. Suddenly cognizant of her new environment, she stopped. Craned her head back. Turned in a slow circle. Wind-blasted spires of tan rock scraped the bleached-white heavens above. On either side of her lonely road towered imposing, rugged cliffs. She saw no sign of caves or other shelter, high or low. As much as the desert had been a wasteland, so was the mountain pass.

Her training asserted itself. Una knew she must have been walking for an extended period of time, but she had only the vaguest memories of nightfall and sunrise, of her shadow circling her as it would the gnomon of a sundial. Had she imagined the suns' transits of the sky? Had the stars overhead been nothing but delusion? It seemed implausible, yet she couldn't deny the obvious: Had she been awake for several consecutive days, in the absence of pharmaceutical assistance, she would now be experiencing severe symptoms of sleep deprivation. Yet she felt almost entirely lucid, rooted in the present moment, however surreal it might be.

Other conundrums nagged at her. She had come well prepared to venture beyond the dimensional barrier, her backpack loaded with water, provisions, and a first-aid kit. But had she eaten anything since her arrival? Had she drawn so much as a sip from the canteen? It hung on the side of her pack, heavy and silent, which suggested it remained full. But if that were so, how had she escaped the effects of dehydration? If she had yet to dig into her rations, why had she not begun to feel the consequences of hypoglycemia?

All the details of her predicament felt remote from her experience, as if she were but a spectator to her own life. *Maybe this is a peculiarity of the alternate universe. If its physical laws differ from those I take for granted, these oddities might be evidence of a new paradigm.*

On its face it seemed a rational explanation, but part of her mind refused to accept it. *Even if this universe operates by different physical laws, wouldn't my biology continue to obey those by which it was made? Is it possible that transiting the dimensional barrier changed me?*

It was a deeply confusing notion. How could she adapt her behavior to suit physical laws of which she had no knowledge? *I can only address the phenomena I perceive,* Una decided.

Resolved to confront her circumstances as they presented themselves, she pressed onward, deeper into the mountain pass, toward what appeared to be a sky rich with hues of waning daylight. Though she hoped the variegated textures and terrain of the pass would keep her mind engaged as she pushed ahead, she soon found herself drifting through the same phantasmagoric haze that had enveloped her on the salt flats. One bit of jagged stone soon came to look like most others, and any hope of remaining rooted in the elusive present to which Una had clung slipped away, lost in the eddies and currents of unchained thought.

Her mind drifted through backwaters of recent memory, then dived into the depths of her life before Starfleet, before her days of being hailed as exceptional, to her developmental years on Illyria, her youth of insecurity and struggle, her childhood of rejections and condemnations. *Never good enough*—that was the lesson she had internalized from her mother, that cruel mistress whose rhetorical quiver had never held one shaft of kindness for all of Una's efforts.

When, at long last, Una's age of independence had drawn near, she had known there would be no path she could take in life that would win her mother's approval. So she had chosen the road that made her happy, that set her on a course to pursue her own dreams and measure out her life not in bitter words but on her own terms, as a grown woman and a freethinking being.

Ironically, that was the only day of Una's life her mother received her not with a frown but a smile, not with criticism but with a hopeful benediction: "Good luck, my dear."

Looking back, Una was at a loss to imagine any other way her mother could have raised her to be the woman she had become.

It's almost as if she spent my youth teaching me to break free of her.

A jab of sharpened stone in Una's ribs disrupted her nostalgic reverie. She halted, lifted her hands slowly, then shifted to look back at whoever it was that had waylaid her on the pass.

A trio of Usildar, their jade-green hair and lithe bodies camouflaged with stripes of stone-colored dust, had ambushed her from behind. Adapted for an arboreal lifestyle, they had long limbs and opposable thumbs on hands and feet alike. Though they tended to cross open ground with their hands swinging low, their lankiness served them well in situations such as this: two of Una's three interceptors dangled upside down from rocky ledges while hoisting spears with flint heads. The third had crept up behind her to jab the business end of his weapon into her back.

They did not appear mollified as she smiled at them. "Hello again."

"Declare yourself, stranger."

She hid her disappointment. Though few of the Usildar she had encountered on Usilde had recognized her after her nearly two decades of absence, she had hoped any of their kin she encountered here might know her face. Instead, she had to hope they remembered her name.

"You know me as Una."

Confused looks passed among the three Usildar. The one who was poking her lumbar region said, "We know of no *Una*."

"My friends and I came from a distant land, to help your people fight the intruders."

This time her words sparked a different, less hostile, but still wary reaction. The Usildar at her back retracted his spear. "You are a friend to the outlanders?"

"I am."

The leader thrust his spear point under Una's jaw. "Prove it."

"I come from the *Enterprise*. My friends' names are Martinez and Shimizu."

The moment she spoke the names, the mood of the Usildar changed. The leader turned his weapon aside, and the dangling pair behind him bowed their heads. Extending his hand in the human fashion to Una, the leader of the trio said, "I am Feneb, Ranger of the Usildar."

She took his hand. "I am Una of the *Enterprise*, and I come to you as a friend."

"Then follow us, Friend Una." He let go of her hand and bounded off, down the mountain pass, with his comrades close behind, his voice echoing off the stony walls: "We go to your kin."

───────

Through the front port of the shuttlecraft *Galileo*, Spock watched the gray-green orb of Usilde grow steadily larger against the starry curtain of the cosmos. He and the rest of the black-clad landing party under his command were nearly at their destination.

"Time to atmosphere, Mister Sulu?"

"Thirty seconds, sir." The *Enterprise*'s senior helm officer guided the boxy shuttle with such ease that he made the clumsy-looking vessel seem downright graceful. Spock considered it a testament to the man's exceptional piloting skill.

Behind the *Enterprise*'s helmsman and first officer, its chief engineer, Lieutenant Commander Montgomery Scott, and its boyish new navigator, Ensign Pavel Chekov, argued under their breath while they tinkered with a cobbled-together gadget Scott had tied into the *Galileo's* navigational deflector. "No, lad," the Scotsman said, his frustration heightening his Aberdeen brogue. "This one goes here, that one goes there."

Chekov's Russian accent was just as heavy as Scott's and tinged with a soupçon of resentment to boot. "In Russia, these connections would have been color coded."

"A shame we're not in Russia, then."

"Gentlemen," Spock said, short-circuiting their argument. "Will the sensor scrambler be ready before we reach the atmosphere? If not, I will give Mister Sulu the order to abort."

"Aye, it'll be ready," Scott said. "If the lad can learn to follow directions."

Chekov tensed to retort. Then he noted Spock's unforgiving scrutiny and kept his protests to himself as he completed the final connections to the sensor-jamming device. "Scrambler ready, Mister Spock."

"Mister Scott, if you would do the honors, please."

"Aye, sir." The chief engineer moved forward to the main console, while Spock slipped aft to make room beside Sulu. With a few swift adjustments to the shuttlecraft's main panel, Scott powered up the device, which filled the passenger compartment with a low-frequency hum and a palpable tingle of galvanic forces coursing over and around the crew. Scott backed away from the console and nodded to Spock. "System engaged, sir."

Spock returned to his station beside Sulu. "Well done, Mister Scott."

It was possible his praise had been premature. Only after the *Galileo* had passed the point of no return would its crew know whether their stealth-approach trajectory, coupled with a jerry-rigged sensor scrambler designed to make them appear as ordinary meteoric debris burning up in the atmosphere, would be enough to fool the Klingon forces on the planet's surface. If they had made the slightest error in their jamming device, or had underestimated the enemy's technological sophistication, they were all about to pay for such a mistake with their lives.

The dark side of Usilde hove into view and blotted out the stars. Unlike the benighted hemispheres of most developed worlds in the Federation, the dark half of primitive Usilde was pitch-black, utterly devoid of artificial light sources. For Sulu that meant flying by instruments alone, because the surface would provide no visible landmarks by which to steer. Fortunately, it was a task for which the native San Franciscan was eminently qualified.

Spock pressed a button on the command panel and extinguished all lighting inside the *Galileo* except for Sulu's piloting console. "Prepare to deploy as soon as we touch down," he said to Scott and Chekov. With a tactile check, he confirmed his compact phaser was in place in the middle of his back and his communicator was secure. His tricorder was inside a slim-profile backpack that he pulled on and fastened with a tug of its straps. Though the rear of the shuttlecraft was steeped in darkness, his sensitive Vulcan ears picked up the soft brush of hands passing over equipment as Scott and Chekov verified their own gear was in order.

Roaring wind noise reverberated through the hull,

and the ship shook—only a bit at first, then with increasing violence—as the *Galileo* plunged toward the surface of Usilde. The more fierce the turbulence became, the more confident Spock was that their arrival had not been detected by the Klingons. *Had they recognized our sensor profile, they would have shot us from the sky by now.* After Spock accounted for all the variables he knew, he calculated the *Galileo*'s chance of reaching the surface intact as greater than ninety-six percent.

Sulu announced over his shoulder, "Thirty seconds to the landing site."

"Mind the local foliage, Lieutenant," Spock said. "it can be quite dense."

"Aye, sir. I have clear sensor readings of the landscape. Our approach is open." True to his word, even in near-perfect darkness, Sulu guided the shuttlecraft down through a gap in the rain forest's tightly packed canopy, into a small and nearly level glade. The *Galileo* touched down with the gentlest of bumps, and then the purr of its impulse engines and thrusters dwindled to silence. "We're down and secure, Mister Spock."

"Well done, Lieutenant. Open the hatch."

Servomotors whined as the hatch slid open. Sultry heat flooded the interior of the shuttlecraft, followed by the sawing song of insects, the harsh screeches of avian life-forms, and the growls of animal hungers echoing in the night.

Spock led the way outside. "Follow me, and stay close."

He heard the other three men's footsteps as they followed him outside. Sulu, the last one to exit the shuttle-craft, closed its hatch. Once the door was shut, the only light in the glade was the weak and distant glow of the stars. As Sulu adjusted the straps of his backpack, Spock said, "Switch to night-vision goggles."

He and the others all had practiced this. Each man retrieved a pair of light-amplifying goggles from an outer pocket on the side of his backpack. Spock secured his in place and powered them up. At once the impenetrable black of night gave way to a surreal scene as the goggles intensified ultraviolet light to render the nightscape in frost-blue shadows and highlights. The other members of the landing party all showed Spock a thumbs-up signal, indicating their goggles were functioning correctly. He signaled them with a gesture to fall in behind him.

Superimposed over his holographic view of the rain forest were subtle scrolls of data from his tricorder, indicating direction and range to the landing party's first objective. Using the heads-up display as his guide, he led Sulu, Chekov, and Scott through muddy paths tangled with roots and low-hanging vines, down a steep slope cloaked in waist-high fronds, then through a gully to another clearing, one smaller than that in which Sulu had landed the *Galileo*.

"This way," Spock said, pointing toward a jumble of broken foliage. The others joined him at the hastily assembled pile of natural camouflage. "Help me remove this." Working as a team, it took them less than a minute to expose the alien travel pod Spock had concealed more than a month earlier, after having stolen it to effect a hectic escape with Captain Kirk from the fortress and dimensional portal the Jatohr called their sanctuary.

Sulu doffed his pack, pulled out his tricorder, and conducted a thorough scan of the pod, employing protocols he and Spock had developed together. "Its security circuit is still responding to external signals," Sulu said. "Scanning for the access codes to the citadel."

Somewhere nearby, a throaty roar gave the impression of a large carnivore with an even larger appetite, on the hunt and keen to make a meal of the landing party. Scott and Chekov both drew their phasers and listened for further warnings of unwanted company, animal or otherwise.

"Got it," Sulu said. "You were right, Mister Spock. The pod does transmit the access code inside a subharmonic of the main response frequency."

Chekov pivoted left, then right, his hand tight on his phaser. "Does that mean we can go now?"

"Yes, Ensign," Spock said. With one tap on his goggles' exterior controls, he instructed his tricorder to switch its guidance circuit to their next destination: the Jatohr citadel. As soon as it locked in he started walking, without fear or hesitation, deeper into the forest primeval. "This way, gentlemen. We have much to do before daybreak."

"Assuming we live that long," Sulu said.

"If all goes to plan," Spock said, "there is no reason to think we won't."

Scott chuckled softly, then said under his breath to

Chekov, "See, lad? What did I tell you? Beneath that cold Vulcan logic beats the heart of an optimist."

Sulu and Chekov laughed. Spock could only shake his head.

"Really, Mister Scott. I see no reason to stoop to insults."

"Sorry, sir," Scott said—yet Spock suspected the man felt no remorse.

I shall never understand the human need for derogatory humor.

A soul could lose itself in the crags and crevices that lined the mountain pass, and Una was all but certain she had lost her bearings as her Usildar escorts ushered her through one fissure after another, ever deeper into the rocky labyrinth.

"Is it much farther?"

"It is as far as it is," said Feneb.

The only thing Una found more maddening than Feneb's tautology was the endless maze of stone paths and switchbacks down which he and his cohort led her.

Before long, the repetition of their surroundings, the perpetual sameness of the landmarks and other features, coupled with the renewed sensation that the twin suns had stalled in the sky, left Una battling disorientation. It was as if every detail she saw had been crafted to sap her will.

In a blink Una found herself in a secluded box canyon at the end of the trail. Caves dotted its red-stone walls;

makeshift rope nets facilitated movement between its upper and lower tiers. A number of Usildar navigated the rope nets with preternatural ease. On the canyon's floor stood a small cluster of tents.

Una had no memory of navigating a turn in the rocky paths that brought her here. One moment she had been in the maze; the next she was in the canyon. All she could think of by way of an explanation was that she had let her mind wander, and so had missed the transition, just as she had when she first found herself in the foothills.

How long ago was that? When did I get here?

There was no time to look for answers. Semifamiliar faces emerged from the tents. Una had prepared herself to confront time-worn visions of her former shipmates, but the people who walked out to meet her looked like her lost friends as they had been when they parted, eighteen years earlier. She set down her backpack and walked toward them.

Lieutenant Commander Martinez was sun-browned but still vigorous—except for his eyes, which looked impossibly ancient. His once indomitable bearing was worn down, beaten into a tired slouch. Beside him was Ensign Tim Shimizu; he had the physique and face of a young man, but all traces of his youthful humor and vitality had vanished, leaving the haunted eyes of one who had seen too much to retain his hold on hope. Behind them were the three security officers who had been part of their landing party on Usilde in 2249—Lieutenant Griffin, Ensign Le May, and Petty Officer Cambias.

Lingering back by the tents were four more lost *Enterprise* personnel, all officers cruelly kidnapped from the ship's bridge by the Jatohr: relief navigator Ensign Cheryl Stevens; Ensign Bruce Goldberg, who had been Captain April's beta-shift yeoman; Ensign Dylan Craig, from the sciences division; and Lieutenant Ingrid Holstine, the relief communications officer.

All of them stared at Una, as if straining to dredge her likeness from their memories. Hoping their chain of command had remained intact despite their long exile, Una made a point of walking toward and addressing Martinez. She raised a hand in greeting as they came to a halt a few yards shy of each other. "Raul? It's me. Una." Not seeing any recognition in his eyes, she reverted to her shipboard nickname: "Number One."

He cocked his head forward and narrowed his squint. "Una? Is that really you?"

"Yes, Raul. It's really me."

She wasn't sure what she had expected. A joyous reunion, mayhap? A firm clasping of hands? Maybe even a vigorous but platonic embrace?

Tears flooded Martinez's eyes, and he dropped to his knees in front of her and sobbed into the sandy earth. "It's been *so long*, Una. It's been *forever*. We thought you'd forgotten us."

Could this really be the same man she had known? The hard-as-nails taskmaster? The proud leader, the fearless soldier? It looked like him, but this man was broken, shattered inside in ways Una would never have thought possible. She kneeled beside him and set her hand on his shoulder, for whatever small measure of comfort that feeble gesture could provide.

A shadow fell over them. Una looked up into the mirthless eyes of Shimizu. He broke his glum frown just long enough to say, "Nice to see you, Number One. Welcome to hell."

Four

There were faster ways to reach the Jatohr fortress than traversing the rain forest on foot, but all of them, Spock knew, were nearly certain to draw the Klingons' attention. One could mask a shuttlecraft from sensors with a measure of technical legerdemain, but concealing one, or an airborne Jatohr transport pod, from the eyes of a Klingon sentry standing watch atop the citadel's eerily organic-looking curved outer walls was nearly impossible without a cloaking device—an advantage that was, for the moment, exclusively in the domain of the Romulans.

Armed with night-vision goggles, he and the rest of the *Enterprise* landing party had moved with stealth down a narrow trail that snaked through dense jungle and thick underbrush. Using narrow-stream aerosol capsules, they had cleared a path, dissolving prickly twisting vines with a substance designed to break down plant fibers while leaving animal tissues and other materials unharmed. Unlike phasers, the spray gave off no light to attract watchful eyes, and it had the advantage of being almost silent. Best of all, after breaking down the branches, the compound turned inert and the dissolved plants became organic fertilizer.

Spock found it noteworthy that only the native Usildean flora was affected by the spray. The pervasive infestation of invasive gray plant species that had taken root along the shoreline and spread deep into the jungle now proved impervious to the defoliant, suggesting their internal chemistry and cellular structures were unlike anything as yet known to Federation science.

Soon the landing party arrived at the forest's abrupt edge and confronted a hundred-meter-wide patch of scorched earth that stood between the jungle and the lake beyond. Great effigies of carved wood and vines, all shaped like Jatohr, peppered the no-man's-land. The rough-hewn scarecrows faced the jungle, the meaning behind their grim presences abundantly clear: *turn back.*

"Use caution here," Spock warned. "Captain Una said the Usildar have set pitfalls and other traps here."

Scott adjusted his tricorder. "Scanning for hidden surprises. Anything we pick up will be relayed to our goggles."

"Good work, Mister Scott." To the others Spock added, "From this point, remain silent until we reach the fungus patch along the lakeshore."

Spock knew the Usildar posted sentries along the tree line to guard against anyone crossing their forbidden zone. He hoped the fortunate combination of moonless darkness, their dark uniforms, and the coal-black burnt ground would make the landing party all but impossible for the Usildar to see.

It took them only a few minutes to traverse the open ground, which was littered with large melons apparently scattered to serve as obstacles and to funnel trespassers into the traps, all of which the landing party evaded with ease.

When their boots squished and crunched across the thick carpet of pungent gray fungus on the other side, it required effort for Spock to mask his displeasure at the odious reek. To the consternation of his shipmates, the stench of decay only grew worse as they neared the gray algae-covered lake, which burbled like a witch's cauldron spewing nitrogen and methane.

They all crouched along the water's edge. From the lake's center rose a structure Usilde's natives called the citadel. Its central tower was ringed by a curve-topped, circular outer wall whose nacreous texture was evocative of the shells of invertebrates—features reflective of the physiology of its architects, an extradimensional species of giant gastropods called the Jatohr. Towering, jagged fingers of pitted rock poked upward from the scum-covered lake at random points around the bizarre alien fortress.

Sulu scanned the citadel with his tricorder. "I'm reading movement along the tops of the walls." He pointed out the Klingon sentinels to Spock, Chekov, and Scott. "Four guards. Each one alone. At regular intervals on the upper perimeter."

The four Klingons were hard to see, even with the light-intensifying goggles, but in seconds Spock observed each one. "Well done, Lieutenant." He reached into a side pouch of his pack and pulled out a full-face diving mask that included a compact rebreather apparatus and a built-in air supply. "Masks on. Mister Chekov, Mister Scott: arm ultrasonic repellent as soon as we're underwater."

The landing party donned its diving masks and followed Spock, who waded with care into the lake. His body sliced a path through the odoriferous tin-colored algae choking its surface. After they all had submerged, Spock's sensitive Vulcan hearing registered the activation hums of Scott's and Chekov's ultrasonic repellent devices. Their pulses' frequencies pitched upward, beyond the reach of even Spock's superlative auditory senses. As they did, he noticed that all the aquatic creatures within view made haste to flee the landing party.

Just as we had desired, Spock noted. He made a mental note to log a commendation for the *Enterprise*'s senior marine biologist, Lieutenant Marina Frants, when he returned to the ship.

Moving in close formation, the four officers crossed the lake to one of the Jatohr fortress's several underwater entrances. Many dozens of meters away, next to the entrance of a more distant landing bay, Spock noted the breach a misdirected Klingon photon grenade had blasted through the citadel's foundation weeks earlier, during his and Kirk's harried escape from the city mere minutes after its occupation by the Klingons.

Odd, he thought. *I recalled that breach being wider.* He attributed the variance between his memory and his observation to the speed of his and the captain's escape. Despite his Vulcan mental discipline, Spock's human half remained vulnerable to adrenaline's sensory distortions.

With a nod, he instructed Sulu to commence his next part in the mission. Sulu activated his tricorder—which Mister Scott had most helpfully waterproofed before they left the *Enterprise*—and triggered the security sequence they had hacked from the Jatohr pod abandoned in the rain forest. Sulu made a few minor adjustments, then one of the citadel's undamaged underwater entrance hatches dilated open like an iris, without a sound, directly ahead of them.

Spock waited for Sulu's all-clear, and then he led the landing party inside. They surfaced inside a moon pool, a hangar for a squadron of amphibious pods. Pale blue strips glowed overhead to light the spacious chamber, in which even the faintest sounds echoed. The landing party waded toward shallower water, then prowled up the gradual ramp that led out of the moon pool to the promenade that encircled it. Their synthetic bodysuits, whose exteriors had been treated with hydrophobic compounds, shed their water with prejudice. It took only seconds for the entire landing party to exit the pool, but by the time they stepped onto the floor, their garments were dry enough that they left not a single footprint to mark their passage.

The four men removed and stowed their rebreathers and diving masks. Spock motioned them toward a door to an airlock, from which they could access a network of corridors that would lead to the control levels of the citadel. He keyed the door's access code into a panel beside it, then it, too, dilated open ahead of them. The four men crowded into the airlock as Spock repeated the process, closing the first portal behind them and opening the one ahead. "This way," he said, skulking down the shadowy passageway, whose walls and ceilings were as curvilinear as the citadel's outer walls, making them seem more like lava tubes or something else wrought by nature than like something engineered by a scientifically advanced culture.

No one spoke as the landing party sneaked through

the alien complex. Halfway to their destination, they took cover behind the walls' protruding, riblike structures as a Klingon patrol marched past ahead of them at a juncture between two intersecting tubular passageways. It was unclear whether the Klingons would shoot to kill on sight, or seek to capture intruders; regardless of the truth, Spock was of no mind to find out firsthand.

They arrived at a spiraling ramp tucked into a recess along the wall. Spock checked to make sure it was clear, then waved the others past him while he guarded their rear flank. Scott descended the spiral ramp first, followed by Sulu, then Chekov. Spock backed down the ramp behind them, watchful for any sign of detection or pursuit.

At the bottom of the spiral, the team regrouped into a forward-facing huddle. Together they looked out at the massive, bizarre machinery that constituted the bowels of what the Jatohr's command consoles had designated the transfer-field generator. Unlike the master control room, which was secured behind a door that could be bypassed only with the aid of a transporter, this sprawling, tiered sublevel was accessible from several different areas of the fortress. Just as Spock had feared, however, it was crowded with Klingon scientists and armed guards.

"There's your gizmo," Scott said. "But good luck gettin' to it."

Chekov wondered, "Are the guards to keep us out, or the scientists in?"

A shrug from Sulu. "Could be both."

Spock lowered his voice as he surveyed the unfavorable tactical situation. "Mister Scott, can we access the Klingons' computers from here?"

"No, sir. They've locked down their circuits, tight as a drum." He pointed toward a secluded cluster of Klingon computer hardware, from which ran a confused tangle of data cables. "We can patch in from there—if I can get to it."

"Then we shall require a distraction," Spock said.

Chekov cracked an impish grin. "Leave that to me."

———

As an engineer, Lieutenant Commander Montgomery Scott was not, by nature, given to taking anything on faith. He liked knowing the variables, the specifications of a situation, and planning his response to fit. Consequently, hearing Pavel Chekov say "Leave that to me" had not exactly filled Scott with confidence.

What's he up to now? Getting us all killed, I'd wager.

After a brief whispered consultation with Spock, the young ensign had stolen away into the shadows alone, back up the ramp to a tier above the large banks of machinery where the Klingons were working. Scott remained baffled as to what sort of "distraction" Chekov could have devised. So far as Scott was aware, the landing party had not brought along any explosives, and none of the pharmaceuticals in their first-aid kits were known to be effective against Klingons. So what was he playing at?

He checked his tricorder's chrono. Chekov had been gone for over ten minutes. Where was he? What was the impetuous ensign doing?

Before Scott was able to waste another minute pondering those questions, Chekov emerged in a fleeting dash from the spiral ramp. The mop-topped, fresh-faced Russian stayed in the shadows along the walls as he made his way back to the landing party. As he fell in at the rear of the group, he couldn't contain his mischievous glee. "Watch this."

Several seconds passed without incident.

Sulu furrowed his brow at Chekov. "Watch what?"

"Wait for it."

It was tempting for Scott to think perhaps Chekov had gone mad. Then he saw signs of confusion and alarm sweep through the Klingons surrounding the generator apparatus, both the guards and the scientists. They were pawing at their uniforms, pivoting back and forth as if looking for something—and then their uniforms and other garments started to disintegrate.

Sleeves decayed and vanished, followed by trouser legs, then tunics and jackets fell apart. Orphaned belt buckles and jacket clasps fell to the hard marble-like floor and plinked away into unplumbed crevices. In less than a minute, the Klingons stationed around the generator were all but naked—and thoroughly perplexed.

Just as baffled, Scott looked back at Chekov. "Laddie . . . what did you do?"

"As I thought," Chekov said, feigning nonchalance, "the Klingons prefer to wear natural fibers." Another flash of that blinding grin. "*Plant* fibers."

All at once, Scott understood. Chekov had deployed what was left of the landing party's plant-demolishing aerosol to deprive the Klingons of all plant-based fabrics in their uniforms. Invisible, silent, odorless, and ineffectual on animal tissue, the spray had proved an ideal means of staging a nonlethal diversion. "Nicely done, lad." He chuckled under his breath at the Klingons as they scurried out of the generator facility. "I'll bet you they'll all be wearing nothing but leather and metal the next time we meet 'em."

"A fascinating prediction, Mister Scott." Spock nodded toward their target. "But we have more pressing concerns."

"Aye, sir."

As the last of the Klingons left the generator area, Scott took point and led the team to the cluster of Klingon electronics. He pointed out some of their more common components. "That's a portable network switch, Mister Spock. And the cylinder? That's a backup data node."

"Excellent," said the first officer. "I will need a few minutes to patch in and download their backup data. Mister Sulu, Mister Chekov: stand sentry at the points where the Klingons exited. Mister Scott, please make a detailed scan of the command console."

Scott nodded. "Aye, sir."

Sulu and Chekov split up to guard the entrances while Spock broke into the Klingons' data network and copied their research findings into his own tricorder. In the meantime, Scott surveyed the generator's main console. The Klingons had ripped the thing open, damaging who knew how many critical systems and components inside. Seeing such an advanced feat of alien engineering savaged by such clumsy hands made Scott shake his head in frustration.

I'll never understand Klingons. They say they want to conquer the galaxy—but if they don't learn to respect technology, they won't stand a chance. What're they thinking?

He was just finishing up his tricorder scan of the generator's control system when Chekov and Sulu started to wave silent warnings that the Klingons were on their way back. Within seconds Spock was at Scott's side, beckoning the two junior officers to regroup. "We have what we need," Spock said. "It's time to withdraw." Once Sulu and Chekov reached him and Scott, the first officer pointed them toward the spiral ramp. "Take point, Mister Sulu."

"Aye, sir."

The four of them climbed the spiral ramp and were halfway to the level at which they'd entered when Klingon disruptor blasts screamed up at them from the generator facility below. Shots caromed off the pearlescent walls, which appeared nearly impervious to directed energy pulses. Sulu sprinted away with Chekov close behind him. Spock and Scott were forced to duck to cover briefly before continuing their own mad dash for escape.

It came as no surprise when Klingon alarms blared down the curving passageways of the citadel. Their reverberating wails hounded the landing party all the way back through the airlock to the moon pool. As the four *Enterprise* officers charged toward the water, a squad of Klingon soldiers raced in through a dilating doorway on the far side of the pod hangar. The Klingons gave no warning—they opened fire, forcing the landing party to take cover behind a pod.

Wild shots tore past over their heads and bounced from one gleaming surface to another inside the hangar, creating an instant cross fire. Chekov flattened himself to the floor and cringed at each near miss that screamed past him. "They have us pinned down."

Spock was unfazed. "For the moment." He activated his tricorder, watched its display, then zeroed in on an oval panel on a wall nearby. "Gentlemen, prepare to dive."

Scott did as ordered. On the other side of the pod the landing party was using for cover, the Klingons advanced two by two in cover formation, darting from one pod or piece of heavy equipment to another. By the time Scott fixed his mask and rebreather into place, Spock had finished fine-tuning his tricorder's settings. "Brace yourselves," he said.

A grouping of lights on the oval wall panel changed colors. Scott felt his ears pop as both the inner and outer doors of the airlock spiraled open.

Then came the water. It swelled out of the moon pool and expanded across the deck, pushing aside anything in its path, including pods, machinery, and the Klingon security team. Moving with tremendous speed and violence, the crashing water swept the Klingons off their feet and slammed them into the hangar's far wall.

Spock sprang into action. "Dive!"

Scott, Chekov, and Sulu followed Spock into the flood. Even underwater Scott felt its surging pressure while he fought his way back to the dilated underwater portal. Only after the landing party had exited into the lake did Scott feel as if they had truly escaped.

Stray shots from the rooftop sentries hectored the landing party's retreat as they reached the far shore and darted through the gap they'd made in the lake's wall of thorns. Back under cover in the rain forest, they ran like madmen, sprinting as if tigers were nipping their heels.

Only once they were aboard the *Galileo* and racing at full impulse away from Usilde to their rendezvous with the *Enterprise* did Scott heave a sigh of relief. Sulu and Chekov manned the shuttlecraft's controls while Spock perused the stolen data files on his tricorder.

In a confidential timbre, Scott asked the half Vulcan, "Did we get what we need?"

"It appears we acquired everything the Klingons know about that facility, as well as what use they plan to make of it." Spock's cool mien betrayed a hint of a frown. "I will know more after I analyze this data on the *Enterprise*." He looked up, curious. "Did you complete your scan of the command console?"

"Aye." Scott was unable to hide his doubts. "But whether I'll be able to make heads or tails of it? That remains to be seen."

Five

On a ship as small as a Romulan bird-of-prey, everything was in short supply at all times: fresh food, stiff drinks, medicine, spare parts, time to sleep—but no commodity aboard ship was so rare as privacy. Tight spaces packed with as many personnel as the ship's systems could support had proved effective at preventing the sequestration of secrets.

Even the sanctum of the commander's quarters offered little relief from eavesdropping. Commander Creelok, like most members of the Imperial star navy, was no claustrophobe, but despite a lifetime of service on starships, he found the confines of his private compartment stifling. They provided him barely enough room to pace a full stride from rack to desk before forcing him to turn about. Tucked into the deepest section of the small ship's disklike primary hull, the single room had no viewport. Creelok knew this was for his protection, but many nights he would gladly have traded safety for a view of the warp-stretched stars outside the *Velibor*.

His door signal buzzed. With a press of a button on his desktop, he unlocked the door, which slid open to admit Centurion Mirat. The silver-haired veteran stepped inside, then manually shut and locked the door behind him. Fear lurked in his weary eyes. "Are we secure?"

Creelok stole a wary look at the overhead. "As much as we can hope to be."

Mirat frowned. He understood Creelok's warning all too well. It was likely the room had been equipped by the Tal Shiar with a number of listening devices. Most of the time they were used by the Empire's political officers to ensure full loyalty and compliance by its command-grade officers. But the surveillance systems were just as often abused by ambitious young field operatives such as Sadira, who Creelok suspected was auditing their every word.

The centurion produced a small device from under his tunic and set it atop Creelok's desk. He switched it on with a tap of his finger. A faint green indicator light blinked on to confirm that it was functioning and had blocked the receptors of one or more listening devices.

"She pulled rank," Mirat said. "Changed our heading during the overnight shift."

The commander reined in his anger at the news. "To where?"

"Unknown. She entered the new coordinates, then locked us out of the helm."

Creelok slammed his fist against the bulkhead. "Damn her! She treats me like a spare part on my own ship."

A solemn look settled over Mirat. "The crew's worried she's taking us into enemy space." He studied the commander's face for any sign of a reaction. "Is she?"

He replied with indignant sarcasm, "I'm just the commander. Why would the Tal Shiar tell me what my ship and crew are being used for?"

"Perhaps it's time we asked her."

"Challenge a Tal Shiar officer? A capital idea, Centurion. But tell me: Do you plan to sleep with one eye open for the rest of your life?"

"I learned that trick growing up in the slums of Ki Baratan, sir."

"No doubt." Creelok pondered their predicament. "Have you spoken with Ranimir? He might be able to patch into the sensors, gauge our heading."

Mirat nodded. "We tried. Sadira isolated the sensor feeds so that only the autopilot can access them. Until we reach our destination, the rest of us will be flying blind."

"So, she expects we'd resist if we knew our journey's endpoint. To me, that suggests she means to place us in peril, but she also needs to ensure none of us can betray her plan."

"We're on the hunt, then."

"Most likely. But who or what is our prey?"

The door signal buzzed, and both men froze. They traded anxious looks. Then the signal buzzed again, drawing their shared attention to the room's sole point of ingress or egress. Creelok reached over to his desk and pressed the button to unlock the door. It slid aside to reveal Sadira. The lithe human woman stepped inside Creelok's quarters without waiting for an invitation. She trained her piercing stare on the commander as she said, "Centurion, get out."

"The centurion is my guest," Creelok said. "He'll go when—"

"He'll leave now, Commander."

There was no reason to think Sadira's threat an idle one, but Mirat held his ground until Creelok dismissed him with a nod. "That's all, Centurion."

Mirat put his fist to his chest, then extended his arm in salute to Creelok before walking to the door. As the centurion left, his only acknowledgment of Sadira was a hateful glower.

She waited until the door closed before she continued. "I'm to understand you and the centurion have . . . *misgivings* . . . about my current assignment."

"Not at all. That would imply we knew what your mission was."

A coy half smirk. "Come now, Commander. Must we play games?"

"Is that what you think this is? A game?" Creelok gestured at the bulkheads. "Because I see a ship and a crew of nearly a hundred brave Romulans—all of which are being put at risk by some *hevam wikah* with delusions of grandeur."

Just as he had hoped, Sadira flinched at the ancient Rihannsu pejoratives. Her lips thinned and vanished into a taut frown, and her hand inched toward the dagger on her belt. He almost hoped she would try to draw her blade. That would be all the provocation he needed to cut her down without risking his career before a military tribunal.

The Tal Shiar officer denied him his revenge once again. She adopted an air of false comity and folded her hands behind her back. "How can I set your mind at ease, Commander?"

"Tell me where you're taking my ship."

"I'm afraid that's on a need-to-know basis."

She'll tell me anything except what I want to know. "Are we crossing the Neutral Zone?"

"I can neither confirm nor deny such suspicions."

All he wanted in that moment was to wrap his weathered hands around her slender neck and feel her cervical vertebrae shatter in his grip. "I don't care what they tell you at the Tal Shiar. There are limits to your authority on this ship." He stepped forward, invading her space. "If you plan to put my crew in danger, I have a right to know. So tell me the truth, you *sussethrai*—are you using my crew to start a war?"

Her smile was as cold and deadly as space. "No, Commander, I'm looking to win one—without anyone ever knowing we were there."

———

The conference room's gauzy curtains were aglow with a blinding splash of golden sunlight as Sarek called the meeting to order. "Fellow delegates, honored guests, I bid you good morning and welcome. Please be seated."

On one side of the table, with their backs to the wall of barely screened windows and its blinding pour of daylight, was the Federation delegation, with Sarek seated in the middle. On his left was his economic adviser, Aravella Gianaris, a human woman with black hair and an olive-tinted complexion who preferred to be described as an Athenian rather than as a Terran. On his right was his military adviser, Beel Zeroh, an irascible Izarian of questionable credentials who Sarek suspected would not last long in the Federation diplomatic corps, but with whose dubious services he was for the moment burdened. To either side beyond them were attachés and various policy specialists in fields ranging from agriculture and aquaculture to transportation, planetary infrastructure management, and general legal counsel.

Lining the other side of the oblong, vaguely oval conference table were the members of the Klingon delegation. Councillor Gorkon sat directly across from Sarek, in the middle of his group. Councillor Prang was seated across from Zeroh, while Durok, a delegate of undetermined portfolio, faced Gianaris. Filling out the Klingons' ranks were advisers and assistants whose job descriptions were roughly equivalent to those of their opposites across the table.

Once everyone had settled into his or her chair, Sarek continued. "If you would all please activate your data slates," he said, leading by example, "I would like to propose that we review today's agenda. Because the first step toward peace—a lasting and enforceable cease-fire—has already been granted us by the Organians, we are free to—"

"We are anything but free," Prang cut in. "Neither of us chose this peace. It was forced upon us, and if we refuse it, the Organians will leave us both at the mercy of our neighbors, none of whom they saw fit to saddle with the same constraints!"

Gorkon leaned toward Prang and said under his breath, "That's enough."

Instead of demurring, Prang stood from his chair, which fell over behind him. "This entire proceeding is a sham! A farce! Klingons do not negotiate! They take what is theirs!"

"The Federation has the utmost respect for your people's ways," Sarek said.

Prang shot back, "Then stand with us! Help us crush the Organians!"

"Just as we have no desire to be your victim, neither do we wish to be your accomplice."

The Klingon spat on the tabletop. Sarek recoiled, more out of reflex than from disgust. "You Federates are all the same!" Prang snapped. "Pretty talk, no action! Useless *petaQpu'*!"

His insult lifted Zeroh from his chair, finger pointed, face contorted in rage. "You're ones to talk! You're just thugs! Half-educated savages! Animals! We ought to do the galaxy a favor and put your kind down like rabid—"

"Sit down, Zeroh," Sarek said, his voice raised but still even in tone. Though he had worked all his life to act free of emotion, Beel Zeroh tested the limits of his Vulcan equanimity.

Across the table, Prang sneered at Zeroh. "Yes! Sit down, *yIntagh*. Let the warriors—" His sentence ended abruptly as he became aware that the blade of Gorkon's *d'k tahg* was under his jaw, just behind his carotid artery. The Klingon delegation's leader applied just enough pressure to draw a thin line of blood from the surface of Prang's exposed throat.

Gorkon's arch tenor was just as icily calm as Sarek's, yet somehow it conveyed a far more palpable sense of impending violence. "You have said quite enough, Prang. Sit. Down."

In measured motions, both Zeroh and Prang sank back into their chairs, humbled but still seething. Sarek feared this would not be the last toxic outburst from either of the two men.

All in all, it was, Sarek concluded, a most inauspicious start to the proceedings. And as distasteful as he had found Gorkon's solution to his belligerent subordinate, he admitted to himself a grudging respect for its simplicity, efficiency, and efficacy.

The Klingons may be violent, cruel, and on occasion

irrational, he mused, *but they do have a knack for accomplishing their objectives in a timely manner.* He spared a moment for a look across the table at Gorkon, who just then happened to be looking back at Sarek.

I can only hope Councillor Gorkon is as committed to securing a true and lasting peace as I am—or else this peace summit is already as good as ended.

———

Threats flying like arrows, knives meeting throats, all in the name of a peace conference—it was as close to a working definition of irony as Elara had ever seen.

She hadn't expected the Federation-Klingon talks to go smoothly—no one had. Back on the Orion homeworld, bookmakers were taking odds on the conference's outcome. The best bet seemed to be a stalemate ending without a treaty; running a distant second was a diplomatic catastrophe culminating in open hostilities that would accomplish little beyond expanding the Romulans' sphere of control in local space.

None of which mattered to Elara. She had no use for gambling or politics. She believed in being well paid for a dishonest day's work. The rest was just theater and excuses.

So far no one inside the conference room had detected the passive sensors she had hidden on the light fixtures, on the corners of the trays used for the beverage service, or in the towering arrangements of fresh flowers tucked into the room's corners beside the windows. Though she, along with the rest of the event's catering staff, was required to wait outside until summoned, she was able to tap into any of the sensor feeds by using the holographic lens in her left eye and the subaural implant embedded in her left ear. With nigh-imperceptible shifts of her gaze and half-blinks, she could switch from one feed to another with great speed, giving her prime vantages on every heated moment of the burgeoning political fiasco transpiring behind closed doors.

To the staff of New Athens University and the organizers of the conference, she was just Elara Soath, a Catullan refugee earning her keep as a waitress while attending classes at NAU on Centaurus, thanks to a generous Federation scholarship. Having tamed her wild mane of pink-and-violet hair into a neat ponytail to comply with the university's health regulations for food service employees, Elara would have been indistinguishable from other colorfully coiffed members of the student body if not for the green-and-yellow geometrically inspired tattoo on her high forehead—a cultural emblem that telegraphed her Catullan origins.

No one who knew her on Centaurus suspected she was, in fact, an expertly trained spy and assassin on retainer to an interstellar crime organization known as the Orion Syndicate.

A blink, and she was in the thick of the fray between Gorkon and his right-hand man, Prang. The insults flew, fast and sharp, and the Izarian from the Federation delegation was only making matters worse. It was clear even to a political novice such as Elara that the only two people in the room who were doing anything to maintain the peace were Gorkon and Ambassador Sarek of Vulcan.

If anything were to happen to the two of them, the

Klingon Empire and the Federation would be at war before we could clear the water glasses from the table.

Elara was not at all privy to the agendas of her employers, or their patrons' true identities, but she could guess at their motivations—and friction between the Klingons and the Federation seemed to be high on their wish list. As she listened to the increasingly fractious argument transpiring inside the conference room, she was certain this was a development her handler would want to be apprised of as soon as possible. It was a breach of protocol for her to access her hidden data recorder in the building's subbasement during daytime hours, when there might be custodial staff working in its vicinity, but that was a danger she was prepared to risk.

The sooner I give them what they want, the sooner I get paid and go home.

Slinking away from the conference room, she caught the eye of another part-time member of the university's catering staff, a young male Bolian. "Yutt? Can you cover me?"

"For how long?"

She pressed her hand to her belly and feigned distress. "Fifteen?"

He looked around, frowned. "Fine. It's not like we're in the middle of lunch. But make it quick. If the Klingons get a hankering for raktajino, I'm not making twelve of them by myself."

"I'll be fast, I promise." She blew him a kiss and slipped out the door.

The main hallway of the university's alumni center was deserted. It had been cleared hours earlier by teams of Starfleet security personnel, followed by a separate inspection conducted by Klingon military security specialists. Elara wasn't sure what she had found more amusing—their mutual, openly demonstrated mistrust, or their shared failure to detect any of her illegal quantum surveillance devices.

She suppressed the urge to smirk. *If they really wanted to find common ground, they'd start by admitting they're both completely incompetent.*

Empty spaces abounded along the main passage. Most of the university's staff who worked here had been relocated for the duration of the conference. Only she and the rest of the skeleton crew assigned to cater the event and tend to the needs of its delegations were allowed to move freely through the open spaces of the alumni center, though much of the building's interior had been cordoned off or secured behind locked doors. In practice, the only areas to which Elara had regular access were the kitchen, pantry, refrigerators, storerooms, and the utilities room in the basement. Though she had yet to see any armed security inside the center, she knew beyond a ghost of a doubt they were there, alert to the least sign of trouble.

Stick to the routine, she told herself. *Do what they've seen you do a thousand times before, just the way you've always done it.*

She paid a visit to the kitchen and made small talk with the cooks for a minute or two. Her own passive sensors had confirmed that while the Federation's security detail was keeping a duotronic eye on the kitchen, they had no ears there. Local laws on Centaurus permitted a limited degree of visual surveillance for security purposes, but it prohibited most forms of eavesdropping on conversations, even for purposes of national security, without a specific court order.

If only more of the Federation's laws showed such concern for the rights of the individual, Elara lamented, *I could almost stand to live in it.*

Satisfied she had dallied long enough with the cooks, she made her way down a back stairwell to the subbasement, where she ducked inside the utilities room. Interference from the room's various power-transfer nodes obstructed most forms of eavesdropping technology. Consequently, this was where she had set up the recording node for her quantum transceivers, which were not affected by the plasma relays that snaked in and out of the cramped space.

The recording module was nondescript; it had been disguised as a power-consumption monitor, a function it performed in addition to its more surreptitious purpose: storing every sound and image received from the conference room while the delegates were in session.

Installing the node inside the building had been an unavoidable risk. To protect the conference, the Klingon Defense Forces had been permitted to erect an energy shield over part of the campus of New Athens University. Though its chief function was to defend the conference from outside attack, it also scrambled unauthorized signals that tried to pass through it in either direction. The node could record signals that originated within the shield's area of protection, but it couldn't retransmit them.

That was where Elara came into play.

She keyed in her codes to access the device's memory banks, then downloaded the morning's handful of recordings to a data card, which she hid inside a pocket of her catering uniform. Her next task would be to carry the card to a transmission point outside the energy shield and relay its contents to her handler on an encrypted channel. There was an ideal transmitter in a laboratory inside the university's engineering building. All she had to do was get there with the data card . . . without being stopped, searched, or questioned.

Back up the stairs, then down the main hall. Out the front doors, and across the quad. No one even looked at her twice. In the drab uniform of a catering waitress, she was nearly as invisible here as she had been on Catulla Prime or Orion. Some experiences were the same, no matter where one went: *No one ever pays attention to a servant.*

Inside the engineering building, she shed her uniform. In that setting, she knew, it would look out of place and attract unwanted attention. Dressed in street clothes, she was once again utterly forgettable, just another young woman roaming the corridors of academia. She found it laughably easy to gain admittance to a subspace communications research lab, upload the contents of her data card to a temporary server, and send it in a hashed burst transmission to an anonymous relay beacon that would pass it along to her handler, the enigmatic Red Man.

Let's see what he thinks of that, she gloated.

Elara left the engineering building and walked back across the quad to resume her mundane catering duties. A glance at her chrono: *Two minutes late.* She was about to castigate herself, then demurred. *Why worry? Yutt always forgives me*

She smiled and shook her head. *Men. They're so predictable.*

Six

Despite her accomplishments and swift ascent through the ranks of Starfleet's command echelon, Una had never accustomed herself to the practice of "holding court." Aboard every ship on which she had served, there had always been one or more officers—and in a few cases, senior noncommissioned officers—who had excelled at compelling the attention of groups great and small, regaling them with ribald jokes and stirring tales of derring-do. Such personalities often became quick favorites with their crewmates, magnets for social activity on and off the ship. All that Una had ever been able to do was watch and listen from a distance, and feel mild pangs of envy at her peers' natural ease in social settings.

Now she was the one surrounded by eager faces, the singular focus of nine of her former *Enterprise* shipmates. None of them appeared to have aged since their abductions to this strange parallel universe, and they all were desperate to learn what had transpired during their years in exile. For what had felt like hours, she had answered their questions as best she could.

Whatever happened to Captain April?

Is Deneva safe? Did my family ever ask you about me?

What new species did Starfleet meet while we were gone?

How many members does the Federation have now?

Did that war with the Klingons ever happen? Did they attack Axanar?

Deceptively simple in their brevity, each query had taken Una nearly an hour to answer, and every detail she offered up spawned half a dozen more follow-up inquiries. At last, with raised hands she stemmed the tide of her old friends' interrogation. "Enough."

The others diminished in the face of her rebuke. Ensign Bruce Goldberg said, "We didn't mean to offend, Captain."

Ensign Cheryl Stevens wore a sheepish grimace. "It's just . . . it's been so long."

"I understand. Really, I do."

"I doubt that," said Ensign Le May. "It's been longer than you think. Time is different here." Her voice took on a haunted quality. "Everything is different here."

"That's as may be," Una said, "but we have—"

A peculiar sound reverberated off the cliff sides surrounding the refugees' box canyon: an eerie warbling electronic music, atonal verging on discordant. Its strangely phased melody rose and fell as its echoes amplified or canceled one another, creating a bizarre Doppler effect.

Una watched the refugees, human and Usildar alike, flee their camp's open areas and scramble to cover under makeshift blinds camouflaged with dirt and rocks from the surrounding area. The only person who paused his flight long enough to look back at Una was Shimizu. "Come on!" He beckoned her with a sweep of his arm. "Take cover!"

Overhead, the dissonant, Theremin-like music grew louder and filled the box canyon. Searching her memory,

Una recognized that haunting sound: it was a Jatohr sentry globe.

She sprinted after Shimizu and Martinez, then crawled under their rocky overhang to huddle with them in its shadow. Seconds after she had settled into place beside them, the silvery white Jatohr sphere floated past a few dozen meters above the ground.

It slowed as it drifted over the campsite. Una found its singsong humming punctuated by low, almost subsonic thumping noises strangely disturbing, though she couldn't pinpoint why.

Perhaps its sonic emissions are meant to provoke anxiety and coax its prey into the open, she speculated. If that was the case, however, it was failing utterly.

After lingering for half a minute, the sphere ascended and sped away, into the mountain pass and its endless maze of crevices. Only once its eerie, haunting music had faded to silence did the Usildar and the *Enterprise* abductees emerge from their hiding places.

Una followed Martinez and Shimizu out from under the rocky overhang and regrouped in the middle of the camp with Goldberg, Stevens, Le May, and a handful of Usildar. Back in the huddle, Una asked Shimizu, "Does that thing come around often?"

"No." He frowned as he squinted into the hazy distance, as if searching for signs of the alien device's return. "Only when we get too close to the Jatohr city on the other side of the mountains, but no one's been there in ages. Before that, they only came when . . ."

He left his thought ominously incomplete.

Una prompted him, "When what?"

Le May answered, "When someone new arrived from the other side."

"How did it know I had come through the gateway?"

"The same way we did," Martinez said. "Whenever the portal opens, this whole world ripples and shimmers like a mirage for a few seconds."

Goldberg looked faintly amused. "How do you think Feneb and his boys got the drop on you in the canyon? They knew you were coming."

Una's mind reeled with questions. "Do new arrivals always land at the same spot on the salt flats?" Everyone around her nodded—even the Usildar. "Then we need to go back there. My friends on the other side are going to open the gateway again, very soon."

Martinez shook his head. "It won't matter. The Jatohr will be watching the gateway now, maybe for years. Going back there would be suicide."

"Well, we can't just sit here," Una said.

Feneb swatted away her protest as if shooing an insect. "There is nothing more we can do. We are trapped here forever. This is our fate, Leader Una."

"Where I come from, we don't believe in fate. Or in luck. We believe in free will. In action." Una stepped into the center of the huddle and mustered her best tenor of command. "Shimizu, you said there's a Jatohr city on the other side of the mountains?"

"That's right."

"Do you know how to get there?"

His eyes widened. "I don't think that's a good idea."

"Answer the question, Lieutenant. Do you know the way?"

Shimizu swallowed his fear, then nodded. "Aye, sir."

"Then it's time to get moving. Mister Martinez, Mister Shimizu, gather weapons and supplies, whatever you think I'll need." She checked her phaser to make sure it was still charged, then turned toward the trail that led out of the box canyon. "It's time to pay the Jatohr a visit."

Seven

The mood in the *Enterprise*'s briefing room was grim. Spock and his covert landing party had returned safely from Usilde, for which Kirk was grateful, but he was finding their after-action report less than encouraging. "How many troops do the Klingons have in the facility?"

"At minimum, one full combat company," Spock said. He switched the image on the table's three-sided screen to show a series of tricorder scans, each pinpointing the locations of numerous Klingon life signs. "I estimate less than ten percent of their personnel are scientists. The rest appear to be armed troops, with the highest concentrations located inside the generator plant and on the fortress's command level."

Kirk shifted his gaze toward Chekov. "Ensign, your tactical assessment?"

"A very hard target, Captain," Chekov said, his Russian accent shifting his consonants and vowels in equal measure. "Now that they know we were there, that trick will not work again. The next time we go back, it will need to be in force."

Exactly what I didn't want to hear. He faced his senior helmsman. "Mister Sulu, your report noted there were no Klingon support vessels in orbit, is that correct?"

"Yes, sir. But based on long-range sensor data, I'd say a D5 cruiser swings through the Libros system at least once every nine days. It might not be there now, but I doubt it's far away."

"A reasonable assumption." Next in Kirk's sights was his chief engineer. "Mister Scott. What did your scans reveal about that generator? Do you think you could rig a new control module to replace the one that was stolen?" Even now Kirk couldn't bring himself to say Bates's name; he knew he would choke on it as his anger at her betrayal resurfaced.

Scott wore a dubious expression. "Not likely, sir. I've just begun to study the data. I might know enough in a few days to jam the original at short range. But build you a new one?" A shake of his head. "I wouldn't know where to begin, sir."

"Then we face a number of new challenges, gentlemen." Kirk leaned forward and folded his hands on the table. "If we can't replace the lost control unit, we'll need to track down the original, no matter how difficult that task might be. But first we need to address the Klingons' interest in the Jatohr's generator. Mister Spock, you tapped into their portable databank. What do we know about their research so far?"

"As we suspected, Captain, the Klingons mean to weaponize the generator, if they can. Fortunately, they remain unaware so far of its origin or intended function. But I suggest we not underestimate them. They *will* obtain those facts, and many more, very soon."

"If they haven't already," Scott added.

"Noted." Kirk glanced at the mission profile, then looked at Chekov. "Ensign, were you able to continue scanning the Klingons during your retreat from the fortress?"

"Yes, Captain."

"Have you identified any flaws in their tactical response?"

"None, sir."

"So luring their sentries out of position with a diversion—?"

"Would be a futile effort," Spock interrupted. "Given the size of their garrison inside the fortress, they could summon sufficient reinforcements to respond to any event, without compromising their basic line of defense."

Kirk nodded. Everything his officers had told him confirmed his own worst fears. "If I were the commander of that garrison, I'd have guards in every submerged hangar. And I'd put antipersonnel mines in the lake around the fortress."

"A logical response," Spock said. "And well within their capabilities."

"Nonetheless, gentlemen, we need to find a way back inside that citadel—one that won't send us to war with the Klingons."

Scott wrinkled his brow in dismay. "Tall order, Captain. The Klingons like doing things the old-fashioned way: never trust a machine when a warm body will do just as well."

"Meaning?"

"If they relied more on automated defenses, it would be an engineering problem. But the Klingons are real belt-and-suspenders types. They'll use a sensor grid, but they'll also post lookouts. They'll put passcodes on doors, but they're just as likely to booby-trap them."

"Mister Scott is correct," Spock added. "The Klingons have a knack for redundancy."

Hoping younger minds might yield fresher ideas, Kirk looked to Chekov and Sulu. "Ensign, if I ordered you to lead a mission back to that fortress, how would you do it?"

"We could tunnel in from underneath."

"That would have the virtue of being unexpected. Unfortunately, it would take years when all we have are days. Mister Sulu: your opinion."

Put on the spot, Sulu reclined and pondered the question. "We've already breached their defenses once by coming in from below, through a pod hangar's moon pool. That trick won't work twice. They have transport-scattering force fields inside the fortress, so we can't beam in." He was quiet for a thoughtful pause. "The one advantage we still have is the ability to mask ourselves from their sensors—but as Mister Scott said, their sentries are watching for us now. So we'd have to come from a direction they wouldn't expect. Since we can't strike from below, that only leaves attacking from above."

"Explain," Kirk said.

"A dive from low orbit, sir, with heat shields and a parachute. If we block their sensors and drop in after nightfall, we could touch down on top of the citadel."

"Right into the arms of their rooftop guards," Scott said.

Sulu shrugged. "I never said the plan was perfect."

Kirk stood, and his officers mirrored him without

delay. "Keep working the problem, gentlemen. If the Klingons weaponize that thing before we can take it back, we'll have no choice but to blow it to kingdom come—and that's *not* an acceptable outcome. Dismissed."

None of the others spoke as Kirk walked out the door, but he felt their eyes on his back—Spock's most of all. And he knew exactly why.

If they destroyed the citadel, Captain Una and her shipmates would never be able to return home.

Eight

"Utterly unacceptable!" Prang pounded his fist on the tabletop to punctuate his thought, a quirk Sarek considered juvenile and somewhat transparent in its affectation. The Klingon councillor continued. "Control of those subsectors is vital to the security of the Empire!"

His outburst drew a reply of equal ferocity from Sarek's portly, white-bearded, and wide-snouted adviser on interstellar communications infrastructure, Gesh mor Tov of Tellar. "Have you lost your mind, Prang? All we're asking for is the right to set up a subspace comm relay!"

"A surveillance array, you mean!" Prang pointed at the star map currently shown on the room's single large viewscreen. "A single spy platform there could intercept signals between all our major star systems along the Federation's border, including those from Qo'noS itself!"

Durok, one of Gorkon's more sanguine advisers, added, "I'm afraid Councillor Prang is correct. Allowing the Federation to establish a communications relay station in that subsector would jeopardize the security of the Empire." His expression brightened. "Perhaps we could establish and maintain the relay, and route your signal traffic for you."

Military adviser Beel Zeroh scrunched his brow at Durok. "You think we'd let a Klingon communications array handle Federation comm traffic? Are you serious?"

"Are you?"

Zeroh clenched his fist and snapped in half the stylus he was holding.

Thinking it might be best to redirect the discussion, Sarek used the panel in front of him to switch the information on the room's main viewscreen. "Let us table that conversation for later in the proceedings. At this time, let me suggest we move on to agricultural issues."

"A capital idea," said Gempok, the Klingons' adviser on matters of the interior. "Can I ask that we begin by addressing the invasive species your people introduced to Homog Three?"

His question prompted looks of confusion among most of the members of the Federation delegation—all except Sarek, who had made a point of learning the Klingon names for the star systems and planets whose disputed sovereignty were items of contention for this summit. "With all respect, Lord Gempok, I believe you mean Sherman's Planet. Though I must admit I am unclear with regard to what 'invasive species' your comment refers. It was my understanding all the tribbles were successfully removed from the planet's surface."

"Not the tribbles, you *toDSaH*! The *loSpev*!"

This time Sarek counted himself among the ranks of the perplexed—and it was his adviser on agricultural affairs, Cellinoor sh'Fairoh, who grasped Gempok's meaning. "Lord Gempok," the Andorian *shen* began, her timbre as gentle as could be, "do you mean to say that the Klingon Empire considers the grain known as quadrot-riticale to be an invasive species?"

"By definition, it cannot be anything else. Your scientists have interfered with Homog Three's natural ecosystem, and my people will not just sit by and watch your Federation infest entire worlds with its genetically engineered crops!"

Doing her best to remain nonconfrontational, sh'Fairoh replied, "Lord Gempok, I assure you, the engineered crops we've introduced to Sherman's Planet are entirely safe, and pose no threat, directly or indirectly, to that world's ecosystem."

Gempok shot a sidelong look down the table at his colleague Mardl, a smooth-headed, almost human-looking female Klingon who served on their delegation as legal counsel. "We've heard that lie from the Federation before," Gempok said.

Sarek knew his peers understood as well as he did Gempok's allusion to the previous century's infamous Augment virus, a genetic-engineering program based on human efforts to create a "superior" species. The virus had conferred some genomic enhancements, but at the cost of humanizing the patients' appearances. That side effect had made its victims, the *QuchHa'*, objects of ridicule and oppression within their own culture.

Even wheat grain has become a source of discord, Sarek reflected. He updated the on-screen information again. "Clearly, agricultural matters require further review before we revisit them. In which case, I suggest we move on to issues connected with currency exchange."

"You mean currency sabotage," said Lord Motas, the emissary of the Klingon Imperial Treasury. His long, thin face was perfectly matched to his lanky physique and his dry, sardonic baritone. "Your economic system has no currency model. How can we set rates of exchange?"

Taking her cue from Sarek, Aravella Gianaris answered the query. "Our economy of surplus might appear confusing, but I assure you, Lord Motas, it has a rational basis. While we no longer use cash, we have a robust system of credit and debit that—"

"A fiat economy," Motas sneered.

"Not exactly," Gianaris said. "It still relies on the conversion of energy to matter, so there are finite resources to consider. However, by leveraging economies of scale, establishing guaranteed personal incomes, and exempting certain sectors of endeavor from being tied to profit models, we've enabled—"

"An interstellar culture of freeloaders," Motas said, his disgust evident. "A Klingon works for what he earns."

"As do Federation citizens," Gianaris said, "if they want anything more than simple state-funded housing and a subsistence income. But by eliminating the threat of poverty, we free our people to pursue lives of self-improvement, excellence, and achievement."

"You coddle your people," grumbled General Orqom, who represented the Klingon High Command at the conference. "You make them dependent. *Weak.*"

"Quite the contrary," Gianaris said. "We achieve strength through unity."

Prang stood. "I have heard enough of this mewling prattle for one day. Ambassador Sarek, let us know when your people are ready to bring ideas to the table that do not insult our intelligence or ask us to be your *chowIQpu'*."

Unfamiliar with Prang's parting epithet, Sarek looked to his delegation's *tlhIngan Hol* translator, Saoirse Liu. The fair-skinned, dark-haired human woman declined to parse the vulgarity, demurring from her duty with a small wave that cautioned Sarek: *Don't ask.*

Across the table, the entire Klingon delegation got up. They departed en masse—all except Councillor Gorkon, who loomed over his place at the table with a grave countenance.

Sarek stood and said to his people, "Give us the room, please."

His subordinates followed the Klingons out of the conference room. The last person to leave closed the room's double doors, offering Sarek and Gorkon a rare moment of privacy.

"A brief adjournment might be for the best," Sarek said. "When we resume tomorrow, perhaps calmer voices will be able to prevail."

Gorkon sighed. "I certainly hope so, Mister Ambassador. Alas, many of my peers are unwilling to accept the truth of our predicament or the necessity of these proceedings."

"It is our job to impress it upon those we lead."

"Quite true." Gorkon's shoulders slumped, as if the burden of responsibility had become all too real. "I will do what I can to move my people toward compromise before we reconvene. But for all our sakes, I hope your reputation as a diplomat is well earned. Your delegation can be swayed by reason. But if Prang gets his way . . . mine will bow only to the sword."

———

Dream logic. In all his many years, never had Sarek ever heard of two words that less deserved to be used in conjunction. Since his youth, he had been trained to hone his thoughts with rigorous Vulcan disciplines designed to keep in check the deep and violent cauldron of his people's emotions, which in eons long past had nearly led the Vulcan race to its destruction. What few non-Vulcans ever learned was that his people's mental training was not limited to the waking hours. Even when a Vulcan slumbered, he or she continued the battle for emotional balance.

He had learned to master the slings and arrows of waking life, to weather the indignities of other, less logic-driven people, with the presence of his conscious mind. But when he slept, he had to contend with the most wily, cunning, and dangerous threat of all—his own subconscious mind, and its endless battalions of surreal imagery and personified anxieties.

To contend with the danger, Sarek, like most other Vulcans, had learned the art of lucid dreaming. He had trained himself to remain alert to the irregularities of a dream state, to note its odd perceptual shifts, irrational physics, and uncanny coincidences.

This evening, his mind had conjured a detailed simulacrum of the conference room, complete with his and Gorkon's delegations in their assigned seats—and giant insects gnawing through the walls, floor, and ceiling, so that the entire space threatened to collapse in on itself.

How trite and easily parsed. I had hoped my subconscious might yield a vision of moderate subtlety. With a mental command he banished the massive termites and willed both teams of delegates—all of whom he knew to be mere extensions of himself within the dream world— into silence so that he could use the dream's slowed perception of time's passage for meditation upon the issues that would top the next day's agenda. *If I am to spend my hours of rest mired in the concerns of work, I shall at least do so on my own terms.*

The first day at the table had been marred by one contretemps after another. Sarek was certain that had been the Klingons' intention from the outset. They had come prepared to stir up controversy on every point of discussion. No matter how Sarek had tried to steer the conversation, the Klingons had found cause for vehement objection. That sort of obstruction could not be counted upon to occur on its own, or even to be reliably improvised in the moment. No, it took careful planning; months of research and rehearsal. Except for Gorkon himself, the Klingons had come ready to provoke a fight.

But why? They must know what will happen if we defy

the Organians. Sarek wondered if that might be the point. *Their bluster might be designed to force us into the role of peacemakers by way of concession. The Klingons seem to think us so fearful of incurring the Organians' wrath that they believe we will accede to all their demands in order to preserve the peace.*

It was a rather logical strategy, viewed in context. But then why was Gorkon not taking the same tack? Were his overtures to peace intended to offset his subordinates' saber rattling and keep the Federation at the table long enough to give the Empire what it really wanted? Or was Gorkon exactly what he claimed to be—a diplomat who truly desired to forge a lasting peace?

Finding the answer to that question, Sarek decided, would very likely determine whether the peace conference was destined to succeed or doomed to fail.

As he began to formulate conversational gambits with which to open the next day's talks, Sarek was roused from his sleep by a shrill wailing of alarms. He opened his eyes and sat up in bed. It was still dark outside; the chrono on the bedside table put the local time as roughly three hours before sunrise. Next to him in bed, Amanda stirred and blinked groggily toward the window. Her voice was dry and brittle. "Sarek? What's happening?"

"I do not know." He got out of bed and grabbed his robe off the bench at the foot of the bed. "Please stay here while—" His personal comm device buzzed on his nightstand. He picked it up and flipped it open. "This is Sarek."

The nervous voice of his Bolian aide Isa Frain replied over the comm, *"Sorry to wake you, Mister Ambas-*

sador, but there's an emergency at the Klingon residence hall."

"What manner of emergency, Isa?"

"They won't say, but they're really angry." Her voice grew more fearful. *"Sir, they're shouting about going to war."*

"I am on my way. Sarek out." He closed the comm and took clean clothes from his closet. Once dressed, he bid Amanda farewell with a look. She reciprocated with a small nod, having long since adapted to the simple gestures of Vulcan courtesy. He pocketed his comm on his way out, then hurried from their suite to fend off yet another diplomatic catastrophe.

Cloaked in shadow, Sarek crossed the New Athens University quad, moving from one pool of lamplight to the next, until he arrived at the dormitory where the Klingon delegation had been housed. A crowd was gathered outside. As he drew closer, he saw that local peace officers and university security personnel had surrounded the Klingon delegates, who shouted threats and profanities in their native tongue.

Sarek shouldered through the wall of police. "Let me through. I am Ambassador Sarek, step aside." When he reached the Klingons, he searched in vain for their one reasonable voice, only to find himself confronted by Prang. The burly councillor seized Sarek by the front of his cassock and almost lifted him off the ground. "You, Vulcan! You did this!"

Three police officers intervened to break Prang's hold on Sarek. Liberated from the grip of the madman,

Sarek asked in a firm but level tone, "Where is Councillor Gorkon? I wish to speak directly with him."

Struggling to escape the police, Prang shouted, "You mock us? How *dare* you!" Spittle flew from between his bared teeth as he added, "Fek'lhr take you, you *petaQ*!"

"I do not understand. Why do you say I mock you?"

"You ask for Gorkon, when you know damned well you're the one who murdered him!"

For half a breath, Sarek's hard-won emotional control nearly deserted him. He answered Prang through a mask of forced grace. "I am sure there must be some mistake, Councillor."

"There is no mistake! He's gone! Vanished from a locked room in the night! And we Klingons all know exactly who's to blame!" He wrested one arm from the police and pointed at Sarek. "I've already summoned our cruiser the *HoS'leth* to show you the error of your ways! You will die for this, Vulcan coward!"

"I assure you, Councillor, there has been a mistake. One that we will investigate and resolve. Until then, I implore you not to make any rash decisions." Sarek turned away and whispered to a nearby police commander, "Take him and the others back to their suites. And summon a crime scene investigation unit at once."

"Yes, Mister Ambassador."

Sarek stepped away as the police corralled the Klingons back inside their dormitory. Once he was well out of the Klingons' earshot, he retrieved his comm from his pocket and flipped it open. "Sarek to Isa Frain."

His aide answered. *"Go ahead, Mister Ambassador."*

"Councillor Prang has summoned a Klingon starship to Centaurus. We must keep that vessel in check, or we will lose control of this conference. Please contact Starfleet Command and let them know we require immediate assistance. We need the *Enterprise*."

Nine

Most nights, Kirk would have resented the aggressive double beep of the comm in his quarters during the small hours of gamma shift. Tonight, however, he had been plagued by restlessness, tossing and turning, unable to find comfort in the spaces between bad dreams, even when he had focused on the soothing hush of the ventilation system and the steady vibrations of the engines through the bulkheads. Liberated from his insomnia by the interruption, he was almost relieved to be able to roll over and activate the comm channel. "Kirk here."

He was answered by Lieutenant Seth Dickinson, a young command-track officer who was earning his stripes standing overnight shifts as the officer of the watch. *"Sorry to wake you, Captain. We've received a distress signal addressed specifically to you."*

"To me? From whom?"

"Ambassador Sarek, sir. He says the talks with the Klingons on Centaurus have broken down—and that the Klingons have summoned one of their starships to the system."

At that, Kirk was out of his bunk and getting dressed. "Do the Klingons realize bringing a warship into Federation space might be seen as an act of war?"

"*They don't seem to care, sir. Should I respond to Ambassador Sarek?*"

"Not yet." He pulled on his trousers. "Did Sarek say why the talks failed?"

"*Yes, sir. Klingon Councillor Gorkon disappeared overnight, and his delegation is blaming it on foul play.*"

Tugging on one of his boots, Kirk said, "Foul play? Based on what?"

"*That's unclear, sir.*"

Kirk put on his other boot. "Have you alerted Mister Spock?"

"*No, sir.*"

"Have him meet me on the bridge in five minutes. Kirk out." He closed the comm channel with a quick press of his thumb on the switch, took a clean green command tunic from his drawer, and pulled it over his head on his way out of his quarters to the corridor and turbolift.

Four and a half minutes later, Kirk strode onto the bridge. Dickinson stood from the command chair and stepped aside as Kirk maneuvered himself into it. "Report, Lieutenant."

"I ordered long-range scans of the sectors adjacent to Centaurus. We've detected a Klingon D7 heavy cruiser moving at high warp toward the system."

It was just as Kirk had feared. "Do we know which one?"

"Its energy signature matches the *I.K.S. HoS'leth*, out of Mempa."

Kirk frowned. "I've heard of the *HoS'leth*. That's General Kovor's ship."

"Is he—?" Dickinson's question was cut off by Spock's arrival in the next turbolift.

The first officer descended into the command well to stand with Kirk and Dickinson. "Reporting as ordered, Captain."

"Mister Spock. Your father, Ambassador Sarek, is requesting Starfleet support at the peace conference on Centaurus."

A quintessentially Vulcan arch of one eyebrow. "Most odd. Did he say why?"

"The leader of the Klingon delegation disappeared. Now his underlings are looking to use his absence as a reason to declare war."

The news caused Spock no obvious concern. "No doubt there are closer vessels to Centaurus than the *Enterprise*."

"Three, actually. But none that are up to facing off with a Klingon cruiser." Noting Spock's uptick in curiosity at that detail, Kirk added, "The *HoS'leth*, out of Mempa."

"General Kovor," Spock said, his manner at once grave.

Kirk shifted his attention to Dickinson. "Lieutenant, open a channel to Starfleet Command. Request permission for us to divert to Centaurus at maximum warp, and make sure Admiral Wong has all the relevant details regarding why."

"Aye, sir." The trim, crew-cut young officer climbed the steps to the communications post, where he relayed Kirk's orders to the gamma-shift communications officer.

Spock dropped his voice and positioned himself to keep his conversation with Kirk isolated from the rest of the bridge crew. "If Councillor Gorkon has been murdered—"

"Then the treaty is at risk," Kirk said, "along with the security of the Federation. But if the Organians step in, they're likely to hamstring the Klingons and us in equal measure."

"A fact of which the Klingons are no doubt aware, Captain."

It was clear to Kirk that Spock was already considering the wider ramifications of the conference's potential failure. "What are you thinking, Spock?"

"Any number of parties in this region of space would have reason to want these talks to fail. If foul play has, in fact, befallen Councillor Gorkon, I think the most likely suspect will be an agent of neither the Federation nor the Klingon Empire, but of a power foreign to both—one that has a vested interest in seeing us and the Klingons come to ruin."

Kirk nodded. "That makes sense. But who would have the resources to bypass all the security at the conference?"

"Difficult to say. But if I were to hazard a guess? I would limit my suspicions to the Orion Syndicate, the Nalori Republic, and the Romulan Star Empire."

Searching his memory for a detail from a day or two earlier, Kirk said, "Spock, wasn't the last reported location of Lisa Bates's Romulan bird-of-prey the Kaleb Sector?"

"It was."

"And Kaleb Sector is adjacent to Alpha Centauri Sector."

"Also true."

"Could those facts be related?"

"Possibly. But without additional evidence, I can't say for certain."

Dickinson returned to the command well to stand with Kirk and Spock. "Captain, we have orders from Starfleet Command to proceed at best possible speed to Centaurus and render whatever aid Ambassador Sarek deems necessary."

"Thank you, Lieutenant." Kirk raised his voice to issue orders. "Helm, set course for Centaurus, warp factor eight." He watched the streaks of stars on the main viewscreen grow longer as the *Constitution*-class starship accelerated to its maximum speed. "Mister Spock, take the ship to yellow alert—and start running battle drills."

Spock balked at the order. "Are you sure that's necessary, Captain?"

"It is, Mister Spock. We might not be looking for a fight at Centaurus, but I have a bad feeling the Klingons will be."

Smoke seared Sadira's lungs and stung her eyes. Toxic fog choked every compartment and corridor inside the *Velibor*; it poured from overhead vents, snaked through the gaps behind the bulkheads, and left the crew of the bird-of-prey hacking phlegm and blood into the sleeves of their uniforms as they toiled to restore the ship's many compromised systems.

No one on the command deck paid Sadira any mind while they worked. Focused on the tasks at hand, they treated her as if she weren't there at all. An engineer reported from inside the smoking husk of a sensor console, "Overloads on all the main circuits. We'll have to bypass."

"Noted," said Subcommander Bedisa. "Helm, how's your control now?"

"Still sluggish at sublight," said Toporok. "Warp navigation still offline."

A flash of light preceded a burst of flames along the compartment's overhead. An officer with a firefighting rig hurried over and squelched the flames before they could spread or devour any more of the ship's suddenly limited and dwindling supply of air.

Lights stuttered and went dark on the weapons console. A garbled hash of static and untranslated alien gibberish spilled from the overhead speakers, thanks to the shutdown of the communications station, which normally buffered and filtered such noise.

In all the confusion and malfunction that swamped the command deck, the only system that still registered as online and operating within normal parameters was the cloaking device. For that bit of good fortune Sadira was thankful—because the *Velibor*'s invisibility was, at the moment, its only defense.

Angry voices traveled up the corridor from the ship's aft sections, announcing the approach of Commander Creelok and Centurion Mirat. The two graybeards traded complaints as they emerged from the hazy veil hanging in the darkness. The first words Sadira heard clearly were

Creelok's: "I think the phrase you're looking for is 'dead in space.'"

"Dead would imply our position was stable, Commander. We're adrift."

"I bow to your vocabulary." As the commander and centurion stepped onto the command deck, Creelok paused to note Sadira's presence with a disapproving glare. "Well, if it isn't our personal saboteur. Come to pour epoxy on the controls? Or maybe erase the databanks?"

She ignored their slights. "I merely stand ready to assist with repairs."

"Emphasis on *merely*," the centurion said as he passed her. He followed Creelok to the compartment's octagonal main console.

Creelok keyed in a command on his panel. "Let's see if this works." He made a final adjustment, then said in a bolder voice, "Engine room, command. Ranimir, can you hear me?"

Over the hastily restored internal comm, the chief engineer's voice was reedy and faint behind a scratch of static. "*I hear you, Commander.*"

Bedisa took her place at the main console, at the node beside Creelok's. "Still no improvement on the helm controls. Databanks remain scrambled."

Mirat asked, "What about environmental systems?"

"All offline," Bedisa said. "Current repair estimate is six hours."

The commander looked displeased. "That's going to make for some stale air."

Mirat dismissed the issue with a grimace. "We'll survive." He shot a venomous look at Sadira. "As long as our power reserves hold."

"We're doing what we can," Ranimir said from engineering. *"But between the cloaking device and that crazy Tal Shiar gadget, we're tapping all our reserves just to keep gravity on."*

"Prioritize the cloaking device," Creelok said. "After that, we need helm functions, then the databanks, and everything else after that. Understood?"

"Perfectly, sir. Engineering out." The channel closed with a scratchy wail of feedback.

The commander confided some further instructions to Mirat, then he stepped away from the console, took Sadira by her arm, and led her off the command deck, down a narrow passageway that led to his quarters. When they reached his cabin, he opened the door using its manual controls, then shoved her inside. He followed her in and stood between her and the open doorway. "Did you know this was going to happen?"

"Did I know your ship would prove defective and your crew incompetent? No."

"Careful, Major. That device you tied into our systems—what is it? Where did it come from? And why did it nearly cripple my ship when you turned it on?"

She couldn't help but strike a haughty note. "Do other people find your bluster intimidating, Commander? Because I find it tedious."

"Answer my questions, or I'll put you out an airlock."

"The Tal Shiar would take a dim view of such action."

Creelok was unperturbed. "They'll be welcome to file a complaint." He prowled forward and loomed over her, his countenance darkening with menace. "Tell me what you've done to my ship, damn you. That thing was active for less than a minute"—he gestured at the emergency lights and smoke—"and it did *this*. Explain. Now."

Sadira took a breath to compose herself. Then she looked Creelok in the eye. "I owe you many things, Commander. My thanks, for your assistance. My apologies, for these unexpected consequences. Maybe even a future debt of obligation, if our mission ends in success. But the one thing I'm certain I don't owe you, in any form, is an explanation. Put into simple terms, Commander, the details of my mission—and those of the alien technology upon which it relies—are so far beyond your security level that if I were to answer your questions, I should be obliged to kill you—and then myself."

"I would have no objection to the latter consequence."

"I'm sure that's true. But it changes nothing."

She moved to step past him. He raised his arm and blocked her way by force. "You're playing with your life here, Major. My crew doesn't like being used as pawns. Push them too far, and I guarantee they'll make you regret it."

"Then I'd suggest you impress upon them the unpleasant truth that I have operational authority for the duration of this mission. And that a mutiny against me will end not just their careers but their lives—and those of their loved ones, their friends, and anyone else they might possibly care about." She made a blade of her hand and thrust it into Creelok's ribs with enough vigor to knock the breath from his lungs but not hard enough to break any bones. He dropped his arm, and she stepped past him, only to pause on the far side of the open doorway.

"Get your ship and your crew in order, Commander. Our mission is not yet over—and I mean to see it finished, at any cost."

Ten

Most of what the Starfleet refugees had been able to break down and pack for travel had been gathered in an orderly fashion, in the center of the camp. Taking a cursory mental inventory, Una noted with some surprise a detail that was obvious in retrospect, but which had jogged her memory only when she had consciously looked for it. She faced Shimizu, who approached bearing another armful of bundled tools. "Tim? Am I seeing things, or does this camp have no stockpile of food and water?"

Her query halted him in midstep. Befuddled, he surveyed the same pile of tools, weapons, and makeshift shelter elements that had led her to ask the question. "I guess you're right. I think I noticed that once, too. But it was a long time ago." He shook his head. "Can't remember the last time I even thought about it."

"When was the last time you ate something?"

Another long, perplexed pause left Shimizu troubled. "I don't know."

It was clear to Una there was nothing to be gained from pressing her old friend further. She waved him past her, toward the load-out stack. "Never mind. Not important. Drop your gear and take a rest before we move out."

"You got it, Captain."

He shuffled away while she looked up at the unchanging sky. *What is this place?*

Her moment of anxious reflection was interrupted by the approach of Feneb, whose arms swung in long arcs as he loped across the dusty ground on a direct path to Una. He had come alone, which Una took as a hopeful sign—a lack of fear if not an outright display of trust.

He greeted her by pressing his hand over his chest and briefly averting his eyes downward. "Leader Una, please do not seek the enemy city."

"I need to, Feneb."

The grizzled Usildar fidgeted and swayed, a behavior she had not seen before, but one that conveyed denial coupled with vehement refusal. "We are safe in the canyon. Soon you will have a way home. You should take shelter and wait with us."

"It's not as simple as that. Time is strange here. If we wait too long in the canyon, we might miss our chance to go home." Pessimism welled up from some dark chasm inside her. "Assuming we haven't missed it already."

Feneb scraped his knuckles in the dirt with each lazy swing of his arms. "It is dangerous to face the enemy, more than you know. Better to hide."

How could she make him understand? "That's not possible anymore. The Jatohr know the gate was opened. Their sentry globes will be watching the arrival point."

Arm outstretched, Feneb pointed a crooked finger at Una's phaser. "But you have fire."

"Yes, but mine is the only phaser that works, and it might not be enough. We saw one globe search the canyon, but there could be more. If we want to go home, I'll need to lure them away from the gateway."

His stare turned hard, and his body language turned defensive. "My people will not leave. We will stay here." He inched closer to Una. His voice became a hoarse whisper. "This place obeys the enemy. No one can fight them here—not even you, Leader Una."

"I'm not looking to fight them. I want to negotiate with them."

"They will not bargain. This is a waste of time and a needless danger."

"You may be right. But I have a duty to seek peace before I accept conflict."

Behind her, the other Starfleet refugees had gathered around the load-out staging point. A dozen meters away, atop a cluster of rocks, a few dozen Usildar observed the discussion. Some looked tense, others frightened. As futile as the effort felt, Una knew she had to make her appeal to Feneb at least once more before she abandoned him and his tribe to their fates.

"Please, go with my people. You'll all be safer together than apart."

"We will not leave the canyon."

"But if the portal opens and you're still here, we won't be able to keep it open long enough for you to reach us. Your only way home is to be there when it opens."

Her entreaty only made Feneb more emphatic in his refusal. "You hear my words, but you do not listen. We cannot go back. The enemy has made certain of that."

Una despaired of reaching Feneb through logic. *How*

do I make a rational argument to someone who still lives in a world of superstition? She purged herself of frustration and adopted her most calming tone of voice. "If the Jatohr had total control of the gateway, I would not have been able to come here by my own choice. The fact that I am here is proof the enemy is not unbeatable. I want to help you and your people get home, Feneb, but you need to trust me."

He looked back and forth between her and his fellow Usildar. Then he backed away from Una. "The risk is too great. We will stay here." He bade her farewell with a broad sweep of his hand. "Safe journey, Leader Una." With that he turned his back on her and loped away to his kinfolk, who retreated en masse into the shadows beneath the canyon wall's rocky overhangs.

One cannot save those who do not wish to be helped, Una reminded herself. She regrouped with the others by the stacked gear and affected a commanding pose. "I want to make clear that my principal objective in approaching the Jatohr is to draw their attention away from the arrival point, so that as many of you as possible can reach the gateway unharmed."

Martinez displayed a hint of his former spark as he asked, "What if the Jatohr don't take the bait, Captain? Or if they recall most of their globes but leave one to guard the gateway?"

She handed him her phaser. "That's what this is for. It should have enough power left to take down one sentry globe."

"No point giving it to me, then." He passed the weapon

to Lieutenant Griffin, then said to Una, "'Cause I'm going with you."

Shimizu added, "That makes two of us."

Their sentiments were echoed by a chorus of the other *Enterprise* personnel until Una raised her hands to quell their spontaneous show of support. "I appreciate your loyalty, really. But the reason I'm here is to bring you all home. Whoever goes with me to face the Jatohr stands a good chance of getting stuck here with me for the rest of our lives."

The others nodded as Ensign Le May said, "We're ready to follow you, Captain. No matter where you need to go." She looked around at the others, then added, "So choose."

It was a moving demonstration, but Una restrained her sentimental impulses. "Very well. Martinez, Shimizu—you're with me. Holstine, you'll lead the others back to the arrival point, or as close to it as you can get without engaging the sentry globes. Avoid a confrontation if at all possible. And if you see that portal open, lead your team through it."

"What about you three?"

"Don't wait for us. We'll find our own way back when it's time." It was a bald-faced lie, but she spoke it with such conviction no one questioned it. She picked up her pack; the others did the same. Putting one foot in front of the other, she led them out of the box canyon. Where the trail met the labyrinth between the mountains, the path split. Una led Martinez and Shimizu one way. Holstine took the rest of the team in the other direction.

It was more likely than not, Una knew, that her team and Holstine's would never meet again. But no one said good-bye, or even farewell. As they parted with firm handshakes and subtle nods, they all encouraged one another with the same simple but heartfelt valediction.

"Good luck."

Eleven

It was rare for Sarek to have cause to second-guess his own judgment, but as Councillor Prang pressed the cold emitter of a disruptor against the back of his head, Sarek had to at least entertain the possibility that he might have overestimated his skills as a negotiator.

"Councillor, I implore you: there is no need for—"

"Silence!" Prang jabbed the disruptor's emitter against Sarek's scalp. "I've had enough of your prattle, Vulcan!" Such had been the tenor of their discourse since Sarek had dared to pay a visit to Prang's suite inside the dormitory reserved for the Klingon delegation. Thinking it would be less provocative to visit without an entourage, Sarek had come alone—a decision he now viewed as another indictment of his hubris.

The entire retinue of Klingon advisers—many of whom Sarek knew to be spies or soldiers in diplomatic costume—huddled around to observe Prang as he taunted Sarek. "I tire of your excuses. Your protocols. Your demands that we be patient." Flecks of spittle struck Sarek's face as Prang shouted, "We are Klingons! People of action, not words!"

For one who claims to eschew words, Prang seems to enjoy hearing himself speak—loudly and at length. Sarek put aside his sardonic criticisms and focused on his dilemma. *I gain nothing by antagonizing him. I must defuse this confrontation.*

Prang circled Sarek while keeping his disruptor pistol steady and aimed at the Vulcan's head. "Is this the true face of the Federation, revealed at last? Under your masks of soft courtesy, cowardly killers who strike from the shadows rather than face their enemies in the open?"

"We are not enemies, Councillor." Sarek dared to look Prang in the eye, hoping it would project confidence and truthfulness. "We must not be enemies, for both our people's sakes."

The Klingon's finger tensed on his weapon's trigger. His hand shook, no doubt a reaction to feelings of overwhelming rage. "Then why murder Gorkon in his sleep?"

"I was told there is no body. No blood. No signs of foul play."

"Because your assassin disintegrated him!"

Contradicting Prang would be a calculated risk, but Sarek hoped the man was not yet wholly beyond the reach of reason. "If Councillor Gorkon had been disintegrated, would there not have been incidental damage from such a powerful release of energy?"

"What?"

"A scorch mark. Traces of ionized dust. Low-level radiation." It was time to attempt a bit of conversational judo. "Perhaps Gorkon left the conference of his own accord."

Frustration and fury contorted Prang's face into an ugly caricature of itself. He turned as if to storm off, then pivoted and lunged, thrusting his disruptor into Sarek's face. "No more games! We know he didn't leave his suite—we checked the sensors!"

"Then who did leave his suite?"

"No one!"

"Then how could he have been murdered? The shields and signal jammers defending the campus prevent the use of transporters on the grounds of the university. So if no one could have entered or departed Councillor Gorkon's suite—"

A white flash of pain—Sarek's head snapped to the side as Prang pistol-whipped him with the disruptor, then was slammed the other way by a second blow that left the middle-aged Vulcan light-headed and his mouth filled with the coppery tang of blood from his split lower lip.

"Done talking yet, Vulcan?"

"In fact . . . no. I am not."

"Then let's see if we can make you tell us something useful." Over his shoulder, Prang shouted, "Bring her in!" The suite's double doors were pulled open. Two Klingons dragged in Amanda by her arms. Prang grinned at the sight of her. "Is she how you did away with Gorkon? Did you send your own mate to seduce him on the dance floor?" When his men presented Amanda to him, Prang leered at her. "Maybe she was the one who did the deed. Came to him in the night. Slipped poison into his drink. Then vaporized him to destroy the evidence."

Amanda was horrified by the accusations. "You're mad!"

Prang backhanded her across the face. Sarek watched his wife fall to the floor. For the first time in his diplomatic career, he contemplated whether it might in fact be logical for him to answer the Klingons on their own terms—by crushing every bone in Prang's body.

The communicator on Prang's hip emitted two long, low beeps. He pulled it off his belt and flipped it open. "Prang here."

"Councillor, this is General Kovor of the HoS'leth. *We have arrived in orbit."*

"Well done, General. Stand by for my order. Prang out." He closed the communicator, then stood over Amanda as he faced Sarek. "Now then, Ambassador. Tell me who gave the order to assassinate Gorkon and how the crime was committed."

"I have no knowledge of such an order, or of any crime against Gorkon."

"I'm going to ask you those questions again. And this time, I want an answer—or else."

"Or else what?"

"We'll find out just how much your wife *really* means to you. And if it turns out you're the sort of man who would sacrifice his mate to conceal his crimes, I will order General Kovor to destroy the *Enterprise*—then lay waste to this entire planet."

———

Kirk strode out of the turbolift onto the bridge of the *Enterprise* to find his crew's preparations for battle well under way. Sulu was at the helm, Chekov at the navigator's station. At the sound of Kirk's first steps onto the upper level of the bridge, Spock swiveled the command chair toward him. As the captain descended the steps into the command well, the first officer stood from the center seat to relinquish it. "Thirty seconds to orbit of Centaurus, Captain."

Pivoting into the command chair, Kirk asked, "What's happening on the surface?"

"Councillor Prang is holding Ambassador Sarek and his wife hostage," Spock said. "Apparently, as a reprisal for the unexplained disappearance of Councillor Gorkon."

It stunned Kirk that his friend could deliver such dire news about his own parents with the same cool detachment he used when reporting on matters trivial and mundane. "How much do we know about the situation on the ground?"

"Prang is threatening to wound or kill Sarek's wife in order to compel information from the ambassador. Based on signals intercepted by Lieutenant Uhura, however, I think it unlikely that Sarek would be able to comply with Prang's demand, even if he wished to."

"Explain."

"He expects Ambassador Sarek to confess to complicity in the murder of Councillor Gorkon. As I consider it doubtful the ambassador was involved in any such crime—"

"Point taken, Mister Spock."

From the helm, Sulu announced, "Assuming standard orbit, Captain."

Chekov added with subdued alarm, "Klingon cruiser, ninety thousand kilometers ahead, running with shields up."

"Helm, close to firing distance. Charge all weapons and stand by to target that ship on my command—but *only* on my command. Clear?"

Sulu activated the helm's targeting viewer. "Aye, sir."

Chekov added over his shoulder, "Now at optimal firing range."

Kirk swiveled his chair toward Lieutenant Uhura. "Hail that ship, Lieutenant."

"Aye, sir." She touched the transceiver tucked into her ear with one hand and worked her console's controls with the other. "The *HoS'leth* refuses to acknowledge our hails, Captain."

Spock, ensconced once more at his post on Kirk's right, looked up from the blue glow of the hooded sensor display. "They've charged their disruptors and torpedo launchers."

"So much for a measured response." Kirk was disappointed to find himself forced into a violent confrontation before diplomacy had been given a chance. "Mister Chekov, lock phasers and torpedoes. Lieutenant Uhura, open a channel to the *HoS'leth*, please."

As Chekov targeted the *Enterprise*'s arsenal upon the *HoS'leth*, which grew larger on the viewscreen with each passing moment, Uhura established a real-time comm link with the Klingon cruiser. "Channel open, Captain."

"Attention, commander of the *HoS'leth*. This is Captain James T. Kirk, commanding the Federation *Starship Enterprise*. Unless you power down your weapons and lower your shields in the next twenty seconds, I will have no choice but to destroy your ship. Respond and comply."

For a long bated breath, there was no sound on the bridge but the chirps and whistles of feedback tones from the ship's computers and the hum of its impulse engines. Then a signal chirruped on Uhura's console. She checked her monitor. "I have General Kovor on visual, sir."

"On-screen," Kirk said.

The Klingon commander's face was a one-eyed horror

of scar tissue. It was easy to see at a glance that this was a man who was on intimate terms with war, and with pain. He was not one to be underestimated or trifled with; this was a warrior in the oldest and most venerable sense of the word. He took Kirk's measure with a fearsome, humbling stare. *"I am Kovor."*

"I am Kirk."

The two captains regarded each other in silence across the subspace channel for a few seconds—and then Kovor raised his chin and cracked a fanged smile. *"You have a good Klingon name. And I see the fire of Kahless in your eyes. Speak and be heard, Kirk."*

Under any circumstances but these, Kirk would not have taken such a comparison as a compliment, but considering the source, it felt warranted. "Our peoples need these talks to win the peace. You know that as well as I do, Kovor. Stand down so we can prevent a war that would destroy us both."

His plea had no effect on the smug Klingon starship commander. Then a female Klingon officer leaned into view along the edge of the viewscreen and whispered something to Kovor, whose smile faded. He nodded once, then dismissed the other officer. In a more reserved manner, he said to Kirk, *"I lack the authority to countermand Councillor Prang's orders. However, in the absence of contrary orders, I can put you in direct contact with him. If your powers of persuasion are sufficient to soothe his fury . . . so be it."*

It struck Kirk as a strangely rational tack for a veteran Klingon general and battle fleet commander. Then again, perhaps the ability to exercise restraint was what had enabled Kovor to climb near to the top of the ranks in the Klingon Defense Forces. He nodded once. "If you're willing to connect us to Councillor Prang, we would be most appreciative, General."

Kovor nodded to someone off-screen. *"May you have better luck talking sense to him than I have, Kirk. HoS'leth out."* His haggard visage vanished from the viewscreen, leaving only the image of the *HoS'leth* cruising in orbit above Centaurus—a reminder to Kirk that its weapons were mere moments from rendering the surface of a major Federation world into molten slag.

Uhura turned her chair toward Kirk. "I have Prang's private communicator channel."

"Hail him."

Prang's voice barked from the overhead: *"What now?"*

"Councillor Prang. This is Captain James T. Kirk of the *Starship Enterprise*. General Kovor and his starship are standing down. Now I need you to release Ambassador Sarek and his wife—unharmed and without delay. Acknowledge."

Kirk could almost hear the Klingon politico grinding his teeth over the comm channel. *"You're bluffing, Kirk. Kovor won't stand down until I say so."*

"Is that so? Then how did we hail your secure comm channel? Who do you think gave us that information?" After a prolonged delay without a reply, Kirk prompted, "Councillor?"

"Don't think this means you've won, Kirk. When the High Council hears of this treachery, your entire Federation will pay with its dearest blood."

There was a faint click on the overhead speakers.

Uhura looked up from her console. "Councillor Prang closed the channel, sir." She touched the transceiver in her ear. "New reports from the surface—Ambassador Sarek and his wife have left Prang's suite. They're being met by local police and escorted back to their own residence hall."

"Good." Kirk used his armrest controls to open an intraship channel. "Bridge to engineering."

"Scott here."

"Do we still have valid command codes for the shield generators protecting the campus?"

"Aye, sir."

"Stand by to open a window for transport. Kirk out." He stood and strode toward the turbolift. "Spock, you're with me. Sulu, you have the conn. Uhura, have Doctor McCoy and a security team meet us in transporter room one, on the double."

A golden shimmer of light, a mellisonant wash of noise— the transporter effect enveloped Kirk on the pad inside the transporter room, then dissipated to reveal the grassy quad of New Athens University on Centaurus. Overhead, a pale dawn sky; around him, the long blue shadows of morning stretched away from the ruddy sun low on the horizon.

On his right stood Spock, tricorder slung at his left hip, ready to work. At his left was Doctor McCoy, who was unarmed and toting a medical kit. Kirk and Spock, meanwhile, both wore pistol-style phasers holstered on their hips—as did the three security officers who had

beamed down with them. As soon as the last flickers of
the transporter beam had faded away, Kirk addressed the
senior security officer. "Lieutenant Patel, have your men
fan out around us. If the Klingons start shooting, take
cover and hold your fire unless I or Mister Spock order
you to do otherwise. Understood?"

"Perfectly, Captain."

"Good. Move out." Kirk and Spock walked quickly toward the residential building that had been designated as
temporary quarters for the Federation delegation. Every
step of the way, he was keenly aware that their backs faced
a different building packed with Klingons who would
likely have little compunction about gunning them all
down from behind.

Let's hope they're not all as bloodthirsty as Prang.

They had crossed half the distance to the residence
hall when the siren-like melody of another transporter
beam filled the quad behind them. Kirk glanced back
long enough to confirm it was a second detail of six security officers from the *Enterprise*. The second group split
into pairs and dispersed to form a wider cordon around
the captain, doctor, and first officer.

McCoy frowned. "I feel like the center of a bull's-eye."

Evincing no pity for the surgeon's anxious complaint,
Spock replied, "Relax, Doctor. It is unlikely anyone would
be targeting you."

"What kind of Vulcan pep talk is that?"

"Gentlemen, enough," Kirk cut in. "We have a job to
do, and there's more at stake here than just our lives. So
let's keep the banter to a minimum."

Spock absorbed the criticism in silence. McCoy

acknowledged it with a contrite nod as he said, "Sorry, Captain."

The trio continued in silence, surrounded by their security phalanx, and approached the entrance to the Federation delegation's dormitory. A knot of local peace officers and university security stood between the walkway and the closed door. One officer, who looked to be in charge, stepped forward and raised his hand toward the landing party. "Halt and identify—"

"Kirk, *Enterprise*," the captain said, leading his team past the local authorities without pausing to entertain questions or doubts. If the officer in charge had any protest, he failed to express it before Kirk, Spock, McCoy, and their armed defenders entered the building and continued upstairs to the delegation's private wing.

The accommodations were less posh than they sounded. Most of the rooms on the upper floors were converted student dwellings. Quite spare in their furnishings, the rooms were devoid of decoration or anything that might be mistaken for luxury. Kirk eyed the nearly empty spaces that typically housed undergraduates and wondered to himself why modern educational institutions still expected students to live like monks.

Even the Academy put a few murals on the walls once in a while.

He and the landing party arrived at the open door to the suite of Ambassador Sarek and his wife, Amanda, whom Kirk knew better as Spock's parents. He looked back at the security officers who trailed him, Spock, and McCoy. "Wait outside," he said to Lieutenant Patel, who nodded once before pointing his subordinates toward defensive positions.

Inside the suite, a nurse and a lone medical doctor tended to Sarek and Amanda. Kirk queried the Andorian physician with a look, and the *thaan* beckoned him and the other *Enterprise* officers inside. McCoy made a point of greeting his peer before anyone else did. "Doctor Leonard McCoy, ship's surgeon, *Enterprise*."

"Doctor Hollishaal th'Carinoor. I am pleased to report that neither the ambassador nor his wife were seriously harmed. Just minor contusions for His Excellency."

"Thank heavens for that." McCoy pointed at Sarek's chart. "May I?"

The Andorian looked at Sarek, who granted permission with one deep nod. "He was my surgeon when my heart failed several months ago." Reassured, th'Carinoor handed Sarek's medical chart to McCoy for review.

While the doctors were occupied, Kirk waited for his first officer to greet his father. Sensing that Spock was not keen to break the ice, he took the task upon himself. "Mister Ambassador, we came as soon as we—"

"You have ruined everything, Kirk."

Sarek's rebuke took Kirk by surprise. "Excuse me? I— that is, we—*my crew* just saved your life, Mister Ambassador. We—"

"Undermined my authority and squandered my last iota of credibility with the Klingon delegation. Really, Captain—for a man who has spent the better part of his career dealing with the Klingons, you seem not to understand them at all."

Kirk felt his blood pressure rising. He turned away from Sarek to tell the local medical and security personnel assembled in the suite, "Anyone not wearing a

Starfleet uniform, get out." The captain noted hesitation from the nurse and physician. He stared them down. "This matter is now under Starfleet jurisdiction. Get out. That's an order."

This time there were no stragglers. All the civilians except Sarek and Amanda made hasty retreats, leaving the diplomat, his wife, and their Starfleet visitors to confer in privacy.

Kirk shot a look at McCoy. "Doctor? The door, please."

McCoy closed the suite's doors and locked them.

Bolstered by a moderate degree of certainty that they were now free from eavesdroppers, Kirk asked Sarek, "What happened over there, Mister Ambassador? The truth, please."

"I went to assess the facts concerning Councillor Gorkon's disappearance. It was my assumption that the Klingons would be willing to entertain reasonable explanations."

An arched eyebrow conveyed McCoy's cynical appraisal of the ambassador's thinking. "And how did *that* work out for you?"

"Less well than I had expected."

"Indeed," Spock said. As innocuous as his reply had been, it still drew a cold stare from his father, which suggested to Kirk that old hard feelings still lingered between the two.

Amanda tried to short-circuit the tension between her husband and son. "We're both lucky to be alive, Captain. I, for one, am grateful you and your ship arrived when you did."

"You're most welcome."

Sarek remained rooted in his icy condemnation. "You will receive no thanks from me, Kirk. You have interfered in a political discourse of a most complex nature."

"Really, Ambassador? It seems fairly simple to me. I'm told Prang had a disruptor to your head, and his friend had a dagger at your wife's throat. From where I'm standing, it sounds as if we saved your lives."

"Perhaps." Sarek affected an imperious manner. "But your intervention may have just squandered this galaxy's best hope for peace."

McCoy chimed in: "It's hard to make peace from the grave, Mister Ambassador."

"He's right, Ambassador," Kirk added. "Klingons have no respect for martyrs."

Sarek folded his hands together inside his cassock's generous, drooping sleeves. "Not true, Kirk. I have heard many tales of Klingons honoring those who died for noble causes."

"Died in battle," Kirk corrected. "Not for peace. There's a difference."

The Vulcan diplomat bristled at Kirk's point. "I lack the time to discuss the nuances of Klingon martial philosophy and its relationship to their politics." He stood and smoothed the front of his scuffed, soiled robe, then extended his arm as an invitation to his wife, who moved to his side and snaked her own arm around his. He nodded once to Kirk. "You did what you thought was necessary, Captain. But I cannot help but be disappointed by the need for your continued involvement. If history is any guide, the presence of military forces at a diplomatic function can only bode ill for its outcome."

"I agree," Kirk said. "And just as soon as the *HoS'leth* breaks orbit, so will we."

Sarek let that condition pass without remark. He led his wife out of the suite's main room and escorted her into the privacy of their bedchambers, whose door he closed quite firmly behind them—no doubt as a signal of his desire for seclusion and an end to Kirk's interrogation.

Only after the door was shut did Kirk realize no words of greeting had passed between Spock and his parents. McCoy, noting with sour disapproval the dynamic that obtained between Sarek, Amanda, and their son, quipped in his dry Southern drawl, "Another happy family reunion, eh, Spock?"

The first officer let the jibe pass unremarked, electing instead to exit the suite in stony silence. Watching his friend leave, clearly stung but too aloof to admit it, left Kirk with a new, more bitter appreciation for the long rift that still lingered between Spock and his father.

Before inspecting the bedroom that had been set aside for Councillor Gorkon's exclusive use, Spock would not have been able to say what it was he was looking for, or what he had expected to find there. In neither case would he have assumed the scene would be so mundane. If there was any aspect of the Klingon diplomat's disappearance that deserved to be termed "baffling," it was the utter banality of the details he had left behind.

Over the objections of the Klingons, more personnel from the *Enterprise* had arrived in the past hour to secure the missing man's personal spaces and effects. In charge of the search had been Lieutenant Ravi Patel from the security division. Backed by a team of forensic investigation specialists from the *Enterprise*, he had been directing the scanning, sorting, and logging of every tiny detail that might at some point become evidence.

So far, however, none of those details appeared to add up to anything at all.

The captain entered the bedroom, and Doctor McCoy was close behind him. The pair took note of the forensic team scouring the room under Patel's supervision, and then Kirk faced Spock. "What have we found?"

"Nothing of note, Captain. No signs of forced entry. And no evidence of a struggle."

Kirk processed that. "Contradicting our theory that he was kidnapped."

"So it would seem." Spock pointed at the empty bed. "Our scans have revealed no sign of Klingon blood and no atomized particles consistent with disintegration by any known weapon, chemical, or process." He directed the captain's attention toward the doors to the suite's main room. "The Klingons have already shared their internal security footage. No one entered or left the room after Gorkon retired for the evening last night."

The captain gestured at the windows. "What about exterior sensors?"

"Also negative," Spock said. "Campus security adjusted all external sensors to provide maximum coverage of the delegates' dormitory facilities, as well as the grounds around them. There was no one outside in the vicinity of either building last night."

McCoy moved along the room's periphery, inspecting small items and scanning things with his medical tricorder. Kirk paid the physician no mind, choosing instead to catch the eye of the security officer leading the investigation. "Mister Patel, do we have evidence that anyone other than Councillor Gorkon or members of his entourage were inside this room before us?"

"None, sir," Patel said. "The only genetic material we've detected that we're sure was here during the over-night hours was Gorkon's. If someone else was here, they left no trace."

Kirk frowned and took another gander at the room, as if he might now notice some vital clue that had eluded trained investigators and the impartial senses of tricord-ers. "So we have no evidence Gorkon left, and none that he was assassinated or kidnapped."

Spock tried to offer his captain a reason for optimism. "The absence of evidence does not negate the fact that Councillor Gorkon is now, indisputably, absent."

"Meaning what, Spock?"

"Regardless of what we can prove, Gorkon is most assuredly gone. If he is gone by his own will, it is without explanation, and we are obliged in the name of diplo-macy to determine why. And if he is gone against his will, our duty is to determine who is to blame and to ensure the councillor's safe return. Either way, it falls to us to determine Gorkon's whereabouts and take proper action."

The proposition drew an outburst from McCoy. "De-termine his whereabouts? And how are we supposed to do *that*, Spock?"

"I didn't say I knew how to locate him, Doctor. If I

possessed such knowledge, I assure you, I would already have done so."

Disgruntled, McCoy turned away and continued his own tedious item-by-item scan of Gorkon's belongings, grumbling under his breath the entire time.

Kirk took Spock aside and lowered his voice. "Bones has a point, Spock. We have no evidence and no options. How do you recommend we continue the search?"

"Difficult to say, Captain. We might wish to gather data from the planetary defense network, to look for signs of anomalous energy signatures, unidentified encrypted signal traffic, or other indications that—"

The doors behind them burst open, flew inward, and rebounded off the walls. A squad of local police backed through the doorway, hounded by an insistent push of enraged Klingons, whose shouted alien vulgarities assaulted Spock's sensitive Vulcan hearing.

The captain intercepted the brouhaha with a fierce bellow. "What's the meaning of this?"

Councillor Prang shouted back, "We want justice!" Behind him, his fellows roared.

"Quiet!" snapped the boss of the local police, Chief Nomi Wreade. She was tall but slight of frame, and her jet-black hair was coiffed in a smart bob. The faintest hint of a deeper register in her slightly nasal voice suggested the transitional nature of her gender, but there was no mistaking her authority as her deputies and their Klingon harassers all froze in place, arrested by the power of her voice. "Councillor Prang! You and your people need to back off. *Now.*"

On a nod from Prang, the Klingons all took a full

step back from their confrontation with the New Athens police. Satisfied the situation was at least momentarily under control, Kirk approached Wreade. "Thank you, Chief."

"Don't thank me unless you've got something. I can't hold them back forever."

Taking his cue from the captain's disappointed expression, Spock told Wreade, "We are still analyzing the evidence and developing our hypothesis."

Wreade shot a nervous glance at the Klingons, then looked back at Spock and dropped her voice to a husky whisper. "Prang wants me to file this as a murder."

Kirk forestalled that notion with a raised hand. "Absolutely not."

The chief turned her skeptical glare on the captain. "You have proof it's not a murder?"

"More to the point," Spock interjected, "you have no proof that it is. And absent such evidence, most notably that of a corpse, you have no basis for labeling this a homicide."

She surveyed the locked room and the team of quiet, methodical Starfleet forensic technicians. "In that case, I have to file it as a kidnapping."

Again, the captain shook his head. "You can't do that, either."

"Why not?"

Spock closed the suite's double doors to render the rest of their conversation private. "Because, Chief Wreade, the moment you do, you will have provided Councillor Prang and the Klingon Empire with a justification for war."

His news flustered the police chief. "So how am I supposed to classify this mess?"

Kirk mustered his most disarming smile. "In the name of interstellar peace, I need to ask that you treat Gorkon's disappearance, for the time being, as a missing person case."

"The Klingons won't like that."

As always, the captain met grim facts with gallows humor.

"True. But the people of Centaurus *really* won't like being exterminated by the Klingons. So do them *and* us a favor, Chief: file this as a missing person until we can prove otherwise."

Twelve

Dawn's cool breezes had given way to a muggy morning on the campus quad by the time Kirk left the Klingon delegation's dormitory. As he had expected, the classification of Gorkon's absence as a missing person without evidence of foul play had enraged the Klingons while simultaneously depriving them of an excuse to begin sterilizing the planet's surface. It was a less than perfect solution, but Kirk's brief tenure as a commanding officer had already taught him the value of expedient delaying tactics when optimal outcomes remained out of reach.

On the quad's well-manicured lawn, Kirk's landing party had gathered to return to the *Enterprise*. Doctor McCoy made a point of standing apart from the rest of the group. As Kirk approached, he noticed his friend was distracted and distraught.

Before Kirk could call out to the doctor, the air between them shimmered with the first sign of an incoming transporter signal. Next came the semimusical droning of a matter-transmission beam. Six humanoid figures took shape inside glittering shells of golden light. Once the coruscating effect started to fade, Kirk recognized Lieutenant Commander Scott, who had beamed down with five other engineers—three women and two men.

He intercepted the chief engineer as the older man surveyed his environs. "Mister Scott. Good of you to join us."

Scott flashed a broad smile. "Wouldn't miss it, sir."

"I didn't think you'd find reinforcing a security shield so exciting."

"It's not the work, sir. It's a chance to observe the Klingon engineers. I've been keen to get a closer look at their tools and their methods."

I should have known. "Very good. But take care, Scotty. If you're watching them—"

"They'll be watching us. Aye, sir. That's the price of admission."

He dismissed Scott with a nod as he stepped past him. "Carry on."

The engineers regrouped and started their hike across the campus to the nearest of the mobile shield generators that were protecting the peace conference from outside interference. Low murmurs of upbeat chatter passed from one engineer to another. Kirk recognized their strange brand of enthusiasm: it was the excitement of specialists who spent most of their waking hours in the bowels of a starship, looking at the same blue-gray bulkheads day in and day out. Any chance to venture off the ship and tinker with something new was cause for celebration.

Kirk waited until they were out of earshot before he sidled over to McCoy. Keeping his voice down, he asked, "Bones? Are you all right?"

His question jolted McCoy out of a somber reverie. "Hm? Oh, yes. I'm fine, Jim."

"Are you sure? It looks to me like something's bothering you."

McCoy folded his hands behind his back, then pivoted to one side, then another, as if worried someone was eavesdropping on them. "I didn't want to say anything . . ."

"Out with it, Bones."

A frown and a furrowed brow deepened the canyons of concern that marked McCoy's face. "It's my daughter."

That caught Kirk off guard. McCoy rarely mentioned his only child. They had been estranged since his bitter divorce from her mother years earlier. "Joanna? What about her?"

"She's a student here, at the College of Medical Science. Second year of nursing school." He looked over his shoulder. "Pretty sure it's a short walk that way."

"You should go say hello."

McCoy regarded Kirk with a stink-eye glare. "I'd sooner eat my phaser."

It was sometimes difficult for Kirk to guess at McCoy's hidden agendas. "Why bring her up if you don't want to see her?"

"Who says I don't want to see her?"

"Bones, I just spent the past hour being verbally abused by Spock's father and a Klingon politician. My patience is gone, so get to the point. What *do* you want?"

The grouchy physician sighed. "I just want to know that if all this goes south, my daughter won't get caught in the cross fire."

Kirk sympathized. He, too, had a child of whom he rarely spoke—his son, David, the product of a years-long, on-again, off-again romance he had enjoyed with Doctor Carol Marcus. The boy had just turned seven—and that was all Kirk knew of him. Kirk's separation from Carol, though less hostile than Bones's acrimonious divorce, still had been unpleasant. And while he had consented to let Carol raise their son free of his "influence," whatever that meant, it was one of his few great regrets that he had let himself be excised from David's life.

If Carol and David were here . . . I'd want to protect them, too.

He set his hand on McCoy's shoulder. "Forget about the past, Bones. You divorced your wife, not your daughter."

McCoy shook his head in denial. "I know Joanna still blames me. She always has."

"How long has it been since you saw each other?"

"In the flesh?" A shrug. "A few years." He thought harder. "Maybe five or so." Then he came clean. "Okay, twelve years and four months. But that's what subspace messages are for."

The longer Kirk talked to his friend, the more certain he became that the man would never just ask for what he needed. It would have to be forced upon him, for his own good.

"Go find your daughter, Bones."

McCoy did his best impression of a man aggrieved. "Now, hang on just a minute, Captain. I've got a lab full of forensic samples in need of—"

"That wasn't a suggestion, Doctor. It was an order. Go. Find her." He softened the directive with a friendly smile. "The samples will still be there when you get back."

An abashed smile brightened McCoy's weathered visage. "Aye, sir."

Montgomery Scott had come ready for a fight. He had five Starfleet engineers at his back and no qualms about throwing the first punch, if someone deserved it. He still savored his memory of cold-cocking Korax, the first officer of the Klingon cruiser *Gr'oth*, aboard Deep Space Station K-7 a few months earlier. *That's what he gets for calling the* Enterprise *"garbage."*

The portable shield generator and signal scrambler was tucked into a tree-shaded corner of the campus, beside a high rock wall whose stones of varying size and color had been assembled with deliberate artlessness. Huddled around the machine, their hands filled with diagnostic tools, were four Klingon engineers. With tensions between the Federation and the Klingon Empire running higher than ever, Scott had no expectation of a warm welcome.

"Look sharp," he muttered to his team.

Scott was still a few paces shy of arm's length when the four Klingons stopped working and turned to face him and his crew. The oldest of the bunch—the only one with a hint of gray in his beard—handed his scanner to one of his subordinates, then stepped away from the machine to meet Scott, his gloved hand outstretched. "Ulgor. Chief engineer of the *HoS'leth*."

The terse welcome surprised Scott. He had tensed to block a swung fist, not grasp a proffered palm. Recovering from his momentary confusion, he shook Ulgor's hand. "Montgomery Scott, chief engineer, *U.S.S. Enterprise*."

Ulgor's grip was firm. "You're the one who beat Korax on K-7."

Proudly lifting his chin, Scott said, "Aye, that was me."

The Klingon released Scott's hand and gave his shoulder a friendly slap. "Well done! I served with that *yIntagh* on the *LoSgor*. Never liked him." He motioned toward the generator. "We ran a full system check of the shield network. No sign of malfunction or breach."

"We'd like to confirm that for ourselves, if you don't mind."

"That is why you're here." Ulgor looked to the largest of his subordinates. "Rathnar, give them the codes for the network's master control panel."

Scott glanced over his shoulder at Lieutenant L'Nar and directed her attention at Rathnar with a tilt of his head. The Vulcan woman nodded in acknowledgment, then primed her tricorder to receive the access codes from the burly Klingon engineer. She silenced feedback tones from her tricorder, then said to Scott, "Codes received and relayed to all team devices."

"Good work, Lieutenant." To the others Scott added, "Get to it." The two engineering teams maneuvered nervously around one another while they worked. Comparing notes, they conducted a new series of hardware, firmware, and software checks of the device and its networked counterparts. Scott watched Ulgor from the corner of his eye. "So. If the shields didn't fail and weren't breached, what do you think happened?"

"I don't know yet." Ulgor noticed Scott's dubious reaction. "Is that not why we're here? To gather facts and learn the truth?"

"Aye. Last I heard."

A cool-headed Klingon? One who cared about evidence? Before that moment, Scott would have called such a notion absurd. Now he pondered Hamlet's words of caution: *There are more things in heaven and earth, Horatio, than are dreamt of in your philosophy.*

Their two teams finished their diagnostics and returned to stand in a mixed huddle around them. L'Nar spoke first. "Our review of the shield generators' logs confirms the Klingons' report, sir. There is no evidence of downtime, power spikes, frequency changes, or other malfunctions, nor is there any sign of a forcible breach of the system."

"All right, then," Scott said. "That means we can rule out Gorkon's abduction by any known type of transporter." He continued to Ulgor, "There's no evidence of foul play in Gorkon's suite, and your security vids prove he can't have left. Which means—"

"That this has been a waste of time," said Rathnar.

L'Nar replied, "Perhaps not." She faced Scott and Ulgor. "Though our diagnostic of the shield network was not able to explain the councillor's disappearance, we were able to assess some flaws in the system's heat-dissipation protocols, as well as minor errors in its field geometry that could be exploited by an attacker. Fortunately, I think I can correct both problems with some adjustments to the system's software." A polite nod at Rathnar. "With your help."

Rathnar looked to Ulgor for permission, which came in the form of a curt nod. The big, brawny Klingon gestured for L'Nar to lead the way back to the generator, and he fell into step beside her, no doubt to supervise her upgrades to the Klingon-made shield network.

Ulgor watched the departing pair for a moment, then

turned back toward Scott. "Most generous of your engineer to offer to improve our system."

"Aye," Scott said. He left unspoken the rest of his thought: *I'll definitely need to have a word with that lass once we get back to the ship.*

As useful as it might have been, in the short term, for L'Nar to have kept her knowledge of flaws in the Klingons' shield network to herself for Starfleet's benefit, Scott had to confess, even if just to himself, a grudging respect for the way her gesture had reduced the tension level between the two engineering teams. And, for that matter, he gave credit to the goodwill shown by Ulgor, his opposite number from the *HoS'leth*.

Maybe we and the Klingons should've sent engineers to get this treaty sorted, he mused. *No way we could gum it up worse than the bloody politicians have.*

———

It had been years since McCoy last walked the halls of a civilian teaching hospital. As odd as he knew it might seem to some people, he looked forward to the hushed atmosphere, the bite of disinfectant in the air, the vaguely pine-scented fragrance of a freshly mopped floor, and even the weak aromas of bland food wafting from a cafeteria.

New Athens University Hospital loomed before him, a Y-shaped complex ten stories tall, with a footprint that occupied most of one square kilometer, including its tastefully manicured grounds. Its exterior was sheathed in the same kind of specially treated transparent aluminum common to large buildings on Centaurus and many other Federation worlds. Amber-tinted, the panels both absorbed solar energy to help replenish the complex's backup batteries as a safeguard against a failure of the planetary power grid and prevented dangerous concentrations of reflected light that could pose a hazard to the planet's indigenous life-forms.

The main entrance was a lobby whose façade consisted of five-meter-tall floor-to-ceiling windows and a broad, three-paneled revolving door that remained in constant gradual motion, sweeping visitors in and out of the lobby with firm but gentle insistence. McCoy followed a handful of civilians through the revolving entrance into the lobby.

He made it as far as the central information desk, which was flanked by security checkpoints. There an Andorian security officer waylaid him. "Can I help you, sir?"

McCoy pointed at the turbolifts on the other side of the checkpoint and flashed his best disarming smile. "Just visiting."

"Not without a pass, sir." The Andorian *chan* directed McCoy's eye to a sign on the front of the ring-shaped information desk. "Access is restricted to staff and approved visitors."

"How do you know I'm not an 'approved visitor'?"

"Biometrics. Your face, retinal scan, and kinetic profile were checked when you came through the door. Plus—" He gave McCoy's uniform exaggerated scrutiny. "You stand out."

His fragile good mood dashed, McCoy glowered at the security officer. "Fine, Sherlock. You've cracked the case. Now what?"

"If you can tell me who you're here to see—"

"I'm here to see nursing student Joanna McCoy."

The guard activated a panel on his side of the desk and mumbled to himself as he accessed the hospital's personnel directory. "McAdams, McAndrews, McCall . . . here we go, McCoy, Joanna." An obsequious smile as he looked up. "And who should I say is here?"

"Her *father*. *Doctor* Leonard McCoy." He hoped that his choice of emphasis might earn him some small measure of additional respect or contrition from the *chan* behind the desk, but his verbal microaggression went unacknowledged. *Typical*.

Some more taps on the screen, another phony smile. "She'll be down as soon as she's able." He gestured toward the padded benches in front of the lobby's dramatically high windows. "Feel free to have a seat and make yourself comfortable."

"I prefer to stand."

"Suit yourself, sir."

Ten minutes later, McCoy started to regret his choice. He was on the verge of swallowing his wounded pride and taking a seat when Joanna emerged from one of the lifts behind the checkpoint. As anxious as he was to see her again after so long apart, he couldn't help but break into a broad grin at the mere sight of her. He threw his arms wide to greet her. "There she is!"

She stepped into his embrace and planted a dutiful peck on his cheek. "Nice to see you, too, Dad." All too soon she pulled away, asserting her independence. "What're you doing here?"

"I came to see you."

"No, I mean, what are you doing on Centaurus?"

He tried to shrug off the question as if it were a trifle. "Ship's business."

Concern darkened her innocent gaze. "It's about the conference, isn't it?"

Out of reflex, McCoy looked around for potential eavesdroppers, then lowered his voice. "Is there someplace more private we could talk?"

She threaded her arm around his and led him toward the revolving door. "Outside." It rankled McCoy to feel as if he were being handled, but it also pleased him to walk with his daughter holding his arm. He wrestled with his confusion in silence as she guided him back out into the crisp autumn morning. They strolled together along a cobblestone path that snaked in languid curves around the complex. Sunlight streaming through a canopy of tree boughs dappled the walkway with a blend of golden light and turquoise shadows.

McCoy wanted to cut to the chase, but the circumstances called for small talk. "So, your second year of nursing school. How are your studies going?"

Her reaction was halting and awkward, as if she sensed he was masking his true agenda. "Um . . . fairly well, I guess. My grades are good. And my performance evals last year were good enough that I'm shadowing the senior RN this year."

"That's good. What's her specialty?"

Another telling hesitation. "Emergent care."

His composure slipped. "The trauma unit? Are you ready for that?"

"Dad, it's fine."

"It's the *emergency* unit. By *definition*, it's the opposite of fine." He could sense her emotional shields going up, so he changed the subject. "Are you still living on campus?"

She rolled her eyes, which made her look like the nineteen-year-old she was. "Not anymore. The peace conference took over my dorm."

"So where are you staying?"

"In town, with friends." She sized him up with a sly look. "What's got you keyed up?"

"Nothing," he lied.

"No, there's something on your mind. Something you want to ask about Mom?"

Now his shields were up. "Not in a million years."

She shook her head. "Still holding a grudge, eh?"

"Might as well. It's all she left me." As soon as he'd said it, he knew he'd crossed the line. Joanna turned around in midstep, and he lurched after her. "Wait, Joanna—"

"No, Dad. If the only reason you're here is to play out this same old song—"

"That's not why I came to see you." His admission halted her retreat. She turned back and with a look prompted him to continue. "I'm here because I'm worried for your safety."

She took a step back toward him. "Why?" A narrowed gaze of suspicion. "It's the peace conference, right? Something went wrong?"

"How'd you know?"

"The news channels can't shut up about the *Enterprise*

and a Klingon cruiser being in orbit. They're trying to say it's no big deal. But it is, isn't it?"

As always, too smart for her own good. He sighed. "Kind of, yeah."

"So what am I supposed to do? Hoard food? Stock up on potable water?"

"I was thinking more along the lines of booking passage back to Earth."

She raised her eyebrows so high they vanished beneath her bangs. "Are you nuts? I'm in the middle of a semester here. I can't just pick up and leave."

He bristled at her hostile tone. "The hell you can't. Three transports to Earth leave every day. I could have you on one tonight."

Crossed arms and a scowl. "Over my dead body."

"Stay here and you might get your wish. If this conference keeps going downhill—"

"Sometimes being a medical professional means working in dangerous places."

"But you're *not* a professional, Joanna. You're just a *student.*"

"No, Dad, I'm a *nurse.*" Her anger boiled over. "You think I'm stupid? That I don't know the peace conference is going south? Thanks for stopping by, but I figured that out myself."

"Dammit, Joanna! You've never seen war, *real* war, up close. I have. It's something I hope you never have to face. And that's why I want you as far from this mess as possible."

A slow, sad nod. "Yeah, that makes sense . . . coming

from you. Cut and run was always kind of your thing, wasn't it?" She turned her back and strode away from him. He stood, stunned and silent, too emotionally wounded to retort or try to follow.

Recklessness, obstinacy, self-righteousness—Joanna's youth was marked by all the same selfish qualities McCoy remembered from his own early adulthood.

With reflection came enlightenment.

No wonder my father couldn't stand me.

Thirteen

It took the better part of an hour for Elara to get far enough from the campus's upgraded security field to feel comfortable attempting to contact her superiors. Ensconced in a cramped hotel room on the outskirts of New Athens, she had taken care while prying up the carpeting and cutting a hole in the floor with a plasma knife, all so that she could tap into the building's communications systems. It had been tedious, but it let her hijack the hotel's link to the planet's orbital subspace signal relay and set up an encrypted real-time signal to her overlord on the Orion homeworld.

Why doesn't he answer? She had been pinging the Red Man for nearly two minutes. He usually answered within seconds. Confused, she checked her wrist chrono again. It was early afternoon in New Athens on Centaurus and late evening in the capital on Orion. The Red Man tended to follow a nocturnal schedule; he should have been awake. *So why doesn't he—?*

His crimson face and bald head filled the screen of her handheld comm tablet. She recalled he wore a black braid of hair on the back of his head, but it wasn't visible on-screen—only the glare of his yellow-gold irises beneath his black peaked brows. *"What, Elara?"*

"My apologies if I've disturbed you, Master."

"You want forgiveness, make this worth my time."

"The peace conference is falling apart because of Councillor Gorkon's disappearance."

That news put a rare smile on the Red Man's face. "*Define 'falling apart.'*"

"Two warships in orbit, one Starfleet, one Klingon. Armed troops from both ships on the ground. And a total halt to the treaty negotiations."

"*Excellent. Just as we'd hoped.*"

Nothing made Elara as suspicious as seeing the Red Man elated. "We *want* them to go to war? Their *last* conflict wasn't good for business. Why would this one be different?"

He suppressed a chortle of sinister mirth. "*Because, my dear—the moment they pull their triggers on each other, they'll both be as good as neutralized.*"

"I don't understand."

He tapped his index finger against his pursed lips, as if considering whether it was prudent to say more. For once, his enthusiasm overcame his caution. "*Thanks to the indiscreet pillow talk of a Starfleet Command officer on Earth, we now know the only reason both sides agreed to this conference was their mutual fear of reprisal by an outside force known as the Organians. The details on this part are, admittedly, hazy—but the gist is that if either side reignites their conflict, the Organians will cripple both their militaries, galaxy-wide.*" A broad, maniacal grin revealed the Red Man's mouthful of perfect, immaculately white teeth. "*It's more than we've ever dared to wish for. And all we have to do to get it is push both sides just a little bit further—then step out of the way when they start shooting.*"

Laid out in such stark terms, the Red Man's interest in the conference became clear to Elara. Goading the Federation and the Klingon Empire into causing their own destruction would be a massive boon to interstellar piracy, smuggling, and sentient trafficking—the principal businesses of the shadowy criminal empire known to outsiders as the Orion Syndicate.

"How do you wish me to proceed, Master?"

"Do whatever you can to turn up the heat under this pot. It sounds like the Klingons are already simmering. Let's see if we can't bring their rage to a boil."

"Understood."

"One more thing. I just put some backup into place for you on Centaurus."

That boded ill. "Might I ask who?"

"Jorncek, the Tiburonian."

The name sounded familiar to Elara. "Isn't he that hitter with a torque problem Ganz kicked off the *Omari-Ekon* last year?"

"A misunderstanding, I'm told."

"A botched heist on a Starfleet pharmaceutical vault is a bit more serious than a 'misunderstanding.' Is he really the best backup you could send?"

"The Terrans have a saying, Elara: 'Beggars can't be choosers.'"

"True, though I don't recall asking for any help." Her suspicious nature asserted itself. "You aren't sending him here just to get him as far from you as possible, are you?"

Her protests had erased the Red Man's good mood as quickly as it had manifested. *"If you do your job and avoid detection, there won't be any need for him to show himself.*

So get back to the university and find some way to make the Klingons do what they do best."

"As you command, Master." She bowed her head in a show of respect and kept her mind blank of all thoughts as she closed the subspace channel.

As soon as it switched off, her buried resentment exhumed itself.

Jorncek. Here, on Centaurus. Just what I didn't need. She yanked her duotronic cables free of their splice to the hotel's comm network. *As long as I don't see him, he can live. But if I catch that fool torqueing when he's supposed to be watching my back, I'll kill him myself.*

———

Days on Centaurus were less than twenty-three hours long, but to Joanna McCoy they always felt longer when she worked a double shift in the university hospital. As a second-year nursing student, she had fewer responsibilities than the full-time staff, but there was still more than enough work to make a night shift drag on forever.

Patient care was only half the story, of course. Thanks to the miracles of modern medicine, it was possible for the doctors and nurses and technicians with whom she worked to cure illnesses and heal injuries once thought to be beyond the reach of science. Damaged digits, limbs, and even vital organs were, as a matter of routine, repaired or replaced.

Still, more often than she had expected before embarking upon a medical career, there were occasional cases that challenged the physicians and their nigh-magical sensors: overlapping conditions that clouded the diagnostic process, rare drug interactions that resulted in bizarre side effects, or sometimes accidental injuries so gruesome or macabre as to be instantly memorable. Moments like those punctuated the long slog of routine and kept the job fresh, even for veterans who had been practicing medicine since the last days of stethoscopes. Oddity, as it turned out, was one of the profession's few true perquisites.

Its ancient and so far unconquered bête noire was, as it had ever been, paperwork. Most of the easily quantified data was reported automatically by the computers built into the biobeds, which collected input from the staff's array of handheld sensors. Limited-function artificial intelligence software transcribed patients' symptom presentations and recorded doctors' initial evaluations and intake sessions in vid files for later review. But at the end of each day, someone needed to sift through those mountains of raw data and qualify the reports with such intangible observations as each patient's mood and presence of mind. Summaries had to be synthesized from multiple charts, vetted, and forwarded to the Federation Surgeon General's office for dissemination to such agencies as Starfleet Medical and the Federation Center for Disease Control, as well as several others, for the purpose of detecting, preventing, and, when necessary, containing epidemics before they got a chance to spread.

Joanna had compiled twenty patient files in the past five hours, and her eyes itched from exhaustion and dehydration. A quick check of the queue on her slate showed she still had another eight cases to review before she could call it a night. She checked the wall chrono, which read 0213, and felt her spirits sink. *I need to be back in class in less than six hours.*

Caffeine was her only hope.

She stood and stretched, arching and twisting her back until she heard the satisfying pops of vertebrae releasing some of their pent-up tension. At this hour, the cafeteria would be closed, but there was a wall of automat food dispensers one floor down where she could score a coffee and a snack to help her soldier on through the end of her shift.

No point waiting for the lift, she decided, detouring into the stairwell. *I could use a bit of exercise. Get the blood moving. Wake me up a little.*

She reached the next floor and found its lighting dimmer than she remembered. The overhead lights were off in its northern corridor, where the automat station was located. At first she feared a circuit had been tripped, cutting off power to the north wing, but then she noticed a faint spill of light on the tiled floor—the glow of the automat machines. *At least those are still working.* She made a mental note to call the maintenance office when she got back to her station.

Halfway down the shadowy passage, an echoing groan, like wind moving through a canyon, turned her head. That was when she saw the doors of the turbolift were propped open with a metal bar, exposing the dark empty shaft on the other side.

She felt the hackles at the back of her neck rise. Paranoid, she looked over her shoulder, toward the lit end of the corridor. She was still alone. Treading with slow, soft footfalls—a task made easier by the soft-soled comfortable shoes preferred by those in her line of work—she crept deeper into the darkness ahead.

Just shy of the automat, the door to the pharmaceutical lockup was ajar. Joanna skulked toward it, listening for any activity from within, but heard nothing. From a pocket on the tunic of her scrubs she took a pen light, a simple tool for testing patients' pupils for reactivity, and shone its beam on the door's handle and lock. Both had been forced open with enough violence to leave them bent and dangling. She took a breath, held it, and nudged open the door.

Her narrow flashlight beam swept across a sprawling mess. The shelves had been raided for a variety of medical supplies, including hypospray dispensers, and the drug cabinets had been broken into and thoroughly pilfered.

"Sonofabitch." She pulled out her personal comm unit and keyed in the code for the hospital's security office.

One of the night-shift desk guards, Sullifeth ch'Laera, and Andorian *chan* she'd blessed with the nickname Sully, answered. *"Security."*

"Sully, this is Joanna McCoy. We've had a burglary up on seven. Someone broke into the north wing's storage—" Her voice caught in her throat as she felt the icy bite of a blade above her carotid artery. Eyes wide, she froze, with her heart slamming inside her chest.

A man's low, hostile whisper was hot against the back of her ear. "One more word, and I'll cut your throat. Drop the comm."

Joanna let the comm fall to the floor. Her assailant stomped it into dust and shards. She felt the trembling of his hand through the blade of his knife. "Please don't hurt me."

His voice was so close, so menacing. "Don't make me. Be a shame to waste a pretty thing like you." He withdrew his blade from Joanna's throat.

She had just enough time to breathe a sigh of relief before the crushing blow hit the back of her head, turning her world white with pain for a moment before she sank into endless black.

———

Consciousness returned, driven by a demon's drumbeat Joanna recognized as her own pulse. She struggled to open her eyes. She was on the floor in the pharma lockup. Her vision was hazy and out of focus; every sound sent throbbing pains shooting through her skull. "What happened?"

"Just lie back and stay still," said a reassuring feminine voice.

The soft hiss of a hypospray accompanied a gentle sting against Joanna's jugular. The pounding rhythm in her head abated, and her vision sharpened by degrees. Able to focus her eyes again, Joanna recognized the woman at her side as Doctor Jennifer Rock, that night's on-call emergency surgeon. Lean and muscular, with a pixie cut of dandelion-yellow hair accented by hot-pink highlights, the striking half-human, half-Argelian physician projected keen intelligence but also an aura of empathy and compassion—qualities that had made her one of Joanna's role models at the hospital. She asked, "How are you feeling?"

"Woozy." Recent events flashed through Joanna's memory. "Someone hit me in the back of the head. Doc, do I have a concussion?"

A sympathetic nod. "A minor one, but yes. I've ordered you a bed in the trauma center, just for tonight, so we can monitor your recovery. We should have you sorted out by morning."

A sudden surge of panic. "Morning? But I have a class at eight."

Rock gave her a reassuring pat on the shoulder. "Relax. I'll write you a note."

Joanna remembered the knife at her throat and reached toward the spot where the blade had kissed her skin. The doctor noticed the gesture and added, "Minor lacerations. Already patched them up." A young man in a mustard-colored Starfleet tunic approached them. The doctor asked Joanna, "Ready to answer a few questions?"

"I can try."

"All right. Joanna, this is Ensign Pavel Chekov, from the *Enterprise*."

Up close he looked even younger than Joanna had first thought; his affect was almost boyish, with his bowl haircut and innocent smile. "Hello, Joanna," he said with a Russian accent.

Sitting up, she winced. "Hi."

"Did you see who attacked you?"

"No, but the voice sounded like a man's."

Chekov nodded. "You reported a break-in."

"Yes, the pharmaceutical lockup." Joanna looked around and saw that the hospital's security guards and some local peace officers were inspecting the burgled storage room while the night-shift duty nurse conducted an inventory to identify missing items. She cast a suspicious look at Chekov. "Since when does Starfleet investigate petty theft?"

"My orders are to investigate any crime on campus, whether I think it's related to the conference or not."

"You think this is?"

"Did the man who hit you do or say anything to make you think so?"

She thought about it. "No."

The young officer shrugged. "Then it might be an isolated event."

Doctor Rock interrupted, "If you have enough, Ensign, I need to take Miss McCoy down to the trauma center for observation."

Chekov's eyes widened. "McCoy?" He now regarded Joanna with something akin to reverence. "You're Doctor Leonard McCoy's daughter?"

A pained nod. "That's right."

He reached for his communicator. "I should let him know you—"

"Please don't," Joanna said. "I'd rather keep him out of it."

"Are you sure? He is your father."

"I'm sure." She took Doctor Rock's hand and, with some help and difficulty, stood on uncertain feet. "I've had enough abuse for one night."

The Russian was unhappy about the bind she had put him in. "As you wish. But I still need to file my report— which means he will find out, sooner or later."

"I know." Leaning on the doctor's shoulder, Joanna shuffled toward the lift. "I just want a chance to finish with *this* headache before I let him give me a new one."

───────────

It was uncommon for ship's time aboard the *Enterprise* to correspond, even approximately, to local time when beaming down to a planet's surface. There were many factors that conspired to keep one feeling out of synch in such scenarios. One was the variable length of a day from one world to the next. Another was the existence of time zones on a planet's surface—dawn in one location meant it was dusk at its antipodal point. Exacerbating the sensation of temporal disconnection was the effect of living without natural light for months on end on a starship.

Consequently, it struck Uhura as a cruel irony that for once local time at the beam-down site on the New Athens University campus—0316 hours—was very close to the time shown on the *Enterprise*'s shipboard chronometer: 0358 hours, the middle of the night or the wee hours of the morning, depending on how one preferred to frame the bad news. Either way, it meant she had been roused from a sound sleep and summoned planetside.

The transporter beam fell away like a dissipating rain of golden light to reveal Ensign Chekov standing in the middle of the campus quad, awaiting her arrival. "Thank you for coming on such short notice."

"What can I do for you, Ensign?"

His shiny disposition tarnished a bit at her gentle reminder that she was his superior officer. "I need your help with a . . . technical matter."

"Care to be a bit more specific?"

He beckoned her to follow him as he walked toward a nearby building. "We asked the campus security office to let us set up our own operations office. They put us in here." He entered an access code into the panel beside the locked front door. Its magnetic bolts retracted with a muffled *thump*. He turned the handle and pushed the door open.

The office inside was dusty and dilapidated, a portrait of institutional neglect. Tucked into the far corner was a workstation with an antiquated computer built into the desk. "They gave us one terminal. Their sick idea of a joke, I think."

Uhura crossed the room and studied the machine. "Is this an optronic system?" She checked its auxiliary data ports. "I haven't seen anything like this since before the Academy." Her fingertips brushed its activation button. "Does it power up?"

"Yes. But that's all it does." When she shot him a questioning look, he added, "They won't let us use their network. Which means I can't monitor current criminal activity, review past crimes, or look for patterns."

She switched on the terminal and noted the boot-up data that scrolled down its monitor. "A system this old? You'd be lucky to get it to play solitaire."

"I already tried. It doesn't have any games."

She asked over her shoulder, "So, what do you expect me to do about it?"

"That is up to you. But if I had your skill for accessing secure networks—"

"Such as the campus security data system."

"For example, yes. Then I could uplink their system with the *Enterprise*'s computers."

"True." Uhura wondered what Chekov was holding back. "Ensign, why not let the local authorities handle their own investigations?"

"Three reasons. First, my orders from Captain Kirk were to investigate all criminal activity on campus and look for threats to the peace conference. But I think the local police and campus security are deliberately preventing me from doing my duty.

"Second, the woman who was attacked in the university hospital tonight was Doctor McCoy's daughter. And I do not want to be empty-handed tomorrow when he asks me what happened and what I did about it.

"Third—" He gesticulated in frustration at their decrepit surroundings. "*This.*"

His first rationale felt flimsy to Uhura, but she couldn't fault his other two arguments. "Fine. But you're going to owe me, mister." She sat down at the terminal and began keying in code injection exploits that she was certain could bypass the software lockouts with which the locals had hobbled the machine's network access.

It took her less than a minute to establish full command-level access to the campus's security data network as well as an interlink to the New Athens Police Department databases. "Better than Christmas morning. What are we looking for?"

"Internal security vids from the hospital. Seventh floor, north wing, starting around two-fifteen this morning local time."

Uhura pulled up a grid of twelve vid feeds, most of

which overlapped one another's fields of view to some degree. "Here we go." She jogged the vids forward at double speed—and in rapid succession they blinked out, one by one, until all were dark. "*That's* interesting." She continued fast-forwarding until the cameras resumed working, shortly after 0231.

Chekov's brow knit with determination. "That was no accident."

"Which means it was either an inside job," Uhura said, "or the thief was a professional, the kind with access to high-tech equipment."

"So much for the easy way. Let's patch in the *Enterprise*'s computer."

"Just a moment." Uhura made more adjustments to create a data link that wouldn't be detected by the locals. "All right, we're up. Now what?"

"Download all security vids from the entire campus, with time stamps from midnight to now. Have the computer cross-reference them for men coming to the hospital before two-fifteen, and leaving the hospital after two-twenty."

"Dumping the vids to the *Enterprise*'s databanks." More lightning-fast keystrokes. "Starting analysis." A dizzying kaleidoscope of high-resolution images blurred past on the screen for several seconds, then there were only three vids, each a compilation of footage from different cameras, tracking three separate persons who fit Chekov's parameters. "Three suspects."

"Not for long." Chekov reached past Uhura to jog through the compiled vid files. "This man must be at least sixty years old." He applied a facial-recognition algorithm to a clear image of the man entering a faculty residential tower on the campus. "Professor Gustav Wanaki, chair of the Philosophy Department. I do not think he is our man."

Uhura scrubbed through the next video. "Our parameters may have been a bit wide. This young man came into the trauma center with a broken arm over two hours before the attack—and he didn't leave until an hour after." She pulled a supplemental vid from the hospital's trauma center, whose cameras had not gone offline. Prominently visible on a biobed in the trauma center, waiting patiently between brief visits by nurses, doctors, and technicians, was the young man with his fractured ulna. "I'd say we can rule him out. Which leaves—"

Chekov sped through the last video. "He wears a hood and stays in the shadows. And he works hard not to show his face to the cameras—as if he knows where each one is, on every part of the campus." A grim nod. "Just like a thief." Then Chekov paused the image and augmented a small portion: a reflection off the window of a parked hovercar. It was only a blurry image, nowhere near enough to confirm someone's identity, but there was something distinctive about the shape. Chekov squinted at it. "I think that is an *ear*."

"Not just any ear," Uhura realized. "That's a Tiburonian ear."

"Good to know." He sent the vid flying forward again. It froze on an ominous report: SUBJECT LOST. "These vids track him only on campus. Can we pull up vids of him from the city's security grid?"

"I can try." Accessing the police databases posed a slightly greater challenge for Uhura; this time it took her almost ninety seconds to obtain full access to their citywide network of automated surveillance systems. "I'm triggering a trace function that should be able to follow our Tiburonian friend by matching his movements from one camera zone to the next."

The lone figure zipped down city streets, which were otherwise empty in the overnight hours. Then the suspect slipped inside what appeared to be a multiunit residential building.

Chekov looked at Uhura. "Any vids from inside?"

She shook her head. "Private property. No surveillance."

He frowned, then an idea put the shine back in his smile. "Is he still inside?"

Uhura sped through a few hours of vid data from the blocks surrounding the building. "Unless there's a secret way out through the basement, I'd say there's a good chance he is."

"Then we've got him." He pulled out his communicator and flipped open its gold grille with a flick of his wrist. "Chekov to *Enterprise*."

He was answered by the overnight watch officer, Lieutenant Dickinson. "Enterprise *here. Go ahead, Ensign.*"

"Lieutenant Uhura is about to send you coordinates for a residential building in the city of New Athens." He fixed her with an expectant look, so she followed his lead and transmitted the building's coordinates to the *Enterprise* with her tricorder.

Over the communicator, Dickinson said, *"Coordinates received."*

"I need you to run a sensor sweep of that building," Chekov said. "Tell me if you read any Tiburonian life-forms inside."

"Scanning now. Stand by." Several seconds passed before Dickinson returned to the channel. *"Ensign, we read one Tiburonian life-form at that location."*

"Can you transport him to the New Athens police lockup?"

"Negative. That's outside our jurisdiction, Ensign. But we couldn't do it even if we had cause—there's too much interference. He must be carrying some kind of data scrambler."

"Like the kind that can black out surveillance cameras?"

"Exactly. Even on stand-by, it would be enough to prevent a pattern lock."

"Understood, *Enterprise*. Beam me and Lieutenant Uhura to the street outside that building, and have a security team join us." Noting Uhura's cautionary glare, he added, "And please warn the local police: we are about to take a suspect into custody."

———

Chekov set his phaser to heavy stun. Under routine conditions, protocol required the weapon stay on light stun unless otherwise ordered by a senior officer. However, in a circumstance such as this—heading into a confrontation to apprehend a suspect known to be violent and possess skills associated with professional criminals—the heavier setting was considered permissible.

He glanced to either side and was satisfied to note that both Uhura and Lieutenant Pran, the leader of the six-strong security detail that had just beamed down from the *Enterprise* to join them outside the suspect's location, had also opted to nudge their phasers up to heavy stun.

Pran, a svelte man whose black hair had recently started to gray at the temples, confirmed his team's readiness with a look, then he nodded to Chekov. "Good to go."

Uhura added, "Ready, Ensign. What's the plan?"

"Lieutenant Pran and I will go in the front," Chekov said. "Lieutenant Uhura, you and Ensign Chapman cover the rear door." He looked past Pran to the other security officers. "Waid, Downing. Stay here, watch the front in case the suspect gets past us. Resnick, Dehler. Have the *Enterprise* beam you to the roof in case the suspect flees that way."

The group fanned out. Uhura and Chapman slipped across the dark street toward a narrow alley that led behind the eight-story residential tower. By the time Chekov, Pran, Waid, and Downing climbed the steps to the front entrance, the street resounded with the gentle droning of a transporter beam moving Resnick and Dehler to the building's rooftop. Pran tried the front door. It let out an angry buzzing noise as it rejected his effort to force it open.

"Locked," Pran said. "I can bypass. Shouldn't take more than—"

His thought was interrupted by the wailing of sirens

from close by, and getting closer by the second. Chekov's hand tightened on his phaser. "I think we are about to have company." He pivoted to face the door. "Stand back!" Pran stepped aside just in time as Chekov fired a phaser shot through the door's locking mechanism. It erupted in a fountain of sparks, and the door lurched open. "Inside!" Chekov snapped.

He looked back as he waved his men past, into the building. Three police hovercars zoomed around corners at either end of the street and converged on the building the landing party was invading. Lights snapped on behind curtained windows in all the nearby buildings as the neighbors stirred to see what all the commotion was about. As Chekov hurried through the doorway, his communicator chirped. He flipped it open on the run. "Chekov here!"

"Chekov, this is Enterprise," Dickinson said. *"Your suspect's moving! Looks like he's in a lift, heading for the roof!"*

"Warn Resnick and Dehler!"

"Already done."

"And beam Uhura and Chapman to an adjacent, higher roof!"

"Acknowledged. Stand by."

Chekov whistled to snag the attention of the men ahead of him. They halted and looked back. He pointed at the lifts. "Get to the roof!"

Pran reached the control pad and called a lift car. The doors opened as Chekov caught up to the three security officers. They piled in as local police charged through the front door into the lobby a dozen meters behind them. "Let's go," Chekov said, pressing the roof button.

The youngest of the security officers, Downing, asked, "What about the police?"

Still annoyed the police had alerted the suspect into fleeing, he grumbled to Downing, "They can catch the next one." Another chirrup from his communicator. He flipped open the grille. "Go ahead."

Over the comm he heard the shrill screech of disruptor fire drowning out Dehler's voice. *"We're taking fire,"* she shouted, more to be heard than out of fear. *"He has us pinned down."*

"Hang on," Chekov said. "We're almost there." He adjusted the device's transceiver settings. "Chekov to Uhura. Can you give Resnick and Dehler covering fire?"

"We're trying," Uhura said. *"We can't get a clear shot."*

Pran tapped Chekov's shoulder. "Five seconds."

"Stay low, fan out." A muted *ding* announced the door was about to open onto the rooftop level. Chekov swallowed hard and tensed to make a run for cover. The doors opened.

In came a flurry of disruptor shots.

His instinct told him to duck into a corner or hit the deck, but he raced forward instead. Behind him, a disruptor blast slammed into Downing, throwing her against the back wall of the lift as if she'd been hit by a charging bull. Pran and Waid evaded the barrage and split up as they fled the lift. In seconds, they and Chekov found cover behind low machinery clusters on the roof, all of them peeking around and over their shelters to pinpoint their foe's position.

A shot screamed past Chekov's head. He ducked and

rolled, then looked again. "He's moving east!" Chekov returned fire. His phaser's blue beams crisscrossed the red streaks leaping from the Tiburonian's disruptor and traced smoldering paths across a stairwell housing and a stand of ventilation pipes. Then they both were back behind cover, plotting their next moves.

Chekov looked around and found Pran and Waid. Downing was still lying in the lift, her feet preventing the doors from closing, which meant the police would be unable to come up that way to provide reinforcements. A stolen peek over another machinery box revealed Dehler and Resnick both were down. He glanced over his shoulder at the tallest adjacent building; crouched at its edge were Uhura and Chapman, both with clear lines of sight to Chekov and Pran.

Simple hand signals made it clear that Uhura and Chapman had no shot. Chekov directed Pran and Waid to flank the suspect while he proceeded directly toward the man. Everyone acknowledged with a thumbs-up and moved out as Chekov broke from cover.

Cold sweat trickled down the back of his neck as he jogged across the roof. He was completely exposed, the bait in the trap. All he could do was hope that when the suspect popped up enough to shoot him, either Pran or Waid would take him down first.

Then came the cross fire.

Blue phaser blasts came from either side; crimson surges from the Tiburonian's disruptor shrieked back in response. Ricochets and stray blasts forced Chekov into a crouch, but he refused to stop, not when he was so close. Then a lucky shot took down Waid—

A retaliation by Pran seared through the suspect's shoulder—

The Tiburonian unleashed a wild spray of energy pulses, then ran toward the ledge.

Chekov shouted to Pran—"Hold your fire!"—as the suspect sprang off the roof.

Too late. Pran's phaser blast hit the Tiburonian square in his back.

Stunned, the suspect dropped his weapon as he tumbled, flailing, across the void between buildings, then dropped like a stone toward the adjacent, lower rooftop.

The Tiburonian struck the other rooftop's edge with a sickening crack of breaking ribs. Even so, he clawed at the raised lip that ringed the rooftop and fought for purchase as he slipped backward, toward the long drop into the alleyway below.

Chekov didn't break stride as he neared his roof's edge. He vaulted from it and leaped across the divide, soaring like gravity's angel, arms windmilling as he dropped, then he crouched and tumble-rolled as he crashed down on the other side. He let his phaser fall away as he skidded to a stop, then he scrambled back to the Tiburonian.

The suspect was dangling by one hand as Chekov reached him—then that hand slipped. Chekov caught the Tiburonian's sleeve as the man fell, and the weight of him nearly pulled Chekov over the edge as well. He wedged his knee against the low raised edge and spread his body out against it to distribute the burden of the hanging man's weight.

"I've got you," Chekov said to the Tiburonian. "Just hang on! We—"

The man's sleeve ripped, its cheap fabric reduced in a blink to tatters.

And then he was gone, falling into the shadows. Seconds later, Chekov winced at the wet slap of a body meeting pavement with fatal velocity.

His communicator beeped. He pulled it free and snapped it open. "Chekov."

It was Dickinson. *"Ensign, we have a lock on your Tiburonian."*

"Beam him up," Chekov said. "And me with him."

"Are you sure? Sensors say your suspect's dead."

"Beam us up, *Enterprise*. And have Doctor McCoy meet us in the transporter room."

"Stand by."

Knowing he had a few seconds to spare, he stood and walked back to retrieve his phaser. No sooner had he tucked it into its loop on his belt than he felt the reassuring embrace of the transporter's annular confinement beam. Next came the familiar rush of mellifluous noise, followed by pale golden light—which intensified to an almost blinding white before fading to reveal Chekov's new surroundings, transporter room one aboard the *Enterprise*.

Next to him on the platform was the bloody, broken corpse of the Tiburonian suspect he and the others had been chasing. True to its species' reputation for rapid decomposition after death, the corpse had already begun to reek.

The transporter operator stared in horror at the mangled body. "What happened?"

"Deceleration trauma," Chekov said.

The door to the corridor swished open. Doctor McCoy hurried in, followed by Captain Kirk. Both men recoiled from the stench of the splattered body spilling blood across the transporter platform. Kirk glared at Chekov. "Explain this, mister."

"Sorry, Captain. I tried to save him, but his sleeve ripped."

"Why didn't you leave him where he landed?"

"If I had left him in the alley, the local police would have blocked our investigation again. At least now we can identify him."

"That wasn't your call to make, Ensign. This planet has laws, and as long as we're here, they apply to us, whether we like it or not." The captain frowned at the corpse, then shot another withering look at Chekov. "The next time you track a suspect, I want them alive. Understood?"

"Aye, Captain."

McCoy stood between Kirk and Chekov. "Jim, go easy."

"I'll ease up when I get some answers, Bones." He glowered at the pulverized body. "But dead men tell no tales."

The doctor turned a sly glance at the corpse. "They say more than you think." He looked back at Kirk. "Give me an hour."

Kirk relented. "One hour, in the briefing room." Without another word, he turned away, walked out the door, and was gone.

McCoy frowned, then shook his head at the mangled corpse next to Chekov. "Just out of curiosity, Ensign . . . what did this man do?"

Chekov saw no reason to hide the truth any longer.

"He assaulted your daughter."

"He *what*?" The surgeon did a surprised double take. "Is she—?"

"She wanted to tell you herself. But she is fine." He glanced at the dead Tiburonian. "Which is more than I can say for him."

McCoy sighed with relief, then regarded Chekov with a new degree of respect. "Remind me to buy you a drink next shore leave, Ensign."

Fourteen

Each passing hour made the *Velibor*'s damage list grow rather than diminish. Despite the engineers' best efforts, cascade effects continued to multiply, all thanks to the alien device the Tal Shiar martinet Sadira had patched into the bird-of-prey's main power relay. Creelok found it hard at times such as this not to succumb to bitterness.

My ship is made of eggshells and Sadira wants to fix everything with a hammer.

Most of the ship's interior was dimmed, and the majority of its onboard systems were in standby mode, as part of a silent-running protocol. Instead of using turbo-lifts, the crew was moving about the vessel by means of its emergency ladderways. Even the life-support systems were operating at a bare-minimum level, making the air on the command deck hot and stale.

Subcommander Bedisa conferred at the weapons station with Kurat, a tactical specialist, then she moved to join Creelok at the central command console. "Passive sensors detect no change in their orbital patterns, and no signal traffic to suggest our presence is known."

"Good." Creelok reached out to call up a tactical chart for the system, then stopped himself as he remembered command systems were still offline—temporary casualties of his chief engineer's need to divert all possible reserve power to the cloaking device. "Any word from

Ranimir on how much longer we'll be working in the dark?"

"Ask him yourself." Bedisa lifted her chin toward the aft hatchway. "Here he comes."

Creelok turned to greet the bedraggled, sweat-soaked, and grime-covered engineer. "I presume you haven't come all the way up here to deliver good news."

"Afraid not, Commander. We're still half a day away from being fully operational. But I did come bearing a proposed solution."

"And that would be?"

"The next time we have the magnetic field of Centaurus's moon for cover, move the ship out of orbit. If we can get behind the moon, we can drop the cloak and expedite repairs."

Before Creelok could voice his approval, Sadira appeared out of the dark recesses of the command deck, as if she were a ghost haunting his every decision. "Absolutely not," the human Tal Shiar agent said. "Our mission profile is simple and precise. We remain in orbit, cloaked, until all operational objectives have been achieved."

Her veto left the command crew in demoralized silence. Ranimir's cool demeanor became desperate as he pleaded with Creelok, "Commander, if we stay in orbit, I can't guarantee we'll finish repairs before the cloak drains our reserves."

"I understand." Creelok stared daggers at Sadira. "But do you? How do you think your secret mission will end if our invisibility fails while our weapons, shields, propulsion, and navigation remain offline? Does that sound to you like a recipe for success?"

A haughty lift of her pale chin. "That's not going to happen."

"And what makes you so certain?"

"Because I have forbidden it. Your men will repair the ship, and we will continue the mission. As planned. As *ordered*, Commander."

His temper blazed behind his eyes, its fury threatening to burn away the core of his being and leave nothing behind but righteous anger and his need for order and respect. *No one speaks to me this way on my own ship. Not some Tal Shiar whelp. Not even the praetor himself.*

He seized Sadira by one arm and all but dragged her off the command deck into the aft corridor. "Why will you not listen to reason?"

"Why can you not just obey?"

It was a struggle not to lock his hands around her throat. "Can't you see we're trying to serve the mission? None of us opposes the objective. Not me, not any member of my crew."

"Then prove it: do as I command."

"Your commands will lead us to failure. I'm trying to salvage your mission." At the edge of his vision, he noticed the centurion's silhouette in the command deck's hatchway. "Taking the ship out of orbit for a few hours will speed repairs and enable—"

"No." Her face was like that of a funerary statue in the *Rikolet* on Romulus: pale, cold, and utterly unmoved by the plights of the living. "I forbid you to take the ship out of orbit."

That was it, then. The gauntlet was thrown, and now the choice was Creelok's.

"Centurion," he called out. "Take Major Sadira into custody—"

Sadira drew her dagger and stabbed at Creelok's gut in a flash, but he caught her wrist and twisted it until she dropped the blade. It clanged across the deck between their feet. Creelok kicked the weapon aside, out of her reach.

Centurion Mirat arrived and seized Sadira's wrists.

Confident his friend had the Tal Shiar brat under control, Creelok let go of her. "Confine her to quarters." As Mirat led the woman away, the commander strode back onto the command deck. "Subcommander Bedisa, on our next orbit, plot a course into the magnetic field of the planet's moon, and put us on the other side of that body. Engineer Ranimir, once we're out of sight, drop the cloak and expedite repairs."

Everyone snapped to, saluted with fists to their chests, and turned his words into action.

This was how his ship was meant to function.

And he had no doubt the Tal Shiar woman would try to murder him for it.

———

All he had to do was lock her on the other side of a door before she started talking. He failed.

"You know this order is illegal—don't you, Centurion?"

Mirat didn't want to hear it. "Keep walking."

They drew inquisitive looks, the two of them. Walking single file through the dim, smoke-hazed corridors, him with his disruptor drawn, her deprived of weapons and being marched aft like a common prisoner.

Curious faces looked out from the compartments they passed on their way to her private quarters. Such accommodations were a rare privilege on a ship where livable space was at such a premium. In Sadira's case, only her status as a Tal Shiar operative and her de facto role as the *Velibor*'s political officer afforded her such consideration.

A coy glance over her shoulder. "I can cite chapter and verse detailing his—"

"Quiet." Mirat suspected he knew what Sadira was trying to say. If he was right, his only defense against a tribunal—or being forced into an unforgivable betrayal— was not to hear it. The only way to ensure that was to prevent her from saying it. He poked his weapon into her lower back. "Keep your mouth shut and your feet moving."

"Or what, Centurion? You'll shoot me?" Now her backward glance had a condescending quality. "Even as a prisoner, I remain a commissioned officer of the Tal Shiar. Fire on me without just cause and you'll be put to death on Romulus."

They were only two sections from her quarters, from his release. He said nothing, hoping his silence would discourage further exchanges with Sadira, but she was incorrigible.

"Creelok has no authority to remove me from the command deck in this manner. My orders carry the authority of the Tal Shiar and the Senate itself. You *know* this, Centurion."

"What I know is that your stubborn refusal to hear reason would get us all killed." He followed her around a corner into the outermost corridor in the bird-of-prey's primary hull. "I don't care if your orders come bearing the signature of the praetor himself. On this ship, I recognize only one authority: the commander's."

The door to Sadira's quarters slid open as she approached it. She halted over its threshold and pivoted back toward Mirat. "This doesn't have to be the end of your career, Centurion."

"It won't be." He ushered her forward with a wave of his disruptor. "Inside."

She held her ground, obstinate as ever. "Why throw your life away?"

He switched his disruptor to a kill setting. It charged to full capacity with a faint whine. "I might ask you the same thing."

"If you were going to kill me, you'd have done it on the command deck. If Creelok possessed real nerve, he'd have ordered you to do it."

He almost pitied the human woman. Sadira could mimic the ways of Romulans, but it was apparent to Mirat she had never truly understood her adopted culture. "The commander does not believe in wasting anything—least of all, lives."

"Yet he has gambled his and yours—for what?"

"The good of the ship and its crew."

"Then he doesn't deserve his command. Any true Romulan knows the good of the mission comes before all else." A coquettish smirk. "Or have you all forgotten your oaths?"

Her smug manner boiled his blood. "We have forgotten nothing."

"Prove it. Fulfill your pledge of loyalty now."

She was waiting for him to make a mistake. He felt it.

He reduced his weapon's power to stun. "The commander would tell me to shoot you."

"Go ahead. Pull that trigger. Then imagine seven of your comrades pulling theirs when they execute you in front of the Senate after this ship returns home." Her arrogance became cold confidence. "But as you hesitate, ask yourself: Are you an oath breaker?"

"No, but I've never had any interest in elected office."

"Clever. But you know what I mean."

He gave a moment of serious consideration to pistol-whipping her in the face, to knock her inside her quarters so he could lock the door and extricate himself from this quagmire of a conversation. "Sorry, Major. I'm at a loss."

"Article Seven of the Imperial Code of Military Conduct," Sadira said. "Section Three, Paragraph Four. 'When any command-grade officer of a ship of the line, battlefield regiment, or strategic military installation defies direct, lawful orders from a duly authorized—'"

"I know what it says," Mirat interrupted.

I should have coldcocked her.

Now he was in a terrible bind. Had he escaped before she invoked the relevant section of the regulations, he could have blamed her for failing to assert her command privilege with sufficient authority to override the orders of the commander. Now he was obliged to hear her out.

Brimming with contempt but bereft of options, he crossed his arms and sighed. "What are you trying to say, Major?"

The cruel ghost of a smile played across her thin lips. She knew she had him.

"Centurion Mirat, as this ship's political officer, I declare Commander Creelok's decision to relieve me of duty to be improper and his conduct to be in violation of the ICMC. It is your sworn duty to enforce the ICMC aboard this ship." With an imperious lift of her chin, she added, "Centurion, I order you to relieve Commander Creelok of his command."

Fifteen

If there was one compartment on the *Enterprise* that Kirk had to say was his least favorite, it was the morgue. Adjacent to the sickbay, it was just large enough to hold a dozen bodies in a grid of stasis chambers containing retractable tables. Four across and three high, the "meat locker," as some of the ship's junior medical personnel called it, was a constant reminder to Kirk that not all of the lives entrusted to his command for this five-year mission were going to return home.

Spock and McCoy stood on either side of one such retractable table. Lying on it was the corpse of the dead Tiburonian whom Chekov had ordered beamed aboard for further analysis. Cleaned and restored to some semblance of order before being sheathed in a synthetic gel that had solidified into a flexible but anaerobic cocoon, the dead man's body no longer gave off any odor that Kirk could detect—a fact for which he was most grateful.

"Hour's up, Bones. What do we know so far?"

"His name is Jorncek." McCoy handed Kirk a data slate whose top sheet displayed the beginning of what looked to be a lengthy biographical profile. "Born on Tiburon Prime, last known to be a permanent resident of the Orion homeworld."

That aroused Kirk's attention. "Orion?"

Spock picked up the conversational baton. "Mister

Jorncek has long been suspected of having ties to the interstellar criminal organization known as the Orion Syndicate." He regarded the dead body with cold detachment. "Most of his criminal record consists of implications unsubstantiated by formal charges."

"Which means he was one slick operator," McCoy added.

Kirk was unhappy with what these new discoveries suggested. "With what sort of crimes did Mister Jorncek find himself connected?"

"Burglaries," Spock said. "However, circumstantial evidence linked him to several high-profile armed heists on three resort planets and one formal charge—later withdrawn—that he masterminded the armed robbery of a mining outpost on Rivos Prime."

"Delightful." Adjusting his tone out of consideration for McCoy's personal link to the dead man's last-known crime, he asked Spock, "Do we know why he broke into the hospital?"

McCoy answered, "I do. He was a drug addict, Jim."

"You're sure?"

A grave nod. "I ran his blood tests twice. Based on the damage sustained by most of his major organs, including his brain, I'd say he must have been addicted for years."

Spock added, "That would explain why he raided the hospital's pharmaceutical locker for charged hyposprays and a variety of stimulants and depressants." A dark and knowing look passed between him and McCoy. "However, I do not believe the robbery was Mister Jorncek's chief reason for being on Centaurus."

Exasperated by his first officer's dramatic pauses, Kirk replied, "Out with it, Spock."

"Inside the apartment he rented in New Athens, local police found plans for guerrilla attacks on the peace conference. Among the methods he planned to employ were bombings, liquid and aerosol poisons . . . and targeted assassinations of key participants."

"Including Spock's father," McCoy interjected.

"And Councillor Gorkon," Spock concluded.

The revelations left Kirk bewildered. "Could the Orion Syndicate be involved in Gorkon's disappearance?"

"Anything is possible, Captain," Spock said. "Though the Orion Syndicate has, until now, been merely a criminal operation, it is conceivable that its capabilities might have expanded as its access to resources has increased."

Kirk's mind was racing. "And this would be a prime opportunity for them. Push us into war with the Klingons, and the Organians rob us both of the ability to project force—leaving dozens of sectors wide open for the Orions to exploit." As quickly as he had embraced the idea, he shook it off. "But how would the Orions even know about the Organians? Or their threat?"

McCoy frowned. "Jim, their chief export is *pleasure*. That kind of business has a way of loosening people's tongues—even at Starfleet Command."

"As disquieting as Doctor McCoy's suggestion is," Spock said, "I am forced to concur."

McCoy pulled a metallic red sheet over the dead Tiburonian, then pushed the sled back inside its stasis tube. "There's one thing about this that still doesn't sit right with me, Jim."

"What's that, Bones?"

"No matter how well equipped or richly financed the Orion Syndicate might be, since when does it have the ability to make someone disappear without a trace from inside a shielded compound the way Gorkon did?" He looked around, as if there might be someone other than the three of them and one dead man inside the tiny, sealed compartment, then lowered his voice. "Am I crazy, or does that sound more like a certain something we recently *misplaced*?"

"One disaster at a time, Bones." Kirk turned and headed for the door, and Spock followed the captain closely as he repeated grimly under his breath, "One disaster at a time."

Sixteen

Discretion demanded that none of the officers be involved. Not that the truth could be hidden for long, not on a ship as small as the *Velibor*. Recruiting the first accomplice was easy enough for Centurion Mirat. One legionnaire moving through the corridors at his side was hardly worthy of notice. After he enlisted a second man to support him, members of the crew started to whisper that something was amiss. Just as he had expected, the ship susurrated with rumors by the time he and four loyal soldiers reached the weapons locker to equip themselves with small arms.

"Set for stun only," Mirat said. "We don't want fatalities or a hole in the ship."

From his men, overlapping hushed replies: "Yes, Centurion."

Bearing compact disruptor rifles, the centurion and his squad left the armory single file. Their quick-march steps resounded on the metal deck. There was no more time for subtlety; speed was paramount now. Mirat knew accessing the armory would trigger an alert on the command deck's main console, telegraphing his action to Commander Creelok and the rest of the ship's officers. It was imperative he and his men reach the command deck before the commander sealed it off—an outcome that would compel Mirat to resort to greater, potentially lethal force in order to accomplish his task.

Ahead of him opened the door to the medical bay. Doctor Pralar stepped into his path, hands raised, his voice pitched in desperate supplication. "Centurion! Wait, don't do this. We—"

Mirat slammed the stock of his rifle into Pralar's chin. The surgeon crumpled and fell backward into the arms of his junior colleagues, who averted their eyes from the centurion and his armed squad as they continued past and climbed the ladderway to the top deck.

At the end of the main corridor, viridescent light spilled through the command deck's open aft hatchway. *There is still time,* Mirat told himself. *As long as we get there before—*

"Halt, Centurion!" The order came from behind him, delivered by Subcommander Bedisa and underscored by the high-pitched hum of a disruptor charging to fire.

Mirat lowered his weapon and looked back. Bedisa and Kurat, the tactical officer, had secreted themselves inside a maintenance crawlspace, where they lay supine, her body half on top of his, both of them with their sidearms trained through the opened access panel at Mirat and his men. Then came the clatter of footfalls in the passageway ahead of them, as more officers loyal to Creelok emerged from the command deck, weapons drawn, ready for battle.

The commander's voice cut through the tense silence of the standoff. "She got to you, did she?" He sounded disappointed rather than upset. "Did she appeal to your patriotism?"

The centurion faced his longtime commanding officer and trusted friend. "She cited the regulations I swore to uphold." He wondered whether his next words might be his last. "I've seen Sadira's orders from the Tal Shiar. She spoke the truth. And we're bound by law to obey."

Creelok absorbed that with a small shake of his head. "You and I . . . we've seen war, Mirat. We know the law is not always just."

"But it is all we have, Commander. Most especially in times of war."

"You're wrong, Mirat. In war, all we have is one another and the ship we serve. Everything else is just an abstraction." Creelok took a moment to survey the centurion's band of armed men, then regarded his defenders. "We seem to be evenly matched, old friend."

Mirat responded with a shrug of pure bravado. "Appearances can deceive, sir."

"Sometimes. But we have you and your men in a crossfire."

"A poorly staged one, Commander. One team in front of us, another at our back? Every shot they miss risks hitting one of your own."

"An unfortunate limitation of the environment."

Fingers hovered above firing studs while a tense and gravid pause unfolded. In the deep silence of the powered-down vessel, the standoff felt interminable to Mirat.

Then the commander asked, "Will you stand down, Centurion?"

"You know I cannot." He took a step forward to stand between his men and Creelok. "If I approach the command deck to carry out my duty, will you give the order to fire?"

The two comrades regarded each other with bitter comprehension. Creelok heaved a sigh and bowed his head, as if surrendering to an oppressive burden. "What are your orders?"

"To relieve you of your command."

A deep frown. "On what grounds?"

"Charges levied by Major Sadira, in accord with Article Seven of the ICMC."

The commander understood Mirat had played him as artfully as the centurion had been manipulated by Sadira. "Officers of the *Velibor* . . . stand down."

At first, no one complied. Creelok said, with greater intensity, "Everyone, stand down. That's an order." This time, the officers guarding the command deck holstered their weapons. As if to reinforce his point, Creelok added, "Stand aside. Let the centurion and his men pass."

Mirat led his team onto the command deck. "Kiril, Valinor: Take Commander Creelok into custody and escort him to the brig. After the commander has been secured, release Major Sadira from her quarters."

Creelok was indignant as Kiril bound his wrists with magnetic manacles. He glared at Mirat. "Tell me you understand why I surrendered."

"To prevent a battle that would have harmed your crew," Mirat said.

"Correct. Now tell me why you put us in this situation."

"You know why, Commander. I had no choice."

Kiril and Valinor prodded Creelok into motion and herded him toward the hatchway. As the commander made his exit under armed guard, he turned one last icy stare at Mirat. "We *always* have a choice, old friend."

No one spoke as the commander was led aft and ushered down the ladderway to the ship's lower decks. Even as the command crew returned to their posts and made a show of going through the motions of their regular jobs, they all avoided looking directly at the centurion. It felt to him as if he himself was now cloaked, unseen and unheard, a *persona non grata* on the ship he had served in good faith for nearly a decade.

The commander's parting words haunted him: *We always have a choice.*

Only now, feeling the full weight of his crewmates' disapproval, did Mirat allow himself to accept the truth that Sadira *had* offered him a choice—and that he had made the wrong one.

Less than two hours after her forced departure in disgrace from the *Velibor*'s command deck, Major Sadira returned with her chin up, her bearing proud. She was met by hateful stares from nearly every direction. Even the lowliest personnel regarded her with naked contempt.

At last—conclusive proof that hatred is stronger than fear.

The one person who didn't shy away from Sadira in revulsion chose to meet her head-on just a few steps inside the hatchway. Subcommander Bedisa blocked her path, eyes gleaming with anger, hand perched on the grip of her sidearm. "You aren't needed here, Major."

"Quite the contrary. As this ship's new commanding officer, I'd say my presence is nothing short of essential."

"What are you talking about? I'm next in the chain of command."

"Not anymore. My orders empower me to assume command if, in my estimation, the success of the mission depends upon it." Sadira leaned in and lowered her voice to add, "Commander Creelok forced me to pull rank. I'd advise you not to repeat his mistake."

Bedisa clenched her jaw, as if biting down on words she knew she might come to regret if spoken. Then she turned her gaze toward the centurion, who shrank from her attention into a shadowy nook of the command deck. When she looked back at Sadira, the ship's second-in-command projected nothing so much as disgust. "Tread with care, *human*."

Sadira cracked a humorless smile. "You invoke my heritage like it's a slur. Yet the Senate and the Tal Shiar trust me with more power than they've ever given you. So perhaps the next time you utter that word, you should consider using it with a bit more *respect*." Then, as if the confrontation had never happened, she turned toward the main console. "Helm! What is our current position?"

Toporok replied, "Far side of the planet's moon."

"Take us back into orbit at once."

The helm officer balked. "I can't, Major. All primary systems are offline."

Bedisa explained, with more than a trace of condescension, "Ranimir disabled the cloaking device and took main power offline to expedite repairs to all the systems damaged by your mysterious artifact."

"Then have him restore main power and engage the cloak."

The subcommander shook her head. "Not possible, Major. Now that he's begun repairs, it would take more time to reverse his steps than it would to let him finish."

"Do we have a repair time estimate?"

"Primary systems back online in four hours," Bedisa said. "Once that's done, we can raise the cloak and return to orbit."

It wasn't what Sadira had wanted, but she couldn't help what had been done in express contravention of her orders. All she could do was cope with the situation at hand. "Very well. Let him use any personnel or resources he needs to speed repairs."

"Understood, Major."

Sadira activated the commander's panel of the main console. "Kurat. Have we continued to monitor signal traffic to and from Centaurus?"

The tactical officer joined Sadira and Bedisa at the main console. "We've intercepted the *Enterprise*'s reports that the Orion Syndicate has operatives near the conference."

"And they base that on what, exactly?"

"They captured one who was suspected in a pharmaceutical theft. When they searched his residence, they found evidence he had been planning to attack the peace talks with a bomb."

"Interesting. Has he confessed? Or named accomplices?"

"Chatter on the police channels suggests the man they caught was already dead."

Sadira chuckled. "Splendid. If we play this right, Romulus will get what it needs, and the Orions will take the blame."

The centurion emerged from the dark and leaned into the penumbra of the main console's lone overhead light. "The Orions might not be blameless for much longer, Major. Reports from our spies on the ground suggest they have another agent in play, one who means to finish what the dead man started. In this case, patience might prove our best ally."

"I don't take your meaning, Centurion."

All eyes focused on Mirat, who reasserted his proud bearing. "If the Orions are this committed to doing our dirty work for us, perhaps we should remain here, monitor the situation from a safe distance, and withdraw in the event that they succeed."

Sadira imagined choking the cowardly old centurion while disemboweling him with a dull spoon. "Are you suggesting we abandon our mission and sit idly by, in the hope that a mediocrity like the Orion Syndicate achieves our objectives for us?"

"I merely propose that it might be more prudent to let them shoulder the risk, since their aims and ours appear to intersect."

"Picture this, Centurion: We stand down and let the Orions blunder their way through this. In their mad flailing, they expose weaknesses in the Klingons' defenses and flaws in the Federation's security protocols—vulnerabilities both sides quickly rectify. Then, after it becomes clear the Orions have failed and been neutralized, we would be obligated to resume our mission—which would then be made all the more difficult because the Orions will have squandered our foes' most exploitable errors." She shook her head. "No, we can't wait for someone else to do our job for us, Centurion. If we want a war between the Klingons and the Federation, we're going to need to start it ourselves."

Seventeen

Kirk knew they were already five minutes behind schedule, but he had to make Sarek see reason. "Ambassador, for your own safety, I think it would be best."

"Absolutely not, Kirk. To let you walk at the head of the procession would diminish the Klingons' perception of my role as the leader of this delegation."

"If I let you take point, I might as well paint a bull's-eye on your chest."

"Unless I command the Klingons' respect, these talks will end in failure."

No wonder Spock hates arguing with Sarek. The man's never wrong.

Behind them in the dormitory corridor stood the rest of the Federation's negotiating team, flanked on either side by three armed security officers from the *Enterprise*. Spock stood a short distance ahead by the door, ostensibly content to let Kirk debate Sarek without his assistance.

The Vulcan diplomat walked toward the door. "We need to go now, Kirk." The others who were queued up in the hallway plodded into motion behind Sarek.

Spock obliged the approaching delegation by pushing open the door, then stepping clear while holding it for them. The security officers kept pace and marched with the politicos across the quad toward the alumni center, in which the talks were slated to resume. Kirk exited the dormitory last. Spock fell in at his side as they hurried to overtake the head of the procession.

Had the choice been up to Kirk, he and his men would not have been involved at all. Their presence had been requested by Sarek—not because he expected to need their protection, but because the Klingons had informed him their delegation would return only with armed escort. Had the Federation representatives arrived without a comparable force at their side, it would have been perceived as a sign of weakness by the Klingons— and, consequently, as an invitation to more egregious abuses and demands at the bargaining table.

Bright sun and a warm breeze made for a pleasant if brief walk across the manicured lawn. Kirk and Spock reached the double doors of the alumni center ahead of the delegation. They each pulled open one door and stood to either side so that Sarek could make his grand entrance. Meanwhile, from the opposite side of the center's main lobby, the Klingon delegation arrived through another pair of doors. Just as Sarek had predicted, Prang was at its vanguard, several steps ahead of his comrades.

A pair of security officers relieved Kirk and Spock at the doors, enabling them to catch up and fall in behind Sarek just as he met Prang in the middle of the lobby. Behind him were several Klingon military officers led by the scar-faced General Kovor and a fierce-looking female officer who wore a commander's rank insignia.

Sarek raised his right hand in Vulcan salute—a V-shape formed by separating the fingers into two pairs at an uncomfortable angle. "Greetings, Councillor Prang."

"You're wasting your time and mine, Vulcan."

"A curious assessment. I look forward to hearing more about it—inside."

The two diplomats stared each other down: Prang, a storm looking for somewhere to rage; Sarek, a mountain cold and immovable. Behind the councillor, General Kovor grinned at Kirk. "Nothing says *peace* like an armed military escort, does it?"

"I guess that depends on the military."

Kovor and his officers stepped off to one side, and Kirk and Spock shifted with them. The general motioned to his comrade. "This is Commander Lomila, my first officer on the *HoS'leth*. Lomila, this is none other than Captain James T. Kirk of the *Enterprise*."

Lomila eyed Kirk in a way that left him feeling almost violated. Then she flashed a smile of fearsome, sharp teeth. "After all the stories . . . I thought you would be taller, Captain."

"I'll try to take that as a compliment."

The general's one-eyed gaze narrowed. "And this must be Commander Spock. Among my people, you're almost as infamous as your captain." Unable to goad Spock into a reaction or a reply, Kovor put his sights back on Kirk. "It's an honor to face you at last, Kirk."

"I'm sure it is." Just as Kirk had expected, Kovor remained calm, betraying nothing—a preview of the cunning reserve that had made him a feared starship combat tactician.

A few meters away, Prang was the first to blink, ending his staredown with Sarek. The grouchy Klingon lumbered toward the conference room. "Let's get this farce under way."

Sarek watched Prang lead the Klingon delegation away, then motioned for his people to follow them. Turning to Kirk and Kovor, he said, "Thank you, gentlemen, but neither of your forces will be required further today. You are both dismissed." And with that he followed Prang.

The declaration left Kirk and the Klingon general speechless at first. They regarded each other with mixed expressions of amusement and suspicion. Kovor nodded to Lomila, who snapped at the armed Klingon guards, "*naDev vo' peghoS!*" The troops turned away from the delegation and marched back the way they had come. A single look from Spock effected the same action by the red-shirted Starfleet security officers shadowing the Federation diplomats.

Kirk nodded at Kovor. "Until we meet again, General."

"I shall look forward—"

A peculiar noise and a brilliant flash of light filled the cavernous lobby. In the space of a single blink both effects had faded—then a woman in the Federation delegation screamed. Spock and Kirk sprinted toward the commotion with Kovor and Lomila at their side.

At the entrance to the corridor that led to the conference room, the two delegations had recoiled from each other. Profanities and threats were shouted in both directions and in multiple languages; fingers were being pointed. The air crackled with the potential for violence.

Kovor silenced the Klingons with one bellow: "*bIjatlh 'e' pemev!*"

"Quiet!" Kirk shouted at the Federation delegates. "What happened?"

Aravella Gianaris, the economic adviser, was on the verge of panic. "They disintegrated him! Or kidnapped him! He was there, then—zap! He was gone!"

Spock asked in a calming baritone, "*Who* was gone?"

"Beel Zeroh," said Gesh mor Tov. "Our military adviser!"

Durok from the Klingon contingent protested, "We did nothing!" He pointed at Sarek. "Your man Zeroh probably misfired his own weapon—the same one he used to kill Gorkon!"

Pandemonium erupted as both sides volleyed accusations and epithets. Behind Kirk and the others, both security squads converged on the scene. Everything was about to spin out of control, Kirk was sure of it. He faced his security team. "Take Sarek and the others back to their dorm! Now!" Then he found Kovor and snapped, "Get your people out of here."

The general barked one order at Lomila, and she gave their troops rapid-fire orders in *tlhIngan Hol*. In a flurry of brutal efficiency, the Klingons mustered their delegation into a tight phalanx and marched them out of the alumni center, back to their own residence hall, even as the *Enterprise* security team herded Sarek and his remaining advisers out the door to the quad.

Kirk, Spock, Kovor, and Lomila were the last four people in the lobby. The two duos said nothing, but mirrored each other's stew of anxiety and regret. Then they turned their backs on each other and went separate ways.

Passing through the main entrance to the quad, Kirk confided to Spock, "That sound we heard, before Zeroh vanished, and that pulse of light. Did those look familiar to you, Spock?"

"Indeed. It was the same as the Transfer Key effect that sent Captain Una into the alternate universe."

Despite his best attempt to present a calm façade, Kirk was unable to keep from clenching his fists in rage. "The Transfer Key is close by, Spock. Which means so are the Romulans—and *her*."

"By 'her,' I presume you mean the Romulan spy Sadira, whom we knew as Ensign Bates."

"Yes, Spock, *her*."

"Regardless of Sadira's involvement, it would be logical for the Romulans to use the Transfer Key to try to disrupt the peace talks." Spock's brow creased. "Which means—"

"This might be our best chance to steal it back."

"Precisely."

Searing-hot phosphors fell like summer rain from the overheads, and the atmosphere inside the *Velibor* was more smoke than air. Auxiliary power stuttered on and off at random. The main console on the command deck showed nothing but garbled computer code and the wild static of cosmic background radiation. Most of the command crew was sprawled on the deck, stunned.

Centurion Mirat stepped gingerly to avoid treading on his fallen comrades. Near the forward bulkhead, he found Subcommander Bedisa collapsed next to the tactical station. He kneeled next to her and fished for a rejuvenating patch in the partially depleted medkit he had salvaged from a lower deck. There was one medicated patch left. He unwrapped it and affixed it to Bedisa's throat, above the collar of her uniform tunic.

It took a few seconds for her to regain consciousness. She awoke with a gasp and sat up quickly. Then she slumped backward. It was a common side effect of *juva* patches, a sudden rush of energy followed by vertigo. Mirat steadied her until she recovered her balance and her breathing slowed to a normal rate. "Are you all right, Subcommander?"

"Yes, I think so, Centurion. Help me up, please."

He stood first, took Bedisa's hands, and hefted her to her feet. He closed his medkit. "I was belowdecks when the ship lurched. What happened?"

The question hardened Bedisa's features into a mask of anger. "She used her toy again." The subcommander eyed the smoldering ruins of the command deck. "I thought she couldn't do any more harm while main power was offline. I was wrong."

Mirat was sure he had heard wrong. "She used the artifact *again*? On whom?"

"I think she was targeting the leader of the Federation team this time." A cynical smirk. "Based on the curses she let slip before the ship went to hell, I'd say she missed." Her mood turned to concern as she searched the deck. "Where is she?"

"Not here," Mirat said. "She must have gone belowdecks." He continued to marvel at the scope of the damage wrought by one alien component wired into their ship's systems. "How did she activate the thing without main power?"

"No idea." Bedisa pulled her mess of black hair from her face and tied it into a regulation tail behind her head. "You'd have to ask Ranimir. Speaking of which—" She walked to the engineering station and tried in vain to coax data from it. "So much for damage reports."

As other members of the command crew groaned back to consciousness and coughed at their first deep breaths of the smoky haze that enveloped them, the centurion inquired loudly, "Can anyone tell me if the cloak is still working?" His question went unanswered while the others pawed at their hobbled consoles.

His comm unit vibrated on his hip. It was standard procedure on a bird-of-prey for personal comms to be silenced, since they were so rarely used while on board. He pulled the device from its pocket and activated it. "Mirat here."

Ranimir's voice was a tense whisper. *"Centurion! It's Sadira! She—"* A howl of noise spat from the comm's speaker.

"Ranimir! What's going on down—" The channel went dead before he finished. He tucked away the comm and faced Bedisa. "We'd better get down to engineering."

They left the command deck, both at a full run, and shouted holes through knots of personnel blocking the corridors and ladderways. Less than a minute later they descended the emergency ladder to the engineering deck, where they found Sadira on a tear, terrorizing the weary mechanics and engineers.

"If propulsion is not restored within the hour," she shouted at one enlisted man, "I'll have your family exiled to the mines of Remus!" She seized another man by the collar. "Get the shields back up, or I'll show you how the Tal Shiar deals with those who fail the praetor." Arriving at a wounded engineer lying on the deck at her feet, she kicked him in his gut. "You can die after you bring the weapons back online. Until then, stand up!"

Bedisa crossed the deck in long strides, her fury rising. "Major! What are you doing?"

Sadira wheeled about and met Bedisa with a manic gleam. "Motivating the crew."

"By abusing them? By making them wonder who their enemy really is?"

The two women stood nose to nose. Sadira's mania turned to malice. "Meaning?"

"Repairs to the ship were nearly complete before you triggered that alien device of yours. Whatever it is, wherever it came from, it's the source of all this damage—and you're the cause. So if you want this mission to go forward, stop using that thing and *let us fix the ship!*"

Everyone watched the human political officer. She raised her chin and wore a smug half smile in the face of Bedisa's open challenge.

A crimson flash and an earsplitting shriek—then Bedisa stumbled backward and collapsed, a smoking cavity burned halfway through her abdomen. The light left her eyes as she struck the deck. Mirat had seen many people meet their end; he recognized death when he saw it. He knew in a glance that Subcommander Bedisa was gone.

Sadira pocketed her compact disruptor and made a slow turn to stare down all the haunted eyes in the room. "Any more questions? Any more complaints? Then get to work." She crossed the deck and paused at Mirat's side just long enough to say, "I am promoting Lieutenant Kurat to second-in-command. See that Bedisa's access codes are transferred at once."

Mirat watched her exit the engineering deck and fantasized about planting his dagger between her shoulder blades.

He was certain her coup would never have gone this far if not for the reputation of the Tal Shiar. *Regulations be damned,* he castigated himself. *I should have trusted my instincts and supported the commander, not this maniac.* He knew what had to be done, but when he pondered the true cost of staging a mutiny, he found his hands unwilling to do the work of his heart.

Standing up to Sadira would be a death sentence, no matter the outcome. If he failed, he would die on the ship; if he succeeded, he would be tried and executed on Romulus.

His eyes fell upon the charred corpse of Bedisa, and for a moment he was surprised to find he envied her, both because she had died with her pride unblemished, and because she now was free of whatever consequences might yet attend this nightmare of a mission.

If only I loved life less and honor more, we could all be free.

━━━━━━━

Kirk let Spock step by him into the faculty office he had commandeered for an impromptu briefing, then closed the door. They turned to face Chekov, Uhura, and Scott, who stood in the middle of a room whose bland décor and sparse furnishings betrayed its institutional nature.

"The good news: the Klingon cruiser in orbit just became our *second* most pressing concern. The bad news: if I'm right, somewhere in this system is a cloaked Romulan ship carrying the artifact recently stolen from the *Enterprise*—and we need to find it before it strikes again."

His officers exchanged anxious glances.

Chekov was the first to speak. "Romulans, Captain?"

"So it seems, Mister Chekov." He turned toward his chief engineer. "Scotty, we—"

The door opened behind Kirk, who turned to see Ambassador Sarek enter the office. "Captain, we need to persuade the Klingons to resume the negotiations as soon as possible."

"This isn't a good time, Mister Ambassador. Please return to your suite."

"I will not be brushed aside, Kirk. This matter demands your immediate attention."

It was an effort for Kirk to restrain his temper when challenged so brazenly in front of his crew, but he knew no good would come from antagonizing Sarek. "With all respect, Ambassador, my crew and I need to contend with a more pressing matter, so if—"

"More pressing than the cause of peace with our most fierce rival in local space? If such a threat to this conference exists, Kirk, I demand to know about it."

Kirk bristled at being badgered into divulging classified information about something as potentially controversial as the Transfer Key. "Unfortunately, it's a top-secret Starfleet matter."

"That may be, Captain, but as a senior ambassador of the Federation Diplomatic Corps, I hold the diplomatic

rank of a Starfleet admiral. If you force me to invoke that
authority, I will, but I would prefer you accord me the
respect due my office and tell me what is going on—not
least because I suspect it relates to the disappearances of
Councillor Gorkon and Mister Zeroh."

Outranked and outflanked, Kirk relented. "Mister
Spock? Care to fill him in?"

Spock shouldered his expository duties with aplomb.
"For some time, commanding officers of the *Enterprise*
have been in clandestine possession of the Transfer Key,
an artifact from an alien universe—a device that by itself
can be used to shift individuals out of this universe into
another, and that when connected to its parent apparatus,
located on a world whose territorial sovereignty is a matter of dispute to be resolved at this conference, might enable much larger movements of personnel and materiel,
including starships, between the two universes."

"Intriguing," Sarek said. "To what purpose?"

"Its creators, the Jatohr, mean to invade our universe,"
Spock said. "Their first beachhead was repulsed eighteen
years ago on Usilde, but in the process several *Enterprise*
crew members were stranded in the Jatohr's dimension.
Several weeks ago, with our help, Captain Una journeyed
there to rescue those personnel—but shortly afterward
the Transfer Key was stolen by a Romulan spy. Unless we
recover the Key, Captain Una's return will be impossible—
and if the Romulans reverse-engineer it, they will have
the Federation at a major tactical disadvantage—one we
might never be able to overcome."

"I see." Sarek returned his attention to Kirk. "Please
continue, Captain."

Only years of hard-won discipline prevented Kirk from making a sarcastic retort about Sarek giving him leave to carry on with his own briefing. He stifled his burgeoning frown and tried to pick up where he had left off. "Mister Scott, I need you to devise some means of blocking the Transfer Key's displacement effect."

"I don't know if I can, sir. It doesn't work by any laws of physics I've ever seen."

"Then learn some new ones, Mister Scott. As long as that device remains unchecked, we'll be fighting a losing battle."

Spock interjected, "I have a few theories you might find helpful, Mister Scott. We should confer after this meeting adjourns." The first officer struck a more cautious note as he faced Kirk. "Captain, if we leave orbit to search for a cloaked Romulan vessel that might or might not still be here, Councillor Prang and General Kovor might take undue advantage of our absence."

"You mean they'll put a gun to Sarek's head the minute our backs are turned. I'm aware of that, Spock. But if I'm right, the Klingons are bluffing to draw concessions, while the Romulans have hit us twice so far. We need to deal with the threat that's already drawn blood."

"A reasonable point," Spock said.

Uhura asked, "Where does that leave our investigation of the Orion Syndicate?"

"In progress," Kirk said. "Just because we have proof the Romulans are in play doesn't mean the Orions aren't also looking to sabotage the talks."

A sage nod from Sarek. "A wise observation, Captain. We should also consider the possibility their efforts are being coordinated. It would not be the first time the Romulans employed a proxy in addition to committing their own resources to this kind of operation."

Chekov added, "If the Romulans hired the Orions through a third party, the Syndicate might not even know who it is really working for."

"Also a reasonable supposition," Sarek said.

Once again, Kirk made an effort to recover control of the briefing. "Uhura, Chekov, have another look at Jorncek's residence. Look for anything that might tell us if he has accomplices. Pay particular attention to his recent communications. I want to know who he was talking to, who was giving him his orders, and who was funding him."

"Understood, Captain," Uhura said.

"Spock, Scotty, get back to the *Enterprise*. Find a way to block the Transfer Key. We have four hundred thirty highly trained personnel at our disposal. Put them to work."

Scott accepted the challenge with his head held high. "Aye, sir."

Finally, Kirk looked to Sarek. Mindful of his inability to pull rank on the man, he moderated his tone to minimize the appearance of confrontation. "Your Excellency, I think that you would be safest in your suite until this situation is resolved."

"I disagree. From what you've said, neither distance nor shields offer any defense against this Transfer Key, so I fail to see what benefit would be realized by confining myself behind closed doors when there is work to be done."

Baffled and annoyed, Kirk furrowed his brow. "What work, Ambassador?"

"You have your mission, Kirk. I have mine. I must return to the Klingon delegation and convince them it is in our mutual best interest to resume the talks in spite of the danger."

Dealing with Sarek made Kirk regret all the times he had accused Spock of being stubborn, because his father redefined the term. "The last time you tried that, you and your wife ended up held hostage."

"I remember. Do you have a point, Captain?"

"My point is, the last we heard, the Klingons blame *you* for this. Right now they're more likely to shoot you than talk to you."

"*That*, Kirk, is exactly why we must continue trying to get them to talk."

Eighteen

Hours, days, weeks—Una wasn't sure such temporal distinctions mattered anymore. Martinez, Shimizu, and she had been hiking mountain trails and dusty low-road passes for what felt like forever. When she concentrated, she could dredge up murky recollections of times spent resting, and maybe even sleeping, though not once had she felt the need to sip from her canteen. There had been hours of darkness, she remembered only vaguely, nights spent under a sky more indigo than black and as starless as the heart of a black hole.

In due course mountains diminished to hills, and those in turn surrendered to a rolling lowland of shingle and sand. Each change of the scenery took Una by surprise, as if each new environment had replaced the last without her detecting the transition. It was the same feeling of disorientation that had haunted Una since her arrival in this dimension, on her first lonely march across the salt flats, and then her trek into the mountains.

At the summit of a low slope, a glare of sunlight along the horizon blinded her. She raised her hand for shade to help her eyes adjust. On the other side of the knoll a crescent-shaped beach stretched away in either direction, its shores vanishing into a haze where land and sky became one. Encompassed by the endless beach was a becalmed sea the color of lead.

Martinez and Shimizu halted on either side of her. Both men shaded their eyes with raised hands. Una was amused by their identical poses. "We look like we're saluting the dawn."

Shimizu grinned. "I said I'd follow you to hell. Never said I'd do yoga."

Martinez squinted. "Hang on—here they come." He pointed.

Several narrow causeways rose out of the gray water—if it was, in fact, water. The paths were all twenty meters wide and equidistant from one another, roughly two kilometers apart. They appeared to radiate from a shared point beyond the horizon, like spokes in a wheel too grand to be observed in its entirety from the vantage of the earthbound.

Una stared in wonder at the causeways. "What are they?"

"Roads to the enemy," Martinez said.

Una hurried down the slope to the beach. The sand was powder soft, and her booted feet sank in almost ankle-deep with each step. The causeway extended all the way onto shore, sparing her the need to wade through the motionless gunmetal liquid to reach it. Her eyes swept over the dreary surface in search of ripples or other artifacts of disruption caused by the rising of the roads, but she saw none. Everything about the vista had a surreal quality, from the disturbing uniformity of color in the sky, paths, and water, to the way that nothing except she, Martinez, and Shimizu ever seemed to move. And the *silence* . . . her surroundings felt eerily quiet.

She halted one step shy of mounting the causeway.

"Do we just walk across and hope it doesn't sink before we get to the center?"

"Don't worry about that," Shimizu said. "The road will do most of the work." An uncertain frown. "Question is: Are you ready to face what's waiting at the other end?"

"One way to find out." Eyes on the road's vanishing point, Una stepped onto it.

Martinez and Shimizu joined her on the end of the causeway. Seconds later, the beach was kilometers behind them, and the glassy smooth, ashen-hued expanse was all around them. Una turned and watched the last remnants of landmarks disappear behind the planet's subtle curve. "This is amazing. I don't feel any sensation of movement. No wind, no acceleration." Looking forward, she perceived no end to the path. "How long does it take?"

"Less time than you'd think," Martinez said.

Shimizu closed his eyes and took a deep breath. "If you want the trip to pass more quickly, just let your thoughts wander." Before Una could ask him why that would matter, she noticed Martinez had done the same thing: he stood with his eyes shut, head tilted back, as if surrendering to whatever lay ahead.

Una was reluctant to follow suit, but soon the monotony of their surroundings made her want to close her eyes just to have a break from the relentless sameness. Isolated with her own thoughts, she wondered whether the causeway had been designed with illusions intended to conceal the true distance between the ends of the spokes and their hub, or if—

"We're here," Shimizu said.

Her eyes snapped open to behold a terrible wonder.

It was a Jatohr city floating on the leaden sea. Its architecture had the same flowing, curvilinear quality Una remembered from the citadel on Usilde: no hard edges or corners anywhere in sight. All the surfaces exhibited the same pearlescent quality, though the range of pastel hues on display was far greater. There were soft streaks of pink and lavender, patches of light bluish gray, gentle whorls of pale sea green and chartreuse. Lording over it all were numerous towers that resembled the spiral horns of a Terran narwhal or a Bolian *ilok*.

The sky above the city was alive with white flashes of motion—Jatohr transport pods moving at great speed and arcing around one another with effortless grace. Some vanished behind the looming bulbous structures of the alien metropolis, while others plunged into the pewter-colored sea—all, Una noticed, without provoking the least trace of a ripple.

Her eyes followed the causeways to a latticework of paths that surrounded the city and continued inside through high arched tunnels that penetrated to its very heart.

Una looked at her compatriots. "So what now? We just walk in?"

Martinez looked at her as if she had gone mad. "Not unless you want to get fried by one of their flying globes. And once you go inside, the damned things are everywhere."

"I didn't come all this way just to give up at their front door." She contemplated the vastness of the alien city. "Sooner or later, it'll get dark again. When it does, we'll go in."

Shimizu cocked an eyebrow. "Pretty sure their killer beach balls can see in the dark."

A scathing glare of reproof. "Would you rather try this in broad daylight?"

The biologist doffed his pack and set it on the city's perimeter walkway, then sat down and used his gear for a cushion. He draped one arm over his eyes and crossed his feet as if to settle in for a long nap. "Okay, Captain. Bivouac 'til nightfall it is."

Nineteen

Jorncek's apartment looked as if it had been ransacked. Chekov and Uhura stepped around overturned pieces of furniture and between scattered personal effects. Drawers had been pulled from dressers and emptied; the contents of closets had been strewn about like refuse. Chekov imagined that if the dead Tiburonian's possessions had been dropped from low orbit they might still have landed in better order than this. "What are we supposed to find in this mess?"

"Look for anything the local police missed," Uhura said. "Hidden data chips. Comm devices. Traces of non-Tiburonian genetic material."

He lifted the tricorder slung at his side and switched it on. Its oscillating whine filled the living room as he scanned for anything that might register as a data storage medium. "Won't the police have already done this?"

"Definitely." Uhura pawed through the pockets of garments draped over a chair lying on its side. "But they don't have Starfleet-grade tricorders. We might find something they missed."

Chekov adjusted the range and direction of his scan as he moved to the open bedroom doorway. "Why don't we just ask them to share what they already have?"

"Because they aren't being very cooperative right now.

Something about a stolen body, they said." She moved to the sofa, which lay on its backrest, and dug through the pockets of a pair of pants. "Be sure to scan inside the walls, above the ceilings, and under the floors."

"Yes, Lieutenant." Once again he tweaked the tricorder's settings.

Uhura stood and looked around. "They seized all the comms and data terminals, didn't they?"

"I think so. I don't read any inside the apartment." He tiptoed through the casual wreckage of the bedroom to make a detailed scan of the bathroom. "No sign of data cards or memory chips. No electronics except clocks and kitchen appliances."

"What about DNA? Any non-Tiburonian traces?"

"Hang on. Changing scan modes." He felt her impatient stare as he keyed in more adjustments. "Filtering out our genetic patterns." Another null result left him scowling at his tricorder. "Nothing. Just half-decayed Tiburonian hair and skin cells." He returned the tricorder to standby mode. "If our suspect had visitors, they left no traces."

Uhura shifted a toppled desk away from one wall. "But the forensics team did." She lifted a data cable. "A standard duotronic local network connector. Jorncek had a terminal, right here."

"A terminal now in the hands of the police."

"True—but they couldn't take the whole local network. Not without cutting off every apartment in this building." She beckoned Chekov. "Let's plug this into the tricorder."

He approached her and handed over his tricorder. "What for?"

The communications officer patched the cable into an auxiliary data port on the device. Keying in commands, she explained to Chekov, "The tricorder should be able to map the local data network and identify any data caches, intermediate nodes, firewalls, or proxy servers being used by this complex." A few more fine-tuning changes, and she smiled. "There we go; all of the above. If I'm reading this right"—she threw a coquettish look Chekov's way—"and I like to think that I am . . . the local network's hub server is located in the basement."

It took a moment, but Chekov caught on. "The local hub has comm and data logs."

"Very good, Ensign." Uhura unplugged the cable from the tricorder and nodded toward the front door. "Let's get down there and see if the police left it in better shape than this place."

They checked the hallway with the tricorder to make certain it was empty, then unlocked the door and slipped out of Jorncek's trashed domicile. Uhura led Chekov through an exit at the end of the corridor, then down the building's emergency stairs.

"The lift would be faster," he said.

"And would run the risk of us being spotted and reported to the locals," Uhura said. "Trust me, this is safer. Besides, a bit of exercise won't hurt you." At the bottom of the switchback staircase they arrived at a door marked BASEMENT. It was unlocked, and Uhura was through it before Chekov could think to reach for his tricorder.

He caught up to her outside a locked door. Next to it was a simple placard: SERVER ROOM. She drew a compact phaser from her belt. "Look for security sensors. If you read one, jam it."

"Scanning," Chekov said. He made a quick sweep of the basement level. "Just smoke detectors and an alarm on the door itself. Signals blocked."

A harsh shriek of phaser fire. Chekov winced at the searing brightness of the blue beam from Uhura's weapon as it sliced through the door's security mechanism. The beam ceased, and the door swung open, smoke rising from its slagged lock.

On the other side was a cool, dry, windowless room. Banks of computers and comm relays stood in racks along the walls to their left and right, and a master control console occupied the far wall, opposite the door. Uhura smiled at the sight of it. "Jackpot."

She moved to the console and sat down. Chekov expected her to ask him to use the tricorder to help crack the system's security, but she accessed the system within seconds. Noting his wide-eyed reaction, she smiled. "Civilian systems have lots of factory-default backdoor codes. Luckily for us, I know most of the ones used in the Federation." Her hands were a blur across the console's controls as she dug into vast troves of archived data. "Here we go. Full comm and data archives for Mister Jorncek's unit."

Chekov perused the data over Uhura's shoulder. "What does it all mean?"

"He hasn't had much contact with anyone on Centaurus." Uhura pointed out some lines of code that looked like gibberish to Chekov. "These are encrypted signals—some incoming, some outbound. Based on the packet metadata, I'd say he was piggybacking on someone else's channel and routing these messages through the planet's subspace comm satellite."

"He was talking to someone offworld?"

"Looks that way." Another flurry of commands into the console. "I'm patching into the satellite and searching its logs for subspace signals relayed with these time stamps. With a little luck, we should be—" A feedback tone and a flood of new data interrupted her. "There we go. Trackbacks indicate most of his messages came from or went to the Orion homeworld."

"So we connect him to the Orion Syndicate—which we already knew."

"Hang on, Ensign. I'm not done yet." Uhura punched in more filtering parameters and initiated another virtual sifting of the data. "Now let's see if his Orion friends know anyone else on Centaurus." In seconds another batch of transmissions was isolated on a tertiary display. "All right, who's this? Another recipient of Orion communiqués, right here in New Athens. I've got their network address . . . identifying their router . . . and now the local hub." A small monitor above the console switched to show a street map of New Athens, with one building highlighted. "Let's ping that hub to see who else the Orions have been talking to."

A name appeared on the main display, along with a face from a New Athens University staff identification card. Chekov leaned forward and read it aloud: "Elara Soath. Catullan. Granted entry as a permanent resident on a work permit with the university catering office."

Uhura looked up in alarm. "She could be on campus, and even inside the conference, right now!" She logged out of the console with one jab at a master switch, then stood, drew her communicator, and flipped it open with one smooth flick of her wrist.

"Uhura to *Enterprise*."

The captain answered, *"Go ahead, Lieutenant."*

"Captain, we've identified a possible Orion agent with access to the conference. Alert all security personnel to arrest university catering employee Elara Soath on sight."

Spock and five *Enterprise* security officers material- ized outside the entrance to the New Athens University catering office at nearly the exact moment that Com- mander Lomila and five armed Klingon soldiers beamed down from the *HoS'leth* to the same location. The two first officers acknowledged each other, then moved together toward the door. Spock reached it first and opened it. Lomila marched through the chivalrously opened portal without a word of thanks, and Spock handed off the door to one of her troops as he followed her inside.

A long corridor stretched away to either side. From the left came the aromas and commotion of a large, busy institutional kitchen. From the right came the low chatter and muted feedback tones of an administrative office. Heads poked out of office doors down the length of the hallway as middle managers overcome by curiosity strained to see what was happening.

Lomila and Spock both headed straight toward the kitchen. He had wondered whether the Klingons had acquired the same intelligence the *Enterprise* had—work schedules and personnel assignments, acquired by means of information-warfare tactics in the name of expediency. The moment Lomila had turned toward the kitchen, without the least hesitation or consideration of the office suites, Spock's suspicion was confirmed: the Klingons on the *HoS'leth* had accessed Elara Soath's work schedule with the same ease as the *Enterprise* crew.

The booted footfalls of the ten armed personnel behind him and Lomila made almost as much racket as the banging of pots and pans that greeted them in the steam-filled kitchen. Flames danced from open grill ranges. Dozens of employees—most of them humanoid—clad in white culinary uniform jackets toiled in long rows at various stainless-steel prep stations inside the massive space, whose walls and floors were dominated by blue-and-white checkered tile.

In unison, Spock and Lomila directed their teams to pair off—one *Enterprise* officer with each *HoS'leth* soldier—and split up around the cavernous kitchen's periphery. The two executive officers remained together as they moved down the kitchen's center aisle, both of them studying the faces of everyone they could see, in search of their target of interest.

At the far end of the kitchen, Lomila and Spock regrouped with their respective teams, having found nothing but the shocked stares of the university's culinary staff. He met his counterpart's simmering fury with a dry observation. "She does not appear to be here."

"Really? Thank you for pointing that out, Vulcan." Lomila seized a young Bolian who was trying to sneak past unnoticed. With one hand the female Klingon hoisted the cook off the floor. "Elara Soath. You know who she is?" A panicked nod. Lomila continued. "Where is she?"

"D—don't know. On break?"

Spock asked, "Where does she go on her breaks?"

The Bolian pointed at the kitchen's rear exit, which stood ajar. Lomila dropped him and marched toward the door with her men at her back. Spock and the *Enterprise* team stayed close beside their Klingon counterparts, determined not to be cut out of any action to come.

Lomila pushed open the back door, which let out onto a pleasant manicured lawn tucked into a U-shaped bend in the catering facility. Beyond its open far side was a promenade around the campus's main quad, which led to both the dormitories that had been commandeered for the delegations to the conference. The two landing parties advanced to the quad and spread out as they searched for their quarry.

A female *Enterprise* security officer pointed and called out, "There!"

Everyone followed her cue and looked north, up the paved walkway that led to the university's medical complex. There, halted in midstep like a prey animal frozen with fear by a sudden bright light, was Elara Soath, staring in abject terror at the combined force of Starfleet and Klingon personnel now charging in her direction with weapons drawn.

The young Catullan woman hurled her comm at the ground hard enough to shatter the device, whose fragments promptly erupted into smoke and sparks. Then she turned and ran. She sprinted with speed and grace, zigzagging through a crowd of passersby who became her innocent living shields. For once the Klingons demonstrated restraint.

Lomila must have warned them to check their fire, Spock reasoned.

On the run, he retrieved his communicator and flipped it open. "Spock to *Enterprise!*"

Captain Kirk replied, *"Go ahead, Spock."*

"Suspect sighted! She's fleeing toward the medical complex!"

"Stay on her, Spock! We're sending reinforcements!"

"Understood. Spock out." He tucked away the communicator, holstered his phaser, and picked up his pace. A dozen strides later he passed Lomila and the rest of her troops to take the lead in the pursuit. Lomila pushed herself to catch up to him.

"In a hurry, Vulcan?"

"We need to stop her before she reaches the hospital."

"You mean before she finds cover and hostages."

For once, Spock appreciated the concision of Klingon discourse. "Exactly."

———

The first thing Elara had done when she saw Starfleet and Klingon military personnel pour out of the university's catering kitchen was activate her Orion-made signal scrambler to hide her Catullan bio-signature from sensors and transporters. The next thing she'd done was trash her comm. Then she ran, faster and harder than she had ever run before in her entire life.

Most of the doors that faced the quad opened only to those carrying authorized ID cards, the kinds with embedded microchips tagged with residents' profiles. If Elara had been lucky enough to see the enemy coming, she might have nicked a few ID cards to get her through those restricted entrances. Instead, with only her scrambler and a miniaturized disruptor in hand, she had no choice but to flee for the nearest building on campus that was open to the public around the clock, every day: the hospital complex.

Far behind her, her pursuers ordered her to halt. She ignored them and darted left, then right, around individuals and clusters of people out strolling the tree-shaded walkways, using them for cover as she risked everything on her headlong flight to the medical center.

She reached the large revolving door, which moved with all the urgency of continental drift. The first shot from her disruptor vaporized one of its three broad transparent panels and scattered the crowd in the lobby. Her second shot drowned out the bystanders' panicked screams as it took down the guard behind the torus-shaped information desk.

No one moved to stop her as she bolted through the lobby, weapon in hand. Elara hurdled over the security checkpoint and reached the lifts as several of them opened.

A warning shot into the ceiling high overhead secured the throng's attention. "Move!" she snapped, eager to clear the riffraff and slip inside one of the lifts. If she could move deeper inside the complex and evade observation even for just a few minutes, it might be enough to find another way out and elude her pursuers. First she needed these stragglers out of her way—

Not her, she realized, her hand snagging a passing young woman's uniform sleeve. The student nurse froze as Elara stared into her eyes. "You," Elara said. "I saw you on the news. You helped them catch Jorncek." She pulled her closer. "You put me in this jam."

"No, please, it was a mistake, I just want to leave, I—"

Elara dragged the young human woman inside a waiting lift. "You're coming with me, sweet-face. Tell me: Where's the drug lockup?"

The question left the terrified human woman perplexed. "Why?"

"I'm asking the questions. Where is it?"

"Upstairs. Seventh floor."

Heavy running footsteps echoed in the lobby. Elara pressed buttons for the top five floors the lift serviced, then thumbed its CLOSE DOORS button to set its ascent into motion. Reassured by the sensation of movement under her feet, she pressed her disruptor to the woman's temple. "What's the access code for the lockup?"

"I don't remember."

A hard punch in the cheekbone left the nursing student on the verge of tears. Elara put the woman's back to the lift wall and pressed her disruptor between her hostage's eyes. "Think—" She read the woman's uniform name tag. "Joanna."

The young woman's jaw trembled, and a tear rolled

from the corner of her eye. "I can open it for you," she said, her voice small and quavering.

"Good. I need you anyway." The doors opened onto the sixth floor. Elara stole a look into the corridor. There were ambulatory patients, half a dozen nurses, and a handful of doctors and specialists moving from one room to another. Elara ducked back inside the lift and moved behind Joanna, in case she had to use the woman as a human shield. As the doors started to close, a young Vulcan doctor caught them and stepped forward to board. He stopped and backed out as Elara lifted her disruptor to Joanna's head and told him, "Wait for the next one, Doc."

The doors closed, the lift ascended, and Elara nudged her prisoner forward. "Take me to the pharma locker. Try to run or fight back, I'll put a hole in you so big you could park a starship in it. We reach, sweet-face?"

A terrified whisper: "We reach."

The lift dinged as it stopped on the seventh floor. A nudge moved the nursing student in front of the doors, which parted with a soft gasp. Elara tucked her disruptor into the small of the other woman's back. "Move." Together they stepped out of the lift, which closed behind them and continued its upward journey. No one noted their presence or the strangeness of their being so close to each other as they progressed in tandem down the corridor.

"Up here, on the left," Joanna said under her breath.

"Good." Wary of an ambush, Elara shifted her gaze from side to side as they walked and shot a quick look over her shoulder to see if they were being followed. So far everything looked calm, a portrait of normalcy. Half a minute later, they reached the pharmaceutical lockup.

"Open it," Elara said. "Quietly."

Joanna took a deep breath and keyed numbers into the lockup's security panel.

Then everything went to hell.

Sirens whooped and emergency lights pulsed on the walls, giving every movement the appearance of stuttered stop-motion. Elara spun to one side, then the other as armed local police charged toward her. She wrapped her arm around Joanna's throat, then put her own back against the wall beside the door to the lockup. "Stop moving or she dies!" The police halted their advance, but their weapons were still aimed in her direction. "Drop your weapons!"

The nearest officer shouted back, "Drop yours!"

"Not happening." She took her disruptor off Joanna's back just long enough to shoot open the door to the pharma lockup. As it swung inward, she backed through it, keeping Joanna squarely in front of her every step of the way. Confident there were no more surprises awaiting her inside the reinforced storage space, she paused to consider her next move. There were drugs here that could counteract and preemptively block the kinds of knockout gases the police and Starfleet were known to use in scenarios such as this. She suspected those would soon be useful.

"You make a move on this room, I'll kill her! We reach?"

The same officer replied from the corridor. "We hear you. Let's just stay calm."

Elara knew this likely wouldn't end well for anyone—least of all her.

So much for a clean getaway.

———

Leonard McCoy emerged from a transporter beam into the midst of pandemonium. Dozens of local law enforcement officers, nearly half the security division from the *Enterprise*, and more than a hundred armed Klingon troops had surrounded New Athens University Hospital.

In the middle of the circus of flashing lights and shouting heads, he found Kirk and Spock conferring in the open, halfway between the gathered official vehicles and the shattered front entrance of the medical center. None of the other assembled authorities paid the two senior officers of the *Enterprise* any mind, a fact that left McCoy flustered and baffled. He marched toward his comrades and, despite having reminded himself several times to remain cool and collected, erupted in a flood of bluster. "Dammit, Jim! What in blazes happened?"

Kirk moved to restrain him. "Bones, calm down, it's under—"

"Don't tell me to calm down! That's my *daughter* being used for a hostage!"

McCoy tried to dodge around the captain, who nonetheless took McCoy by his shoulders. "Bones! We have the suspect cornered! Every exit is covered. She's not going anywhere."

"Great news, Jim—unless she decides not to go down without a fight. Then this mess turns into a crossfire, with Joanna smack in the middle of it!"

Spock edged between Kirk and McCoy. "Everyone is aware of the risk to your daughter, Doctor, and all possible steps are being taken to ensure her safety."

"Are you out of your Vulcan mind? How can she be safe with a gun to her head?"

No matter how furious McCoy became, Spock remained calm. "In scenarios such as this, negotiation often proves effective. The suspect has no viable means of escape."

"I don't give a damn about the suspect! I just want my daughter. Can't we beam her out?"

"Not at this time," Spock said. "Her captor is using a data scrambler to block unwanted transporter activity, preventing us from establishing a lock on either her or Joanna."

McCoy trembled with rage. "So what are we doing about it?"

Spock remained unfazed. "Our best strategy is to provide the suspect with face-saving concessions in exchange for Joanna's safe release."

Kirk relaxed his grip on McCoy's shoulders. "Listen to him, Bones. We can do this."

Under any other circumstances, McCoy knew he could be a reasonable man. His training as a physician and as a Starfleet officer compelled him to seek peaceful resolutions to crises such as this—or, if force became necessary, to mitigate its use so that it caused a minimum of harm. But this was his little girl being used as a pawn. As a father, he wanted blood.

Listen to your head, not your heart, he counseled himself. *Hear your better angels. This isn't a time for violence. Let cooler heads talk this out.*

It was one of the hardest things he'd ever done: he ceased his struggling and backed away from Kirk and Spock. "All right, Jim. We'll do this by the book."

Kirk gave him a sympathetic nod, then turned to Spock. "Where do we stand?"

Spock pulled out his communicator. "Spock to Uhura. Status, please."

"Setting up a secure comm link to the suspect now, Commander. She won't negotiate with the local authorities or the Klingons—she only wants to deal with Starfleet."

"Understood. Spock out." The first officer closed his communicator and said to Kirk, "Curious. Why would she rather speak with us than with the local authorities?"

"Let's just get her talking. Where are we with a tactical plan? Do we have schematics for the seventh floor yet?"

"Ensign Chekov is retrieving the blueprints for the complex. As soon as he has them, he'll route them to my tricorder, along with real-time sensor data from inside the hospital."

"Very good."

Spock's communicator beeped, and he flipped it open. "Spock here."

"Mister Spock," Chekov said, *"hospital schematics uploading now."*

The first officer glanced at his tricorder. "Acknowledged. Status of preparations inside?"

"All patients and staff evacuated from the seventh floor. The rooms above and below the lockup have been cleared and are under guard. Your suspect isn't getting out those ways."

"Well done, Ensign. Stand by for further instructions.

Spock out." He tucked away the communicator and faced Kirk and McCoy. "The comm channel and location are secure. We should initiate contact and attempt to begin negotiations."

The captain took out his own communicator. "Maybe let me handle that part, Spock." He flipped open the device's grille. "Kirk to *Enterprise*."

Uhura answered, "*This is* Enterprise. *Go ahead, Captain.*"

"Patch me through to the suspect, Lieutenant."

"*Stand by, sir. Hailing her now.*"

McCoy grabbed Kirk's wrist and made him lower the communicator. His voice a rasping whisper, he said, "Jim. Joanna's my only child. She's all I have left in this life. I can't lose her."

Kirk allowed the gravity of the moment to rest between them. "I understand," he said. "I give you my word, Bones—as your captain, and as your friend—we will get her back, safe and sound. But I need you to trust me."

A leap of faith—that was what the captain was asking of him. After all they had been through, and all the times Jim Kirk had proved himself brave and loyal to a fault, McCoy knew he owed the man at least this much trust. But the price of failure—his daughter's life—was so high that he couldn't help but harbor doubts, even when he knew the matter was in the best hands possible. He swallowed his anxiety and nodded once to grant his blessing to the operation.

Over the communicator, Uhura's voice: "*Channel open, sir.*"

Armed with McCoy's consent, Kirk swung into action.

All McCoy could do now was hope he hadn't just gambled away Joanna's life.

———

There wasn't much to talk about as the kidnapper wrapped Joanna's wrists with medical tape. The Catullan woman had already bound Joanna's ankles with most of another roll of tape, all while keeping one wary eye on the doorway, as if in anticipation of a fast-strike rescue mission.

"Do you really need to use that much tape?"

A sour look from the Catullan. "You want me to put you down like an animal?"

"It's cutting off the circulation to my hands and feet."

Her complaint was answered with a few more twists of tape. "You'll live."

The panel on the wall buzzed, indicating an incoming call. Setting aside the tape, the captor put her back to the wall and sidled over to the comm, then thumbed open a channel. Her anxiety was telegraphed by her gruff salutation: "What do you want?"

A charming male voice replied, *"A better question would be: What do* you *want, Elara?"*

The question deepened her scowl of distrust. "You know my name. Who are you?"

"This is Captain James T. Kirk, of the Starship Enterprise. *You asked to talk to Starfleet; here we are. So let's talk."*

Elara snuck quick peeks into the corridor outside the

lockup, then ducked back inside. "How do I know this isn't a trick?"

"You don't. But neither do we. Which is why we're hoping for a show of good faith."

"Like what?" The Catullan drew her disruptor and aimed it at the open doorway.

"If you wouldn't mind, we'd be grateful if you'd let us talk to Miss McCoy, to confirm she's alive and well." Kirk was trying to adopt a deferential tone, but Joanna could hear the strain in his voice, as if kowtowing to a kidnapper offended the captain's nature.

After a brief bout of indecision, Elara returned to Joanna, seized her by one arm, and hoisted her to her feet. Then she dragged her closer to the comm, all while keeping her disruptor pressed against Joanna's rib cage. Next came an evil whisper in Joanna's ear: "Talk, sweet-face. Try to tell them anything tactically useful, and I'll scramble your guts into soup."

Joanna took a breath to calm her nerves. "Captain, this is Joanna McCoy. I'm unhurt."

"We're all very glad to hear that, Miss McCoy."

All? Did Kirk mean her father was with him? Joanna imagined the manic state her dad must be in, then felt a sting of regret for the note on which they'd last parted.

Before her maudlin reflection could manifest as a faux pas, Elara pushed her to the floor in the far end of the room. "You have your proof of life, Captain. Now what?"

"You tell me, Elara. You hold all the cards here."

"Don't try to flatter me. I'm alone, backed into a corner. If I didn't have a hostage, you'd have stormed me already. Meanwhile, you have legions and all the time in the world."

"We're still waiting to hear an actual demand, Elara. What do you need?"

She eyed the tiny space with keen eyes. "A small portable commode. Ten liters of potable water. And something to eat. Preferably something nonperishable."

"All right," Kirk said. *"We can arrange all that. Anything else?"*

A mischievous gleam lit up Elara's eyes. "I want all your people out of the hospital in the next ten minutes. In half an hour I want a warp-capable transport, fully fueled, its transponder disabled, on the roof. And I want safe passage for me and my hostage, to neutral space."

This time her demands were met by a pause. Joanna imagined the incredulous stares among the forces assembled outside the complex. Then Kirk said, without a hint of irony or condescension, *"We'll start working on that now, but it might take closer to an hour."*

"Forty-five minutes," Elara said. "Not one second longer. Or I start carving up this pretty young thing, bit by bit, until you learn how to follow directions." She closed the comm channel without waiting for another round of hot air from Kirk.

Joanna wondered if Elara was stupid, confused, panicked, or feigning those qualities for the sake of deception. Meanwhile, Elara rooted through the drug cabinets and assembled a number of vials onto the countertop beside a fresh hypospray.

It was a risk for Joanna to struggle too hard against the tape on her wrists or ankles; if she was able to stretch the tape enough to free herself, she had to do so when Elara wasn't watching. If she miscalculated and broke the tape, her efforts were almost certain to be detected.

She doesn't like to make eye contact when she speaks to me, Joanna noted. *Maybe if I keep her talking, she'll avoid looking my way while I work at the tape.*

"You know they'll never let you just walk out of here, right? With me or without me, there's no way you're getting out of this alive."

"No one told you to talk." As Joanna had hoped, Elara's focus remained on her search of the cabinet's upper shelves for more drugs. "Do us both a favor and sit quietly until this is over."

From the floor, Joanna couldn't see what vials Elara was collecting. "You already inoculated yourself against knockout drugs. What else do you think they'd throw at us?"

"No idea. But whatever they send in, you'll be my early warning system." Her eyes shifted Joanna's way. It was just a quick glance, but enough for Elara to realize her every move was being observed by her prisoner. Her gaze narrowed, and she gathered up a roll of gauze and a roll of tape. "I think you've seen enough for now."

Joanna knew there was no point protesting. It wasn't as if Elara would listen. The Catullan wrapped the gauze around Joanna's head, over her eyes, five or six times, until the only sliver of a view Joanna could find was when she looked straight down. Then came a couple rounds of medical tape to fix the improvised blindfold into place.

Elara returned to the counter to continue her experiment in pharmacology. In the corner, Joanna wrestled discreetly with her bonds—determined not to meet her fate as a bystander.

———

If there was one thing worse for McCoy than letting others take the lead in the rescue of his hostage daughter, it was listening to them argue in circles about how to get the job done.

"We can't just sit here and do *nothing*," Chekov said.

"That's *exactly* what we're going to do," Kirk said. "The best strategy in a hostage crisis is to bide your time and wait for the captor to make a mistake."

McCoy felt his temper rising. "And if that mistake gets my daughter killed?"

"It won't come to that, Bones. We won't let it."

Chekov remained impatient. "Why not seal the floor and pump in anesthezine gas to put them both to sleep?"

"Plenty of reasons," McCoy said, his tone sharp. "For one thing, anesthezine affects humans faster than it does Catullans. If this Elara woman sees Joanna pass out, she might kill her before she loses consciousness too. Second, she didn't choose a drug lockup by accident, Lieutenant. By now she could have dosed herself ten ways to Sunday to preempt any knockout drugs we might try to push through the ventilation system."

A new idea possessed Chekov. "Wait! She asked for water. We could lace it with something more potent, something strong enough to overcome her dosing."

His suggestion drew Spock's dry disapproval. "And what if Elara insists Joanna drink first from each container? How might such doctored water affect her when she likely has not had a preemptive dose of stimulants?"

"Not to mention the native differences in their blood chemistries," McCoy added. "If Elara's using stims, any dose strong enough to put her down might kill Joanna."

"All right," Kirk said. "That tactic is off the table for now. What's left?" Before Chekov could say the words, Kirk cut him off: "Aside from a direct assault."

Spock said, "We could offer her amnesty in exchange for surrender."

"She'd never believe it, and there's no way I can sell it to the JAG or the local magistrate."

McCoy heard footsteps. He turned to see three local police officers approach. One held a lightweight box with an open top; the other two carried reinforced crates loaded with lightweight metal canisters filled with potable water. "Here come Elara's first two demands."

Watching the police deliver the prepackaged snacks and bottled water, Spock looked troubled. Kirk took notice and asked, "What's wrong, Spock?"

"I find myself perplexed by the contradictory agendas implicit in Elara's demands. Asking for food, water, and a commode suggests she means to fortify her position and remain inside the hospital for the immediate future. However, requesting a shuttle and free passage out of Federation space represents an open declaration of her intent to flee. Why demand both?"

Uhura shrugged. "To keep her options open?"

"No," Kirk said, "to sow confusion. To keep us guessing and delay our response."

McCoy let slip a bitter harrumph. "It's working."

The sonic whitewash of a transporter beam filled the air. The *Enterprise* officers turned toward the golden shimmer forming on the quad behind their command post. It was a single person materializing inside the brilliant glow, which faded to reveal Lieutenant Commander Scott. The chief engineer held a squat contraption—a Starfleet standard field-issue portable commode. The devices weren't used often, only when landing parties needed to be careful about conserving their water during extended planetary deployments without support from a starship. Until that moment, McCoy hadn't been certain the *Enterprise* even had one on board.

Scott stepped forward and offered the commode to Kirk as if it were a treasure beyond price. "Here you go, sir. One commode, ready to serve"—he winked as he continued—"with a few wee modifications, made to order."

"Well done, Mister Scott." Kirk set the commode next to the food and water.

It was impossible for McCoy to miss the broad, Cheshire-cat grin on Scotty's face. "All right, Scotty, I'll take the bait: What's so special about this portable toilet?"

"A microsensor hidden inside the seat," Scott said. "Passive until there's weight on the hoop. Then it scans the person using it. If it reads anything but a Catullan, nothing happens. But if it senses our Catullan friend on the privy . . . let's just say she'll be in for a *doozy* of a jolt."

It was the most preposterous thing McCoy had ever heard. "Of all the cockamamie, half-baked . . ." He turned an accusatory stare at the captain. "Your idea, I presume?"

An abashed deflection. "I'd say it was more of a group effort."

The doctor shifted his reproach toward Spock. "You knew about this?"

Predictably, the first officer hedged. "While I concede the proposal lacks a certain dignity, it has the benefits of being well-targeted, non-lethal, and difficult to detect prior to being triggered." He traded an uncomfortable look with the captain. "We also found ourselves at a loss for a better idea, and time does currently appear to be a factor."

"Which leaves one last question," Chekov said. "Who takes it in to Elara?"

In unison, Spock, Kirk, Scott, Chekov, and no fewer than three nearby security officers all volunteered, then regarded one another with confused apprehension. McCoy took that moment to interject, "It should be me, Jim. I'll go."

Spock stepped closer to Kirk and lowered his voice. "I would advise against that, Captain. As noble as Doctor McCoy's motives may be, his emotional involvement could lead him to make irrational and even dangerous choices at key decision points."

McCoy suppressed the urge to slap his half-Vulcan shipmate. "Key decision points? I'm volunteering to be a glorified delivery boy! I'm dropping off snacks, water, and a traveling toilet. How many 'key decision points' do you really think that entails?"

"If Elara takes you as a second hostage, perhaps more than you expect," Spock said. His point made, he bowed his head to signal he was standing down from the debate. "Of course, the decision is yours, Captain."

"So it is." Kirk was less than happy about that fact. "Bones, you know you'll have to go in there unarmed, right?"

"I know the risks, Jim. I also know it's my little girl in there—and that if Elara was holding your son, you'd already be inside."

The captain nodded. "Then good luck—and be careful."

They shook hands, then McCoy waited while Scott and the security officers loaded the food, water, and commode onto a small antigrav pallet. Scott handed him the remote control for the floating load-lifter, then bid him farewell with a grim nod.

McCoy set the pallet into motion toward the hospital's blasted-open main entrance. The rational side of him worried Spock was right—that he might make a foolish mistake when he saw Joanna as a captive. But his paternal instinct knew he had to do this—because if he had left it to anyone else and it went wrong, he would never be able to forgive himself.

Let's just hope that when this is over, there's nothing to forgive.

———

Slack but unbroken: that was the state of the medical tape binding Joanna's wrists. When her captor wasn't looking, she twisted her bonds slowly back and forth. Shifting her ankles to weaken the tape holding them was more difficult to accomplish without being noticed, but she had forced some pliancy into the thick coil of white adhesive above her feet.

Just a little more time and I can break them, she assured herself.

She peeked under her blindfold. It wasn't easy. It required her to turn her head at an uncomfortable angle and look down past her nose, but it let her keep tabs on Elara, who lurked just inside the open doorway. The Catullan was on alert for any sign of someone drawing near. Her disruptor remained always at the ready, which suggested to Joanna that the other woman expected their predicament to lead to violence. The notion of becoming collateral damage galled Joanna, but she vowed not to go down without a fight.

Joanna pulled her right leg upward until the tape refused to stretch. Then she pushed that leg down and lifted the other. Behind her back, she stressed the tape around her wrists with the sort of patience that enabled wind and rain to wear down mountains. All it would take for her to break free was pressure and time. Pressure she could apply at will. She hoped to have enough time to finish what she had started.

In the corridor a soft electronic chime announced the arrival of a lift car. Someone was coming. Correctly anticipating Elara's reaction—a quick check of her prisoner before turning to face the newcomer—Joanna ceased her escape efforts and sat still. After Elara turned away, Joanna put her head to the floor so she could steal a better look at whoever was outside.

There was only a single set of footsteps. Whoever it was had come alone.

Elara called out, "Stop! Who are you?"

A man answered. "I have the food, water, and commode you requested."

The sound of her father's voice made Joanna freeze and gasp ever so slightly. She wondered if Elara had noticed, but couldn't dare to sneak a look at her.

The Catullan remained suspicious. "Turn around. Lift your shirt."

"I'm not armed," he said. "I didn't bring anything except what you asked for."

Joanna resumed her fight to break her bonds as the conversation continued.

"You're no security officer," Elara said. "What are you?"

"I'm a doctor. If it's all right, I'd like to make sure neither of you is hurt."

"We're fine. Leave the supplies and go."

The tape on Joanna's wrists tore. One good pull and her hands would be free. But even through the blindfold she sensed Elara was watching her—or was that just paranoia? Still, she paused her efforts while her father pleaded with Elara.

"I just want to know that she's all right."

Elara grew angry. "I gave Kirk proof of life ten minutes ago. I'm not doing it again."

"Please, just let me see her. It's not that much to ask."

"Hang on—who is she to you? Do you two know each—?" Realization dawned upon Elara. "She's your daughter! That's it, isn't it!"

No more waiting. Joanna broke the tape on her wrists with a final jerk.

"Trade me for her," her father begged. "Let her go!

She's just a child." His pleading covered the soft rip of Joanna severing the tape on her feet. "I'm a Starfleet officer, a much more valuable hostage. Take me and let the girl go free."

"I don't think so."

Joanna could hear the sneer behind Elara's words.

She pulled off her blindfold and leaped at the Catullan without a word of warning.

The rest happened so fast that Joanna barely registered any of it. Her fist connected with Elara's face, then she grabbed the woman's wrist as the disruptor in that hand went off. They tumbled through the lockup's open doorway, into the corridor. Noise and light, smoke and the reek of scorched tile. Elara elbowed Joanna in the throat. As Joanna staggered from the blow she tore the weapon from Elara's grasp but couldn't hold it. It clattered to the floor and bounced out of reach. Then Elara's foot struck Joanna's jaw and launched her backward.

Her father grabbed Elara, but the Catullan threw her head back and smashed it into his face. He let go of her and stumbled, his eyes watering and blood spilling from his nose. Elara drew a stiletto from under her kitchen uniform jacket and lunged toward him.

Joanna saw the disruptor and dived for it. Her hand closed on it, and she rolled with her arm outstretched. Acting on instinct, she aimed down the length of her arm and fired.

The crimson beam struck at the speed of thought and slammed into Elara's chest.

Only when the knife fell from Elara's hand did Joanna cease firing.

The Catullan's eyes went blank, and she pitched face-first to the floor.

Joanna's father stumbled toward her. She struggled to her feet and met him in a tearful embrace. He peppered the side of her face with grateful kisses of relief. "Are you okay?"

"Yeah, are you?"

He regarded her with amazement. "Where did you learn to do that?"

"There's a Krav Maga class in the rec center on Tuesdays and Thursdays."

A hearty laugh shook his entire body as he held her close again. "I want to yell at you, but you just saved my life."

She sleeved away some of the blood on his upper lip. "Let's not keep score."

"Deal." He let go of Joanna and kneeled beside Elara. He pressed his fingers to the fallen woman's throat, then with his free hand pulled out his communicator. "McCoy to Captain Kirk."

"Go ahead, Bones."

"Bit of a snafu up here, Jim. The good news is, the suspect's down."

"What's the bad news?"

"I think she might be dead."

Joanna stared in disbelief at the weapon in her hand, then handed it to her father. "Dad, how can she be dead? It's only set for stun."

"Stand by, Jim." He closed his communicator, examined Elara's disruptor, then cocked one eyebrow. "That's odd. Did she inject any drugs from the lockup? Maybe as a precaution against sedatives being snuck in?"

"She was mixing something before you contacted her," Joanna said. "Hang on—the vials she pulled must still be in the trash." She went to the lockup, dug through its refuse bin, and returned to her father with several half-drained medication vials. "Are these what killed her?"

His keen eyes perused the various labels, then his expression brightened with the ghost of a devilish smirk. "No, but that's what she wants us to think." He flipped open his communicator. "Jim, cancel that call to the morgue—and have security prep a spot in the brig."

"Acknowledged. They're on their way up. Kirk out."

Joanna was baffled as her father put away his communicator. "Wait—she's *alive*?"

"Yup, and due for one hell of a headache when she wakes up—on the *Enterprise*."

Twenty

Always in motion. That was what Una saw most clearly about the Jatohr's city on the sea. Everywhere she looked, something was moving. The airspace above its organically rounded megastructures was perpetually choked with fast-moving transports; its promenades were busy with the massive sentient gastropods. Every plaza stood packed with bulbous vessels that harbored other, smaller craft, giving Una the impression she was looking at an attack fleet.

She moved from one concealed space to another, with Shimizu and Martinez at her back. The city's strangely organic shapes exhibited a tendency to be separated by irregular gaps where the curves of one structure intersected those of another. The three Starfleet officers made use of those hidden spaces—though it sometimes meant crawling on all fours—to move unseen from the city's periphery almost to its core and their objective: the Jatohr's headquarters.

At an open patch between two vaguely conch-shaped towers, Una held up a hand to halt her companions. "Sentry globe. Back." They retreated deeper into the shadows of cover.

A prismatic spill of light danced over the ground beyond their shelter as an eerie atonal keening resounded into a haunting chorus with itself. Within the city, these were the telltale signs of a sentry globe passing close overhead. A half dozen or so of the radiant spheres—similar to the automated sentry devices she had seen the Jatohr use on Usilde many years earlier—circled the megalopolis on a fairly regular schedule. Because of what Shimizu and Martinez had told her about those unlucky enough to be intercepted by the spheres in the past, Una had made avoiding the automated guardians a mission priority.

Darkness returned, along with blessed silence.

"Okay," Una said. "Let's go." She crawled out first and led the way.

The trio stole forward, vigilant for any sign of the Jatohr or their sentries. Hunched over, they scurried along a narrow ledge that circled the great onion-shaped dome of what Martinez had said was the Jatohr's headquarters. Far below, in a vast common at the heart of the city, stood an armada of asymmetrical vessels attended by legions of armed and armored Jatohr.

"They look ready for business," Shimizu said, careful to keep his voice down.

Martinez eyed the alien attack force with fear and hatred. "Look at them all. If they ever break through to our universe—"

"That's what we're here to prevent," Una said. She hoped the reminder would keep her friends focused on the mission rather than on the odds against its success. Ahead of her, their narrow ledge was intersected by a vertical groove that narrowed as it traveled up the curving slope of the dome to its apex. At the intersection, it was just thin enough that she could reach either side without fully extending her arms, and angled sufficiently away from a vertical drop that she could hope to shift herself inside it without immediately going into free fall.

Prudence compelled her to wick the sweat from her palms with her uniform tunic before she began her ascent. A nervous look back at Martinez and Shimizu netted her two in return. "Are you men ready for this?"

"No," Shimizu said.

Martinez looked stricken. "Not even remotely."

"Good. If you'd said yes, I'd have declared you mentally unfit to continue."

Shimizu frowned. "I knew it had to be a trick question."

Una knew the transition into the vertical channel would be the most perilous phase. Rather than dwell on it, she committed to it, in one smooth leap, arms apart, feet following.

She landed with her back in the groove, then slipped several centimeters before her palms and boot soles found traction on the dome's nacreous surface. Her muscles ached and her limbs trembled at the strain of supporting her weight while pressing outward against the groove's walls to keep from plummeting—a technique one of her mountaineering instructors at the Academy had called chimneying. With effort, she shifted one extremity at a time and started her long climb toward the dome's distant, flattened apex.

There was no point looking down to gauge Martinez's and Shimizu's success at the transition or their progress in the climb. They would either stick or fall, complete the ascent or slip down the groove to certain death. Watching them would have no effect on their performance, so Una kept her mind trained on her own predicament.

One hand at a time. Then the opposite foot. Lift and set. Lift and set.

If I have timed this correctly, we should be able to summit the dome and have ninety seconds to find an ingress point before the next sentry globe passes this building.

The climb was slow and arduous. Unable to see above and behind herself, Una trusted her senses of orientation and gravity to tell her when she was close enough to the top of the dome to risk turning over to continue the ascent on all fours. Gazing out at an unnervingly dark seascape, she found herself curious at the absence of wind buffeting her and the others. At this altitude she expected at least mild turbulence, but the air was as calm as the sea had been. Before she could speculate about this new peculiarity of the alternate universe, she realized she was lying nearly flat on top of the dome, so she relaxed her handholds. Stable at that angle, she turned over and clambered forward onto the structure's level rooftop.

Shimizu and Martinez joined her roughly one minute apart. As the two men caught their breath, Una studied the entranceway in the center of the rooftop. It was sealed with an irislike portal similar to those the Jatohr had used for doors inside the citadel on Usilde.

"Does either of you know how to open this?"

Alarmed, Shimizu said, "We thought you knew."

Martinez thumped the side of his fist against the doorway's contracted iris. "Bet you wish you'd held on to your phaser now, eh, Number One?" He corrected himself: "Sorry—Captain."

"I'm not sure we could shoot through it even if we wanted to. Not without bringing the city down on our heads. Look for anything that might be a control mechanism."

The trio split up and pawed at the glassy-smooth surfaces around the doorway. Shimizu looked skeptical. "Wouldn't the door be locked?"

A shrug from Martinez. "Why would it be? Who expects someone to come in through the roof? And it's not as if the Jatohr are used to thinking in terms of internal security."

"True," Una said. "The Jatohr aren't even used to sharing a universe with other intelligent life-forms. The concept of a locking door—" The portal dilated open, interrupting her thought.

Shimizu smiled and pointed at a grouping of five colored dots on the surface of the raised dome housing the portal. "Found it. Touch the bottom three dots at once and 'open sesame.'"

"Good work, Tim." Una led them inside, eager to get off the roof before the next pass of the sentry globes. "Move quickly, but tread lightly."

The curving passageway was roughly oval in shape, with a flattened bottom. Every surface Una could see was composed of the same pearlescent substance that was ubiquitous in the Jatohr city. As she, Shimizu, and Martinez followed the corridor, Una got the impression it sloped downward in a gradual spiral. Then it let out onto a platform surrounded by a vast expanse of shadowy open space. She halted at the end of the passage and signaled Martinez and Shimizu to hang back while she scouted the path ahead.

Outside, the platform appeared to be deserted. A deep humming of great machines filled the cavernous interior of the dome, which Una realized was hollow. In the darkness, distant lights of many colors flickered, pale and spectral. "Okay," she whispered over her shoulder. "Stay with me." They advanced onto the circular platform, which vibrated under Una's feet.

The trio reached the edge of the platform and peered over it.

Beneath their stationary top platform rotated a succession of ever-wider platforms, which were evenly spaced along the vertical axis of the building's core pillar. It was a design Una had seen before: it was a much larger version of the tower inside the citadel on Usilde.

This one was also far more densely populated. Clusters of Jatohr moved about on the lower levels, their origins and destinations as inscrutable to Una as their objectives. Just like their kin whom Una had seen on Usilde, the ones toiling below were enormous gastropods. Their bodies were mostly armored in synthetic, opalescent shells, but their undersides were bare to facilitate their sole means of locomotion: a single great rubbery foot that propelled them slowly by means of muscular undulations. Protruding from each Jatohr's upper body was a pair of limbs sheathed in metallic coils and terminating in clasping extremities. To Una, a Jatohr's most disturbing feature was its bare, glistening head crowned with six pairs of sensory tentacles.

Martinez said softly, "This definitely looks like the party we came to find."

"Agreed," Una said. "Though I doubt we'll be welcomed as guests if they see us."

"It's our own fault for coming empty-handed," Shimizu said. "We should've brought a bottle of wine or a nice dessert."

"Save the jokes, Tim," Una said. "Find a way to access their computers." She regretted having to rebuke him. Secretly, she was glad he was rediscovering his sense of humor.

The trio retreated from the platform's edge and moved toward the wide core cylinder. Circling it counterclockwise from the entrance to the spiral ramp, they arrived at a bank of consoles that resembled the ones Una had seen inside the Usilde citadel. "Here we go. Now let's see what we can learn about the Jatohr and their mission."

Martinez was confused. "You know how to use this thing?"

"I've spent the better part of two decades studying every scan I made of the Jatohr and their technology. I still don't know it as well as I know the helm of a starship, but I think I've got a handle on the basics." She keyed in commands, grateful once again for her eidetic memory and the years she had spent cracking the Jatohr's programming language with help from dedicated Starfleet computers. Then she noticed how fixated Shimizu and Martinez were on her work. "Would one of you keep an eye out for armored slugs, please?"

Shimizu backed away, his mien apologetic. "Aye, Captain."

As Una resumed her efforts, Martinez asked, "What are you trying to do?"

"First, I'm tapping into the Jatohr's sensor logs, to see exactly how long it's been in our universe since I arrived in this one." The system behaved contrary to her expectations a few times before she found what she sought. "Forty-five days. Good. That means we still have fifteen days to make the rendezvous." She stopped and thought about time's passage. "Wait. How can it have been forty-five days? It didn't . . . I mean, I don't . . ." Then, reflecting on her time since stepping through the doorway, her memories of crossing the desert suddenly felt longer and more surreal than ever before. She looked at Martinez. "Raul, how long do you think it's been since you were sent here?"

"A hundred years? Maybe a hundred and ten?"

"So your perception of time's passage here is slower than real time at home, but mine is faster? How can that be?"

"I don't know. Maybe because I'm human and you're Illyrian?"

It was a reasonable hypothesis; residents of the Illyrian colonies were raised with far more rigorous mental training than were most of their fellow Federation citizens. "Maybe. Something to think about—after we get home." She entered more commands into the Jatohr's computer system. "Now I'm sending all the sentry globes on a permanent vacation. That should clear the way for our people to reach the gateway when it opens and make it easier for us to get out of here in one piece."

"Neat trick. What else have you got up your sleeve?"

"If this works, I should be able to program one of the Jatohr's transport pods to pick us up on the roof and take us to the gateway site. Which means we don't need to be—"

Shimizu cut in: "Um, Captain?"

She and Martinez turned to see a matte-black sentry globe hovering in the dark above Shimizu, who was trapped in a silent, sickly green beam emanating from the sphere.

Creeping onto the platform from the entranceway in the main pillar was a line of armed Jatohr. The first three had already cleared one another's lines of fire and aimed their stafflike weapons at her and Martinez. The triangular mouth of the lead Jatohr contorted as it spoke in a string of gurgling noises that Una's communicator translated with immediate ease:

"Surrender or die, creatures."

Twenty-one

"How's your head?" Kirk's question lingered without an answer as he watched Elara stir to consciousness on the other side of a force field in the *Enterprise*'s brig.

The young Catullan woman sat up on her bunk and massaged the back of her neck, then glared from under her tousled pink-and-violet hair at him and Spock. "Not bad, considering I expected to wake up in a body bag." A sweep of her hand pushed her hair from her eyes and revealed the lime-and-yellow tattoo on her high forehead. "Don't suppose I could get a drink?"

Spock motioned toward the bulkhead opposite her bed. "There is a water dispenser behind that panel and a refresher nook in the aft corner."

"I was hoping for something a bit more intoxicating."

"Life is full of disappointments," Kirk said.

She rolled her eyes. "No need to tell *me* that." A sullen stare. "So, what do you want?"

"Information," Spock said. "We have confirmed you are Elara Soath of Catullus, and that you have, until recently, resided on the Orion homeworld. Why did you come to Centaurus?"

Her brooding became an air of jejune mischief. "To get an education."

Kirk's patience frayed. "Enough games. We know the

university job is just part of your cover. We want to know who you're *really* working for."

If she felt the least bit intimidated, she hid it well. "Who do *you* think I work for?"

"I think you're on the Orion Syndicate's payroll."

"Never heard of it." She reclined on her bunk, a portrait of sublime indifference.

While Kirk simmered, Spock carried on. "We can prove that you have sent and received numerous messages from an individual on the Orion homeworld since your arrival on Centaurus. Do you deny this?"

"Why would I? I lived on Orion for years. Just because I moved to the Federation doesn't mean I cut all my old friends out of my life. Don't you ever talk to people from home?"

"No, not as such."

A feigned frown of insincere pity. "Must be a bore being you."

Her insouciance grated on Kirk. "The same person you talked to on Orion was also in regular contact with a known Orion Syndicate operative—a Tiburonian man named Jorncek. Who, it turns out, just yesterday robbed the very same pharmaceutical lockup in which you staged a hostage crisis." He waited for any sign of a reaction, to no avail. "Care to explain that?"

"I'm no solicitor, but I'm pretty sure guilt by association doesn't actually count as evidence in a Federation court of law."

"True. Let me tell you what *does* constitute evidence in our legal system. Firing a deadly weapon in a public place. Taking a hostage. Assault on, and attempted murder of, a civilian and an unarmed Starfleet officer. Being arrested in possession of a deadly weapon and a contraband signal scrambler. Resisting arrest."

Elara sighed. "Is that all you have? My lawyer will say I fled from the Klingons, whom I saw first. What you call assault and attempted murder I'll claim was self-defense. I'll cop to the weapons charge and the contraband, then plead to a reduced charge of destroying public property. I'll serve twenty months, tops, in one of your cushy penal resorts."

With a look, Kirk cued Spock to deliver their retort.

"I suspect your sentence will be greatly extended when the Starfleet Judge Advocate General files charges of espionage, illegal surveillance, and treason. Once convicted, you will be sentenced to no fewer than fifteen years at the maximum-security Tantalus Penal Colony."

His threat made Elara sit up and face them, this time without pretense. "What are you talking about? What do you mean 'treason'?"

"As you noted, Miss Soath, you emigrated to the United Federation of Planets. If you were merely residing here on a vocational or academic permit, you still would be charged with espionage and illegal surveillance. But as a provisional émigré, you agreed to be subject to the laws as they apply to citizens of the Federation—including the statutes that govern treason."

Her intense façade melted away, leaving only the frightened eyes of a young woman fresh out of options. "You're bluffing."

"We're not," Kirk said. "We found your DNA on hidden surveillance devices inside the conference room where the peace talks took place. That's enough to indict you as a spy—and make you an accomplice to the disappearances of Councillor Gorkon and Mister Zeroh."

Elara's face blanched. "No, you don't understand—"

"Then *make* me understand," Kirk said.

She struggled to collect herself. "I need legal counsel. I want to cut a deal."

"Talk to me," Kirk said. "Right here, right now, or no deal. Ever."

It was clear she knew she was in no position to make demands. Suddenly a bundle of nerves, she started to pace inside the confines of her cell. "Yes—I was hired to spy on the conference and report back. But that was all. It was just intelligence gathering. We had nothing to do with the people who vanished."

"Who's 'we'?"

"Me and my boss. The Red Man."

Intrigued, Spock asked, "Why do you call him 'the Red Man'?"

She looked at Spock as if he had grown antennae. "Because he's *red*."

Sensing that wasn't going to be a productive avenue of discussion, Kirk asked, "How do you know your boss wasn't involved?"

"Because he was even more shocked by the news than I was."

"So if your people didn't get rid of Gorkon and Zeroh, who did?"

"I don't know! But it wasn't me. Okay?"

Kirk kept his countenance stern. "We'll see." He walked toward the exit. "Spock."

They left the brig and halted in the corridor as soon as the door slid closed behind them. Kirk looked to his friend for counsel. "What do you think of her story?"

"It does comport with the facts we already possess. And her reactions were consistent with genuine surprise and fear."

"Good enough for me. Hand her over to the planetary authorities—then put all our people to work on finding that Romulan bird-of-prey. Because it's here, Spock—I can feel it."

Spock lifted an eyebrow. "We should use caution, Captain. If Major Sadira has returned with the Transfer Key, there is no telling how much damage she might be able to inflict with it."

"Exactly why we need to stop her now, Spock—and at any cost."

———

McCoy switched off his medical tricorder and reset the biobed's overhead display to standby. "That should do it. You're fit as a fiddle."

Joanna sat up and swung her legs off the bed. "I've never understood that phrase. How fit is a fiddle, exactly? Fitter than a flute? What about a piano?"

"How would I know? I'm a doctor, not a linguist." His remark earned a smile from his daughter, who had been hearing his *I'm a doctor* quips all her life. He set aside his diagnostic tools. "I guess I owe you a real thank-you for saving my life down there."

She tried to deflect his gratitude. "No, you don't."

"Yes, I do. That crazy little minx would've skewered me if not for you. *Thank you.*"

A warm and heartfelt smile. "You're more than welcome, Dad."

He helped her off the biobed. "I still can't get over you—throwing punches, firing a disruptor, all like some kind of daredevil." He regarded her with a newly deepened sense of paternal pride. "When did you get so strong?"

"When you weren't looking."

"That's always when it happens, isn't it?"

Suddenly concerned, she looked around. "What time is it?"

"Just after fourteen hundred."

"No, I mean, what time is it in New Athens? I have a class at three o'clock."

"Don't worry about it." He gestured toward himself. "Stay. Have dinner with me."

Her chipper mood started to fade. "Thanks, Dad, but I really should get back down to campus. Can you walk me to the transporter room?"

"Actually, I plan on walking you to some guest quarters."

She pulled away, suspicious. "What're you talking about?"

"Sweetheart, you've had two brushes with death in less than twenty-four hours—"

"And I'm still standing," Joanna cut in. "Damn it, Dad, when are you going to stop trying to protect me?"

"Never."

Her raised hand prevented him from blurting out any more mawkish sentiments. "This has to stop, Dad. There's a fine line between protecting and *over*-protecting. And you're crossing it." She gathered her personal effects from a low rolling table at the foot of the biobed. "I know I'm only a student, but I'm serious about being there for my patients and my coworkers."

How could he make her see things his way without divulging classified information she wasn't allowed to know? He couldn't tell her of the captain's suspicion that a Romulan warship was in the system, threatening not only to derail the conference but perhaps ignite a war and condemn countless innocent souls to exile in a strange parallel universe. He wasn't allowed to warn her or any other civilians just how close they all were to becoming the flash point of a war that would be exceptionally brief but, for everyone on Centaurus, horrifically final.

"One day," he said, blocking her path to the door. "That's all I'm asking for. Stay on the ship for one day while we try to sort out this mess with the conference."

"You're asking a lot more than that, Dad. You're asking me to let you make my decisions for me. To go back to being a child instead of a woman living her own life."

She had spoken softly, but her words cut like a blade through his heart. He knew she was right. Even in the face of all that he knew but couldn't say, she was still right. It was her life, not his. *If I really love her, I need to respect her and her choices.*

He stepped out of her way.

Joanna walked past him, then paused as the door opened. She looked back. "Thank you." A wan smile of forgiveness. "I could use some company for the walk to the transporter room."

He beamed with delight. "It would be my honor." He offered her his arm, and she looped hers around it. Walking with her, he longed for the time when he had held her tiny toddler hands and swung her through the air—but those days were gone.

All these years, when I wasn't looking, my little girl grew up . . . without me.

━━━━━━━

Sulu stood back from the panel. "What do you think, Mister Spock? Could it work?"

"The principle is sound. But its implementation could prove challenging." Spock looked up from the science console when he heard the turbolift doors open. As Kirk stepped onto the bridge of the *Enterprise*, the first officer said, "Captain, we may have something."

Kirk detoured off his route to the command chair and circled the aft upper deck to join Sulu and Spock. "Good news, I hope."

"Perhaps. Mister Sulu has suggested a means of finding the cloaked Romulan vessel."

"Let's hear it," Kirk said, pivoting toward the helmsman.

Sulu eyed the schematic he had sent to Spock's station. "Triangulation, sir. It's something I've been thinking about since we tracked that bird-of-prey after the attacks on the Neutral Zone outposts last year." He called up additional data on a secondary screen. "Our sensors registered fleeting contacts, but couldn't pinpoint their source when the Romulan ship maneuvered while cloaked." He nodded at the plan on the main display as he continued. "But, if we can coordinate three synchronized sensor fields, spaced far enough apart, we might be able to maintain a sensor lock long enough to resolve a firing solution."

The captain studied the proposal with shrewd focus. "It's a good idea, Mister Sulu. But if the Romulans learned as much from our last encounter as we did, it might not be enough."

Spock said, "A concern I expressed as well. However, if the ship we mean to find is armed with the Transfer Key, we possess an advantage we lacked in our previous meeting."

"Explain."

"The Key needs vast amounts of energy to function, even at short range. If, as we suspect, the Romulans have been using it from orbit, or perhaps from even greater distances, its power consumption will be considerable—as will its emission of tau neutrinos, charge-free leptons that, in theory, should be able to escape the Romulans' cloaking field."

Kirk was dubious. "Leptons aren't the easiest particles to detect."

"True. But a targeted sensor protocol, combined with Mister Sulu's triangulation method, could track even small quantities of tau neutrinos at ranges of up to twenty-five light-minutes."

"How long to make it work?"

"Modifications to the *Enterprise*'s sensors would take less than one hour," Spock said.

Sulu added, "We'll need ninety minutes to prep the second node."

"What *is* the second node, Lieutenant?"

"An equatorial sensor station on the planet's surface. It's operated remotely by the astronomy department of New Athens University."

"We're commandeering a *civilian* observatory?"

Spock interjected, "It is the only facility on the planet with the requisite hardware, software, and power supply to serve as part of our detection network."

It became evident the captain's appraisal of Sulu's plan was souring with each new detail. "Spock . . . dare I ask what the third node is?"

"For maximal effectiveness, it will need to be another starship, one with sensor capabilities comparable to those of the *Enterprise*."

Kirk's brow knit with irritation. "You mean the Klingons."

"The *HoS'leth* would be a viable candidate, yes."

Noting the captain's displeasure, Sulu said, "I just provided a theory."

Kirk pondered the data on the displays. "Including the Klingons isn't something we can do on a whim. For one thing, it would mean sharing classified sensor protocols."

"Not to mention persuading them to help in the first place," Sulu said.

"Be that as it may," Spock said, "without their participation, we have no reliable means of locating a cloaked Romulan vessel in time to halt further attacks."

The captain sighed, then turned toward the communications post. "Lieutenant Uhura. Get me a priority-one channel to Admiral Wong at Starfleet Command. Let her know it's a matter of Federation security."

"Aye, sir."

Pivoting back toward Spock and Sulu, Kirk added, "It won't be easy, but I'll get the brass to sign off on sharing sensor protocols with the Klingons. Which means our last hurdle is going to be convincing the Klingons to cooperate. Any ideas on that front?"

Spock concocted a plan. "Securing their help will require diplomatic skills far beyond our experience. . . . Fortunately, we are acquainted with someone eminently qualified to assist us."

Twenty-two

For the second time in as many days, Ambassador Sarek found himself surrounded by Klingons in the foyer of Prang's dormitory suite with a disruptor aimed at his head. Repetition failed to make his predicament any less vexing on this occasion than it had been the day before.

Prang said with a sneer, "You should not have come back, Vulcan."

"I am a patient man, Councillor, but, having come in pursuit of our mutual interest, I must confess I find your incivility most counterproductive."

His sangfroid irked the brash Klingon politician. "What 'mutual interest'? And don't tell me 'peace,' because that's the Federation's desire, not ours."

"I speak of turning our strength against our shared enemy—our true foe: the cowards who strike from the shadows to fan the flames of our mistrust." When he saw Prang lower his weapon by the most incremental degree, he added, "The Romulans."

His invocation of that reclusive interstellar power gave Prang pause. The councillor lowered his weapon a few degrees further, though it remained at the ready. "You have proof?"

"We have compelling evidence," Sarek said. "Proof will come in the form of their starship brought to heel by our combined efforts. Assuming, of course, you wish to avenge yourselves upon the *petaQpu'* who took Councillor Gorkon from you." Sarek found it distasteful to resort to such aggressive proposals, but this negotiation needed to appeal to the Klingons' sensibilities rather than his own.

Durok, a junior member of the Klingon delegation, pulled Prang aside and confided something to him while their backs were turned. They returned to the conversation once again masked with distrust. Prang said, "We know of no Romulan weapon that could have taken Gorkon without breaching our shields."

"I am informed the weapon they used is one not of their own design, but plundered from an alien race of unknown origin. Some of this device's properties are known to Starfleet, as are certain weaknesses of the Romulan cloaking device." Sarek folded his hands at his waist, to enhance his professorial demeanor. "The Federation has granted me permission to share this and other classified intelligence with you, in exchange for the assistance of your vessel in orbit."

Prang holstered his disruptor and, with a downward sweep of his hand, ordered all his compatriots to do the same. "What sort of assistance?"

"A hunt. The *Enterprise* will share with the *HoS'leth* special sensor protocols for tracking the Romulan ship. An observatory on the planet's surface will help triangulate the position of the cloaked bird-of-prey that has been playing us for fools and pitting us against each other."

A murmur circuited the room, passed from one Klingon to the next, until once again Durok pulled Prang aside. When the aide finished, Prang nodded, then returned to face Sarek. "A generous offer, Ambassador. And exactly the sort of cunning trick we have come to expect of Starfleet—and Captain Kirk."

"I assure you, we are engaged in no deceit. Our intentions—"

"Spare me, Vulcan. How do we know these so-called sensor protocols aren't a sly means of sabotaging our starship?"

"We would have nothing to gain by such action."

"Wouldn't you? Crippling the *HoS'leth* would certainly enhance your bargaining position. You would have a capital ship in orbit, and we would be defenseless."

Their illogic confounded him. "An irrelevant detail. The original terms of our talks specified there were to be no capital ships in orbit. Though, as I recall, your side was the first to abrogate that clause of our prenegotiation agreement."

"Stop splitting hairs, Vulcan. For all I know, this is just a distraction—an attempt to deny your role in Gorkon's murder! We're not giving you access to our ship!"

"We have not asked for any access. Quite the contrary, in fact. We are offering to share our sensor protocols with you." Sarek directed a look at Durok, who he suspected was likely an intelligence operative posing as a political adviser. "I should think that would be incentive enough to merit your aid against a foe that wishes to see us both hobbled as interstellar powers."

As he had hoped, his criticism compelled Durok to whisper once more in Prang's ear. This time the councillor listened with narrowed eyes, as if being told something he did not want to hear. As his frown deepened, Sarek became certain Prang was being handled by his apparent subordinates and that he had just been given directions he found galling.

"For the sake of discussion," Prang said, "let us assume I accede to your request. If your story turns out to be true, and we expose a Romulan vessel shadowing the conference, what action is Starfleet prepared to take?"

"They have been ordered to neutralize any Romulan interference." Hoping the question implied they were close to an agreement, Sarek asked, "Does this mean you will instruct General Kovor to join the effort?"

Prang clenched his jaw. He approached Sarek, set a hand on the ambassador's back, and guided him out of the foyer, into another room away from the rest of the Klingon delegation. In a harsh whisper he said, "I can try, but I cannot promise Kovor will listen."

"Are you not a member of the High Council?"

"I am. But Kovor is a powerful general from a noble house, one long opposed to mine. If he refuses an order to cooperate with the *Enterprise*, my ability to compel his obedience will be quite limited." He glanced over his shoulder, as if fearful of eavesdroppers. "I also would not be surprised if Kovor used a battle against a Romulan ship as cover for a 'friendly fire' strike against the *Enterprise*. He would call it an accident, but the Organians might not see it that way."

The profound shift in Prang's outlook did not escape Sarek's notice. "You have shown little regard for the Organians' reactions up until now. Why exhibit such abrupt concern?"

"I posture out of political necessity. If I do not cry for war at every turn, my rivals on Qo'noS will brand me as soft, and my father will send my younger brother to represent our house on the High Council. At which point I'll become superfluous—which means I'll be expected to fall on my *tIq'leth*, to shed my dishonor along with my blood." Prang's disgruntled sigh devolved into a low growl. "I will tell General Kovor to help the *Enterprise* with its hunt—but you need to warn Kirk: the general is *not* to be trusted."

———

As soon as the *Velibor*'s sensors came back online, bad news followed.

Centurion Mirat leaned in beside tactical officer Pilus, who had taken over the command-deck post to replace the ship's newly promoted second-in-command, Subcommander Kurat. Pilus was young and nervous and eager to please, and the tremors in his voice betrayed his fear that he would be punished merely for reporting facts—an apprehension Mirat found more reasonable the longer Sadira remained in command. He tried calming the young officer by speaking in dulcet tones. "What have you found, Pilus?"

"New active sensor frequencies from the *Enterprise*," Pilus said. "And matching frequencies from a subspace radio observatory on the planet's surface."

"What do I need to know about these frequencies?"

Before the young tactical specialist could answer, Mirat became aware of people at his back. Not wanting to compound Pilus's fears by reacting with alarm, Mirat made a slow turn to face Kurat and Sadira. The human woman got to the point. "What has he found?"

"New sensor protocols from the *Enterprise*," Mirat said.

The news put Sadira on her guard. "What of them?"

Pilus adjusted his stance to let the senior personnel see his console displays. "They're using amplified harmonics in their subspace pulses."

Kurat and Sadira looked as confused by Pilus's technical jargon as Mirat was. To spare the senior officers the potential embarrassment of having to admit ignorance, Mirat asked Pilus, "Why is that significant, Sublieutenant?"

"It means they're looking for something different."

Mirat filled in the rest: "Which means there's something new they expect to find—something that will lead them to us."

Kurat shouldered past Mirat to gain access to the tactical console, which he knew better than anyone else on the ship. "If we know their sensor frequency, can we work backward from that to figure out what they're seeking?"

"Possibly," Pilus said. "But it could take days, and it would be guesswork, at best."

This could be an opportunity, Mirat realized. "Major, if we're in danger of being revealed by the *Enterprise*, perhaps now would be a good time to withdraw to the outer edge of the system and engage silent-running procedures."

"Don't be a fool, Centurion. For all we know, the *Enterprise* is cycling through a range of frequencies, hoping to get lucky."

Pilus interjected, "Then why is the observatory on the surface using the same frequency?"

His question drew a hard look from Sadira. "What did you say?"

"The observatory," Pilus said. "It's using the same frequency as the *Enterprise*."

Sadira pointed at the tactical console. "Show me."

Pilus called up multiple screens of sensor data. "They appear to be creating overlapping scan fields, though their angles of detection are limited by the planet and its moon."

Mirat saw the trap taking shape and was in no mood to watch it snare the *Velibor*. He left Pilus to stand by the communications officer. "Nevira, are we picking up any signal traffic between the *HoS'leth* and the *Enterprise*?"

"Affirmative," Nevira said.

Fear began to crack Sadira's mask of arch superiority. "What are they saying?"

Nevira covered the wireless transceiver in her ear and concentrated while working her panel's controls. "Unknown, Major. I'm unable to crack the channel's encryption."

Time was running out, Mirat was certain of it. He hurried to Sadira's side and prayed he could make her see reason. "Major, if the *Enterprise* has a new detection method that can pierce the cloak, and they give it to the *HoS'leth*, they'll have three active sensor matrices—"

"And they'll triangulate our position," Sadira said. "I know, Centurion."

"Then you agree: it's time to withdraw."

Her anxiety turned to mania. "Quite the contrary. It's time to land the killing stroke."

Mindful of what had happened to Bedisa when she

challenged Sadira's command decisions, Mirat chose his words with care. "Major, it is my duty as centurion to advise you in good faith. Even under the best of conditions, our ship is no match for two heavy cruisers. Right now, our only remaining advantage is the cloaking device. But if the *HoS'leth* joins the hunt, the cloak might cease to be of use—and we would then find ourselves outgunned *and* defenseless."

"True," Sadira said. "Which is why we can't afford to wait for that hammer to fall. We need to strike first, and in a way that will guarantee the peace talks collapse." Her next orders came in rapid succession. "Nevira, put together a message on a coded Starfleet frequency, one we know the Klingons recently broke. Relay a message through the planet's satellite network to the *Enterprise*, confirming we are ready to attack the *HoS'leth* on their signal. Pilus, arm a spread of plasma torpedoes—tight grouping, proximity detonation. Toporok, move us into an attack profile against the *HoS'leth*'s aft port quarter, ventral approach." As the junior officers swung into action, she ordered Kurat, "Start scanning the Klingons' compound on the surface. Find me high-value targets. And charge up the Transfer Key."

This time, even Kurat balked. "The Key? Now? After what it's done to the ship?"

"Ranimir says he solved the buffering problem," Sadira said. "Do as I command, Kurat—or I'll have you replaced by someone who will."

Kurat put his fist to his chest and saluted her. "Yes, Major."

Mirat watched the cowed young officer retreat to

the sensor console to look for targets. Shaking his head in dismay, the old centurion made his way to Sadira's side. "Have you ever commanded a starship in combat, Major?"

"No," she said. "But that's what I have you for."

"Major, please—this is madness. We've struck our blows for the Empire, but it's time to withdraw, while we still can."

Her steely gaze remained fixed on the viewscreen image of the *Enterprise* and the *HoS'leth*, cruising together in orbit of Centaurus. "Not yet, Centurion. Not while there remains any hope of peace between the Federation and the Klingons." A cruel smile tugged at the corners of her mouth. "Hate must win the day."

Twenty-three

Overkill. That was the word that sprang unbidden to Una's mind as she eyed the Jatohr platoon tasked with escorting her, Shimizu, and Martinez out of the headquarters building and across a ramp whose smooth white surface gleamed like porcelain. Her disbelief at the Jatohr's obvious fear of her and her comrades amused her so much that they were halfway across the hundred-meter-long bridge before she noticed the city was once again bathed in daylight.

We couldn't have been inside that *long, could we?* She searched for the directions of shadows, expecting to find long stretches of shade thrown by a rising sun, but the pitiless twin suns blazed from high overhead. *How can it be midday again so soon?*

The bridge was wide enough that she and her friends walked side by side with several meters to spare on either flank. A dozen armed and armored Jatohr pushed forward ahead of them, their massive, undulating foot muscles leaving a slick sheen on the bridge's surface. It wasn't slippery enough to prevent Una and the others from following, but it made their footing too uncertain to attempt making a run in any direction.

Shimizu spoke from the corner of his mouth, his voice low. "Why didn't they kill us?"

His question earned a disgusted scowl from Martinez.

"Heaven help us—are you complaining about *not* being executed?"

"No, I'm just asking: Why are we alive?"

Una thought back to her first mission on Usilde. "I once spoke to a Jatohr scientist named Eljor. He said his people were peaceful by nature. That they abhor violence."

A sidelong glance from Martinez. "Maybe your translator parsed him wrong."

"I don't think so," Una said. "Tim's right. If they wanted us dead, we would be."

"Right," Shimizu said. "So what's going on?"

Ahead of them, at the far end of the bridge, a massive round doorway dilated open on the side of a pear-shaped building composed of the same nacreous substance as everything else in the Jatohr's floating metropolis.

Una stared into the shadows beyond the doorway. "I think we're about to find out."

The trio followed their guards into the towering open space of the bulbous structure. Once inside, the eerie silence that blanketed the city gave way to a buzz of muted chatter. At first it sounded like a hiss of escaping gas, a burbling of liquid leaking from a pipe, and the buzzing of an insect hive of mind-boggling proportions. Then Una's eyes adjusted to the dim conditions inside the vast chamber. A tier spiraled up the interior of the dome above and was dotted at regular intervals by platforms jutting off the tier into the open air of the atrium. Perched on the platforms were Jatohr whose shells bore what looked like ornamental or ceremonial markings, perhaps badges of office. The floor level of the atrium was packed with Jatohr, their giant sluglike bodies pressed together in a teeming, ever-restless mass of striped orange flesh.

The slug scrum parted. The soldiers leading the trio formed a wedge and pushed their way to the great chamber's center. There the triangular formation split to either side, forming a narrow channel that led to a dais with gently sloped sides. The guards behind Una and her friends made them keep walking until the three stood on the dais, surrounded by a sea of alien faces.

A sustained near-subsonic note filled the cathedral-like space, hushing the Jatohr even as it made Una feel as if her teeth might rattle free of her jaw. She imagined she could sense her internal organs vibrating against one another as the deep, muffling drone overwhelmed her. On either side of her, Martinez and Shimizu likewise winced before the sonic onslaught.

Silence washed over them like absolution.

Then came an amplified voice full of hatred and contempt, a baritone roar Una hadn't heard in eighteen years, and had hoped never to hear again: Woryan.

"Some among us have long wondered: Will the doorway ever open again? I always knew it would. Just as I always suspected it would be you who opened it, creature Una."

A blinding spot of light drew her gaze upward, to Woryan's exalted place inside the hall. She regarded the ruthless Jatohr leader with the same contempt s/he exuded toward her and all the other denizens of the universe she considered home. "Woryan. I would say it's been too long, but that would be a lie. If I had never looked upon your face again, it would've been too soon."

"Yet here we are, creature. And this time you'll find no traitors in our ranks. No quislings waiting to aid your escape." One of hir mechanical arms reached over to a console beside hir platform and manipulated its controls with the limb's prehensile clasping digits. A harsh white light snapped on directly above the dais, cocooning Una, Martinez, and Shimizu in a blinding glare that left them unable to see any of the Jatohr in the shadows beyond.

Una smiled. "Is this meant to frighten me?"

"I ask the questions here, creature. Do you still have the Transfer Key?"

Lies seemed to be in order. "The what?"

"The master control device for the sanctuary's transfer-field generator! Do you have it?"

She turned out her pockets and shook her head. "Nope. What does it look like?"

Woryan's temper worsened. "Lies! You must have had the Key! There is no other way you could have come here." Hir outburst led to waves of gurgle-hiss chatter among hir peers. Another subsonic pulse quelled the susurrus, enabling hir to continue. "If you came here without the Key, then it must be on the other side. Is someone waiting to reopen the doorway?"

"I wish I knew. I just cross-wired your sanctuary's main console and hopped on through. I thought I left it open behind me, but I guess it closed as soon as I got here." Una shrugged. "What is one to do?"

"Do not mock me, creature."

"You need to lighten up. If you ever get your wish and

bring your band of refugees over to my universe, you'll have to get used to this kind of thing."

"She's right," Martinez added. "One look at you guys and the Tellarites won't stop dreaming up insults for at least a decade."

Woryan bellowed, "Silence!"

Una scrunched her brow. "If we're silent, we can't answer questions. Are we done?"

"Do not test my patience further, creature."

Shimizu pointed at Woryan and stage-whispered to Una, "You heard it. Don't tempt the wrath of the whatever from high atop the thing." A crackling jolt of electrical energy shot down from outside the tower of light and left a smoking scorch between Shimizu's feet. "Like that."

"Enough!" Una shouted up at the imperious Jatohr. "This is all a waste—of energy, lives, and time. We don't need to be enemies. You don't have to invade our universe, or even our galaxy. I don't know what conditions you're used to, but our realm, as you call it, has more than enough room to accommodate all your people without violence."

"That is not our way," said a different Jatohr voice.

"Wrong," Martinez hollered back. "It's not the way you knew. But it could be your way forward. Our people could help you colonize new worlds, planets you could have to yourselves."

"Planets are not enough," Woryan said. "We have always been alone in our universe, and so will we remain."

"Not in *our* universe, you won't," Shimizu quipped.

His moment of snark gave Una an idea. "Here's a

question, Woryan. If you and your people like your universes empty, why not just look for one that—and this is just a suggestion, mind you—isn't positively crammed with *billions* of other intelligent species?"

"Finding other universes that are hospitable to life but not already overrun with semi-sentient creatures such as yourselves has so far proved impossible. Every universe we have found beyond our own has either been inimical to the sustenance of organic life, or it has been infested with native forms in need of removal as a condition of our settlement." The brilliant pillar of light snapped off, leaving Una seeing a dark haze between herself and the ocean of Jatohr swaying in waves around her. Woryan continued, "This universe is dying, creature, and soon we must depart or else perish with it. Your realm is the closest dimension, and therefore the one that takes the least energy to reach. So it is there we must go."

A sickly green ray streaked down from the underside of Woryan's platform and seized Una. Like a tractor beam it lifted her half a meter off the dais—but then it began to twist the upper and lower halves of her body in different directions. She tried to hold in her cries of pain and alarm, but failed. The first of her screams echoed off the chamber's pearlescent walls as Woryan demanded, "Tell me when the portal to your universe will open again."

"I don't know," she said through teeth gritted in agony. "It's already late! Something must have gone wrong!"

The viridescent beam released her. She dropped into the waiting arms of Martinez and Shimizu, who eased her down onto the dais.

"So the gateway could open at any time," Woryan said.

"Then it is time to make ready the next phase of our invasion. When next the gateway opens, we must be there to launch our attack." Hir next words dripped with condescension. "On behalf of my people, I thank you, creatures. You have been most helpful."

The surface of the dais, which had been smooth only moments earlier, opened wide beneath them until just a narrow ring around its edge remained. Una and her friends dropped into a black pit whose rocky nadir she met with enough force to plunge her into the deeper, colder darkness of oblivion.

Twenty-four

Kovor's face filled the main viewscreen just as his rasping voice thundered in the close quarters of the *Enterprise*'s bridge. *"I don't know what trickery your ambassador worked on Prang, nor do I care. He can order me to help you—but you and I both know that's not why we're here."*

"I can't speak for your motives, General," Kirk replied, "but I make no secret of mine. I'm here to do whatever is needed to secure the peace treaty."

His declaration made Kovor sniff and growl with disdain. *"Lies, Kirk! We are men of war. Always have been. Always will be. Why deny it now?"*

"Because war has . . . *outlived* its usefulness. A new age is coming, General. We can either take a hand in building it—or we can become obsolete."

Even across the subspace channel, Kirk felt the Klingon general size him up. It was hard to tell if he was getting through to Kovor—or whether it would matter if he did. The scarred old warrior brooded behind his gray bramble of a beard. *"Had I not seen your delegation's man vanish, I wouldn't believe your story of a weapon that disappears people without a trace. But I'm not ready to put the blame on a third party when the one in front of me is far more plausible."*

"You can't be serious," Kirk said. "We have nothing to gain by—"

"*Don't you? What about the sabotage of my ship? Did you really think I'd lower my defenses and let you transmit an attack into my vessel's own memory banks?*"

Invited by a look from Kirk, Spock stepped to the captain's side to respond to Kovor. "General, if preserving the integrity of your ship's systems is your concern, I can beam over to the *HoS'leth* with the necessary sensor protocols on a data card."

"*What difference would that make?*"

"You could verify the benign nature of our shared intelligence on a dedicated system, one separate from your ship's network. When your crew has verified the data is safe, only then would it be introduced into your sensor matrix." Prodded by another glance from Kirk, the first officer added, "However, I should stress, General, that time *is* a factor."

The general swiveled his command chair away from the screen to confer with one of his off-screen subordinates. While the Klingons huddled, Kirk shot a glance to port, where Mister Scott worked at the bridge's engineering station, revising formulae he had been developing with Spock in an effort to block the targeting capabilities of the Transfer Key. Based on the engineer's angry grimaces and frustrated thumpings of the console, Kirk guessed their progress was proving slower than either of them had expected.

On the viewscreen, Kovor turned back toward the conversation. "*Very well, Kirk. Send me your first officer, and have him bring these 'upgrades' for our sensors. I'll be the judge of whether they live up to your boasts. But if I see the least hint of sabotage, I—*"

A searing flash filled the screen as an unearthly *whoop* resounded over the speakers. When the whiteout on the viewscreen faded back to a normal image, Kovor was gone, and the command crews of both ships stared in mute horror at each other across the subspace channel.

Then a geyser of Klingon epithets erupted on the bridge of the *HoS'leth*. Kirk didn't recognize any of the words he was hearing, but he would have understood their tone in any language: the Klingons wanted blood. *Most likely, mine.*

Lomila hurled herself into the command chair of the *HoS'leth*, and with one shouted command from her, the intership channel was closed. The *Enterprise's* viewscreen reverted automatically to the ship's forward view—of the *HoS'leth* coming about to face them.

Sulu declared with alarm, "Captain! They're assuming an attack posture!"

Beside him at the forward console, Chekov kept his eyes on the viewscreen as he reached for the defensive controls. "Shields up, Captain?"

At the sensor controls, Spock peered into the blue glow of the hooded display. "The *HoS'leth* has raised its shields and is charging disruptors and torpedo tubes."

From the other side of the bridge, Scott asked, "Should I sound red alert, sir?"

In the span of mere seconds, Kirk watched his mission start to unravel. He thought of the *Enterprise's* mission the year before to Organia, and of his and Spock's confrontation there with Kor, the Klingon commander who had tried in vain to subjugate the Organians, a species of energy beings who had been masquerading as mere mortals of flesh and bone. Then, too, Kirk had stood at the flash point of what had threatened to become a war between the Federation and the Klingon Empire—one the Organians had forced both sides to abandon, lest the two rival powers see their formidable militaries permanently enfeebled.

This was supposed to be the beginning of the end of all that useless posturing, a step toward a day when we can put an end to our saber rattling. Now one traitor—he corrected himself—*one spy has us back at each other's throats? Are we really this foolish? This insane?*

Spock's voice arrested his introspection. "Captain."

Kirk blinked, then remembered Sarek's criticism: *"For a man who has spent the better part of his career dealing with the Klingons, you seem not to understand them at all."*

He set his mind on a path of action. *I know them better than Sarek thinks.*

"Uhura, hail the *HoS'leth*, all frequencies."

As the lieutenant transmitted the hail, Chekov asked again, "Shields, Captain?"

"Negative, Ensign. Shields stay down. Mister Sulu, do not charge weapons."

Frightened looks were volleyed from one officer to another on the bridge, but no one spoke a word of protest. In the tense hush, Spock's voice rang out clearly. "They are locking disruptors onto multiple areas of our saucer and engineering section."

Uhura swiveled her chair toward Kirk. "Channel open, sir."

"Commander Lomila, this is Captain Kirk. We are *not* your enemy. Our shields are down, and our weapons are not charged. We are on a mission of peace and self-preservation. If you care about *either* of those things . . . hold your fire. Please respond."

On the screen, the D7 cruiser slowed its approach, then came to a halt. Its forward torpedo tube shone bright red, a harbinger of an imminent launch.

Kirk looked to Spock for new information. His first officer lifted his eyes from the sensor hood. "They are holding station six hundred kilometers off our bow. Their shields are still up; their weapon systems remain charged and locked on to our key systems."

Rising from the center seat, Kirk repeated, "Commander Lomila, please respond."

All was quiet on the bridge except for the low thrum of air moving through the vents overhead and the gentle feedback tones from the ship's computers.

Scott muttered, "What're they waiting for? They've got us dead to rights!"

"Don't rush them, Mister Scott." Kirk couldn't take his eyes off the smoldering crimson glow of the Klingon ship's torpedo tube. "If their response turns out to be bad news . . . I'm just as happy to wait for it."

———

Never in her life had Commander Lomila felt so close to being the target of a mutiny as at the moment she roared out, "Hold!"

On the main screen was the *Enterprise*, its most vulnerable points plotted and locked into the gunners' sights. Sensors had confirmed the infamous Starfleet battle cruiser was running with its shields down and its weapons disengaged. Kirk and his ship—a prize that had taunted and eluded so many Klingon starship commanders—was about to become her most decisive victory.

Then she'd heard Kirk's appeal for reason.

It stirred no pity in her warrior's heart—but it did arouse her curiosity. Why would he stand down rather than defend himself and his crew? How could he be so cavalier with his ship? Then a deeper misgiving filled her heart; who would sing songs of her victory over a vessel that had put up no defense? What honor would there be in so hollow a triumph?

Something was very wrong. She felt it.

Lieutenant Marga, the senior weapons officer and next behind Lomila in the ship's chain of command, rushed to the captain's seat and pressed himself against the base of its elevated dais. "Why do we hold? They are right there!"

"We hold because I have said it. That is all you need to know."

Gunner K'mgar looked over his shoulder at Lomila and squinted against the bright white battle lights that had switched on when the ship went into attack mode. "Commander, we can finish them in one salvo. If the enemy wants to fall on our sword, should we not oblige them?"

Grumblings of concurrence came back from all around the bridge. Lomila wondered if any of these bloodlusting *yIntaghpu'* understood the true gravity of the Organians' threat, or if they had dismissed it as a bluff, the way General Kovor had.

Marga stole a look at the *Enterprise*, then peered up at

Lomila, his whole body shaking with excitement, like an inbred *targ* at feeding time. "What now, Commander?"

"Return to your post." She swiveled a few degrees toward the communications officer. "Kowgon, tell the *Enterprise* to send us its sensor protocols. Route them to Marga's console."

"But Commander—what of the intercepted signal from the Romulans to the *Enterprise*?"

"It could easily be a ruse by the Romulans, part of their plan to sabotage the conference."

"But if our enemies are working together—"

"Then this is our chance to prove their treachery." She swung her chair aft, toward the tactical console, where Marga stood. "Check their software. If it's a trick, we vaporize them, then we crush their Romulan allies. But if these new protocols are real, I want to know."

Kowgon looked up from his station. "Sending the protocols to Marga now."

Everyone waited while Marga analyzed the files from the *Enterprise*. As he worked, Lomila kept her focus on the Starfleet vessel itself, wary for the first sign that its shields were going up or its weapons were charging. Even an attempt at retreat would be all the evidence of duplicity she would need to justify opening fire.

It took nearly a minute before Marga finished. "The protocols check out, Commander."

"Are you sure?"

"They work on the same principles we've been developing, but Starfleet's intelligence is more complete. Also, the parts of these protocols that track the alien weapon Kirk blames for the disappearances match energy waveforms recorded by our research team on the planet Usilde, where a massive installation of unknown alien origin was recently discovered."

"Understood." She returned her chair to its forward position. "Marga, release target locks on the *Enterprise*, then install the new sensor protocols. Kowgon, inform Captain Kirk we stand ready to assist him in hunting our shared but presently unseen enemy."

K'mgar looked back again. "Commander, what of General Kovor?"

"Kovor is gone," Lomila declared. "This ship is now mine. Which means from this moment forward, you will obey my orders, or you will die. Do any of you want to test me?" No one answered her challenge. "That's what I thought. Man your posts."

She looked at the *Enterprise*, shocked to think she was about to take her ship into battle beside it instead of against it. *If the Organians have their way, this will be the shape of things to come.* She shook her head. *May Kahless forgive us all.*

Twenty-five

Had he been raised a man of superstition rather than reason, Mirat would have called it a miracle. For the first time since Sadira brought the Transfer Key aboard the *Velibor*, she had succeeded in triggering it without crippling the bird-of-prey as a consequence.

Power levels continued to fluctuate throughout the ship, of course. Garbled hash stuttered across every screen on the command deck, and damage reports filtered up from the lower decks, complaining of overloads in several of the auxiliary power relays. But all those glitches could be overlooked as long as the *Velibor* retained its cloak, helm control, and weapons array.

Ensconced at the main console, Major Sadira looked pleased with herself. "Now we'll see the end of these peace talks," she said. "As soon as the *Enterprise* and the *HoS'leth* exchange fire, our mission will be accomplished, and we can set course for home."

The sensor readouts in the middle of the command console bore out Sadira's prediction. The Klingon cruiser reversed its orientation and maneuvered to engage the Federation ship in orbit of Centaurus. Mirat noted that Sadira's belief the Klingons would be more easily goaded into violent action had also proved correct—though, in hindsight, it seemed trite and obvious to the centurion.

Starfleet's way was to question first; the Klingon way was to kill.

Then both ships came to a halt facing each other . . . and nothing happened.

Sadira tensed. "What's going on? Why don't they fire?"

Nevira reacted to new intel at the communications console. "Encrypted signals are passing between the *Enterprise* and the *HoS'leth*," she said. "*Enterprise* hailed the Klingon ship. After a delay, the Klingons are responding."

Desperation crept into Sadira's tone. "What are they saying?"

"Unable to crack their cipher, Major. Trying all known keys."

Mirat had a premonition the *Velibor*'s fortunes were about to take a turn for the worse. "Pilus, focus all passive sensors on the *HoS'leth*. Tell me if their emissions change." To Sadira he said under his breath, "I suggest we shut down the Transfer Key and withdraw. *Now.*"

"Based on what? Our enemies' reluctance to fight? I can fix that." She opened a channel to the engineering deck. "Ranimir! Charge up another pulse for the Transfer Key."

"*Understood, Major. We'll need a few minutes to buffer the charge.*"

"Make it fast. We need to strike before it's too late. Command out." She closed the channel, then activated the Transfer Key's targeting interface. "We'll hit the Klingons again. That should be enough to push whoever's left on that ship into a berserker rage. Helm! Take us out of the polar magnetic field and put us on a heading for another pass at the *HoS'leth*."

The *Velibor*'s impulse engines made the hull resonate with sympathetic vibrations as the bird-of-prey sped toward another perilous flyby assault on the Klingon cruiser. Speaking out against Sadira's plan was pointless, Mirat knew. All he could do was stand at her side as she fought to lock the Transfer Key's targeting sights on to a new victim inside the *HoS'leth*.

Then came Pilus's report: "Major! The Klingons are generating new active sensor frequencies—the same kind being used by the *Enterprise* and the planetside observatory."

If Mirat was ever going to have a chance of talking sense to Sadira, this was it. "Major, they're triangulating our position!"

"No, Centurion, they're just *attempting* to. Continue the attack."

Kurat was the next to deliver bad news. "Both ships are changing course—coming about to intercept us! *Enterprise* is raising shields and charging weapons!"

Sadira jabbed at her controls. "Engineering! Why isn't my weapon ready yet?"

"Still buffering the charge," Ranimir said. *"Fire too soon and we'll fry half the ship!"*

The two starships loomed larger on the viewscreen, both speeding toward the *Velibor*. Pilus called out, "Enemy ships targeting our position!"

The major reached toward the trigger button of the Transfer Key. Mirat abandoned caution and decorum to grab Sadira's arm. "No! You'll cripple us! We must re-treat!"

She yanked her arm free, then elbowed his chin. His head struck a low bulkhead hard enough to leave him seeing spots. Sadira raged at him, "Don't you dare touch me, Centurion! I should—"

"Incoming!" Pilus shouted. "Two salvos! One from each ship!"

Sadira stared in horror at the incoming torpedo bar-rage. "Evasive!"

The *Velibor*'s engines moaned like spirits denied peace in the grave. On the viewscreen, stars wheeled and streaked into sloppy twists as the ship rolled and yawed through a desperate series of maneuvers, all in a panicked bid to escape—

Thunder and darkness, the stomach-turning lurch of chaotic motion as inertial dampers succumbed to over-whelming violent force. Mirat felt his feet leave the deck. Bodies flew and tumbled in stuttered motion as consoles flickered between life and death. Then he met a bulk-head with his shoulder and the side of his head. Gravity vanished for half a breath, then reversed, throwing him against the overhead.

Normal gravity returned and pulled him to the deck. He, like the rest of the *Velibor*'s command crew, struggled to stand and return to his post. A ghastly pall of dark gray smoke lingered at eye level inside the compartment and snaked away into the connecting corridors. Torched con-soles crackled and spat white-hot sparks. He brushed the glowing motes from his uniform and sleeved green blood from his gashed forehead. Light-headed, he staggered to his place at the main console, where he opened a channel to engineering. "Ranimir! Damage report!"

"*The cloak . . . is offline*," the chief engineer said between coughs. "*Shields . . . up.*"

Sadira, her face decorated in Terran crimson, clawed her way back to her feet. "What about the Key? Is it intact?"

"*Barely,*" Ranimir croaked.

"Forget that," Mirat cut in. "Do we have weapons?"

"*Affirmative. Plasma torpedoes . . . ready!*"

Pilus called out, "Both ships are locking weapons!"

"Plasma torpedoes on the *HoS'leth*, disruptors on the *Enterprise*! Lock and fire!"

"No!" cried Sadira, adamant in her madness. "Finish charging the Key! We—"

Mirat returned Sadira's backhanded swat and knocked her to the deck. It meant the end of his career, but that was the least of his troubles now. "This is *real* combat, you *hevam wikah*! Fight like a soldier—or make way for those who know how!"

———

There she is! Kirk gloated at the sight of his phantom foe made real in a flash of antimatter annihilation. "Stay with her, Sulu! Chekov, switch to phasers only."

The red-alert siren wailed as Spock stared into the hooded sensor display. "The Romulans are raising their shields, charging weapons, and changing speed and heading—"

"To an attack profile," Kirk interrupted. "I see it,

Spock. Scotty, more power to the forward shields. Sulu, keep showing them our nose. Chekov, status."

"Still working to lock phasers, Captain!"

"Work faster, Ensign—because here they come!"

On the viewscreen, the bird-of-prey made a rolling turn as it fired. A huge, expanding plasma charge slammed into the engineering section of the *HoS'leth* as the Romulans' disruptor banks raked the *Enterprise*'s starboard shields. The crash and boom of the shields dimpling before the attack resounded through the hull, followed by Chekov's report—"Firing!"—and the whooping cry of the phaser banks nearest the bridge being discharged.

"Report," Kirk said.

"A glancing blow off their aft shields," Spock said. "No damage."

Chekov looked over his shoulder just long enough to show Kirk an apologetic frown. "Sorry, Captain. They're just too fast!"

"Keep after them, Ensign. Increase your lead time, and let the targeting computer help." He swiveled left, toward Scott. "Damage?"

"Shields took a bruising," the engineer said. "Nothing we can't handle."

Uhura pointed at the main screen. "Captain!"

Kirk looked back to see the image of the *HoS'leth* drift across the screen as the *Enterprise* continued its mad chase of the *Velibor*. The Klingon cruiser was listing, and its port warp nacelle had gone dark. As the ship yawed to expose its underside, the massive breach in its secondary hull became visible. "How bad were they hit?"

Spock adjusted the sensors. "Scanning. . . . Major internal damage. Their warp core has been breached, and they have lost main power."

"Which means they're running without shields or disruptors," Scott added.

Sulu warned, "The Romulans are making another pass!"

White-knuckling the arms of the command chair, Kirk snapped, "Full impulse! Overtake them before they—"

The bird-of-prey unleashed another plasma torpedo, as well as a broadside with its disruptors, all of it targeted onto the *HoS'leth*.

On the *Enterprise*, everyone winced as the plasma munitions flared on impact and shredded the aft quarter of the D7 cruiser. Kirk felt a queasy sympathy for its Klingon crew as he saw the Romulan ship's disruptor beams slice through the *HoS'leth*'s engineering section, pylons, and nacelles before it banked hard to port, a split second ahead of Chekov's latest counterattack.

"They're accelerating," Sulu reported. "Moving out of phaser range and circling around for another run." He looked back at Kirk and shook his head. "We can't overtake or outmaneuver them at impulse."

Looking up from the sensors, Spock added, "I estimate we have less than ninety seconds before their next attack run, Captain."

"Sulu, put us within transporter range of the *HoS'leth*. Spock, scan for survivors." As they executed his orders, Kirk turned aft toward Uhura. "Lieutenant, hail the Klingons, tell them to stand by for evacuation. Mister Scott—"

"Charging transporters now, Captain. Standing by to drop shields and relay coordinates."

"Look sharp, Scotty. We'll only have a few seconds." On the viewscreen, a red-and-silver streak of motion, an omen of the next cycle of punishment. "Spock?"

"Reading approximately three dozen survivors on the *HoS'leth*, all in the forward section. Sending transport coordinates to Mister Scott now."

Kirk knew the timing would be close. "Sulu, try to anticipate the Romulans' attack vector, then put us between them and the *HoS'leth*. Chekov, prepare to lay down suppressing fire. Force the Romulans off their optimal firing trajectory while our shields are down."

Uhura's voice cut through the excited chatter. "Captain! Commander Lomila of the *HoS'leth* demands we not evacuate her crew."

That news drew looks of surprise from around the bridge and a glance of curious interest from Spock. Kirk took it in stride. "They want to go down with their ship. I understand that. I even respect it. But right now they're the only ones who can verify to the Klingon High Council that we were both attacked by the Romulans. If they die, the Klingons will blame us and say we faked the sensor logs." He made eye contact with Scott. "Beam them over, now."

"Aye, sir. Dropping shields. Energizing." The engineer set to work, taking remote control of the ship's multiple transporter platforms to pluck the Klingon survivors off their crippled ship.

The bird-of-prey's narrow outline took shape on the main viewscreen. Its forward plasma torpedo launcher began to glow as it charged to fire.

Still gathering sensor data, Spock announced, "The Romulan ship's energy profile is a match for the *Velibor*—the ship that aided Lisa Bates's exfiltration from the *Enterprise* with the Transfer Key." He looked up at Kirk. "Your hunch appears to have been correct, Captain."

"Then we need to find a way to stop that ship without destroying it—and get the Key back before they use it again." The bird-of-prey was close enough now for the viewscreen to render in crisp detail the stylized raptor emblem on its dorsal hull. "Time to phaser range?"

Chekov's hand hovered above the firing switches. "Fifteen seconds."

"Sulu, arm a full spread of torpedoes. Fire on my mark."

Working quickly, Sulu replied, "Photon torpedoes standing by."

Scott's hands flew from one part of the engineering console to another. "First round of transports done. We need thirty seconds to finish!"

"Stay on it, Mister Scott. Spock, can we raise just the forward shields?"

"Attempting to angle deflectors," Spock said as he worked.

"Here we go," Sulu muttered under his breath.

Chekov declared, "Firing range in four, three—"

"Fire!" Kirk bellowed. "Keep firing! Alternate phaser batteries!"

"Torpedoes away," Sulu said over the howling clamor of the ship's weapons.

"The Romulans are locking weapons," Spock said. "Firing—"

On the viewscreen, the image of the *Velibor* was blotted out by the all-too-familiar sight of a plasma torpedo hurtling toward the *Enterprise*. It had been over a year since the ship had last faced the Romulans' terrifying new armament, and Starfleet still had no solid defense against it.

Sulu asked, "Evasive maneuvers, Captain?"

"Hold station, Lieutenant! Keep firing!"

Searing white light flooded the main viewscreen. The *Enterprise* shuddered as an impact like a thunderclap echoed through its groaning hull. Then the blinding glow faded to reveal the *Velibor*, changing course with a hard turn as the *Enterprise*'s phaser beams deflected off its shields at oblique angles before one lucky shot slipped through and blazed a red-hot scar across the Romulan vessel's bow.

"Their plasma torpedo deflected off our shields and detonated six kilometers above us," Spock said. "Damage to both our warp nacelles and dorsal hull."

Adrenaline surged through Kirk and impelled him to spring from the command chair. "What about the Romulans? I'm sure I saw Chekov score a hit."

"Affirmative, a phaser strike to their torpedo launcher," Spock confirmed. "The weapon has been neutralized. If they continue their attack, they will have to rely on disruptors."

Kirk gave Chekov a congratulatory slap on the shoulder. "Good shooting, Ensign!" He looked to Scott. "Transport status?"

"All survivors aboard and shields back up, sir. But I suggest we move clear, on the double. That ship's warp core could go at any second."

"Noted. Chekov, snag the *HoS'leth* with a tractor beam. We need to send it away from the planet. Sulu, once that's done, get us out of its blast radius." Confident the derelict D7 was being handled with dispatch, Kirk moved to stand with Spock at the sensor console. "How long until the Romulans' next attack run?"

"They do not appear to be making one. At least, not against us."

"Explain."

Spock straightened, his expression grave. "They are headed into the atmosphere of Centaurus, on a direct heading for New Athens."

All at once, Kirk understood. "They must think the Klingon crew is dead."

"Which means," Spock concluded, "the Romulans must now eliminate the last Klingon witnesses who might testify to their involvement in this incident: Councillor Prang and the remainder of his delegation."

There was no time to waste. Kirk bolted back to the command chair. "Sulu! Pursuit course, full impulse!"

The helmsman shot a petrified look at Kirk. "Sir? Into the atmosphere?"

"You heard me, Lieutenant."

"But, sir, we're not designed to operate in atmosphere."

"Neither are they, Mister Sulu. Which means this might be our one chance to catch the *Velibor* before it kills the Klingon delegation. But if we fail . . . all of this will have been for nothing." He pointed at the planet on the viewscreen. "Take us in, Mister Sulu. Full impulse."

———

Between the red-alert siren and the hectic chatter of the *Enterprise*'s superficially wounded crew and its terminally put-upon nursing staff, Doctor McCoy could barely hear himself think.

Trailed by Nurse Christine Chapel, he moved down the triage line of *Enterprise* crewmen in the main compartment of sickbay. He assessed the waiting patients with clinical efficiency. "First-degree burn. Give him some ointment and cut him loose. . . . Minor laceration. Antibiotic cream and a quick pass of the dermal regenerator. . . . Hm. Shrapnel, but not deep. Hand me some tweezers." He held out his hand; Chapel planted the requested sterile instrument into his palm. He extricated a sliver of metal from a female Caitian officer's neck, then passed the tweezers back to Chapel. "Antibiotics and a dermal re-gen."

The door slid open behind McCoy, who turned to see a quartet of crimson-shirted *Enterprise* security officers usher more than a dozen scuffed-and-scorched Klingons into sickbay. "What the devil is this?"

Before the ranking security officer could reply, the Klingons turned in unison against his team, pummeling the four men to the deck in a matter of seconds. Their leader, a wild-eyed woman, seized McCoy by his throat. "What has Kirk done?"

He would have answered if only he had been able to breathe.

Chapel raced to intercede. "Let him go! He's a doctor!" The Klingon officer tightened her grip on McCoy's esophagus.

Then Chapel decked her.

It was a solid punch, a hard jab to the Klingon's nose. Cartilage and bone collapsed with a satisfying crunch, and magenta blood spilled from the Klingon's crumpled nostrils. She let go of McCoy and stumbled backward two steps before falling unceremoniously on her ass.

"If you're smart," Chapel said, pointing at the Klingon, "you'll *stay* down!"

McCoy stepped between the women and waved Chapel back. "It's okay. . . . But get more security down here, just in—" Before he finished, the door to the corridor opened again, and six armed security officers hurried in to stand between him, Chapel, and the Klingons. The four *Enterprise* crewmen assaulted by the Klingons struggled to their feet with bruised chins and wounded pride. Massaging his throat, McCoy grumbled, "Better late than never."

The female Klingon on the deck got up, with one hand pressed to her face to stanch the bleeding from her broken nose. She glared at McCoy. Her new injury gave her voice a flat, nasal quality. "I told your captain to leave us on our ship!"

"You'll have to take that up with him. I'm just the ship's surgeon." McCoy frowned at her. "Are any of your people hurt?"

She looked offended by the question. "We will live."

"Suit yourself." He turned away to tend patients still awaiting his attention.

The Klingon's enraged lament turned him back. "Kirk should have let us die with honor! He robbed us of our glory in *Sto-Vo-Kor*!"

McCoy had never understood the Klingon mind, and

he suspected he never would. All he could do was scowl at the Klingon woman's outburst. "I believe the phrase you're looking for is 'Thank you.'"

Speechless, the female Klingon stewed in her rage as McCoy and Chapel walked back to the triage line. Once they were a few meters away from the altercation, Chapel confided to McCoy in an embarrassed whisper, "I think I broke my hand."

He smiled at Chapel, touched by her loyalty. "Thank you."

"My pleasure, Doctor."

Twenty-six

Wind and fire buffeted the bird-of-prey. Arrowing through the skies of Centaurus, falling like a meteor meeting its destiny, the *Velibor* resonated with the howls of displaced air and hull plates buckling under pressure. The enemy was at best a heartbeat behind and growing closer with each passing breath. Every part of the ship shuddered with dread at what was coming, from the dimming lights to the engines screaming like a choir of the damned.

Mirat clutched the sides of the main console with both hands, doing his best to be a rock amid the chaos. "Pilus! Lock disruptors onto the Klingons' compound!"

"I can't get a lock through the shields," said the young tactical officer.

This all would have been so much simpler with plasma torpedoes, Mirat fumed. It was just bad fortune that a wild shot by the *Enterprise* had deprived the *Velibor* of its most powerful weapon, leaving its disruptors to break down the ground-based energy shield over the university campus. Where the Transfer Key had struck with ease, the *Velibor* now would have to force a breach before it could finish this ugly, hateful mission for the Tal Shiar.

"Concentrate fire on the shield," Mirat said.

Pilus scrambled to comply. "What part?"

"*Any* part! Just hit it with everything we have! We

need to overload its emitters. Helm, level out at eighteen thousand and circle the target so we can maintain fire."

Toporok, the helmsman, pulled the ship out of its near-vertical dive and banked the bird-of-prey into a tight circling pattern. "Ready, Centurion!"

"Fire, Pilus! Alternate disruptor banks! Keep hitting that shield until it falls."

Across the main console, Subcommander Kurat updated the tactical display. "The *Enterprise* is starting its descent!" His eyes bulged. "It's entering the atmosphere!"

"Curious," Mirat said. "Why descend when they can strike from orbit?"

No one offered a guess, so the high-pitched cries of the *Velibor*'s disruptors filled the abrupt lacuna in the bridge's backdrop of chatter. Shimmering streaks of orange crisscrossed on the viewscreen, always converging just in time to hammer the campus's hemispherical energy shield, which was invisible until it was hit, at which point its outline was revealed by a fast-fading nimbus generated by the system's energy-dissipation matrix.

An internal hail flashed on Mirat's screen. He opened the channel. "Report!"

Ranimir answered, *"We have power spikes in all systems! We need to break off!"*

"Not an option. How long until the torpedo launcher is repaired?"

"We can't make a full repair under these conditions!"

"Then a partial repair. The *Enterprise* is almost on top of us. We need torpedoes!"

Over the comm came static, a hiss of escaping gas,

something spitting sparks. Then the voice of the belea-guered chief engineer. *"I can have it up in ten minutes."*

"Five minutes, or we're all dead! Command out!" Mirat closed the channel. "Pilus! Status of the surface shield!"

The tactical officer's reply was cut short by a humbling blast that rocked the *Velibor*. Lights went dark on the command deck for several seconds before hiccuping back to life, only to reveal the smoke belching from mul-tiple failed consoles. Then, as if anyone needed to be told, Kurat reported, "We're taking fire from the *Enterprise*."

Pilus, at least, stayed focused on his task. "The shield is contracting!"

"Keep at it! Hit it with all we have! We need that shield down *now*."

"Firing again," Pilus said, triggering the next salvo from the disruptor banks.

Another bone-rattling series of blasts shook the *Ve-libor*. Sparks rained from the overhead, and the veils of smoke in the corridors behind the command deck thick-ened to curtains.

Sadira, who had been observing from the periphery of the command deck, inched toward the main console. "Centurion? Shouldn't we engage the *Enterprise*?"

"Not yet. One miracle at a time, Major." Another bar-rage from the *Enterprise* shook the bird-of-prey. "Kurat, damage report."

"Our shields are holding." Surprise lifted his brows and added a note of hope to his voice. "The *Enterprise* isn't firing at full power."

"Just as I thought," Mirat said. "They don't want to

risk civilian collateral damage if they miss. The same reason they can't use photon torpedoes—a detonation this close to a city would level it. Pilus, keep disruptors on the campus shield." He opened the internal comm channel. "Ranimir! Plasma torpedoes! Status!"

The engineer sounded frazzled. *"Still a few minutes away."*

"Work faster, damn it!" As Mirat closed the channel, he noticed Sadira was still staring at him. "What do you want?"

"The plasma torpedoes—you're not going to fire them at the city, are you?"

"Of course not. How stupid are you?" He pointed at the tactical display. "They're for the *Enterprise*, so we might actually get out of this alive. We need to take out the Klingon delegation, then break off the attack. That way, it'll look to their High Council like the Federation betrayed them and tried to blame it on us."

She nodded. "Most wise, Centurion. I'm sorry I ever doubted you."

A look around confirmed the rest of the crew was focused on their duties, so Mirat locked his hand around Sadira's throat and forced her back to the shadowy edges of the command deck. He put her back to the wall and let his hate-warmed breath wash over her face as he leaned in to make his point. "I'm not doing this for *you*, Major. I'm completing a mission for the Star Empire, in the way I think gives my ship and my crew the best chance of survival. If not for the pain it would bring down on my family, I'd have already gutted you like a bait fish and shoved you out an airlock. Do we understand each other, *Major?*"

She hid her fear like a master. No tears, no tension, barely any reaction at all. It was true, all that Mirat had ever heard about the clandestine services: the Tal Shiar trained its people well. Sadira lifted her chin and spoke without a trace of vibrato. "As long as the mission succeeds and the Empire is served, I don't care what your motives are . . . *Centurion.*"

He backed away from her. "Good."

From behind him, Pilus called out, "The shield is down!"

Mirat spun on his heel and marched back to the main console.

"Commence strafing run. Target all Klingon life-signs—*and fire at will.*"

Blue skies and a cool breeze gave way to the roar of disruptor blasts and the acrid bite of smoke. Crimson beams slashed massive, burning wounds into the ground and through the buildings that bordered the quad. Trees burst into flames. Stone façades crumbled. Innocent people ran for their lives, desperate to escape the spreading conflagration.

Heedless of the danger, Sarek dashed through the chaos with Amanda and the rest of the Federation delegation close behind him. He darted from one fallen civilian to another, stopping each time just long enough to assess their injuries and give orders.

"Where are you hit?" Sarek asked, kneeling beside a young Andorian *shen.*

She nodded at her lower left leg. "There."

Despite his lack of medical training, Sarek could see the wound was serious; there was evidence of partial disintegration and third-degree burns. "Can you walk?"

"With help," the *shen* said in a calm, level voice, exhibiting a degree of emotional discipline Sarek found quite admirable.

He beckoned his Bolian assistant. "Isa!" Once she was close enough to hear his instructions, he continued, "Help her inside the alumni center."

A roaring blur coursed past overhead and scored the front of the alumni center with a fresh salvo of disruptor fire. Isa and the *shen* both winced at the attack. The young Andorian turned a pleading look back at Sarek. "Is there anywhere else?"

"Nothing close enough to offer shelter." To Isa he added, "Get her inside and head for the subbasement. The foundation will provide additional protection." He helped Isa lift the fallen *shen*, set them in motion toward the only viable shelter, then searched the smoky quad for his wife. Squinting against the sting of hot fumes wafting past, he found her.

Amanda was a dozen meters away, tending a young male humanoid whose right arm had been vaporized, leaving a smoldering stump of charred flesh at his shoulder. Around her, the other Federation delegates had each gravitated to other wounded civilians, including at least one seriously wounded police officer. Campus security guards fanned out across the quad, dodging panicked students and faculty who ran in random directions, without strategy or agenda, just an instinctual desire to be anywhere that wasn't under attack.

Sarek squatted opposite Amanda, who administered a hypospray of analgesic medicine taken from an emergency first-aid kit they had pulled off a wall in their residence building. She looked into the frightened man's eyes as the medicine flooded into his shocked system. "This should relieve a bit of the pain, or at least make it easier to manage." The youth's eyes took on a glassy affect. Amanda grabbed his chin and turned his head to face her. "Stay with me, Joel."

It was evident to Sarek the young man was slipping into shock. He waved over an officer from the campus's security department. "This man needs medical attention."

"So does everyone else," the guard replied, masking his fear with sarcasm.

"This man's wounds are critical," Amanda insisted. "We have to get him to a hospital."

A thunderous explosion echoed across the campus, and a ruddy fireball drew Sarek's eye. Whoever was strafing the campus had just blown a hole in the university's hospital complex.

The security guard coughed out a lungful of smoke. "You ask me? He might be better off where he is." Then he pointed. "Here come the medics now."

A crowd of nearly three dozen people sprinted toward the burning quad. Decked out in white medical jackets over scrubs of blue, green, or pink, they came bearing satchels and cases, stretchers and surgical kits, blankets and water.

Flames erupted from the shattering windows of the Klingon delegation's residence hall, followed by dense gouts of black smoke. A dusty cloud vomited into the sky from the top of the building, suggesting to Sarek its roof had just collapsed—or been destroyed. Either way, the interior of the building was likely to be a crumbling disaster, with several Klingon diplomats trapped inside it. Faced with the shape of the attack, Sarek now realized the Klingons were its principal target, and all the other wounded merely collateral damage.

Sarek stood but motioned for Amanda not to follow him. "Stay with him." The medics drew near. "I must help the Klingons."

Amanda reached out, as if she could arrest him with a word or a gesture. "Sarek!"

There was no time to wait for firefighters to respond to the disaster; it was all unfolding far too swiftly for civilian organizations to cope with effectively. If the Klingons were to have any hope of escaping from their residence building, someone needed to come to their aid now.

After running halfway across the quad, Sarek spied a Starfleet security officer tending to a fallen comrade. The Vulcan ambassador stopped at their side and held out his hand to the security officer. "Hand me your phaser."

Squinting with suspicion, the lantern-jawed human man replied, "Are you crazy?"

"I am Ambassador Sarek of Vulcan. Hand me your phaser or I will have you cashiered out of Starfleet before your shift ends." His hand remained outstretched, his palm open.

Whether he was reacting to Sarek's force of personality or the power of his reputation, the security officer drew his weapon and handed it to Sarek. "I'll need that back, sir."

"Of course. Thank you, Ensign."

Sarek raced across the quad toward the blazing husk of the Klingons' dorm. He vaporized the front door with one high-power shot from the phaser, then took the deepest breath he could hold for more than three minutes, and charged into the inferno.

Ceilings fell in from above, floors tumbled away underfoot. In every direction, flames danced and stung Sarek's face with deadly heat. His eyes watered from the toxic fumes, and even though he held his breath and resisted the urge to gasp and inhale, he felt a cruel burn of superheated air snake up his nostrils and down his throat.

He knew the lifts would be useless. *The Klingons must have figured that out by now,* he reasoned. A hit from his shoulder opened the door to one emergency stairwell. On the other side he found a furnace whose hungry pull nearly dragged him into its blazing heart. He pulled the door shut and moved on to the next emergency staircase.

He kicked open the next door to find the stairwell mostly clear of heat or smoke, but also steeped in darkness. From somewhere above the ground floor came the chatter of angry voices. Sarek started up the stairs and shouted into the gap between switchback flights, "Who is there?"

Loud coughs preceded the reply: "Councillor Prang!"

"Hurry, Councillor! This exit is still clear!"

"But the stairs are not!"

Two and half flights up, Sarek saw the obstruction that had hindered the Klingons' escape. A stray disruptor shot had reduced the stairs to a twisted knot of concrete and steel.

Sarek adjusted the settings on his borrowed phaser. "Stand away from the edge! Now!" Above, he heard the scrapes of shuffling feet. The moment they settled, he fired.

A single bluish-white beam disintegrated the cluster of wreckage blocking the path—but also left a full flight's gap in the stairwell, a perilous vertical drop from where the Klingons were to where Sarek stood. "The rest of the stairs are structurally sound. You will have to drop down."

He expected argument, perhaps an expression of denial. Instead, the Klingons sent their two strongest delegation members first—Prang, followed by Orqom. Next, Marbas and Gempok lowered a wounded colleague over the edge and let him drop—so that Prang and Orqom could catch him. They repeated the process once more before following the others down.

A quick head count left Sarek concerned. "Three of your delegation—"

"Are dead," Prang said. "And unless we move, we'll join them in *Sto-Vo-Kor*. Move!"

They were pragmatic, results-oriented, and coped with the present while thinking of the future and letting go of the past. Perhaps these were people Sarek could negotiate with after all.

Moving as a unit they left the staircase and navigated the burning ruins of the building's ground floor. Collapsing timbers blocked their route to the front door until Sarek blasted the debris into free radicals. Then they left the imploding building double-file and regrouped on the quad, well away from the biting heat of the fire.

Amanda jogged toward Sarek from the far end of the

quad, while the Klingons brushed the soot and dust from their clothes. Councillor Prang regarded Sarek with a new eye, one less tainted with hostility or suspicion. "After all our slights against you and your mate, you would run into a burning house for our sakes." A slow nod. "Maybe you *are* someone we can make a deal with, Vulcan." He offered Sarek his open hand.

Sarek took Prang's hand and shook it. "I look forward—"

Fiery pain, a roar that swallowed the world: those were the last things Sarek knew before the darkness took him.

———

In all of her nineteen short years of life, Joanna McCoy had never seen an explosion bring down an entire building in a flash of fire and fury.

She and the other volunteers from the university hospital were far enough from the blast not to feel its first pulse of heat, but its shock wave threw them and everyone else to the heat-brittled grass of the quad. She winced at the knifing pain in her ears, then watched in horror as the residence hall—where she had lived before being temporarily displaced to make way for the peace conference—fell in upon itself. Then a cloud of ash and dust, of pulverized concrete and aerosolized flesh and blood, rolled away from the razed structure's smoldering footprint.

Utterly opaque, the cloud consumed everything in its path. It swept over the Klingons who had just escaped the building as well as Ambassador Sarek and his wife.

Then it reached Joanna, and all she could do was plant her face in the ground and wrap her arms around her head. Hot winds coated her in the greasy filth of the implosion's aftermath. Joanna didn't dare breathe in for fear of filling her lungs with fine particles of death.

Gravelike quiet settled over the quad. She lifted her head.

Around her, few people were moving. A pall of smoke lingered over everything, and the golden haze of dust obscured anyone and anything more than a dozen meters away. Joanna searched her tunic's pockets for a sterile face mask, then freed it from its hermetically sealed wrapping and pulled it on over her mouth and nose. The toxic fog stung her eyes, but she let her tears flow and kept her thoughts focused on those with more grievous problems.

On her left, a staggering medical technician. He didn't appear to be wounded. Joanna snapped her fingers to get his attention. "Hey! You with me?" He nodded, so she pointed at a ring of stunned civilians closer to the fallen building. "Get over there and triage the wounded. We need to figure out who's critical and who's ambulatory. Move."

Overhead, the skies thundered with distant explosions, but she had no time to dwell on that. Scores of wounded and dying people lay at her feet. She had work to do.

She kneeled beside a shuddering Tellarite to tie a tourniquet on his leg that would stanch his blood loss long enough to evacuate him to a city hospital. A Klingon who was holding his midriff together with both hands and sheer stubbornness tried to shout her away, but she knew he couldn't stop her from rendering medical treatment without letting his intestines spill out, so she sprayed an aerosolized antibiotic over his injuries, then closed the wounds—albeit temporarily—with a liberal dose of liquid dermis.

Then she pivoted to her next patient—and found herself poised between Ambassador Sarek of Vulcan and his wife—both of them unconscious, scorched, and bleeding from multiple shrapnel wounds. All her training abandoned her for seconds that her fear stretched into an eternity. Her fear overcame her paralysis, and she shouted to everyone and no one, "Over here! The ambassador's been hit! I need a stretcher! Get me a surgical kit! And find me a Vulcan blood donor!" Twisting left, then right, she found no one rushing to her aid. "Dammit, people! Ambassador Sarek is hurt! I need tools, drugs, a doctor— anything!"

Sarek's eyes fluttered open. He caught Joanna's wrist. "I . . . am stunned . . . but will live. Help . . . my wife. Please." Joanna hesitated, then chose to trust the famous Vulcan. She pivoted away from him to tend to Amanda, who re- mained unconscious. When the folds of the woman's dark outer garment were pulled aside, the bloody wound be- neath became clearly visible.

Another detonation, much closer this time, shattered windows and shook the ground. Screams were followed by the percussion of running footsteps—the music of panicked flight.

Fighting back against a flood-crush of primal urges that told her to run, Joanna calmed herself and pressed her hands against Amanda's chest, to cover wounds that pulsed with dark red blood, all while the older woman's pulse faded with each struggling beat of her heart.

"Keep after them, Sulu!" Kirk was half out of his chair, grasping one arm as he leaned forward to point at the madly banking Romulan bird-of-prey on the main viewscreen. "Chekov! Don't let them make another pass over the campus! We can't give them another shot at the Klingons!"

The screeching of the *Enterprise*'s phasers traveled up from several decks below to echo inside the bridge. On the viewscreen, twin beams of fierce blue energy shot forward and converged on the Romulan ship's aft quarter in a brilliant white flash. A secondary explosion tore a hull plate off the bird-of-prey, which trailed smoke as it yawed to starboard and climbed into an evasive corkscrew maneuver.

With one hand to the transceiver in her ear, Uhura swiveled away from the communications panel. "Captain, reports of multiple civilian casualties on the surface."

"Noted, Lieutenant." Kirk had seen the *Velibor*'s disruptor beams lance through crowds of innocent people on the New Athens campus. Watching buildings erupt into deadly shrapnel, seeing trees burst into flames, he had known blood would be shed and lives would be lost. His mission had been to prevent such a calamity; now his remit was to minimize the damage and neutralize the threat, as quickly and with as little risk of additional collateral damage as possible. "Scotty, tell your people on the ground to get the campus shield back up, on the double."

"They're doing the best they can, sir," the chief engineer protested.

A viewscreen full of blue sky turned to star-flecked darkness as the *Enterprise* pushed through its own awkward rolling climb, in pursuit of the *Velibor*. Banshee howls registered the engines' displeasure. Just as quickly as the cerulean glow of atmosphere had faded it returned, engulfing the viewscreen as the Romulan vessel slipped past the top edge of the frame, only to be recovered briefly before vanishing once more to screen right.

Atmospheric turbulence buffeted the *Enterprise*'s hull and made its duranium plates rattle like bone china during an earthquake—an experience Kirk recalled from a formal dinner during his Academy days in San Francisco, and one he would have been happy to forget.

Clouds parted ahead, no doubt shredded by the supersonic passage of starships running with shields raised. Kirk strained to spot the *Velibor* over the curve of Centaurus. He wondered whether he had lost the enemy ship in the skyline of New Athens.

"Chekov, where the hell are they?"

The young Russian stammered, "I . . . I don't know, Captain. They are not on my targeting scanner!"

"Behind us," Spock declared in a firm but level voice.

"Scotty," Kirk snapped, "more power to—!" Before he could say *aft shields*, a crushing blow rocked the *Enterprise* from stern to bow. The jolt launched him from the command chair. He landed on the deck, his shoulder against the forward console, between Chekov and Sulu.

On the upper level of the bridge, Uhura, Scott, and a relief officer had also been hurled from their chairs, while

Spock clung to the edge of the console and the hood over his sensor display. The first officer reported above the continuing rumbles transiting the hull, "A hit by one plasma torpedo. Minor damage to the hull, aft shields are losing power."

Kirk pulled himself up the forward console until he was standing. "Sulu, evasive maneuvers. Get us back into firing position. Mister Scott, we need you back in engineering."

The engineer sprang from his seat and strode into a waiting turbolift. "You read my mind, Captain. Full damage reports in three minutes."

Another jarring blast sent Kirk staggering backward, this time to fall against his own command chair. "Hard to port! Chekov, suppressing fire—and don't hit any civilians!"

"Trying, Captain! But there's still heavy air traffic over the capital—"

"Just . . ." What could he say? "Do your best." A new idea struck him. "Sulu, can you force us into a stall during a climbing turn? Trick the Romulans into closing the gap to give Chekov a better shot?"

"I can try," Sulu said, already plotting the dangerous stunt.

Spock left his station to counsel Kirk in confidence from beside the command chair. "Captain, in an atmosphere, such a maneuver could inflict catastrophic stress on our dorsal connecting hull. In a worst-case scenario—"

"I might snap the saucer clean off," Kirk said under his breath. "I know, Spock."

Again, a punishing detonation hammered the *Enterprise*'s shields, stuttering the overhead lights and sending the bridge consoles into flickering spasms of malfunction. The normally unflappable first officer remarked with an almost glum affect, "The bird-of-prey is making short work of our defenses."

"Good," Kirk said. "Every shot they land on us is one they aren't taking at the surface—and I mean to keep it that way as long as possible, until we can finish them."

Sulu looked over his shoulder at Kirk. "Ready for the stall."

Kirk seized his chair's armrests and let Spock hurry back to his own post on the bridge's upper deck. Then he ordered Sulu, "Execute."

Unlike the momentary disruption caused by sudden shocks such as disruptor blasts or torpedo detonations, the sustained overload of the ship's inertial damper system by a wild maneuver inside a gravity well was a uniquely gut-wrenching experience. Kirk tried to steel himself as he watched Sulu enter the commands at the helm—but when the ship's momentum arrested as its bow climbed and yawed into a near standstill, then rolled through its free fall, he remembered the nausea and vertigo of his first day of zero-g training.

His breakfast did all it could to push its way back up his esophagus. It took every bit of discipline and experience Kirk possessed to keep his morning meal in his stomach.

Then Chekov cried out, "Firing!"

All that was visible on the main viewscreen was a blur of motion and color, pulses of sapphire and emerald light, crimson flashes—and then a hash of static and distorted images as the latest enemy salvo pummeled Kirk's ship.

Next came the crushing pressure of acceleration, until the inertial dampers recovered and made it possible for Kirk to breathe again. "Spock, report!"

"Two direct hits on the *Velibor*. Her shields are buckling."

"And how are we?"

This time, Spock's demeanor took a turn for the grim. "Numerous hits in the engineering section. Shields are failing, and main power is at fifty percent and falling."

Kirk's eyes were fixed upon the retreating aft quarter of the *Velibor*, which vanished into a cloud bank dozens of kilometers ahead. "They're faster than we are, more agile. But we have more mass, more power. Let's start using it. Sulu, do whatever you have to, but do *not* lose that ship. Chekov, keep firing until we get their shields down, then put a tractor beam on them."

The ensign asked, "Then what, Captain?"

"Then," Kirk said, "we teach them what it means to get dragged out to the woodshed."

Twenty-seven

No matter how many accolades the captain heaped upon Montgomery Scott, at moments such as this the engineer felt less like a miracle worker than he did like a conductor leading an orchestra composed of chaos, blood, and fire.

The master systems display in main engineering was a snapshot of the *Enterprise*, from the inside out. All the major components of the ship, and their countless interactions—from here Scott could witness them all at a glance: the power-relay undervoltages between sections C and D below deck nineteen; the power-coupling overloads in starboard phaser control; the failure of the CO_2 scrubbers serving the auxiliary control center; firmware failures slowing the response time of the forward phaser bank's targeting system; jammed valves fouling the deuterium flow to the main impulse reactor up at the rear of the saucer section. He saw them all, and much more, with what was at times a horrifying clarity.

A ferocious cannonade rocked the ship. Scott held the edges of his console and prayed to his beloved: *Hold together, my beauty. I believe in you.*

Alarms flashed across his system board. Fires had broken out on multiple decks. He triggered manual warnings, as a precaution in case the ship's automated alerts had malfunctioned, then opened an internal channel to the firefighting dispatcher: "Scott to damage control! Fires on decks twenty and twenty-one, all compartments aft of section delta!"

"*Acknowledged,*" came the response. "*Firefighters responding.*"

Just as he closed that comm circuit, the captain's priority channel from the bridge flashed for Scott's attention, accompanied by Kirk's stressed voice: "*Bridge to engineering!*"

He opened the two-way comm circuit. "Scott here."

"*I need more speed at impulse, and I need the tractor beam ready at full power!*"

More enemy fire racked the ship and reduced auxiliary stations on either side of Scott to heaps of sparking junk. "I'm doing all I can just to hold her together, sir!"

"*This isn't a request, Mister Scott! We have to match the Romulans' speed and be ready to drag them back to orbit. And it needs to happen in the next three minutes.*"

It was clear the captain had a bee in his bonnet; when that happened, there was nothing for it. What he wanted had to get done, come what may.

"Aye, sir. I'll do what I can. Scott out." The chief engineer sighed as he closed the channel. Then came the next series of blinking red warnings on his master systems display—a series of alerts he had hoped never to see lit up in dire crimson. The antimatter containment pods were swiftly losing power. If their magnetic fields dipped below safe levels for even a microsecond, the resulting mutual annihilation of matter and escaping antimatter would release enough uncontrolled energy to reduce the *Enterprise* to a cloud of superheated vapor.

Scott's blood ran cold as he remembered where the

ship was. *In atmosphere, we'll go up like a bomb! We'll cook this planet in a flash!*

He opened channels to every damage-control team he had. "Scott to all DC teams! We're losing antimatter containment! I need fast-response on deck twenty-one! Acknowledge!"

Someone should have answered immediately. Instead, precious seconds wasted away, until Scott tore his eyes from the warnings of antimatter containment failure to see another system failure light: internal comm circuits for his master systems display.

There was no more time to delegate.

Scott bolted from his station and ran aft. As he passed another engineer, he pointed the young woman back the way he'd come. "Alspach! Man the MSD! Get its comms working!"

The flummoxed blond lieutenant shouted at fast-retreating Scott, "Wait, sir! Where are you going?"

"To keep us from going up like a bonfire!"

Ahead of him, a medic was treating an engineer felled by a burn to the side of his face. Scott slowed just enough to snag the other engineer's tool kit off the deck and sling it over his shoulder, then kept sprinting aft, to the nearest access panel that led into the bowels of the ship, down to the antimatter pods.

The panel was hot enough to sting his hand as he pulled it up and pushed it aside. A blast-furnace gust struck his face. Scott worried his hair might singe as he lowered himself into the cruel heat that filled the belly of the *Enterprise.*

Can't worry about that now.

Descending the scalding hot rungs of the ladder, Scott felt his palms blister. Every breath was an assault on his respiratory system; his nose parched within seconds, forcing him to breathe through his mouth, which left his throat burning with pain. Arcs of electricity danced around him and stung his face with sharp licks of forked lightning.

Just a little farther . . .

His boots touched down on the catwalk between two rows of antimatter pods. Painful coughs racked his chest and doubled him over as he trudged ahead toward the severed relay he knew was threatening to reduce the ship, its crew, and every living thing on Centaurus to dust. Irregular jets of white-hot leaking plasma crossed his path, nearly close enough to strip the flesh from his bones. Navigating the accidental death traps was like braving the Devil's funhouse.

Almost there . . .

He reached the juncture, barely able to breathe, his legs threatening to betray him at any moment. His eyes scratched in their sockets like they were made of sandpaper as he searched the area for the severed power line that had put so many lives in jeopardy. Then he found its halves, dangling beneath his catwalk.

Of all the bloody stupid places to put a—

He decided to save his complaints for after the work was done. There was no remedy for his current predicament but an act of inspired foolhardiness. He squatted and lowered his legs over the sides of the narrow catwalk.

Underneath it he crossed his ankles. Then he pulled off his toolkit, selected the right implement for the job, and leaned over the side.

Half a second later he dangled, upside down, from the catwalk, supported only by his own crossed ankles and quaking leg muscles. In his right hand he held the coupling fuser; with his left he seized the nearest end of the severed line.

Aided by the kind of ease that only comes from decades of practice, he secured the first end of the line in the fuser, then reached for the other end. It swung and eluded him at first, but a few choice epithets known only to true Scotsmen proved enough to scare the swaying cord into his hand. He lifted it to the fuser and repaired the broken coupling with the press of a button.

An inverted sit-up enabled him to set the fuser back on the catwalk; a second sit-up let him reach the edge and pull himself back onto the walkway. As he lay gasping in the brutal scorch of the ship's lowest deck, too tired to move, sprays of fire suppressant rained down from above, followed by rushes of cool, filtered air that washed away the sting of unseen flames. Supine and spent, Scott afforded himself a rare five-second break to enjoy the moment.

Now I feel like a miracle worker, he mused behind a satisfied grin.

———

To some people, operating the helm of a starship looked like nothing more than pushing buttons and flipping switches, but Sulu knew better. From his seat on the bridge of the *Enterprise*, he felt the ship's every movement as if it were an extension of his own body.

More than one doctor had suggested he was imagining that connection, but he knew they were wrong. A galvanic tingling made hairs on the backs of his hands stand tall when he fired the phasers. When he pushed the ship through hard turns and wild rolls, maneuvers for which its stately frame had not been designed, the groaning of its spaceframe felt the same to him as the aching in his joints when he lunged beyond his comfort zone while fencing, or landed without grace after being thrown by an opponent during judo practice.

Today he was putting the *Enterprise* through its paces in a way few helm officers had ever tested a starship as large as the *Constitution*-class heavy cruiser. So far it had survived every punishment he had imposed—but the pursuit of the *Velibor* wasn't over yet.

"Range closing to five hundred kilometers," Sulu said loudly enough for everyone on the bridge to hear. "The bird-of-prey is shifting its heading back toward the New Athens campus."

Captain Kirk watched the elusive silver shape dart through cloud banks on the main viewscreen. "We need to make sure they don't get there. Chekov, hit them again."

The navigator adjusted the controls at his station, then halted his efforts with irritation. "Still too much air traffic, Captain! If I miss, I might hit civilians."

Spock pivoted away from his console. "We have another problem, Captain. The firing of phasers and disruptors in the planet's atmosphere has generated unusually high levels of ionized particles, which are interfering with the planet's civilian data network."

"Add it to Mister Scott's repair list," the captain said. "Job one is capturing the *Velibor* intact and recovering the Transfer Key. Speaking of which, we need to get closer, Sulu."

"Trying, sir." There was no more speed left to wring from the ship's impulse engines, but Sulu did his best to coax one more bump of acceleration from the overtaxed fusion cores.

"Traffic clearing—I'm taking the shot," Chekov declared. He unleashed another phaser salvo at the *Velibor*, which dodged to starboard, then dived, skirting beneath and away from the phaser blasts in a fraction of a second. Then the bird-of-prey vanished inside another sea of clouds lingering over the coastline. In the scant seconds it took Sulu to switch from visual scanning to check his instruments for a sensor reading on the enemy ship's position, it had come hard about, speeding straight toward the *Enterprise*, disruptors blazing.

"Evasive!" Kirk shouted, even as Sulu steered them clear of the incoming barrage. Violent shakes launched Sulu and the rest of his shipmates from their posts. They all landed on the deck as the lights blinked off and deafening rumbles reverberated through the hull.

Sulu and Chekov were only halfway back into their chairs as Kirk demanded, "Sulu, get back on their tail! Spock, damage reports!"

"Structural damage to the starboard nacelle pylon," Spock said. "I suggest we head back to orbit as soon as possible."

"Not while the *Velibor*'s harassing the surface at point-blank range," Kirk said.

"Captain, may I remind you that our nacelle pylons are not designed to endure any degree of wind shear. In its compromised state, it—"

"Your concern is noted, Mister Spock, but we're staying in the hunt. Helm, do we have a fix on the *Velibor*?"

Chekov responded first. "Tracking her now, Captain. She is still moving too fast for a manual phaser lock, and fire-control systems are sluggish."

"Setting a new pursuit course," Sulu said. "Thirty seconds to intercept."

Visualizing the encounter to come, Sulu realized a direct assault on or pursuit of the Romulan ship would continue to prove futile. The smaller ship was just too nimble, both in vacuum and in atmosphere, for the *Enterprise* to match its hard turns and sudden changes of speed and direction. *Going head to head is a losing battle for us. Time to change the game.*

He leaned toward Chekov. "I have an idea. Target their port nacelle and fire."

"Targeting." Chekov thumbed the trigger. "Firing!"

Under his breath, Sulu said, "Yaw to starboard, roll to port and climb—" Half a second later, the *Velibor* executed that exact series of maneuvers as it dodged Chekov's latest barrage.

The Russian gazed wide-eyed at Sulu. "How did you know?"

"I think I have their pilot figured out." He swiveled his chair to look back at the captain. "Sir, we'll never catch them following their trail. We have to get ahead of them—by figuring out where they're going to go, then getting there first."

"You feel up to that, Lieutenant?"

"I think so, sir. But I'll have to act on instinct."

Kirk nodded. "Understood. Maneuver at your own discretion."

"Aye, aye, sir." Sulu reached over to Chekov's side of the helm console and plugged coordinates into the firing panel. "Your first shots will be a feint, to force them into evasion mode. If I'm right, her next escape will be a starboard roll followed by an inverted dive—and this time, we'll have phasers locked on her exit trajectory."

Chekov cracked his knuckles, grinned, and set his hands into ready positions above the tactical controls. "Sounds good to me."

Sulu patched in the last reserves of auxiliary and battery power to drive the impulse engines toward their best possible speed. On his console, the range to the *Velibor* shrank.

"Here we go," Sulu said. "Pavel, on my mark, fire the warning shot off her port side." The range ticked downward toward optimal firing range. He programmed his anticipated response maneuver to keep the *Velibor* in Chekov's sights during its imminent escape attempt. "Three. Two. One. Fire!"

Two phaser beams, close together, ripped past the *Velibor*, an apparent near miss.

Then the bird-of-prey's helm officer did exactly what Sulu had predicted: a starboard roll into an inverted dive—and directly into Chekov's next two phaser blasts, which slashed a pair of black, smoking scars across the *Velibor*'s dorsal hull.

"Direct hit," Spock declared. "The *Velibor*'s shields have collapsed, and her power levels are dropping."

Sulu added, "She's losing speed, Captain, and her maneuvers are turning sluggish."

In the command chair, Kirk permitted himself a restrained fist pump of satisfaction. "Well done, gentlemen! One more hit like that and we've got them." An overhead panel collapsed to Kirk's left, mangling the empty chair in front of the engineering console and showering the deck with radiant phosphors. The captain grimaced at the mounting damage on his bridge. "As long as they don't hit us first."

What I wouldn't give for a tricorder right now. Enveloped in smoke and surrounded by people overcome by panic, Joanna fought to keep Amanda Grayson from slipping into shock or, worse, a coma. The middle-aged human woman had a number of obvious external injuries from shrapnel or flames, but as Joanna palpated the woman's midriff and listened for pained reactions, her greatest fear was that her patient had suffered internal injuries, the kind Joanna was neither trained nor equipped to treat.

It didn't help her confidence that her every move was being observed by Sarek, who kneeled a couple of meters behind her. His distance was clearly meant as a gesture of respect, an effort to give her space to work. Unfortunately, even with her back turned she felt the weight of his gaze as she struggled to tend his wounded spouse. *If his wife were giving birth, I could send him to fetch hot water and towels. Instead, I'm stuck with an audience.*

After several minutes of frantic work, she had stanched the bleeding of Amanda's myriad small punctures and lacerations. By touch alone she had pinpointed one broken rib, and she suspected Amanda's left radius and ulna might also be fractured, though she was at a loss to identify any actual break in the bones. She turned away to paw through her partial medkit.

Amanda's voice was a dry scratch of fear and pain. "What are you doing?"

"Just looking for this," Joanna said, holding up a simple pen light. "I need to check for a concussion." She switched on the light and pointed its narrow beam into Amanda's eyes. "Normal response, no sign of ocular bleeding. That's good." She turned off the light and held up her fingers in a V shape. "How many fingers?"

"Two."

"You're doing great. Any headache, dizziness?"

A weak, small shake of her head. "Not yet. But I'm thirsty."

"Don't worry, that's normal," Joanna lied. She didn't want to alarm Amanda by raising the possibility that her thirst was the result of internal bleeding. Especially when she had no way of knowing for certain whether that was—

Running footsteps, close by, somewhere beyond the curtains of smoke that surrounded Joanna and her two VIP patients. She called out, "Hey! Who's there? We need help!" To her relief, the sprinter halted, then changed direction toward her.

From the gray veil emerged a familiar face. The young Bolian man was one of the hospital's second-year medical students. "Um—" It took Joanna a few seconds to dredge up his name from her memory. "Nett, right?" He nodded, so she continued. "I need a full medkit. Dammit, even a working hypospray and some painkillers."

He hurried to her and kneeled on the other side of Amanda. "I don't have much, just a few basics. I'm doing my psychiatric residency right now."

"What about a tricorder? You still carry one on psych rotation?"

"Sure." Nett retrieved his medical tricorder from under his white lab coat and handed it to Joanna. As she took it from him, her pale fingertips brushed the back of his blue hand, and for the blink of an eye, the hue of his cheeks deepened from azure to indigo—confirming what Joanna had suspected for the past month: *I knew it! He has a crush on me!*

She switched on the tricorder and made a fast scan of Amanda's torso. The first pass revealed nothing unusual, but Joanna wanted to be certain. She reset the device for a deep-tissue scan and started over. It took several seconds for the tricorder to assess Amanda's vital organs, nervous system, and blood chemistry. When the analysis appeared on the device's compact display, Joanna was relieved to see healthy results. "Good news," she told Amanda with a smile. "No sign of internal damage. You're going to be just fine."

Amanda set her hand on Joanna's forearm with a feather-light grip. "Thank you."

"You're welcome." She turned to share the good news with Sarek. "She's all right, Mister Ambassador."

The Vulcan looked weary beyond words. He nodded once. "Good," he said, as if with his last breath. Then his eyelids closed, and he slumped sideways, deadweight surrendering to gravity. He landed in a heap on the trampled grass before Nett and Joanna could catch him.

In a flash they both were at Sarek's side, hands and voices trembling. Nett stared at the unconscious diplomat with the terror of a man who expected to be blamed for a tragedy based on nothing more than his proximity to it. "What happened? He was fine a second ago!"

"Vulcans are very good at hiding their symptoms." Joanna focused the tricorder on Sarek. "He had me fooled too." Data packed the display. "Dammit! Internal bleeding!"

"Where?" Nett plundered his medkit for tools.

Joanna refined the analysis. "Inferior vena cava."

"All right, pull down his collar." The medical student loaded a hypospray, then pressed it to Sarek's throat, which Joanna had obligingly exposed. A sharp hiss announced the injection. "That'll slow the bleeding and keep his blood oxygenated until we get him into surgery."

"And how do we do that? Got a stretcher hiding in that bag?"

Before Nett could answer Joanna's sarcastic jab, Amanda interrupted, "What's wrong with my husband? Is it his heart again?"

"No, ma'am," Nett said. "Shrapnel pierced his abdomen and hit a major vein. He's bleeding internally and needs surgery." He stood and handed his medkit to Joanna. "I'll round up a stretcher and someone to help us carry him. Watch his vitals on the tricorder. If his bleed rate increases, give him another dose from the hypo. It's loaded and ready to go."

"Got it." She added quickly, "Hurry."

"Count on it." He ran toward the hospital; within seconds the drifting smoke on the quad had swallowed him up, leaving Joanna alone between Sarek, whose wounds she couldn't heal, and Amanda, whose fears she couldn't calm.

And for the first time in years, Joanna wished her father was at her side.

The only thing failing faster than the *Velibor* itself was the morale of its crew. Sadira smelled the fear in the air of the command deck: all around her, the Romulan officers were abandoning their faith in the mission, losing their nerve to soldier on. All she could do was try to be an example for the others to follow. "Continue evasive maneuvers! Get us back over the campus!"

At the helm, Toporok did his best to obey, but across the main console her orders were met by Centurion Mirat's furious stare. "Damn you, Major! Can't you see we're finished?"

"Not until the mission is accomplished."

Kurat was back at the tactical console, his old post, having taken over for the slain Lieutenant Pilus. "Major! We're losing power to the weapons! Disruptors at one-quarter power."

"Focus both banks on the same target, and choose your shots with care."

The acting second-in-command struggled against his console. "It might not be enough. Parts of the surface shield are back online, and the Klingons have moved into underground shelters." His dismay deepened. "And they've scattered, sir."

He relayed the sensor readings to the command console. Sadira felt the centurion's ire as he observed the same discouraging facts she did. "They've split up, Major, and they're moving farther apart by the minute. We can't target them all."

Crushing blasts from the *Enterprise*'s phasers battered the *Velibor*. Failing consoles filled the command deck with weltering light as the droning of the impulse engines cycled into longer, sadder frequencies. Toporok looked up from the flight console. "We're losing speed!"

"Dive into the attack," Sadira said. "Let the planet's gravity work for us."

"Belay that," Mirat said. "Break off and head for orbit."

"Ignore the centurion," Sadira snapped. "Hold your course!"

The centurion growled through clenched teeth, "This is a suicide mission!"

"We all knew we might be asked to die for Romulus."

"For the Empire, yes. Not for you and your mad ambition." He opened an internal comm channel. "Ranimir, decouple the Transfer Key from—"

"You'll do no such thing," Sadira cut in, closing the channel as she spoke.

Mirat pointed at the tactical display. "Our gunner

can't target all the Klingons before the *Enterprise* takes us down, and we can't outrun her with that infernal contraption of yours eating all our power! We need to shut it down before it's too late."

"For what? Surrender?" She had come too far to back down. "I just need one more shot."

"What difference will one more shot make?"

"That depends on its target, doesn't it?"

He circled the main console to confront her, nose to nose. "You're insane! Your weapon can't target more than one person at a time, or a small area, and any shot you take will be a death sentence for this ship! Let go of your delusions, Major! This is *over*."

"In case you've forgotten, Centurion, that decision isn't yours to make." She took a deep breath and savored the acrid bite of burnt wiring and the sting of hot smoke; it hurt to take it in, yet she had never felt more alive than she did in that moment, facing death's morbid grin. "Helm, start our next attack run, best possible speed. Tactical, target—"

Kurat stood back from his post. "Centurion, I am relieving the major of command. Collect her sidearm and take her into custody."

Before Mirat could reach for Sadira's disruptor, she had it aimed at his face. "One more step and I'll kill you and both the men behind you. Now . . . hand me *your* weapon." As she extended her open hand to Mirat, she kept one eye on Kurat. "I see you tensing, Kurat. Reach for your weapon and I promise you and the centurion will be dead before you pull that trigger."

Mirat handed over his sidearm. Everyone on the

bridge froze, and Sadira knew that was a disaster waiting to happen. "Nevira, take over for Kurat. Toporok, continue the attack run." She aimed her newly acquired disruptor at Kurat. "Draw your weapon with two fingers, set it on the deck, and kick it over to me." The young officer's movements were exaggerated in their sloth. "Hurry up." He put his disruptor on the deck and hit it with the side of his boot. It skittered across the deck to Sadira, who trapped it under her left foot. "Good. Now go get Commander Creelok and bring him here, on the double. Move!"

Kurat was more than happy to flee the command deck. As he left, Sadira pivoted atop the captured sidearm to keep the entire command crew in her sights. "Back to stations, all of you."

The centurion backed away from her, then side-stepped to his place on the other side of the main console. "What do you think you're doing, Major?"

"Whatever is necessary—just as I swore I would."

Nevira fumbled to make sense of the tactical controls. "Trying to lock in Klingon targets," she said. "Signals are weak. Too much interference. I can't—"

Then came the deathblow—a brutal direct hit by the *Enterprise*'s formidable phaser banks. Knowing it had been inevitable made it no less dispiriting for Sadira as the *Velibor*'s key systems all went dark around her. Next came the violent lurch of inertial damper failure, followed by the sickening free fall that signaled the bird-of-prey was in an uncontrolled spin through the atmosphere. At last, another jarring jerk as its tumbles were halted—and the hull of the *Velibor* creaked and whimpered under a strain it hadn't been made to withstand.

Despite being a hostage in all but name, Mirat continued to wield the authority of command. "Damage reports! What hit us? All stations, check in!"

"Two phaser hits to our primary reactor," Nevira said. "Main power is gone. Shields are down. Weapons are offline."

Toporok gave up trying to coax or coerce the helm back into action. "We're in a tractor beam," he said. "We're being towed out of the atmosphere."

"Don't fight it," Mirat said. "You'll just shred us if you do."

For once Sadira concurred with Mirat's counsel, but not for the same reason. She found a working internal comm channel to engineering. "Ranimir, respond!"

An unfamiliar voice replied, *"Ranimir's dead. This is Lieutenant Canok."*

"Canok, this is Major Sadira. I need all remaining power, every reserve, every battery, patched into the Transfer Key immediately. That's an order!" She saw Mirat inhale as a prelude to voicing an objection—which she silenced by raising her disruptor as a warning.

After a delay filled with noises concussive and sibilant, Canok responded, *"Understood. We'll have all reserves patched into the Key in sixty seconds. Engineering out."*

Diagonal slashes of static on the viewscreen resolved into a shaky image of the ventral aft quarter of the *Enterprise*, as seen through the silvery blue radiance of its tractor beam.

If only we still had weapons, this would be an ideal angle from which to target their antimatter containment pods, Sadira reflected.

Her musing was cut short by the return of Kurat and Creelok. The commander looked around his smoking, shattered bridge in horror. "What have you done to my ship?"

She aimed her second disruptor at him, just to ensure there would be no misunderstandings with regard to who was in control of the vessel. "I've put it to the test and found it wanting. But I'm going to give it one last chance to redeem itself."

His fury decayed into stunned disbelief. "You brought me here to tell me that? To gloat?"

Sadira pitied his inability to see what was obviously the only endgame left to them. "No. I need you and the centurion to prevent our enemies from capturing the Transfer Key."

"And how are we supposed to do that?"

She prefaced her reply with a sinister smile.

"How else? With a glorious, final act of pure *spite*."

Twenty-eight

Taken prisoner: a humiliating end to what had promised to be a glorious career. Mirat seethed as the *Enterprise* towed his ship away from Centaurus, back into the cold void of space, to face whatever passed for justice in the decadent corruption of the Federation.

The enemy captain's voice crackled over the intership comm. "*. . . repeat, please acknowledge, Velibor. This is Captain James T. Kirk of the* Starship Enterprise. *Prepare to surrender your vessel and be boarded. If you resist, we will have no choice but to use deadly force. You have thirty seconds to acknowledge, Velibor. Enterprise out.*"

No one sent a reply because Major Sadira—the usurper, the fool, the quisling human in Romulan dress—hadn't ordered one. Instead they all stood like statues, bearing mute witness to the result of her gross incompetence, her arrogance, her unchecked zealotry. Instead, all anyone paid any heed to was the shared effort of Mirat and Creelok, who labored in vain to make the ship's half-demolished main computer accept their command codes.

The commander sighed. "Let's try again. Computer, acknowledge Creelok, Commander Tevan. Authorization code seven, nine, green, three, *t'liska*."

The synthetic voice of the computer spat back a garbled mess of nonsense syllables. Did that mean it understood the code? Or that its inputs were as fouled as its verbal interface? There was no easy way to tell. Creelok signaled Mirat to continue the process.

"Computer, acknowledge Mirat, Centurion Tulius. Authorization code six, zero, white, four, *dhael.*" Clicks, scratches, and a long rasp of distortion constituted the computer's response to his command codes. As before, there was no way to tell what the hashed audio signified.

Sadira stared daggers at the two of them from behind the barrels of her disruptor pistols. "What's taking so long?"

"The computer's too badly damaged," Creelok said. "We can't tell if it's accepting our codes for the self-destruct sequence, or if it will know what to do once it has them."

The human woman trembled with rage. "Can't you detonate manually?"

Mirat took umbrage at her tone. "We can, but we'll need to stall the *Enterprise.*"

"I'll buy you what time I can. Work quickly." She opened the intership channel to the Federation vessel and marshaled a cruel smirk as Kirk's face appeared on the main viewscreen. "We meet again, Captain. I trust you remember me."

"All too well," Kirk said. *"And I look forward to questioning you in my brig. Tell your crew to stand down and prepare to—"*

"I wouldn't do that, Captain." Sadira punched commands into her panel on the main console. "I've targeted the Transfer Key for one last demonstration. And unless you release this ship from your tractor beam and permit us to depart, I intend to trigger it."

Kirk's eyes narrowed. He said nothing, but looked

toward someone out of frame. Meanwhile, on the *Velibor*'s command deck, Creelok and Mirat lifted a deck panel to expose the manual activation controls for the bird-of-prey's self-destruct package.

The Starfleet captain lifted his chin in defiance. *"You'll find me hard to bluff, Major."*

"Oh, this is no bluff, Captain, I promise you that." She keyed in another command, and the main screen split into two images: Kirk on the left, and on the right, the pair caught in the crosshairs of the Transfer Key's targeting mechanism, a Vulcan man and a human woman. With a single tap on her console, she sent the targeting scanner's image to Kirk's screen. "If even one of your men sets foot on this vessel, you can kiss those two souls good-bye."

"Hold your fire." Under his breath, Kirk passed orders to someone off-screen.

At Sadira's feet, Mirat's and Creelok's labors met with success. The manual triggers switched into place as designed, and the countdown began. Mirat watched the commander look up to catch Sadira's eye and confirm with a nod that the ship's self-immolation was under way.

The major kept her expression neutral as she noted Creelok's signal, then she returned her focus to Kirk. "I applaud you, Captain. Advising the Klingons to scatter was a wise move."

"I wish I could take the credit. It was Ambassador Sarek's idea."

"Really? Then I salute your humility in giving credit where it's due—or should I say blame?" Her index finger pushed the Transfer Key's trigger.

What happened next unfolded in the wink of an eye.

The middle-aged Vulcan man and the human woman vanished in a blinding pulse of light that whited out the right half of the viewscreen before it blinked off for the last time.

Aboard the *Velibor*, the handful of systems still functioning on the command deck dimmed and faded to black. Sadira's parting shot had left the ship dead and dark.

Acting on nothing more than his last memory of where Sadira had been standing, Mirat sprang through the darkness and seized a wrist. Brittle bones splintered in his grip—it had to be the human woman's hand. He wrested one disruptor from her control—

She fired her other disruptor and vaporized part of his left hip, along with most of the main console behind him. Then he fired—and the crimson burst showed him the side of her skull cooked off in a fatal blast.

Then all was quiet inside the *Velibor* . . . all except the synthetic voice of the self-destruct package, an isolated system with its own power supply, capable of operating even when all other systems on the ship had failed. Mirat dropped his disruptor beside Sadira's corpse, then collapsed on top of her, broken in body but not in spirit.

Creelok kneeled and put his hand on Mirat's shoulder. "Well done, Centurion."

"Thank you, Commander. It is . . . an honor . . . to die in your service."

"The honor is mine, old friend." He turned a rueful look toward the dwindling digits on the self-destruct's countdown display. "If only the choice had been ours, as well."

———————

"Time, Spock," Kirk demanded, keenly aware it was running out.

"Twenty-six seconds until the *Velibor* self-destructs."

Sulu added, "Five seconds to minimum safe distance from the planet."

As always, they were cutting this far too close, but Kirk hid his anxiety behind a mask of confidence. "Stand by to deactivate tractor beam, on my mark." He opened an intraship channel. "Bridge to transporter room. Do you have a lock on the Transfer Key?"

"Trying, sir," answered Lieutenant Galloway. *"It's a slippery little—"*

"Just beam it aboard, on the double." Seconds ticked away on the ship's chronometer. "Chekov, deactivate tractor beam. Sulu, keep us just inside maximum transporter range."

"Releasing tractor beam," Chekov confirmed, keying in the command. The *Velibor* glided into frame on the main viewscreen. Its ventral raptor art was scarred and blackened, and burning vapors trailed from its ravaged warp nacelles.

"Fifteen seconds to self-destruct," Spock said.

Chekov reached for the tactical controls. "Shields up, Captain?"

"Not until we have the Transfer Key." It was a calculated risk, lingering without shields inside the *Velibor's* projected blast radius, but the moment the *Enterprise* raised its shields it would be unable to beam over the alien device.

Spock's baritone was devoid of inflection: "Ten seconds."

Kirk thumped his fist on the arm of the command chair. He was about to give the abort order when Galloway's voice trumpeted over the internal comm, *"The Key's aboard, sir!"*

"Shields up! Hard about, full impulse!" The deck and bulkheads sang with the rising hum of the impulse engines pushed suddenly into overdrive, and the *Velibor* slipped out of sight as the *Enterprise* veered away. "Chekov, aft angle, on-screen!"

Pinwheeling stars blinked to an image of the bird-of-prey, which shrank to a dot as the *Enterprise* accelerated back toward Centaurus. The *Velibor* was little more than a dim gray dot on the curtain of night when it bloomed into a series of fiery white detonations, each larger than the last. Within seconds the pyrotechnics faded; no trace of the Romulan vessel remained.

Spock descended into the command well to stand beside Kirk's chair. He reported with cool efficiency, "The *Velibor* has been destroyed, Captain."

Kirk admired his first officer's stoicism; despite having seen his father blinked into the alternate universe by the Transfer Key, Spock exhibited no dismay, no agitation. It was an impressive display of emotional control, but Kirk knew it was a charade. *Underneath that veneer of calm, he's got to feel something. Rage? Regret? Worry?* There was no point asking about it. *The only trait Vulcans seem to prize more than logic is privacy.* He stood from his chair. "I'm going down to get the artifact. Spock, you're with me. Sulu, you have the conn."

"Aye, sir." Sulu handed off the helm console to a relief

officer and moved to the command chair as Kirk and Spock walked to the turbolift.

The battle was won, but Kirk felt no sense of triumph. Too much blood had been shed and too many lives had been lost for him to call this a victory. Worst of all, the day's most bitter task still lay ahead.

He had to tell Doctor McCoy his daughter was gone.

Twenty-nine

Una jolted back to consciousness with a start and a gasp, then looked around to get her bearings. Martinez and Shimizu sat on the glassy-smooth floor of what she presumed was a cell, their heads drooped in defeat. A narrow shaft of light angled through a pinhole in a mostly contracted iris that blocked the only means of egress from the dungeonlike chamber.

A tingling sensation lingered on the nape of her neck and sent a shiver down her back. "Guys? Did either of you feel that?"

Martinez's reply was monotonic. "Feel what?"

"That electric prickling feeling, like cold fire. I'd swear that's what woke me up."

"It means someone just passed through the gateway," Shimizu said.

"You're sure?" She thought back to the first time she had noticed the peculiar flash that they'd said heralded new arrivals. "Why didn't I feel it before? Back in the canyon?"

"Maybe you weren't acclimated yet." Martinez projected morose disengagement. "None of us noticed it at first, but we all felt it when you arrived."

She didn't doubt a word they were saying, but she also failed to imagine how it might be true. What did it mean?

What was the significance of becoming acclimated? Why did so much about this place feel off-kilter?

Her limbs and back ached as she stood. Neither of her friends stirred as she walked the perimeter of their cell and examined its walls, floor, and ceiling for any signs of weakness. Even one vulnerability could provide them their first step toward escape and freedom. Hoping to revive her friends' spirits, she asked, "Tim? How long have we been down here?"

"Who knows? Hours? Days? I can't tell anymore."

"Damn it, Tim, get it together. I need you men sharp if we're going to get out of here." At the end of her first circuit of the room's periphery, she moved to its center and looked up. At first she thought her eyes hadn't adjusted, but then she blinked in surprise. "Where's the pit?"

Martinez groggily lifted his head. "What pit?"

"The one we fell through." She pivoted one way, then the other. "Were we moved after we hit the bottom?"

"No," Shimizu said. "This is where we've been the whole time."

"This is where we've always been," Martinez added. "You, too."

"Neither of you remembers being on the dais? Or having it swallow us and spit us out down here?" Nothing but blank looks from her comrades. She turned away from them.

What's going on? Why don't they remember? Were they mind-wiped? Do the Jatohr know enough about our neural biology to do something that sophisticated?

She plumbed her own memories and made full use

of her powers of perfect recall. The atrium chamber, the meeting with Woryan, the dais, the pit—she could recollect it all in perfect detail. It had happened, she was certain of it. But if that was true, where was the pit? How had it vanished, leaving not even the outline of a portal?

Wait, the portal on the dais—it appeared the same way. The dais was smooth and solid one second, spiraling open the next.

Una knew there were a number of smart materials that could do what she had seen. It was reasonable to think a species as technologically sophisticated as the Jatohr should be able to manufacture and control such substances. *But that fails to explain Martinez's and Shimizu's gaps of memory. Or the strange passage of time in this place. Or our perpetual lack of appetites.*

Her thoughts drifted back to their crossing of the gray sea: the way the pathways had appeared without making ripples in the water, the lack of any sensation of movement, of acceleration or deceleration, or of wind resistance as the three of them had sped to the city seemingly without moving. Then she remembered the way one place in this realm would become another, but only when her attention and focus wandered, a psychological phenomenon a Terran psychiatrist had once dubbed "highway hypnosis."

It's all so surreal, like a permanent waking dream . . . .

Clarity dawned inside her mind. The very act of recognizing the dream changed her perception of it. She felt its falsity now. As if the stone walls of the cell were nothing more than painted papier-mâché, the forgotten horizon nothing more than an ever-shifting backdrop. It reminded her of the telepathic illusions foisted upon her and Captain Pike years earlier by the Talosians. Those fantasies they had overcome by channeling violent, primal emotions. Might that work here? She cast off her Illyrian discipline and tapped into her deep well of anger.

She walked to the contracted iris barring the cell's exit. The hole at its center, through which a narrow shaft of light speared the cell's darkness, was just wide enough for her to slip her index fingers through. Behind her, Martinez and Shimizu got up and loomed at her back.

Shimizu's voice trembled as he asked, "Captain? What're you doing?"

"Getting us out of here." She visualized the iris expanding at her tactile command—then she pushed her fingers apart. With a grinding of metallic plates against stone and one another, the iris dilated and vanished into the walls. She cracked a manic grin. *It works!*

Shock and wonder pitched Martinez's voice. "How'd you do that?"

"Lucid-dreaming techniques," Una said. "Plus a little trick I learned from an old friend."

Shimizu peeked out the open portal. "What does this mean?"

"That this place isn't what it appears to be." Una led her friends out of the cell and down the empty corridor, whose surfaces had the look and texture of bleached, petrified coral. "None of this is real. It's possible we ourselves aren't what we think we are, not in this place."

"I don't understand," Martinez said, jogging to keep up with Una's long, proud strides. "You're saying we might not be us?"

"No, I'm saying we've been changed. I don't know how, or how it affects our chances of going home, but this universe is an illusion. A prison for our minds more than our bodies."

The corridor terminated in a dead end. Una closed her eyes and pictured the rough coral walls melting into a smooth, opalescent texture, then spiraling open. When she opened her eyes, the wall obeyed her desire and dilated a doorway to the sprawl of the Jatohr city on the other side of a closed lagoon of gray water.

"Amazing," Shimizu said, his voice a shocked whisper. "Let me try." He stared at the water. Closed his eyes and creased his brow with strained concentration. He opened his eyes and his face drooped in disappointment. "I guess some of us are better at dreaming than others."

Stepping forward, Martinez asked, "What were you trying to do?"

"Raise a bridge to let us cross the lagoon."

"Okay." Martinez shut his eyes and took a deep breath. Una watched him raise his hand, like a stage illusionist cuing a trick—only to register the same dismay when he opened his eyes to find nothing had changed. "I don't get it. If we know it's fake, why can't we shape it?"

"I don't know," Una confessed. "Maybe it's my Illyrian conditioning or my experience with lucid dreaming and telepathic illusions. But whatever it is, I'm not sure how much difference it'll make." She looked out at the city and realized that it, like the rest of this reality, was all just an extension of the same virtual jail. "Wherever we go, we're still prisoners."

Thirty

Doctor McCoy stepped onto the bridge and made a bee-line for Kirk. "I came as soon as I—"

Kirk raised a hand to forestall McCoy's question and kept his attention on the main viewscreen, where the bloodied and soot-blackened visages of Councillor Prang and his fellow Klingon delegates regarded Kirk through veils of black smoke.

Prang grinned. *"Don't mince words, Kirk! Is it true? You vanquished the Romulan* taHqeqpu'?"

The captain answered without pride, "The Romulan bird-of-prey was destroyed."

Prang raised his arms in celebration. *"Qapla', Kirk!"* Behind him, the other Klingons echoed his cheer, drawing fearful stares from many of the nearby civilians.

Being praised by Klingons heightened Kirk's visible lingering discomfort regarding the day's events. "You're welcome. But that's not—"

"This is the second time today we've had to reconsider our opinions of your kind," Prang continued. *"My colleagues and I would be dead if not for the bravery of Sarek."*

That news prompted Spock to lift an eyebrow in surprise. "How so?"

"He charged into a burning building," said Durok, *"shot his way through flaming debris, and led us out of the inferno."*

Anger twisted Prang's features. "*Then those Romulan* petaQpu' *murdered him and that human woman with their cowards' weapon.*" He spit on the ground. "*Fek'lhr take them all.*" He lifted his chin as he added, "*But your father died with honor, Spock. If his spirit should find the gates of* Sto-Vo-Kor, *my ancestors will welcome him.*"

"Most kind," Spock said. "Though we are not yet certain the ambassador is dead." The Klingons exchanged confused looks, prompting Spock to explain further. "We believe the weapon used by the bird-of-prey displaces persons into an alternate universe—one from which it might be possible to return."

Prang immediately grasped the possibilities implicit in that notion. "*If that's so . . . then it might be possible to bring back Councillor Gorkon, as well.*"

Kirk nodded. "We hope so, yes."

"*Most intriguing.*" Prang lost himself briefly in thought. "*Bring back Sarek and Gorkon, and maybe these talks will resume. Until then, fight and die with honor, Kirk.*" He turned and marched away, with the Klingon delegation tight around him, as the channel closed and the image on-screen reverted to the orbital view of Centaurus.

"So much for the peace talks," Kirk grumped.

Reflecting upon the Klingons' furtive glances and hunched body language, McCoy couldn't help but suspect they were once again up to no good. He muttered to Kirk, "Are you sure telling them the truth about the Transfer Key was a good idea?"

Spock's expression betrayed a hint of regret. "Time

will tell, Doctor." To Kirk he added, "With your permission, I would like to beam down to be with my mother."

The captain nodded. "Of course, Spock."

The first officer headed for the turbolift. McCoy waited until Spock was away before he pulled Kirk aside. "Jim . . . didn't Prang say Sarek and Amanda were both disappeared by the Transfer Key?" The look on Kirk's face turned from concern to pity. It was clear he knew something McCoy didn't—something terrible. "Jim . . . what is it? What's happened?"

Kirk lowered his voice, which was heavy with regret. "Bones . . . the woman who vanished with Sarek . . . wasn't his wife. It was the student nurse tending his wounds."

Bitter understanding dawned. At once, McCoy understood the reason for Kirk's urgent summons, yet he refused to believe it. "No. . . . Jim, it can't be. There has to be some mistake!"

Kirk shook his head. "I'm sorry, Bones. It was Joanna."

McCoy's stomach became an abyss of acid. Breathing in became impossible. It felt as if his feet had turned to lead and his knees to rubber. He began to sink to the deck. Kirk caught his shoulders but couldn't hold him up—the weight of McCoy's anguish was too great for anyone to bear. Driven to his knees by sorrow, he buried his face in his hands. "I tried to warn her, Jim. I did all I could . . . but it wasn't enough. Now she's gone . . . and it's my fault."

"No," Kirk insisted, "it's not. This was *not* your fault, Bones. And it wasn't hers."

Fury swelled inside him, overpowering his grief.

"Romulan bastards!" The bridge crew averted their eyes as McCoy raged, "They took her from me, Jim! Took my little girl!"

"I know they did," Kirk said, looking McCoy in the eye, as if that might let McCoy share some of his courage and certainty. "But she's still alive, Bones. I know it. And so do you."

In the face of failure, all McCoy wanted to do was fall apart. But he knew that wasn't an option, not for him. He was a doctor. A Starfleet officer. A father. He would get up and do whatever was necessary to get his daughter back. He swallowed hard, collected himself with a deep breath. "You're right, Jim. She's alive, and she needs our help. So what do we do now?"

Kirk clasped McCoy's shoulder. "We move heaven and earth—and we *bring her home*."

———

Spock greeted his materialization on Centaurus with a wince as ragged drifts of smoke stung his eyes and burned inside his nostrils. The New Athens University campus had been reduced to a smoldering war zone. Its quad now was bordered by half-imploded buildings whose wreckage was scored with carbonized streaks from the Romulan ship's disruptors. Firefighters squelched several small blazes still crackling at various points around the site, and a legion of police and medical personnel had arrived to tend the wounded now that the shooting was over.

Locating his mother amid the chaos proved easy

enough for Spock—a few simple inquiries was all it had required. The difficulty lay, as he had known it would, in contending with her torrent of desperate emotions.

"One moment they were there, then a flash! And they were just *gone*," she recounted, her manner verging upon hysteria. In spite of knowing Spock's preference for eschewing physical contact, she had thrown herself against him the moment she saw him. Now she clung to him like a stranded sailor to a hunk of flotsam bobbing in the sea. "They just disappeared, Spock!"

"I am aware of what happened, Mother. I witnessed the event from the *Enterprise*."

Shocked, she pulled back and fixed him with an accusatory stare. "And you didn't do anything to stop it?"

"There was nothing I could have done. The *Enterprise* was beyond transporter range of the planet's surface, and though I have tried to devise a means of blocking the device responsible for the abductions, my efforts have, so far, been unsuccessful."

A cascade of emotions played across her features— anger, frustration, fear—until at last she slumped into a melancholy despair. "Forgive me, Spock. I know I shouldn't have blamed you. It wasn't your fault." Tears fell from her blue eyes. "I just can't believe he's gone."

He wondered how much he dared confide to her. Some of the secrets to which he was privileged might offer her solace. But sharing classified intelligence with her would be a grave violation of Starfleet protocols.

His hard-won Vulcan discipline, refined by decades of emotional training, told him to say nothing, to comfort his mother with platitudes—as if parroting empty phrases could make her forget the sorrow of thinking her husband had been slain before her eyes.

The buried part of his soul that was human wanted nothing more at that moment than to give his beloved mother a reason to dry her tears.

"Sarek might yet live, Mother."

Shock, then a glimmer of hope. "How, Spock?"

"The weapon Sadira used . . . was a dimensional shifter. It moves people from one universe to another. And before the bird-of-prey was destroyed . . . we captured the device."

She revived at once and seized the front of Spock's tunic. "Does it still work? Can you really bring him back?"

"I have reason to think it might be within the realm of possibility."

Her sadness reasserted itself, but Spock could see her subdue her darker emotions with a conscious choice of courage. "Promise me, Spock. Promise you'll bring him home."

"I give you my word—as a Starfleet officer, and as a Vulcan—that my shipmates and I will do all that we can to bring home the victims of the device."

A single nod conveyed her faith in him. "I know you will, Spock." She relaxed her grip on his shirt. "If anyone can save them, it'll be you."

"And when I do, Sarek will no doubt expect you there to welcome him back." He took a half step away from Amanda and pulled out his communicator. "We should return to the *Enterprise*, Mother."

"You go on ahead. I'll follow after I gather your father's effects."

"As you wish. Signal the *Enterprise* when you're ready for transport." He flipped open his communicator. "Spock to *Enterprise*. One to beam up."

In the delay before the transporter beam engaged, Amanda said, "I love you, Spock."

He stood frozen, at a loss for a response. He knew what she wanted him to say, but he had spent his entire life being conditioned not to express such sentiments. Could love possibly have any office more lonely and austere than that of mother to a Vulcan child? All Spock could do was look into Amanda's eyes and hope she understood his boundless affection for her.

The champagne-colored sparkle and musical wash of the transporter field enveloped him.

Watching his mother fade from his sight, Spock thought again of Sarek's displacement into a strange and hostile universe, and resolved to do whatever proved necessary to bring him home. Not for Sarek's sake, or for his own, but for Amanda's.

I will not fail you, Mother.

━━━━━━━

Anxious, expectant stares greeted Kirk's return to the bridge of the *Enterprise*. Damage-control teams had removed most of the debris, but the bulkheads and work stations still bore the dark scars of battle damage. Scott and McCoy were huddled over the scorched wreck of the engineering console to his left. On his right, Uhura looked up from her post just as Sulu and Chekov swiveled around from the conn. Evincing a bit more restraint, Spock was the last to turn his attention toward Kirk as he stood from the command chair.

McCoy was the first to say what they all were thinking. "Well? What'd they say?"

Kirk knew better than to sugarcoat the outcome of his subspace-radio conference with Starfleet Command. "As we feared," he said, descending the steps to his chair, "the Klingons once again embody the phrase, 'No good deed goes unpunished.' They've put the peace talks on hold, and they're still blaming us for the disappearance of Gorkon."

Scott erupted in righteous indignation. "Have they lost their minds? What about the Romulans? They saw them, clear as day!"

"Apparently, the *HoS'leth* survivors experienced a collective memory failure after we beamed them down to the planet," Kirk said. "Once they were debriefed by Councillor Prang, none of them could recall what type of ship attacked them—so they can't 'rule out the possibility' it was one of ours."

Horror contorted Chekov's face. "They must be joking! There are witnesses! Evidence!"

"All of which they will claim have been falsified," Spock said. "They are maneuvering for political advantage."

"And doing a bang-up job of it," Kirk said as he pivoted into his chair. "If Prang gets his way, we'll be daring the Organians to cripple our fleets any day now."

McCoy moved to Spock's side next to Kirk's chair. "But the Transfer Key—what did the brass say about that?"

"They want us to hand it over to Starfleet Research and Development."

The doctor fumed, but it was Scotty whose temper flared first. "You cannae do that, sir! If it goes in there, we'll never see it again!"

"I concur, Mister Scott. There's a reason the device was kept off the books and on the *Enterprise* all those years. Just between us, the last thing I want to see is someone reverse-engineering that thing."

Sulu had the quality of a spring coiled for action. "What do we do, sir?"

Kirk had pondered this predicament on the walk from his quarters to the bridge. The longer he considered the facts, the more inescapable his conclusion became.

He looked at McCoy, who wore his anguish on his sleeve, and at Spock, who buried his pain so deep that it might be a mystery even to himself. Two men with loved ones now trapped in a mysterious parallel universe, along with a Klingon diplomat whose life was now more valuable than ever, a fellow Starfleet captain on her own mission of redemption, and any number of other innocent souls condemned to extradimensional exile. Kirk weighed his oaths of service against the magnitude of their losses, and he knew without a doubt what his loyalty demanded.

"Without Sarek and Gorkon, there's no way to salvage the peace talks," he told his crew. "Not in time to prevent a war that would ruin both sides." A tired sigh. "I tried reasoning with admirals; I failed. Meanwhile, the Federation Council minces words with the Klingons, who gave up on peace the moment Prang realized the military potential of the citadel on Usilde."

Kirk looked at the viewscreen, as if the answers to his troubles lay hidden in the dark between the stars. "There's only one path left to us, whether we like it or not. We need to rescue our people from the alternate universe— without starting a war."

He swiveled his chair so he could face aft. "Lieutenant Uhura, send a priority message to Starfleet Command. Tell them I'm taking the Transfer Key and the *Enterprise* back to the Libros system." Turning forward, he gave the only order that made sense to him now.

"Mister Sulu . . . set course for Usilde."

Acknowledgments

First, I must thank my wife, Kara, who remains my sounding board, my cheerleader, and my rock during the long labor that is crafting a novel.

I owe a major debt of gratitude to my literary co-conspirators: Dayton Ward, who conceived this project, and his writing accomplice, Kevin Dilmore; and Greg Cox, who agreed to join the three of us on this damned-fool idealistic fiftieth-anniversary crusade. This wasn't the first time the bunch of us have collaborated, and I certainly hope it won't be the last.

Riding the next float in my thank-you parade is John Van Citters of CBS Television Licensing. Or, as we writers like to think of him, "the man with a plan." His enthusiasm for this trilogy helped it go from being a mere gleam in our authorial eyes to an ink-on-paper (or pixels-on-screens) reality. *Muchas gracias*, John!

Our hardworking editors, Margaret Clark and Ed Schlesinger, also deserve their fair shares of gratitude and congratulations for jobs well done. Thanks, you two!

Let me also say *merci beaucoup* to my superb agent, Lucienne Diver, who ties up all the loose ends of my business dealings so I don't have to.

Also, thank you, vodka. This book would not exist without you.

Last but not least, live long and prosper, *Trek* fans!

About the Author

David Mack is not taking questions at this time.
Find the answers you seek on his official website:

davidmack.pro

STAR TREK: LEGACIES

WILL CONCLUDE IN

BOOK 3:
PURGATORY'S KEY

by Dayton Ward & Kevin Dilmore

Turn the page for an exciting excerpt . . .

Pivoting on her heel and flattening the wooden training *bat'leth* as she lifted it from its resting place on her left shoulder, Visla swung the weapon with her right arm and let its heavy blade arc across her body. The impact against her opponent's simulated blade made her arm shudder, but she ignored it. Instinct guided her to her left and she ducked under her adversary's counterattack, feeling the rush of air as the training weapon sliced through the air above her head. Adjusting her stance and raising her own *bat'leth* in preparation for another attack, Visla realized something about her counterpart's movements was not quite right.

"Mev!"

The response to her command was immediate, with her opponent, Lieutenant Koveq, halting his own movements and returning to a basic ready stance. With both hands, he held his *bat'leth* before him, cutting edge pointed toward the deck plating.

"Commander?"

Visla eyed him. "You do not attack me with full force. Why?"

"I do not understand," replied Koveq, his heavy brow furrowing in confusion. "This was to be an exercise interval."

"I have no wish to be coddled like a child." Feeling her grip tighten on her own weapon, she relished the anger flowing through her for another moment. "Attack me. Spare none of your strength and skill."

Regarding her with obvious doubt, her weapons officer replied, "Are you certain, Commander?"

It was not an unreasonable question, Visla conceded. Her subordinate was well trained in close combat, both with bladed weapons and his own hands. He outweighed her by a considerable margin, and there was no denying that his brute physical strength was superior to her own. There also was the simple fact that she had engaged Koveq in this exercise as a training bout for which there were rules and protocols in order to reduce the number of preventable, even stupid injuries.

She cared nothing about any of that today.

"Stop questioning my orders, attack me!"

In response to her command, Koveq said nothing more. His expression darkened and Visla recognized the determined set to his jaw. He raised his *bat'leth* blade, angling the weapon so that the end to Visla's left was higher and tilted toward her. With skill born from countless hours of training and actual combat, he advanced, neither rushing his movements nor offering any insight into what he was planning. Visla felt her pulse quicken in anticipation, and she could not resist a small smile of satisfaction as she hefted her blade and began stepping to her right.

She expected Koveq to feint to his left before launching an assault to her left flank, but the weapons officer surprised her by lunging left, shifting the angle of his *bat'leth*, and then continuing with his original attack angle. Visla brought her blade up and over in time to block the strike, by which time Kotaq was pivoting away, using his momentum to swing his weapon with one hand back toward her head. She parried that attack, backpedaling to give herself maneuvering room, but her subordinate had already gathered himself and was charging again. She started to counter his move, but he spun at the last instant, turning away from her blade as she took one step too far and overextended her reach. Koveq's *bat'leth* swung across his body, and Visla felt the sting of the training weapon across her back. The force of the strike pushed her off her feet, and she stumbled, stopping her fall with her free hand and pushing herself back to her feet.

"*Mev*," said Koveq, dropping his *bat'leth* to a carry position that indicated he was neither attacking nor defending.

Visla glowered at him. "I did not command you to stop."

"I know, Commander. As the ship's combat training officer, it is my prerogative. This exercise is concluded."

"Why?" She used her forearm to wipe perspiration from her brow. "You were winning."

"Training is not about winning or losing, Commander," said Koveq, his voice calm. "It is for learning."

Growling in irritation, Visla shook her head. "You sound like a Vulcan when you talk like that."

"Despite their annoying tendencies to incessantly ramble about subjects of little consequence, Vulcans are quite adept in the fighting arts." Crossing the room, Koveq paused before the bench that angled outward from the training room's slanted bulkhead. There, he retrieved a towel and began to wipe down his training *bat'leth*. "I have studied some of their unarmed combat disciplines. There is much to learn and to admire."

Her ire rising, Visla held up her own simulated weapon. "Before I find a way to kill you with this toy, what does any of the nonsense you spout have to do with anything?"

Setting the *bat'leth* on the bench, Koveq turned back to her. "The Vulcans are masters of opening their minds to new ideas and new ways of doing things. For this reason, they are most adaptable to almost any situation, including combat. It is this attitude that facilitates their learning and their ability to meet any challenge. For one to learn, one's mind must be attuned to the task at hand. Your mind is elsewhere, Commander."

She was opening her mouth to respond when Visla caught herself. Several heartbeats passed before she took a step backward, drawing a deep breath and letting the wooden *bat'leth* drop from her hand. The weapon clattered as it struck the metal deck plating. For the first time since entering the training room, she smiled and released a small laugh.

"You understand that not even my first officer is permitted to address me in such a manner, and I actually like him."

The comment elicited a deep belly laugh from the weapons officer. "Yes, but you have entrusted me with being the keeper of your conscience, Commander. It is not a responsibility I take lightly. You are obviously troubled, and it affects your focus."

Though Visla valued his counsel, there were times

when Koveq's calm, unflappable demeanor made her want to drive his face into the nearest bulkhead or simply fire him from one of the ship's torpedo tubes. When he spoke to her this way, it only heightened her annoyance because she knew he was well aware of the source of her anger.

"You know I hate it when you cloak your words," she said, reaching for the *bat'leth* she had dropped and returning it to its place with the other training weapons on the far bulkhead's storage rack. "Say what you wish to say, Lieutenant."

Moving to stand beside her, Koveq placed his own weapon on the rack. "You are conflicted. You are grateful that your son lives, and yet you feel that he, much like yourself, has had his honor taken from him through forces over which he has no control. You fear that he will be reduced to a mere servant of the Empire—fated to serve in obscurity, with no opportunity for advancement, commendation, reward, or respect."

Her jaw clenching as she listened to her trusted friend, Visla turned and punched the bulkhead. The force of the strike did nothing to damage the metal plating, of course, though she felt the satisfying jolt of pain in her hand even through the heavy leather glove designed to protect it. Still, the punch produced a dull echo in the wall, and she imagined the reverberation carrying through the entire skeleton of her ship. Then she laughed at the absurdity of such thinking.

You and I, we are both stubborn. We never buckle. We never surrender.

While this old bucket might be well beyond its prime, the *I.K.S. Qo'Daqh* still retained some measure of mettle and pride. The D5-class battle cruiser was a relic, an obsolete deathtrap that should have been consigned to scrap a generation before Visla even was born, but it possessed a history filled with both glory and shame. The latter, of course, was all that mattered, along with the dishonor brought to it and the Klingon Empire in a battle lost decades earlier. Like the battle, the commander of that ill-fated campaign, Visla's grandfather, had been all but erased from official records, and no one she knew had spoken aloud of that ignominious day. He had never spoken of it, preferring to shoulder the burden of humiliation in silence until the end of his life.

Under almost any other circumstances, the *Qo'Daqh* would have been destroyed, but someone somewhere decided that it retained some small portion of value. As those who had crewed it were consigned to disgrace, so too was this vessel damned in similar fashion. It was forever barred from performing anything save the most menial of tasks, let alone taking any action that might see its honor and legacy restored. Anyone sent to serve aboard it did so knowing that the Empire held them in the lowest regard, and that was especially true of the Klingon condemned to its captain's chair. It was to be Visla's punishment for having the temerity to be born into a house that had dishonored the Empire.

"My son was already doomed to follow me down the path of disgrace," she said, moving from the weapons rack to where she had left a coarse canvas towel lying on the nearby bench. "It was his misfortune to have me as his mother. His shame is only compounded now."

Visla had not slept since receiving word the previous evening that the *I.K.S. HoS'leth*—the cruiser to which her son, K'tovel, was assigned—had been lost in battle against a Romulan ship near the planet Centaurus. The location of the battle was itself interesting, given that peace talks had been under way between envoys from the Federation and the Klingon Empire. The *HoS'leth*, under the command of a renowned Klingon general, Kovor, had fought the Romulan vessel with the unlikely assistance of a Federation starship, the *U.S.S. Enterprise*. Details of the encounter remained unreported, though Prang, the Klingon attaché assigned to Councillor Gorkon during the peace talks on Centaurus, had told Visla that the confrontation was an outgrowth of some important discovery on Usilde, a remote world in the Libros star system. Prang had not offered any other information, leaving Visla to speculate that whatever had been found on that planet, it obviously was of great interest to the Romulans as well as the Empire and the Federation.

Further, someone had deemed that discovery to be of sufficient value to spur General Kovor to ally himself with the captain of the Federation ship, James Kirk. Visla had found this hard to believe, considering what she had read of the Earther's recent engagements with other Klingon vessels. Those encounters had earned him scorn as well as grudging respect within the High Command. Numerous ship commanders had already made clear their desire to engage the human captain in combat, to see if the reports of his tactical prowess and guile were true. For her part, Visla suspected the accounts had been embellished to mitigate the incompetence of the Klingons who had suffered defeat at Kirk's hands.

As for the *HoS'leth*, all Visla knew at this point was that a group of survivors from the destroyed cruiser awaited pickup on the planet Centaurus, and that K'tovel was among them. How her son and his shipmates had evaded their vessel's destruction during the battle also was a question that would remain unanswered until the *Qo'Daqh* arrived to retrieve them. Visla was already anticipating the reaction she would receive from the Klingon High Command when it was learned that K'tovel was among the *HoS'leth* survivors.

More dishonor upon our house.

"I have read the report," said Koveq. "Though it lacks detail, it is obvious that the Starfleet captain acted without regard for our traditions. The *HoS'leth* crew, including your son, were prepared to die with their vessel, but were robbed of that honor. This should be taken into account when passing judgment upon the survivors."

Wiping her face with her towel, Visla scowled. "And how likely is that to happen?" She shook her head. "No. The High Command has never squandered an opportunity to remind my family of its place. They will not do so here, and the insult is only compounded with me being sent to retrieve them. It is an endless cycle, Koveq, and one from which there is no escape." Pausing, she regarded him for a moment. "How is it that you don't allow your feelings to spill forth? You have also had your honor stripped away. Does it not anger you?"

"My dishonor is by my own hand, Commander." The weapons officer stared at the metal deck plating. "I hesitated in battle. It was my first time facing an enemy, and one might look to youth and inexperience as an explanation, but the simple fact was that I was afraid. That fear kept me from acting, and that failure resulted in the death of two warriors. I live with that knowledge, and with each new day I try to be a better warrior than I was the day before, but I know that I can never atone for that mistake. All I can do is work to ensure it never happens again."

Visla nodded. Like her and Koveq, every member of the *Qo'Daqh*'s crew had such a story, some failing or shortcoming that was viewed as having brought discredit to the Empire. There were other ships just like this one, filled with castoffs and rejects who ultimately possessed but one purpose: die so that other warriors, better and more honorable, might live to fight another day.

We shall see about that.

"You and I are of similar mind, my friend," she said. "I have no concerns over restoring my own personal honor, as doing so is not within my control. However, that does not free us from our duty as warriors, and if that means correcting an insult directed against the Empire, then that is what we should do."

Koveq eyed her with confusion. "I do not understand, Commander."

The intercom panel near the training room's entrance emitted a series of beeps before a deep male voice said through the panel's speaker, *"Bridge to Commander Visla."*

Smiling at her trusted friend, Visla said, "You will understand in due course, Lieutenant." She gestured for Koveq to follow her to the communications panel, and she pressed the unit's activation control. "This is Visla."

"I apologize for interrupting your personal exercise period, Commander," said Woveth, the *Qo'Daqh*'s first officer, *"but we have received a subspace message from the Klingon High Command. They are demanding to know why you have not acknowledged our orders to set course for Centaurus."*

Visla exchanged a glance with Koveq, whose brow had furrowed.

"That is because we are not going to Centaurus, Lieutenant," she said. "Plot a course for the Libros system and engage at maximum speed. Once we are under way, notify me with our time of arrival."

A pause was Woveth's initial response, and Visla thought she could hear him breathing through the open channel. Then the first officer said, *"Commander, I do not understand. Did I fail to note a change in our orders?"*

"No, Lieutenant, you did not. This is at my discretion, and I accept full responsibility. We will discuss it in detail when I return to the bridge. For now, execute the course change."

The first officer, obviously confused, nevertheless offered no resistance. *"Understood, Commander. Plotting the new course."*

"Excellent." Visla pressed the panel control to sever the communication.

"Commander?" Koveq was making no effort to mask his skepticism. "An unauthorized deviation of our course will not go unnoticed by High Command."

Visla nodded. "Quite true. My hope is that they will not notice our attempt to redeem the *HoS'leth* crew and restore the honor taken from them."

"The crew." Koveq's eyes narrowed. "Including your son."

"Yes, including my son." Visla turned to face her weapons officer. "Do I have your loyalty, Lieutenant?"

Koveq nodded. "Always, and without question, Commander."

"Good."

Feeling the all but imperceptible tremor in the deck plates beneath her feet that signified the *Qo'Daqh* was increasing speed and drawing more power from its engines, Visla allowed herself a smile of satisfaction. She, her misfit crew, and her dilapidated vessel were going to seize back for the Empire and the *HoS'leth* that which had been taken from them by one foolhardy Earther.

James Kirk would pay for his insolence.